SHADOW OF THE MOUNTAINS

LYNN MORRIS & GILBERT MORRIS

W0010374

BETHANY HOUSE PUBLISHERS
MINNEAPOLIS, MINNESOTA 55438

BOOKS BY GILBERT MORRIS

Through a Glass Darkly

THE HOUSE OF WINSLOW SERIES

1. *The Honorable Imposter*
2. *The Captive Bride*
3. *The Indentured Heart*
4. *The Gentle Rebel*
5. *The Saintly Buccaneer*
6. *The Holy Warrior*
7. *The Reluctant Bridegroom*
8. *The Last Confederate*
9. *The Dixie Widow*
10. *The Wounded Yankee*
11. *The Union Belle*
12. *The Final Adversary*
13. *The Crossed Sabres*
14. *The Valiant Gunman*
15. *The Gallant Outlaw*
16. *The Jeweled Spur*
17. *The Yukon Queen*
18. *The Rough Rider*
19. *The Iron Lady*
20. *The Silver Star*
21. *The Shadow Portrait*
22. *The White Hunter*
23. *The Flying Cavalier*
24. *The Glorious Prodigal*

THE LIBERTY BELL

1. *Sound the Trumpet*
2. *Song in a Strange Land*
3. *Tread Upon the Lion*
4. *Arrow of the Almighty*
5. *Wind From the Wilderness*
6. *The Right Hand of God*
7. *Command the Sun*

CHENEY DUVALL, M.D.
(with Lynn Morris)

1. *The Stars for a Light*
2. *Shadow of the Mountains*
3. *A City Not Forsaken*
4. *Toward the Sunrising*
5. *Secret Place of Thunder*
6. *In the Twilight, in the Evening*
7. *Island of the Innocent*
8. *Driven With the Wind*

THE SPIRIT OF APPALACHIA
(with Aaron McCarver)

1. *Over the Misty Mountains*
2. *Beyond the Quiet Hills*
3. *Among the King's Soldiers*
4. *Beneath the Mockingbird's Wings*

TIME NAVIGATORS
(for Young Teens)

1. *Dangerous Voyage*
2. *Vanishing Clues*

BOOKS BY LYNN MORRIS

The Balcony

CHENEY DUVALL, M.D.*

1. *The Stars for a Light*
2. *Shadow of the Mountains*
3. *A City Not Forsaken*
4. *Toward the Sunrising*
5. *Secret Place of Thunder*
6. *In the Twilight, in the Evening*
7. *Island of the Innocent*
8. *Driven With the Wind*

*with Gilbert Morris

Published by Bethany House Publishers
A Ministry of Bethany Fellowship International
11400 Hampshire Avenue South
Minneapolis, Minnesota 55438
www.bethanyhouse.com

Printed in the United States of America by
Bethany Press International, Minneapolis, Minnesota 55438

Library of Congress Cataloging-in-Publication Data

Morris, Gilbert
    Shadow of the mountains / Gilbert Morris, Lynn Morris.
        p.   cm. — (Cheney Duvall, M.D. ; #2)

    1. Women physicians—Ozark Mountains Region—Fiction. 2. Mountain life—Ozark Mountains Region—Fiction. I. Morris, Lynn. II. Title.
III. Series: Morris, Gilbert. Cheney Duvall, M.D. ; 2.
PS3563.08742S49   1994
813'.54—dc20   94–32698
ISBN 1-55661-423-3   CIP

For Dixie—

the best thing
that ever happened to me.

GILBERT MORRIS & LYNN MORRIS are a father/daughter writing team who combine Gilbert's strength of great story plots and adventure with Lynn's research skills and character development. Together they form a powerful duo! Lynn and her daughter live near her parents on the Gulf coast in Alabama.

CONTENTS

The Satterfields and Carters of Black Arrow

The Satterfields

Enoch and Leah (Trask) Satterfield
  T. R.   Abe
  Lorine   Frannie
  Caroline   Prince
  Jimmy Dale   Cassia

Noah and Peggy (Harrison) Satterfield
  Six children

Ben and Gloria (Sikes) Satterfield
  Four children

Hiram and Lettie (Wilkes) Satterfield
  Eight children, including sons Jude and D. K.

Caleb and Amelia (Redden) Satterfield
  Four children, including son Will

Levi and Ruthie (Trask) Satterfield
  Wanda Jo   Shirl
  Eulalie   Isaac

Judith (Satterfield) and Latham Trask
  Rafe (deceased)
  Booth
  Dorcas

The Carters

Lige Carter and Katie (Rawlins) Carter
  Josh and M. Sharon (Bateman)
  Bobbie Jo
  Dane
  Glendean

Deak Carter and Mary (Redden) Carter
  Six children

Flave Carter and Faye Jean (Smithton) Carter
  Eight children

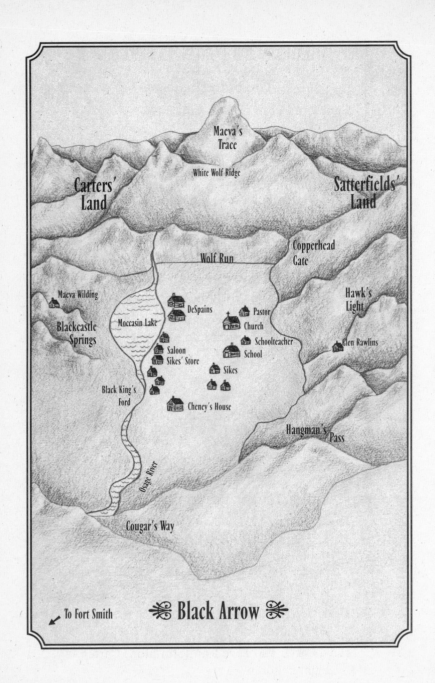

Maeva's
Trace

White Wolf Ridge

Carters'
Land

Satterfields'
Land

Copperhead
Gate

Wolf Run

Maeva Wilding

Hawk's
Light

Blackcastle
Springs

Moccasin Lake

DeSpains

Pastor

Church

Glen Rawlins

Schoolteacher

Saloon

School

Sikes' Store

Sikes

Black King's
Ford

Cheney's House

Hangman's
Pass

Osage River

Cougar's Way

To Fort Smith

❈ Black Arrow ❈

NEITHER SHADOW
✳ P·A·R·T · O·N·E ✳
OF TURNING

*Every good gift and every
perfect gift is from above, and
cometh down from the Father of
lights, with whom is no variableness,
neither shadow of turning.*

James 1:17

1

Time to Move On

The gambler's smoke gray eyes turned to cold flint as the words cut through the low roar in the Logjammer's Saloon.

"I say you're a dirty, card-cheatin' dog!" Axel Tarver jumped out of his chair, knocking it sprawling, and drew his gun. It was a long-barreled .38 Remington, and Axel's draw was slow and clumsy.

"King Red" Jackson sat very still as Axel leveled the gun at Jackson's heart.

"I'm going to stand up now," Jackson said quietly, "and raise my hands. You just be real still, and I'll show you what's up my sleeve. You ready?"

"Yeah," Axel grunted, "I'll be still—if you move real slow and careful."

The three men still seated with King stood up and moved quickly away. One of them, Shiloh Irons, took a long backward stride into the shadows, his eyes never leaving the two men, now alone in the circle of amber light shed by the kerosene lantern suspended low over the littered card table.

"King Red" Jackson slowly rose, a slender figure dressed in solid black, the only color about him the red ruby flashing on his pinkie finger. With exaggerated, cautious movements, he raised both arms above his head. Slowly his left hand went to his right sleeve.

"You just pull that card outta your sleeve, King—" Axel began.

In a blur of movement, King kicked over the large round table, pulled a small silver gun out of his sleeve, leveled it at Axel

Tarver, and shot as he threw himself to the floor behind the table.

Axel lurched to the side, gun blazing, as soon as King's boot touched the table. But he was like a great blond bear, bulky and clumsy, and the three shots he pulled off went wild. One hit a whiskey bottle that had taken flight from the table, and it exploded into a thousand green shards. Another hit the table square center, and the last hit the wall where the gambler had stood a moment before. When the black smoke from his gun cleared, Axel rolled on the floor in agony, holding his belly. Already there was a puddle of dark blood on the floor.

Six feet away from the overturned table, King rose and dusted himself off. The small gun had disappeared, and King's clothes were soon a spotless, severe black once again. Deliberately he picked up his black hat, dusted it off, and placed it squarely on his head.

As he pocketed some of the scattered money, he came to stand over Axel Tarver and Shiloh, who knelt beside the wounded man.

"Tried to wing him," King muttered with a trace of regret. "Wouldn't gutshoot a stray dog."

He crossed the floor, and the other men parted to open a way for him, glancing nervously at his dark form. The swinging doors creaked loudly in the silence, which was broken intermittently by the groans of the injured man.

"We've got to get him to a doctor," Shiloh snapped as he examined Tarver.

"Waste of time," a tall young cowboy muttered as he turned back to the bar. "Saw lots of gutshots in the war, and can't rightly remember a man Jack of 'em livin' through it. Might as well take Axel home and let him die in as much peace as he can get in the next hour or two."

"Help me," Shiloh grunted as he struggled to lift the huge timber man. Several men, all of them dressed as lumberjacks, rushed to help. The three largest finally wrestled Tarver up and staggered toward the door.

"Where you goin'?" the tall cowboy asked idly as the men struggled by him.

"To Doc's, down the street," Shiloh panted.

The cowboy shrugged. "Okay. Reckon if you can carry that big ox, I kin carry Doc Guinness." He took a last swig of beer, wiped his mouth, and swaggered over to a man sitting at a table alone, his head down on his arms. A half-empty bottle of whiskey sat on the table next to one smudged shot glass. "Doc!" the young cowboy yelled. "Git up! You got a patient!"

"Huh? What?" the old man asked. Bleary-eyed, he lifted his head and looked around. The cowboy threw Doc Guinness's arm around his shoulders, pulled him upright, and followed the procession carrying the wounded man out the door. Beside him, Doc Guinness hung on tightly, stumbling blindly as they went.

★ ★ ★ ★

Cheney Duvall sat in a burgundy velvet chair at a small mahogany table by the window. The tiny sitting room was elegant but dark, with heavy velvet drapes and a patterned blue-and-burgundy carpet. Bleak afternoon light filtered through the open window. Distant thunder grumbled for long seconds, and a cool, wet breeze stirred a thick curl that hung over Cheney's shoulder.

A gunshot cracked in the sullen silence, and Cheney looked up from her embroidery to search the street two floors below. *Must have been in Logjammer's,* she thought anxiously. *Hope Shiloh's all right. . . .* Nervously she watched the swinging doors directly across the street from the Empire Hotel.

She made a lovely picture framed by the gray aura of the window. She had washed her waist-length auburn hair that morning, and it had taken her over an hour to brush it out. Now, at three-thirty in the afternoon, her hair was finally completely dry, but Cheney had tied a simple black ribbon around it instead of elaborately dressing it. Thick curls covered her shoulders and back, and though the light was dim, an occasional glint of red fire flashed as she moved her head.

Her eyes were sea-green, with thick dark lashes and rather heavy dark brows. A beauty mark, inherited from her mother, adorned her left cheekbone. With her short, small nose, wide mouth, and determined chin, Cheney's face was too strong to be called beautiful, but it was an expressive, interesting face. She was twenty-four years old, tall—five feet, ten inches—and slender, and her movements and gestures were deft and purposeful.

Cheney sat up a little straighter to watch as a tall man dressed in black pushed through the swinging doors of the saloon. He mounted a glossy palomino that was tied outside, and horse and rider disappeared from Cheney's view. In a few moments four men struggled through the doors carrying another man, and even from two floors above and across the street Cheney could see the dark bloodstain on the man's tan shirt. She breathed a sigh of relief when she saw that Shiloh Irons was one of those who carried the injured man.

Setting her jaw in a stubborn line, she sat back, picked up her embroidery hoop, and stabbed it vengefully with a large needle. *Cannot imagine why I waste my time worrying about him! Why can't I remember that he's a big boy—he can take care of himself?*

For fifteen minutes she sewed with more determination than skill, until a knock sounded on the sitting room door. Glancing ruefully at her handiwork, Cheney quickly stepped through the door behind her into the small bedroom and thrust the embroidery hoop under her pillow. She stopped briefly in front of the mirror to smooth her hair and called, "I'm coming," then hurriedly crossed the sitting room floor.

"It's me, Doc!" Shiloh called. "Can I come in?"

Cheney opened the door and started to say something, but she stopped before a word came out. Her eyes wide, she sniffed and made a face. "Shiloh! You smell as if you'd bathed in whiskey!"

"Can I come in anyhow?"

Cheney stepped back a little, her face stern. "I don't know—

16

can you? Walk straight enough to come through the door, I mean?"

Shiloh entered the room and went to the window. Pulling the heavy curtains aside to let in more of the dim light, he stared down at the street below. "Don't worry, Doc," he muttered, "it's all over me, but not in me. Bottle got shot, and I was standing too close." His face was glum as he stared out.

How is it that when he's serious, he looks younger? Cheney wondered. *Or maybe that's when he seems most vulnerable. . . .*

Shiloh was a little younger than Cheney, about twenty-three. He had been abandoned on the steps of an orphanage in South Carolina when he was a baby, so his exact birth date was unknown. The only identification he had was that he lay in a crate stamped "Shiloh Ironworks." The women who had attended the orphanage had questions about his exact age as he grew, for they had based their estimate on the size of the baby. Shiloh grew to be a tall child, though not large, and he was now a man of six feet, four inches. His shoulders were wide, his body well-muscled, lithe, and quick.

Cheney noticed as she studied him that his blond hair had grown—it brushed his eyebrows and fell down over his collar. His cornflower blue eyes were set in a wedge-shaped face that was burned a dark tan. A network of scar tissue surrounded his eyes from his prizefighting days, and a pronounced scar under his left eye made a perfect V, discernible even from a few feet away.

Cheney moved very close to him and lifted her face to his.

He glanced down in surprise and asked, "What—?" Then he grinned and put his hands on her slender waist. "I'm glad to see you, too, Doc, even though we just had breakfast this morning—"

"Never mind!" she snapped, pushing him away. "I was just checking—the only thing that doesn't smell like whiskey on you is your breath. What happened?"

"Axel Tarver got shot." He turned to stare again out the window. "We took him to Doc Guinness's."

"How is he?" Cheney asked with concern, in spite of the fact that she had never met the man.

"Axel's gut-shot," Shiloh answered matter-of-factly, "and Doc Guinness is drunk. And they wouldn't let me come get you."

Cheney moved around the small table, sat across from Shiloh, folded her hands, and looked up at him, expressionless. "I'm used to it. Aren't you?"

"No. And when I do get used to it, I'm still not going to like it."

Cheney had gotten her medical degree from the brand-new Women's Medical College of the University of Pennsylvania. A prestigious school, it was run by esteemed Quaker physicians. Cheney had graduated with honors and proved to be an excellent doctor. Yet everywhere she went, she met with raging disapproval and distrust. There were very few female physicians in 1865, none of them universally well-respected. In spite of her bold statement to Shiloh, Cheney was by no means "used to it." Anger seethed inside her as she considered the treatment the injured man was likely to have from Doc Guinness—Seattle's resident doctor, dentist, and veterinarian, and also one of the town drunks.

Shiloh and Cheney were silent for a while, each deep in thought, both thinking of the same things. They had worked together for two months, traveling by steamer from New York to Seattle. Cheney had been offered a position as physician to one hundred Eastern women traveling to Washington Territory, accompanied by an energetic young man named Asa Mercer. Mercer had made two such voyages now, bringing women— mostly widows—from the war-torn East to the newly settled, predominantly male Northwest. Almost all of "Mercer's Belles" married within a year.

Cheney had engaged Shiloh Irons as her nurse for the voyage. He had received his training as a medical corpsman during the War Between the States. They reached Seattle the first of July. A month later they weren't technically working together, but they were friends and were in each other's company every day. Both of them were now thinking of the hardships of that voyage and of what a good medical team they made. They also thought of the refusal of most of the people in Seattle to acknowledge Cheney as anything but another of "Mercer's Belles"—just another woman looking for a husband.

A knock sounded on Cheney's door, and she hurried to open it. A tall redheaded woman stood in the hall, her face grim. Swiftly she looked Cheney up and down, nodded to Shiloh, and lifted her chin. "I'm Jenny Tarver. Are you Dr. Duvall?"

"Yes. Won't you come in, Mrs. Tarver?"

"No, thank you, doctor. I'm in a hurry. My man's been shot, and that fool Doc Guinness says he's done for." She held her head high, but Cheney noticed that the large, rawboned hands that clutched her shawl trembled slightly. "I've heard some of the ladies that Mr. Mercer brung here talk about what a good doctor you are. Will you come?"

Cheney hesitated, glancing up at Shiloh, who had come to stand by her side. "Has Dr. Guinness agreed—?"

Jenny Tarver frowned and shook her head. "No, but he's just gonna stand there and watch Axel die! My Axel—he's strong, you know—" Her voice grew ragged, but she bit her lip, straightened her shoulders, and looked Cheney squarely in the eye. "I ain't asking for charity, Dr. Duvall," she went on proudly. "I can pay you. And this ain't no last-ditch gesture, neither. I believe you can help Axel."

"That does it!" Shiloh grunted, turning to Cheney with a stubborn look on his face. "I can persuade Doc Guinness, Cheney. Let's go."

Cheney nodded her agreement, and within minutes the three were marching into Dr. Guinness's office. The brass bell on the door tinkled loudly, and from a back room came a hoarse call. "Be there in a minute!"

Shiloh made the back room in three strides. Cheney and Jenny glanced at each other as they heard first a low growl, then a soft answer, and then a loud thump.

"All right!" Doc Guinness yelped in a creaky voice. "I cain't git outta here 'til you let me up, Irons!"

In a few moments Doc Guinness came stumping through the front office, clapping a dusty brown bowler on his head and grumbling. "Female doctors and giant nurses! Like he had to flatten me like a pancake to get me outta here! Man's dying—I don't wanna stay here and watch it, anyways!"

Completely ignoring Cheney and Jenny, he slammed out the door, setting the bell jangling as a groan sounded from the back room.

"Doc!" Shiloh called. "Come on! Doc Guinness said for you to make yourself at home!"

"Stay here, Mrs. Tarver," Cheney ordered sternly. "We're going to take care of Axel, but you must stay here, out of our way."

"But I want to help. Please let me," Mrs. Tarver protested.

Cheney stopped before opening the door of the back room and looked back at Jenny Tarver. She was a strong woman, Cheney saw, who worked hard and loved her husband very much. Only now was she showing fear and worry, her plain face twisted with lines of pain.

"There's one very important thing you must do to help me, Mrs. Tarver. Will you?"

"Anything!"

"Pray. Pray for me, pray for Shiloh, pray for your husband—and pray for yourself, that God will give you grace and peace, no matter what happens." Cheney slipped into the back room, and Jenny Tarver slowly sank into a chair, buried her face in her hands, and let the tears flow.

"He's not dead yet," Shiloh muttered grimly as he bent over the man lying on the high wooden table, "but he might die from the morphine Guinness gave him. Don't know how much, but he's out cold, barely breathing, and his pulse is erratic."

Cheney could barely control her anger as she looked around the room. It was dusty and dark, and smelled of whiskey and sickness. The operating table was covered with black stains that Cheney suspected were blood. Mixed in with the medical supplies and instruments were empty whiskey bottles, dirty cups, and odd pieces of saddle tack.

With quick, impatient movements she swept aside the litter from the wheeled table next to the operating bed and placed her large black medical bag on it. Opening it, she yanked out a starched white apron and pulled it over her head. "Is there any chloroform?"

"I dunno," Shiloh grumbled, rummaging through an assortment of bottles on a nearby shelf. "Here. Can't tell how old it is, but it looks like it's never been opened."

Cheney examined the unconscious man. Shiloh had already cut his shirt and pants off and covered him with the cleanest sheet he could find. Cheney picked up the bloody towel that Shiloh had been pressing to the wound and bent close. "Did the bullet come out his back?" she asked hopefully.

"Nope."

"All right. We're going to have to operate. I can't just go digging around in there; I've got to see what the bullet's hit, and if it shattered at that close range. You've administered chloroform before, haven't you?"

Mutely, Shiloh shook his head.

"What! Not in the war?" Cheney began to pull gleaming surgical instruments out of her bag. She was grateful that she had a full array of tools; she didn't even want to see Dr. Guinness's equipment.

"By the time I got hit and ended up limping around the field hospital, chloroform, ether, and morphine were long-gone dreams, Doc," Shiloh answered. He was moving quickly as he spoke, pulling on the apron Cheney handed him, rolling up his sleeves, and pouring carbolic acid on his hands to clean them. "But you just tell me what to do. I can handle it."

"I know you can, Shiloh," Cheney answered gratefully. "And this is going to be difficult, since he's had too much morphine. Put a small amount of chloroform on a clean towel. I'm just about ready to make the incision." She was putting instruments in a silver bowl and pouring carbolic acid on them. The acrid smell of the disinfectant stung her nostrils, and it had stained both hers and Shiloh's hands a lurid yellow. "When I do, you're going to have to start a drip, once a minute. Watch Axel's breathing. If it gets too shallow, you're giving him too much. If he starts to rouse, you're not giving him enough. Don't let him start to regain consciousness! If he thrashes around while I'm operating, even a tiny cut from the scalpel could do more harm than that bullet might have!"

"I understand," Shiloh answered, and his voice was steady and confident.

Cheney took a deep breath and held a scalpel above Tarver's midsection. "There's more, Shiloh." She frowned and tentatively placed the scalpel on the man's stomach, just above the bullet hole. "You have to watch him. When a patient's getting chloroform, he can swallow his tongue and choke to death. Turn his head slightly to the side."

Shiloh obeyed, his movements gentle.

"Good. Also, he may vomit, and that could choke him to death, too. So you have to watch!"

"All right. I can do it."

"And you have to watch me, too," Cheney said matter-of-factly as she began the incision. "B-because I may need help."

This was the first telltale stutter in Cheney's speech since they had begun. As always, Shiloh knew it meant she was frightened and unsure of herself. "Just relax, Doc," he said softly. "You're doing great. I know you're going to save this man. I'll watch, and I'll be able to tell if you need help."

"Shiloh," she murmured absently as she bent close over Tarver and began to expertly tie off veins and arteries, "seems like you always know I need help long before I do. . . ."

★ ★ ★ ★

"It's raining," Cheney said softly as she stared out the window.

"It's been raining for quite a while, Doc," Shiloh answered lazily. He stretched his long legs in front of him, crossed his

22

hands over his flat stomach, and yawned. They were back in Cheney's sitting room, and Shiloh was lounging all over one of the small, elegant armless velvet chairs. On the small mahogany table between them was a silver tea service, a platter that held only crumbs, and two china cups, half full of tea.

"What time is it?" Cheney asked wearily, propping her chin on one hand.

"I don't know."

"Don't you have a watch?"

"Nope. Don't you?"

"Yes, but it's in my medical bag, and I'm too tired to get up and go see." Cheney sighed, picked up her tiny silver fork, and started arranging the crumbs on the platter into straight lines.

Just like her! Shiloh thought with amusement as he watched her. *She always wants everything just so, filed away neatly, in the right compartment on the right shelf.* His amusement faded a little as he thought of her sudden lapses into insecurity and sometimes outright fear. *What a waste—she never should have to worry, or be scared—of herself, anyway—she can do anything!*

"Think it's about nine o'clock or so," Shiloh mumbled, and yawned again. "What time do you think it is? Want to put a small wager on it?"

Cheney ignored his teasing and moodily smashed crumbs beneath the fork. "I think . . . that it's time for me to go home."

Shiloh became very still, although his face kept its light expression. "Why?"

"Because—because—" Cheney murmured, almost speaking to herself. "I don't feel as though I'm supposed to be here anymore. Until now, I just couldn't face getting back on a ship for the return trip. . . ." Her voice was slow and quiet, and Shiloh's face grew tight as he strained to hear her. "I thought about staying here, you know—Asa and Annie have tried to talk me into opening a practice—maybe for just a year or so—" Her voice dropped off and silence filled the room for a few moments.

"You saved Tarver's life tonight, Cheney," Shiloh said. "They need a real doctor here, just like the Mercers have been trying to tell you. Are you sure—?"

Cheney roused herself from staring unseeing at the platter of crumbs, now arranged with military precision and flattened to uniform shapes. "Yes," she answered quietly. "I don't exactly know where I'm supposed to be—yet—but I feel that it's time to move on. And I do want to go back to New York for a while. I want to go home."

"Me, too," Shiloh nodded with determination. "I'm coming with you."

"To New York?" Cheney asked, astonished. "But—but— New York's not your home. You were only there for two days before we sailed!"

Shiloh shrugged carelessly and grinned at her. "You know what they say about home, Doc!"

" 'Home is where the heart is?' " Cheney quoted, mystified.

"That's it!"

"But—but—I thought your home was—well, it's. . . . Where is your home, Shiloh?" Cheney asked with consternation. She knew he had been raised in South Carolina, had traveled as a prizefighter up and down the eastern seaboard, had joined the Twenty-second Alabama Regiment in 1861, and had been all over the theaters of war. But now she realized he had never spoken of any place as "home."

"Never have had one," he answered airily, "so I thought I'd just follow *your* heart and borrow *your* home, Doc. That okay with you?"

Cheney considered his words carefully, and she was not nearly as casual as Shiloh seemed to be. "Shiloh," she said softly, "you don't need to follow *my* heart, you know. My father and mother practically adopted you as soon as they met you. So— let's go home!"

2

DINNER AT EIGHT: UPPER MANHATTAN

"What do I have to wear for dinner, Irene?" Richard Duvall's disgruntled voice floated faintly into his wife's dressing room.

"It doesn't matter, dear!" Irene answered as sweetly as she could, considering the fact that she was obliged to yell. Between them was a cozy sitting room that connected Irene's room to their bedroom, where Richard was dressing for dinner.

Irene was seated at a large dressing table with a triple mirror mounted on top. Behind her, Dally—a former slave, now the Duvalls' housekeeper—was brushing Irene's long, gleaming auburn hair with a silver brush.

"Don't you 'uns niver git tired o' having this here conversation at the top o' your lungs ever' night, Miss Irene?" Dally asked sarcastically.

Irene smiled playfully at Dally's reflection in the mirror. "I got tired of it about twenty-five years ago, Dally. But Richard seems to enjoy it so much."

"What did you say, Irene?" Richard demanded plaintively. "I thought you said that it didn't matter what I wore—"

"That's right, dear," Irene called. "Whatever you want!"

Dally and Irene nodded at each other with amusement.

" 'S'bout time fo' him to git in heah," Dally sighed. "I better go 'head and git through." Nimbly she twisted Irene's hair to the side, pushed four hairpins into it, wound some curls around the silver brush, and stood back, surveying the results of her work in the mirror with satisfaction. Irene's hair gleamed with a soft burnished copper glow from the firelight behind them, elegantly arranged with four long ringlets over her left shoulder.

Richard's uneven footsteps whispered on the deep carpet,

and he entered the room, holding a black velvet frock coat and frowning. His thick silver hair was slightly mussed, and again Irene and Dally exchanged amused looks in the mirror. "Did you say I can wear whatever I want for dinner, Irene?" he demanded. "I could've sworn that's what you said!"

Dally went to the door leading out into the hall grumbling, "If you'll 'scuse me, Miss Irene, Mistuh Richard, ah gotta go tackle that Miss Cheney's hair, an' that's a job for a strong woman! Miss Cheney's hair *looks* lak your hair, Miss Irene, but it sho don't behave lak it!"

"Thank you so much, Dally," Irene called as the woman slipped soundlessly out into the hall. As big as Dally was, she moved without making a sound. Irene turned back to her husband, who stood looking quizzically at her. "Yes, Richard, that's what I said. You don't have to dress for dinner tonight. You can just wear a shirt and breeches."

Irene was glowing in a green satin dress with a wide scooped neckline. Holding up an emerald-and-diamond necklace, she looked invitingly up at Richard.

Smiling, he tossed the frock coat onto the "fainting couch" by the door and walked to stand behind Irene. Leaning his lion's-head cane against the dressing table, he fastened the necklace and caressed Irene's ivory shoulders, looking at her reflection in the mirror appreciatively. "Irene, you're still the most beautiful woman I've ever seen."

"Thank you," she answered softly, and reached up with one hand to hold his. "I love you so much, Richard."

"And I love you, Irene." They stayed still for a few moments, smiling at each other in the mirror.

Richard gave Irene's shoulder a gentle squeeze and reached for his cane. Returning to the sumptuous brocaded chaise, he sat down on top of the velvet coat, leaned back, stretched his legs out, and watched his cane as he waved it back and forth in small arcs. "Now, explain to me again about dinner, Irene."

Irene picked up a crystal decanter with a gold tassel and delicately sprayed the air above her shoulders. A spicy-sweet scent of gardenias filled the air, and Richard sniffed appreciatively.

"It's simple, dear," she replied patiently. "Shiloh doesn't have any evening clothes, so dinner isn't formal tonight."

Richard wrinkled his brow and waved the cane in slightly larger arcs, making a swishing sound in the air. "Oh," he finally said, and shrugged. "Guess men don't think about little social niceties like that. I'm glad Shiloh's staying with us for a couple of days, anyway—you are, too, aren't you, Irene?"

"Yes, dear."

"But, I mean—I've spent a lot more time with him than you have, and I really like him a lot. Do you?" Richard put the cane to his eye like a telescope and squinted down the length of it.

"Yes, dear." Irene watched her husband's antics with amusement.

Richard swung his legs back over the side of the chaise, sat up, balanced the cane between his hands, lion's head down, and bounced it up and down. "What do you think Cheney's going to do?"

"I don't know. She hasn't mentioned anything to me," Irene answered, leaning close to the mirror to apply a feather-light touch of rice powder to her small nose. "Has she said anything to you?"

"No, or Shiloh either, or Dev either."

Devlin Buchanan, M.D., was almost as much a part of the Duvall family as Cheney. Though the Duvalls had not formally adopted him, they had raised him as their son since he was seven years old. Educated along with Cheney by private tutors, Dev had received his medical degree in England, then had returned to New York to open an extremely successful private practice.

"Richard." Irene rose from the dressing table and moved across the room to sit by her husband. "You know what a difficult time I had when Cheney decided to go to Seattle."

"Yes. I did, too—"

"I've prayed about it so much—about us worrying all the time about Cheney. We can't do it, Richard. She's a grown woman, a professional, and"—Irene smiled warmly, her eyes reflective—"she knows her own mind."

"She certainly does!" Richard agreed fervently.

"The Lord has finally made me see that, no matter what she decides to do, you and I need to be completely supportive. I think—no, I'm *sure*—that I made it harder on her last time. I didn't really mean to, but I guess I just hadn't faced the fact that her decisions, her surroundings, the people she associates with—everything about her life is different from mine. From most women's, as a matter of fact." Irene tucked her hand around Richard's arm and watched his face carefully as she spoke.

"More difficult than most women's—in so many ways," Richard sighed as he patted Irene's hand.

"Yes, but it was her decision to be a doctor. It's what she wanted, and obviously she made the right choice."

"That's true! She's a wonderful doctor, Irene," Richard said, his face glowing with pride. "Wasn't that an outstanding reference Asa Mercer gave her!"

" 'An excellent doctor, and an honorable and courageous woman,' " Irene quoted, gazing at the fire. "She's not our baby anymore, Richard. She's a woman, a strong woman, and she deserves respect—from us, from Dev, from everyone. I'm not going to burden her with fears and sorrow—we don't do that to Dev, do we? We've supported everything he's done, and I'm going to make sure that Cheney has the same assurance that we've been so careful to give him. Whatever she does, and wherever she goes."

"Irene," Richard murmured as he put his arms around his wife and pulled her close, "she's not the only strong, courageous woman around here."

★ ★ ★ ★

Richard and Irene went downstairs to the drawing room at seven-thirty. A fire had been built in the massive fireplace early that afternoon, and now small blue flames flickered around a huge oak log, and a three-inch bed of red embers glowed underneath it. The room was warm and inviting on this frosty November night. Two royal blue velvet couches faced each other in front of the fireplace with a low mahogany table between them. Frosted white lamp globes diffused the harsh gaslight into a comfortable glow.

Within five minutes they heard Shiloh's voice in the hallway. "Aw, c'mon, Dally! Just give me a hint!"

"No, suh! You want some o' Dally's Double Cream, you jist come heah and git you some!"

"But, Dally—"

Dally entered the drawing room, her hands folded in front of her spotless white apron, her face set. Behind her, Shiloh, a pleading look on his face, was carrying a large tray with a tea service on it.

Dally shook her head and said stubbornly, "An' if you thinks that carryin' that tray for me is gonna make me tell you—"

Shiloh set the tray on the low table in front of the couches and turned back to Dally, who made shooing motions at him with her hands. "Why, Dally, I'll carry trays for you anytime!" he declared.

He moved hastily out of her way as she bent over the table to fix three cups of tea with deft movements.

"Hmph!" she grunted.

"You might as well give it up, Shiloh." Irene smiled as she took the cup of tea Dally offered. "She won't tell anyone where she gets this cream. I've tried everything!"

Dally served everyone tea and glided to the door. "Hmph!" she grunted again as she left, and her voice drifted back to the sitting room. "I'll do all the worryin' 'bout where to git that there cream, an' Miss Irene needs to be a-worryin' 'bout eatin' it, and Mr. Richard, too. Ever'body in this house is too skinny."

Irene shook her head. "It's a wonder we all aren't round and jolly, with Dally's cooking."

Cheney appeared at the door of the drawing room. She was wearing a dress of deep blue velvet trimmed with white lace, and a sapphire-and-diamond pin that Dev had given her, on a velvet ribbon around her throat. Her hair was swept up, with long ringlets and wisps of curls in the back and over her shoulders. Gracefully she glided into the room and settled on the couch across from her mother.

"Hello, everyone! When's dinner?" She smiled. "I'm starving, and I don't care if I do get as round as a tub!"

"We can't eat yet, dear," Irene said placidly as she poured a cup of steaming, fragrant tea for Cheney. "Dev's not here. But I told him dinner was at eight o'clock, and he won't be late."

"No, he won't. He never is," Cheney agreed, accepting the tea Irene offered her. "By the way, who won the chess tournament?"

Richard looked pained, and Shiloh moved slowly to the fireplace to stand beside him. Shiloh was simply dressed but elegant in fawn breeches and a white cotton shirt with full sleeves. His knee boots were spotlessly shined.

"We're four and three," he answered with a sly look at Cheney's father.

"Darnedest thing I ever saw!" Richard shook his head. "Like trying to plan a strategy against an earthquake or a flood!"

"When I win, sir," Shiloh amended. "But you gotta admit, when I lose, it's just as dramatic."

"True. Might as well just pick up your king and toss it into the fireplace sometimes—"

"Queen probably feels that way, anyway," Cheney commented nonchalantly, and Irene smiled to herself.

The brass bell at the front door jingled.

Cheney jumped up to answer it, but Dally soundlessly sailed by before Cheney reached the door into the hallway. In passing, she mumbled, "When is they ever gonna learn that I kin answer this here do'? I dunno, after twenny-five years, if they ever gonna unnerstan' who's s'pose to be answerin' this here do'...."

Cheney turned abruptly, shook her head, and returned to the couch.

"Good evenin', Mistuh Dev," they heard Dally say. "They in the sittin' room waitin' fo' you. . . ."

After a few moments Dev entered the drawing room, going at once to kiss Irene, shake hands with Richard, nod at Shiloh, and accept a cup of tea from Cheney. Striding to the fireplace, he backed up to the fire between Cheney's father and Shiloh. "I'm cold," he announced, sipping the steaming tea. "Fire feels good."

The dinner tonight was in Dev's honor, for he had just been invited by Guy's Hospital in London to study surgery and function as a staff physician for a year. Cheney had ambivalent feelings about Dev's acceptance of the position, for she and Dev were very close; in fact, Dev had asked her to marry him the previous April. But they had not spoken of it since Cheney had returned five days before, and now Dev was leaving for England in two days.

Richard inquired about the weather in England, and he and Dev spoke for a few minutes about Dev's trip and some arrangements with which Richard was helping him.

Curiously Cheney studied Dev and Shiloh as they stood side by side. *Two men were never so different—looks, personality, attitudes, preferences, demeanor. Father says Shiloh always plays the black in chess . . . Black Knight . . . White King. . . .*

Dev spoke in a low, controlled baritone, his sentences concise, his words chosen carefully. He wore a velvet frock coat, a white linen shirt, a complicated black cravat with a small diamond stud, black breeches pressed with a knife crease, and black boots. His dark hair was groomed carefully, and his classical Greek face was sharply delineated by the firelight.

Shiloh's hair was tousled, his stance loose and relaxed, his drawl pronounced. Suddenly, over his teacup, his blue eyes caught Cheney's intense gaze. Cheney felt her cheeks redden, and dropping her eyes, she sipped her tea in confusion.

Dally announced dinner promptly at eight o'clock, and the group went down the hall to the dining room, where another fire welcomed them. The Duvalls' mahogany dining table was lavishly set with shiny brass chargers, simple white china, gold-trimmed crystal goblets, and goldware utensils. A glorious centerpiece of chrysanthemums brightened the room, which was lit only by the firelight and candles.

Richard was at the head of the table, with Irene on one side and Cheney on the other. Dev looked disgruntled as Shiloh was seated beside Cheney, and Dev across from them, but his face smoothed out instantly as he held Irene's chair. Richard said grace, and Dally began to serve.

"First of all, a toast to Devlin Buchanan, M.D." Richard beamed and lifted his crystal goblet. "Your new position is quite an honor, son, and Irene and I are very proud of you. Congratulations."

They all saluted Dev, who looked exceedingly pleased at Richard's praise.

After they drank, Dev said simply, "So many times before, I've thanked you, sir, and Miss Irene—and Cheney." He turned to include her with a glance. "Now I must thank you again, because without you, I would never have been, or done, anything."

A shared understanding and warmth passed between the Duvalls and Dev Buchanan, and even seemed to encompass Dally, who stood silently smiling at the oak sideboard. Shiloh was excluded, and he dropped his eyes and toyed with the stem of his crystal goblet.

Richard glanced at him quickly and began eating his soup, signaling that the meal should begin.

Dev took a tiny sip of the soup as his dark eyes went to Cheney. "Congratulations may also be in order for Cheney."

"What? Why?" she asked with surprise.

"I spoke to Dr. Judson Walters at Massachusetts General last week, Cheney. After the glowing article about you in the *Herald* and the commendation you received from the Washington Territorial Governor—"

"Asa Mercer received the commendation," Cheney interrupted with a sidelong glance at Shiloh, who continued to eat his soup unconcernedly. "And he was kind enough to include me—and Shiloh—in his acknowledgment. And Shiloh should have been in that article, too."

"Yes—well—" Dev shrugged. "The point is, Cheney, that Dr. Walters is reconsidering your application for staff physician. I believe he's going to offer you a position."

"That's wonderful!" Richard exclaimed. "Cheney, Massachusetts General! Wasn't that your first choice after graduation?"

"Yes, Father, it was," Cheney answered dryly, "and my first rejection. Dev, I suppose *you* suggested to Dr. Walters that he reconsider my application? If I remember our interview correctly—and unfortunately, I think I always will—Massachusetts General was not at all interested in physicians of the female persuasion. And I don't think articles in the *Herald* or some lowly governor of a mere territory would make much of an impression on the august members of that hospital board! I think their mutton-chop whiskers and handlebar mustaches have weighted down their brains!"

"Cheney!" Irene chided in mock horror. "Such personal comments on grooming!"

Richard and Shiloh were amused, but Dev regarded Cheney rather severely. She winked at her mother, who refused to acknowledge it, but Irene's mouth twitched slightly as she lifted her soup spoon.

"You're right, Mother," Cheney amended. "It wasn't ladylike of me to mention their ferocious whiskers. I'll just say that it appeared that they'd been sniffing too much formaldehyde!"

Shiloh laughed aloud, and Richard and Irene looked mystified, but Dev burst out, "Really, Cheney! Jokes about embalming fluid, and at the table!"

"Dev!" Irene protested.

"I didn't say it! Cheney said it!"

Richard, Irene, Cheney, and Shiloh laughed, and finally Dev smiled, his deep dimples flashing.

"We've heard variations on that theme for twenty years," Richard explained to Shiloh. "But the sense of humor you medical people display—" He shook his head ruefully.

"You medical people," her father had said. Not "you doctors." It didn't escape Cheney's notice that her father deliberately included Shiloh in his teasing rebuff.

Dally cleared the soup plates and served the main course. It was Richard Duvall's favorite, Beef Wellington. The crust was flaky and golden, and the tender beef fell away from the knife smoothly as Richard carved.

"Anyway, Dev," Cheney continued, taking a sip of water. "I want to thank you, because I'm certain that you had a lot to do with Dr. Walters' consideration."

Shiloh and Dev were both watching her intently, and she found she was slightly nervous. Unconsciously she glanced repeatedly at Shiloh as she spoke, and he nodded at her with encouragement. Then she sat straighter in her chair and went on, "But I've already found another position."

Silence fell in the dining room; even Dally halted for a moment as she served the diners. Again Cheney's eyes went to Shiloh. He smiled and started to say something, but Irene spoke first.

"Really, Cheney? What is it, darling?"

"Well—w-well—" Cheney faltered slightly, took a deep breath, and tried again. "I had a letter from Sharon Bateman waiting for me when Shiloh and I returned from Seattle."

Dev frowned at Cheney's easy coupling of names, and shot an appraising glance at Shiloh, but he had turned slightly toward Cheney and didn't seem to notice.

Cheney went on, "It's Sharon Carter now. She married a man named Josh Carter last year. He's from Arkansas, and that's where they live now, in Wolf County. It's a town called Black Arrow."

"Yes, of course. We remember, dear." Irene smiled reassuringly at Cheney, who looked rather surprised.

She had expected signs of protest from her mother and father, but they merely listened eagerly.

Dev frowned and asked in a mystified voice, "Sharon Bateman—do I know her?"

"Yes." Cheney smiled. "You remember Sharon, don't you? The pretty girl with brown hair and big brown eyes? We've met her several times—"

"Oh, yes, at the Vandivers' and the Nelsons', right? Everyone always asked her to play the piano."

Shiloh's face grew carefully expressionless, and by very subtle body language he withdrew slightly from Cheney. She gave no sign, but seemed to sense it, and now she turned slightly toward him as she ate. Dev's eyes narrowed, and Irene and Richard exchanged questioning glances.

His eyes on Shiloh, Dev went on, "Sharon was very charming and seemed to be extremely intelligent. She was attending the Academy of Arts and Letters, wasn't she?"

"Yes," Cheney answered, "but when the war broke out, she hurried back home to her parents' plantation outside Richmond. She hated to leave the Academy, but she's an only child, and she felt she needed to be home with her mother and father. She volunteered to help with the hospital at Chimborazo, and evidently that's where she met Josh Carter. Anyway, she's having a baby soon, and she wrote me that they have no doctor within miles of Wolf County, Arkansas."

Her parents were watching her gravely, and she dropped her eyes from her father's gaze.

Deliberately Shiloh took a long drink of water, and the ice tinkling in his glass was the only sound in the room. Then he turned to Cheney, nodded, and lifted his glass in a slight salute.

She gratefully returned his smile, and then looked up at her father. "I'm going to Arkansas . . . for Sharon, and to see if I can help those people."

Her father's eyes softened, and he reached over to put a hand on her arm. "Are you sure this is what you want to do, Cheney?"

"Yes, Father," she replied softly, and glanced back and forth from him to her mother. "I've prayed about it, and I just . . .

know that this is where I'm supposed to go." Her eyes lingered beseechingly on Irene.

"Cheney, dear," Irene said softly, "I think that's wonderful! We'll help you any way we can."

"You do? You will?" Cheney asked, her green eyes wide.

"Yes," her father added firmly, but his eyes were on Irene. "We do, and we will."

"Wait a minute!" Dev exclaimed. "You can't mean that you're going to let her do this! Arkansas!"

"Why not, Dev?" Irene asked, her sea green eyes sparkling, "We're letting you go to England."

"But—but—that's different!" Dev exclaimed.

"Why?" Cheney demanded instantly. "Because you're a man?"

"Yes! I mean, no!" Dev frowned darkly and tried again. "Cheney, be serious! You can't go to Arkansas! Alone, out there in the wilderness! Arkansas!"

"Actually—" Shiloh began.

"Dev, stop saying 'Arkansas' that way!" Cheney interrupted.

"How else can you say it, Cheney?" Dev countered, a sardonic look on his face. "Because you might as well be saying 'the other side of the moon' or 'the red planet Zeron'!"

"Well, Arkansas is—" Shiloh tried again.

"It is *not* like the red planet Zeron!" Cheney said indignantly.

"Cheney, Dev—" Irene's voice was soothing but firm. "I'd like to hear what Shiloh's trying to say."

"You would?" Shiloh grinned.

"Shiloh's been trying to say something?" Richard asked in surprise. "We've got to get the hang of refereeing three of them, Irene."

"No, you don't," Dev retorted with a meaningful look at Shiloh.

Cheney looked up at Shiloh with interest. "What did you say, Shiloh?"

Shiloh looked around the table expectantly. Then, when no

36

one spoke, he smiled lazily down at Cheney. "I was just going to say that I agree with Buchanan."

"What!" Cheney demanded.

"Listen, Cheney—" Dev began.

"It's *my* turn," Shiloh said reproachfully, and the table grew silent again.

Richard and Irene exchanged amused glances.

"I was just saying that Arkansas is kind of a wilderness—and the people are sure different, especially the hill people."

"Different?" Cheney asked. "From us?"

"Yes, and from most of the rest of the human race," Shiloh drawled. "They don't like strangers at all—"

"I can understand that." Cheney lifted her chin. "And I can deal with it."

"And they don't like educated strangers," Shiloh told her gravely. "Like doctors. And they don't like educated women, either. Or Yankees."

"But—" Cheney began.

"Listen to him, Cheney," Dev said severely.

"Guess you could just say," Shiloh told Irene and Richard woefully, "that they most especially don't like strange, educated, Yankee female doctors."

"Arkansas!" Dev muttered with disgust. "And that's why—"

"Yeah, that's why I've gotta go, too," Shiloh announced, popping a huge piece of Beef Wellington—his third helping—into his mouth.

"What!" Dev exploded.

"What?" Cheney demanded.

"What'd he say?" Richard asked Irene.

"Shiloh's going, too," Irene answered softly, her eyes on Cheney.

Richard's glance went back and forth between Cheney and Shiloh, his eyes grave.

"You can't do that, Irons," Dev snapped.

Shiloh shrugged carelessly, but his eyes were intense as he challenged Dev's hostile gaze. "I can if the Doc wants me to,

Buchanan," he said evenly. "And if Mr. Duvall and Miss Irene don't object."

Richard and Irene glanced at each other, and Cheney studied their faces carefully. Something seemed to pass between them—a look of understanding and encouragement—and Cheney marveled again, as she had so many times, at how her parents seemed to communicate so well without words.

Slowly Richard said, "If I understand the situation correctly, Shiloh is applying for a position as Cheney's nurse, and it's perfectly logical to assume that a nurse will be needed just as badly as a doctor." He glanced at Irene again, and a smile lingered in her eyes as she nodded almost imperceptibly. "I think," he went on slowly, "that it's Cheney's decision to make—and just as Irene said, we'll do whatever we can to help her."

All eyes turned to Cheney, who was watching her father and mother with pleased surprise. "Thank you, Father," she almost whispered, "and you, too, Mother. I—know it's difficult for you, in some ways."

Richard and Irene took each other's hands and smiled at Cheney with encouragement.

"Yes, it is, Cheney," Irene answered, "but we're very proud of you, and we trust you. We know you'll do the right thing."

"Taking me would be the right thing, Doc," Shiloh assured her somberly. "I know these people. I grew up with people like them in South Carolina, and remember, I was in the Twenty-second Alabama in the war. I can help you, and them, too, Doc. I know I can."

Cheney took a deep breath, glanced for the slightest instant at Dev, who was frowning, and turned back to Shiloh. "You're hired, Shiloh!" She smiled. "That is, you have a position. No money, but lots of advantages—travel, the mountains, meeting new people—"

"Cheney—" Dev controlled his voice with an effort, turned to Irene, and began again. "Miss Irene, surely you can see that this is a delicate situation? Cheney, and this—this—" He motioned to Shiloh with uncharacteristic awkwardness.

"Nurse," Shiloh said helpfully, "*Cheney's* nurse."

"Nurse!" Dev exclaimed. "You're a *man*! That's what I mean!"

"I know what you mean, Dev," Irene responded quietly, laying a soft, white hand on his arm. "We all do." Turning to Cheney she added soberly, "Darling, that is the one question I have. I do think it would be advisable for you to be accompanied by a chaperone, don't you?"

Cheney was silent for a moment, considering, her brow furrowed. Finally she looked up at Shiloh, who seemed to be trying to look as innocuous as possible, and smiled faintly. "You're right, Mother."

Richard and Irene looked immensely relieved, but remained silent, and Cheney went on almost to herself, "But—I was hoping to leave this week—and I just don't know anyone offhand. . . ."

Dev shifted restlessly in his seat and finally muttered ungraciously, "Well, there's Rissy."

"Of course!" Irene exclaimed. "Rissy! What was she going to do after you left, Dev?"

He shifted again in his seat, still eyeing Shiloh sourly. "I hadn't found anything for her. I was going to keep her on full salary to care for the house—but I could make other arrangements for that."

"Tansy an' Jake kin look out fo' dat house," Dally's voice sounded behind them. Surprised, everyone looked back at her as she stood at the oak sideboard at the far end of the room, by the kitchen door. "Rissy better go to dat Arkinsaw wi' Miss Cheney, to look out fo' her. Rissy kin do it." Dally nodded with satisfaction.

Rissy was one of Dally's daughters—a carbon copy of her, in fact, except that she was slightly smaller. Born exactly one month before Cheney, Rissy had spent a great deal of time with Cheney and Dev when they were children, as had all of Dally's children. When Dev had returned from school in England, he had hired Rissy as his housekeeper. She treated him exactly as

Dally treated the Duvalls—with exasperated affection, firm in the belief that he was helpless without her. Which was—as far as keeping a house went—very true.

"If anyone can look after Cheney—" Dev nodded with satisfaction. "Rissy can."

"I promise I'll look after Cheney, too, Dr. Buchanan"—Shiloh grinned and lifted his glass in a mock salute. "So you don't have anything to worry about."

"Wish that were true," Dev grumbled.

"Neither of you has anything to worry about," Cheney told them calmly, "because I promise *I'll* look after Rissy"—she nodded imperiously at Dev, then turned to Shiloh—"and you, too."

"Wish that was true," Shiloh mumbled.

3

STAGES

Traveling from New York to Springfield, Missouri, by train took five days—and nights.

"I thought the train trip we took across the Isthmus of Panama was bad," Cheney grumbled to Shiloh on the fourth day as they pulled out of St. Louis.

"Nah," Shiloh shrugged. "All we had to deal with then was a hurricane, a tornado, banditos, a nitroglycerin explosion, and"—he shuddered—"snakes.'"

"Yes—but at least it was exciting. This is so boring and miserable, it just grinds you to pieces."

"I know, I'm really bored," Shiloh mocked. "Wish we'd have some train robbers or at least a band of wild Indians attack us."

Cheney elbowed him sharply in the ribs, and turned again to the dirty train window to watch the miles roll by.

During the entire fourteen-hundred-mile trip, the train was crowded, noisy, smoky, dirty, and uncomfortable. When they closed the windows, the cigar, pipe, and cigarette smoke from the numerous male passengers soon clouded up the cars with a dense tobacco fog. When the windows were opened, the cars were cold, and cinders blew in. Within minutes the passengers' clothes were a uniform shade of dirty gray, and everyone sported dark hair and red eyes.

Sleeping was impossible. Cheney found that each night she would eventually slip into a nightmare unconsciousness sometime after midnight. When she awoke, she was practically lying in Shiloh's lap. Across from her, Rissy would be asleep, with her head back on the seat and her mouth open.

Shiloh never seemed to sleep. Each time Cheney would wake

up and jerk away from him in embarrassment, he would grin at her and make some remark such as, "Make a good pillow, don't I, Doc?"

In spite of his teasing and mockery, Cheney enjoyed Shiloh's company. They talked about new medical treatments and medicines, which Cheney assiduously studied. Although he had no formal training as a nurse, Shiloh had gained experience in the war with all types of medical problems, and he was an astute learner.

From time to time he would go to another car where a continual poker game was in progress. One afternoon Cheney sat alone, Rissy dozing across from her. She was totally absorbed in Rudolf Virchow's *Archive of Pathological Anatomy and Physiology and of Clinical Medicine* when a low, hoarse voice next to her ear made her jump.

"Ma'am, they's something I been wantin' to tell you ever since I got on this here train."

Cheney looked up in surprise. Bending low over her was a muscular man dressed in buckskins, with a brown western hat and knee-high fringed moccasins. Cheney had noticed him before because his moccasins, with their silver conchos in a twinkling line down the sides, were the first she had ever seen.

"What?" Cheney asked in confusion.

Buckskin slid his arm along the back of Cheney's seat and leaned in next to her. Cheney recoiled from the stench of tobacco and whiskey, but he moved in so close she could feel his breath on her ear.

"I b'lieve you're the purtiest woman I ever set eyes on. Why don't I just set down and keep you company for a while?"

"No!" Cheney snapped, and scooted as close as she could to the window. "Leave me alone!"

"Now, that ain't no way for a purty lady like you to talk! Here, lemme just move this here nice skirt over so's I won't dirty it up when I set down." Cheney looked down with horror as the man reached down to rub the material of her skirt between his grubby thumb and forefinger.

With a loud slapping sound, a hand clapped around Buckskin's arm at the wrist. Cheney watched, frozen with fascination, as the hand began to squeeze, the tendons standing out in thick cords. Simultaneously Cheney's and Buckskin's eyes went upward.

Shiloh Irons loomed above the man, grinning down with a smile that didn't reach his eyes. Buckskin let go of Cheney's dress and spread his fingers wide. Shiloh let go of his wrist, straightened, and shoved the side of his long coat back—behind a holster slung low on his hips.

"Can I help you?" Shiloh asked Buckskin, his eyes glittering.

"Colt .44 six-shot single action, ain't it?" Buckskin asked in a high voice.

"Yep."

"Thought so," Buckskin muttered. "No, don't b'lieve I need no help. I kin throw my own self off the train . . ." His voice faded as he backed down the aisle, nodding apologetically to Shiloh.

By the time they reached Springfield, Missouri, Cheney's green traveling dress and velvet mantle were in a sorry state. Shiloh, too, looked bedraggled and dirty.

As they left the train, Rissy glowered at them and direly muttered, "If you 'uns don't look awful! My mama'd hev my head if she saw you goin' about in public lookin' like—like—"

"Don't worry, Rissy," Shiloh said with a grin. His white, even teeth and blue eyes looked startling in his cinder-grimed face. "We just look like your brother and sister. Maybe we could do a minstrel show or something."

Rissy sniffed disdainfully, took a handkerchief out of her sleeve, and thrust it into Cheney's hand. "At least clean *yo'* face, Miss Cheney," she ordered. "If'n he thinks it's fun to be colored down heah in dis heathern Arkinsaw, let him stay dat way."

"This is Missouri, Rissy." Cheney scrubbed at her face with the handkerchief and succeeded only in turning the dirty film covering her face into a uniform muddy smudge. "We still have a two-day stagecoach ride to Fort Smith. Thank the Lord we're off that train! I'm looking forward to the stage for a change!"

Shiloh chuckled, low in his throat. "You ever ridden a stage before, Doc?"

"No. Why?"

"You'll find out. They're as much fun as a five-day train ride."

"What? Why's that?" Cheney and Rissy exclaimed in unison.

Shiloh shrugged. "Well, maybe they aren't quite as much fun as the train. Stage doesn't have the creature comforts—like water, air, and light, and an inch or so to move in. But it'll be real fun, Doc! You'll have an excuse to sit on my lap, instead of pretending like you're asleep!"

While Cheney spluttered, Rissy gave Shiloh a murderous look and pointedly moved to walk in between them as they made their way to the stagecoach office.

Shiloh was right. The stagecoach was dark, cold, and crowded, and the ride was painfully jarring. All of the six passengers were tossed back and forth onto their neighbors and up and down and almost off the seats. Cheney's memories of the two-day trip were of a teeth-clenching headache, constant apologies to her fellow passengers for kicking them, and literally ending up square on Shiloh's lap twice.

The overnight stage stop was a rough log cabin that sat by itself in the lonely Missouri woods. The front half of the cabin was a long, dark room with a fireplace at one end. A silent Flathead Indian woman served them a thick vegetable stew that was surprisingly good.

The back half of the cabin was separated into two rooms with four bunks each. Shiloh turned around at the door of the men's bedroom, announced, "Think I'll go bunk out in the stable," and disappeared.

Cheney's and Rissy's room had a leprous brown floor, grime-gray walls, and lumpy bedding complete with bedbugs. Rissy fussed loudly and tried to shake out the blanket and pillow on one of the lumpy bunks, but Cheney fell across the other one and passed out.

★ ★ ★ ★

The mountains in the near foreground looked blue and misty, even though the day was dry and clear. High above the wagon and team making their way slowly across the plain, a hawk soared effortlessly, the only mark upon the deep blue sky. He escorted the travelers for a brief time, then disappeared behind one of the sharp-peaked hills.

Aside from the hawk, the travelers saw two rabbits, three deer, and eight squirrels the entire day after they left Fort Smith. Cheney was aware that they were gradually ascending to higher elevations. The air grew keener and sharper and steadily colder toward noon and into the afternoon. The plains leading to the Moccasin Mountains were wooded in places, mostly along the Osage River to their left, but most of their journey was through wide fields, now brown and bleak.

"How do you know where to go?" Cheney asked Shiloh curiously. To her, the terrain was generally unremarkable, with no distinctive landmarks. There was a semblance of a road, but it sometimes forked, and to Cheney one track looked much the same as the next.

"I asked the stable hand in Fort Smith, where I bought the horses and team, Doc. Wolf County is northeast of Fort Smith. Just keep the sun to your right and a little behind in the morning and to your left and behind in the afternoon."

Cheney digested this in silence, but on her other side Rissy remarked acidly, "An' where does you keep the moon while youse traipsin' along out heah? It's gonna be dark soon, Mr. Shiloh!"

Shiloh leaned over Cheney to speak reassuringly to Rissy. "When we get to the foothills, Rissy, we just follow the river right through what they call Cougar's Way. We didn't follow the river all the way out of Fort Smith because it winds around too much. But in case anything happens to me—you know, if the cougars get me or somethin' "—he sat back and winked at Cheney—"you just follow the river from here on in."

45

"Don't you go makin' funnies about that, Mr. Shiloh," Rissy chided, her brow wrinkling as she looked about them. "Dis heah's a spooky place, if'n you ask me."

Shiloh looked amused, but Cheney secretly agreed with Rissy. The mountains ahead were not high by Alpine standards, but they seemed remote and inhospitable in the pale yellow winter sun. And it was so quiet! Occasionally a bird would call, but it always sounded far-off and mournful.

The setting sun threw Shiloh's face into sharp relief, and his blond hair glowed with pale fire.

Cheney broke a long silence as they neared the pass that marked the southwestern boundary of Wolf County. "Shiloh?"

"Hmm?"

"Do you think we've gone totally mad? Coming out here to this remote wilderness?"

Shiloh looked puzzled, and Cheney went on hastily, "Well, I suppose you might not see it that way—you've been in places like this before, and gotten to know the people. But I—I've never been anywhere but New York and Philadelphia! How—"

"And halfway around the world when we went to Seattle," Shiloh chimed in.

"But that was different! Mr. Mercer and the ladies were just like the people I've known all my life. And being on ship—well, that was dangerous, sometimes, and maybe not as—nice as my home, but it was—it was—"

"It was a place and a way of life that was familiar to you, Doc. So it was easy for you to be in charge." He glanced obliquely at Cheney, who was beginning to look rebellious, and Shiloh went on hastily, "But people are the same everywhere, you know. They may talk different, or be different colors, or wear clothes that aren't like yours, but they're pretty much alike. Some you care about, some you like, some you trust—"

"Some you beat up," Cheney put in smartly.

"And some beat you up." Shiloh grinned. "Anyway, Doc," he finished with a shrug, "when we were in the war, we all liked to sit around and talk about this battle and that battle, and what

46

we'd do and shoulda done. But when it came time to go into battle—well, we all turned a little white-faced and clench-jawed."

Cheney sighed loudly. "But you went, and you fought, and—"

"Some I beat up, and some beat me up."

Cougar's Way was mostly a trough cut by the Osage River between two high peaks, with narrow beaten tracks on either side of the river. It was heavily wooded on both sides, and in places the wagon was hub-deep in water as they struggled through. Twilight overtook them. The wind picked up through the pass and made plaintive moans in the thick pines along with crackling noises in the bare hardwoods, and the cold grew more piercing. Shiloh was vigilant, but he seemed relaxed, and reassured Rissy often that they were fine and would be at the settlement soon. Cheney knew that the confident words were for her benefit too, but still she grew uneasy in the semidarkness.

When they came through the pass, a three-quarter moon peeked over the ridge ahead of them, on the other side of the valley. Below, they could see the river flowing into a small lake, and Cheney thought she saw symmetrical outlines of buildings. But there were no lights.

Eagerly the two horses began the gentle descent. The road was wider on this side of Cougar's Way, and the horses seemed to be as glad to be out of the oppressive passageway between the mountains as Cheney and Rissy were. Within an hour they had reached the valley, and slowly followed along the river to the lake.

"I see buildings, but no lights," Cheney worried. "I was afraid Sharon wouldn't get my letter in time. No one's here to meet us. How are we going to find the house—and who are we going to see about staying there?"

Sharon had said in her letter that there was a house in the settlement that would be perfect for a doctor's office. Some timber company had built it for their offices on the first floor and living quarters on the second, but now it was empty. Sharon

47

didn't say why, but she did say that she was certain they would "let Cheney have it." Cheney thought that was very strange, so in her letter to Sharon she told her that she planned to lease it or buy it, whichever the owners preferred.

"Shouldn't be too hard, Doc," Shiloh drawled. "From what I see, there's not that many buildings here, and only one of 'em looks like a two-story."

With a shock, Cheney realized Shiloh was right. She had seen the few buildings, but somehow had persuaded herself that the city streets and all the businesses and houses were just out of view. Now she realized that Black Arrow consisted of a few buildings dotted along Moccasin Lake in Wolf County, Arkansas—and that was it.

Shiloh pulled the horses up in front of the two-story house and jumped out of the wagon. Cheney looked anxiously at the building, squinting in the darkness. It seemed taller than it was wide. She couldn't tell what it was made of in the darkness, but it looked like some kind of shingles. The front door was centered. There was a window on either side on the first floor, and two windows above on the second. Two steps led up to a front porch that had a small roof made of the same shingling, but there were no sides to the porch.

Shiloh looked around quizzically, yanked on the horses' harness, and pulled them up close to the house, where he tied them securely to one of the porch pillars. His voice sounded quietly amused as he muttered in the darkness, "Here we are! Duvall Court, Black Arrow, Arkansas!"

4

ALL APPEARANCE OF EVIL

The room was filled with an aromatic, woodsy scent, and the faintest whiff of coffee and bacon enticed Cheney to stir. Her eyes didn't open, but her nostrils flared as she breathed deeply. *Fires in autumn . . . breakfast . . . Father's study . . .*

Slowly sitting up, she hugged the thick down comforter closer and looked around owlishly. She was in a small attic room—the ceiling was slanted with the roof line—made entirely of some fragrant reddish wood boards, some with white stripes through them. A cheerful morning sun glowed through plain white muslin curtains covering a small window at the far end of the room. Tucked in the opposite corner from the small bunk was a large brown overstuffed chair next to a small table, which held a kerosene lantern.

Cheney yawned and stretched. *The cabin . . . Black Arrow . . . no gaslights . . .* Her eyes fell on the "thunder mug" underneath a small washstand to her left. *And no indoor water closet?* Cheney blinked rapidly as she stared at the white porcelain pot.

"Ah hears you, Miss Cheney!" Rissy's deep voice drifted up the stairwell. "Coffee's 'most ready! Ah'm comin' up dere in a minute!"

How'd she hear me? Cheney wondered as she reluctantly pushed back the down comforter and climbed out of the small bed. *Just like her mother! I always swore Dally could hear Mother's eyes open in the mornings!* "No, I'll come down, Rissy!"

"Don't you be a-runnin' down here in yo' never-minds! Mistuh Shiloh's here!"

"Yes, Rissy!" Cheney called back obediently. Quickly she pulled on a simple gray skirt made of the softest cashmere and a plain white cotton blouse, and grabbed a matching cashmere shawl. Hurrying down the narrow steps, her mouth watering at the smell of bacon cooking, she looked curiously around the cabin. When they had arrived the previous night, Cheney had been too tired to notice much of anything by the dim lantern light. Rissy had checked the rooms upstairs and sternly ordered her to bed, and Cheney had obeyed without protest.

The entire cabin seemed to be made of the unusual red wood. A merry fire crackled in a large fireplace on the right side of the front room. Cozily arranged around the fireplace were a small settee and two rocking chairs. To Cheney's left, a large businesslike oak desk was centered between two big windows.

Two smaller windows framed the heavy oak door, and all of the windows had sturdy hinged shutters, which were now opened to admit the pale yellow sunlight into the small but cozy room. Cheney noticed that the floors were covered by some type of rug that she had never seen before; it seemed to be woven of long loops of cotton material. All the rooms, and even the stairs, were adorned with the same type of rug. Basically white, with occasional threads of red, yellow, and blue, the rugs warmed and brightened what would otherwise be rather dark and somber rooms.

"Whut breakfast they is, is ready," Rissy bellowed from the kitchen as Cheney hurried through the door to the back half of the cabin.

Shiloh glanced up from a small wooden table by a window. An enormous pile of bacon was in front of him, and steam rose from a plain white mug by his plate. He nodded at her, noisily crunching a mouthful of bacon.

"Mmm, smells wonderful!" Cheney exclaimed. "I want lots of bacon, and no peaches! I had enough peaches on the train to do me for a long time!"

"Ain't a fittin' breakfast for a lady," Rissy grumbled as she poured coffee from a blue tin coffeepot on top of the potbellied stove. "Jest coffee an' a big pile o' bacon! Ain't no aigs, ain't no biscuits! You cain't be eatin' like a plowhan' ever' mornin', Miss Cheney!"

Cheney giggled as she slid into the rough wooden chair across from Shiloh, and Rissy put down a plate of bacon and her coffee. "You have to make up your mind, Miss Rissy. You think if I just eat bacon, I'm eating like a plowhand, but if I also had four eggs and half-a-dozen biscuits, I'd be eating like a lady?"

"Well—they is most sartainly *ladies*," Rissy asserted stoutly, "and then—they is *ladies*."

Shiloh's mystified eyes met Cheney's as she munched contentedly on the crisp bacon, and finally he was able to speak. "Good mornin', Doc. What do you think of your new home?"

Studying the small kitchen—built also of the reddish wood, with a wooden floor—Cheney chewed and thoughtfully licked her fingers. "Quaint," she pronounced carefully.

"Picturesque," Shiloh suggested.

"Distinctive—"

"Pastoral—"

"Rustic—"

"Foolishness," Rissy sniffed as Shiloh and Cheney grinned at each other, "is whut I'd call it. Considerin' that we 'uns jest galloped up heah an' decided this must be Miss Cheney's house 'thout askin' somebody first."

"Don't worry, Rissy." Shiloh shrugged. "I've already talked to the owner, and we're legal now."

"You have?" Cheney asked in surprise. "Where is he? Who is he? He doesn't mind us renting this place? For how much?"

"Yes—down the road—Waylon DeSpain—no—and he'll exchange rent if you'll doctor his men," Shiloh answered briskly as Rissy poured him more coffee and rolled her eyes upward.

"He will? How many men does he have, and what are they doing here? How long can we have it? The cabin, I mean?"

Shiloh took a sip of the scalding coffee. "Yes—five, counting himself—they're in the timber business—and as long as we want. The cabin, I mean," he added mockingly.

Cheney smiled and relented. "All right, suppose you just tell me about him."

"But that's no fun."

"Shiloh!"

"Okay, okay. During the war, Waylon DeSpain met a man from here named Enoch Satterfield. DeSpain owns a timber business in Missouri, and Satterfield told him about Wolf County. So DeSpain came here after the war to look around, and he seems to think this is ideal timber country. This was his and his foreman's cabin when they first came. Now he's built a big office and a house and quarters for his men down the road, and he's brought some other men in. He didn't have plans for this place, so he said he'd let you have it if you'll tend his people."

Cheney thought carefully as she nibbled at the thick bacon and sipped the strong coffee. Sighing slightly, she asked in a low voice, "Did you tell him I'm a woman?"

"Nope." Shiloh grinned. "I'm gonna let him have the pleasure of finding that out for himself. Shouldn't make any difference anyway."

"It shouldn't, but it does," Cheney muttered.

Shiloh shrugged and went on thoughtfully, "He offered to let me stay in the quarters he's built for his men, but I don't think I'll do that right now. Don't want to be beholden to anyone until we get the lay of the land. . . . He said something about feudin'."

Cheney had no idea what "feudin'" was, but she was distracted by the thought of quarters for Shiloh. "But—but wherever did you stay last night?" she asked anxiously, looking around the kitchen as if there might be a bunk somewhere that she hadn't noticed. "Did you stay here?"

"No, ma'am, he sartainly *didn't*, an' *won't!*" Rissy huffed.

"Rissy wouldn't let me," Shiloh replied unnecessarily. "She made me stay out in the stable, and it was cold." He let his broad shoulders droop sorrowfully, but he spoiled the melancholy effect by picking up a piece of bacon and munching with obvious relish.

"But that's—I don't want you to—" Cheney began uncertainly, feeling rather guilty that she hadn't made some kind of arrangements for Shiloh.

"Dat's right," Rissy retorted as she began to sweep the spotless wooden floor, "an' what do you thinks I'm heah fo'? To chaferone them hosses?"

"But Rissy—"

Rissy's mouth tightened, but her voice was gentle as she stopped sweeping and turned to face Shiloh and Cheney. "It ain't dat I think nothin' mismannered 'bout neither one o' you two. But the Lawd tole us to 'stain from all 'pearance of evil. An' dat's why I'm here, Miss Cheney, and you knows it, too, Mistuh Shiloh."

"I know," Shiloh answered, "but you remind me again tonight when I go out to sleep in that cold, lonely stable, Rissy."

Rissy again began to sweep with vehemence. "Souns to me lak them heels o' yours needs some coolin' off anyways, Mistuh Shiloh Arns!"

★ ★ ★ ★

"They're a kind of new breed," Shiloh told Cheney as he slapped the muscular rump of one of the horses, "called Standardbred. More suited to driving than quarter horses, but they're good saddle horses, too."

"They certainly look good," Cheney answered, expertly running her hand down the horse's near foreleg. "Good girth, wide chest, and the legs are sturdy and muscular. But aren't they rather long-legged?"

"Both of them are sixteen hands," Shiloh admitted, moving to rub the other horse's nose, "but Mr. Jack said they're a really sturdy breed, as long as the muscles of the legs are proportionate to the girth. What do you think?"

Cheney stepped back to study the two geldings. Both were a rich chocolate brown color, their coats thickened for winter so they were shiny but not glossy. One had a white sock on his near hind leg, and one had a stocking on his off hind leg. As far as she could see, their conformation was excellent, their musculature well-pronounced. Squinting, Cheney decided that they were simply large, well-formed horses, and their legs were well in proportion. As she studied them, they seemed at the same time to be assessing her with intelligent, liquid brown eyes. One of them snorted slightly, the puff of breath from his nostrils steaming in the cold air.

"I think you did very well." Cheney nodded with satisfaction. "They look wonderful. And now that I think about it, I can see why you'd need a saddle horse of sixteen hands or so." She crossed her arms and looked Shiloh's six-foot-four-inch frame up and down critically. "Guess your heels drag the ground on fourteen hands."

Shiloh laughed as he petted the horse, who seemed to enjoy it immensely. The other horse whickered impatiently and, to Cheney's surprise, moved up and nudged her hand insistently. She began to stroke his silky muzzle and he, too, stood still. "Looks like this one chose me," she smiled, "and that one chose you."

"Suits me." Shiloh turned to her, and the horse impatiently nosed his back. "Why don't you go get something warm on, and I'll saddle up Stocking for you and Sock for me."

Cheney agreed and hurried back to the cabin. Rissy called from the kitchen, "Your wool cloak's down heah by the fireplace, Miss Cheney! Don't you be a-sashayin' aroun' out there in jest dat shawl!"

Cheney went into the kitchen to filch another cup of coffee, then went to the small front room to stand by the fire and sip it. Looking around speculatively, she planned the conversion of the room into an examining room, thinking about where to put shelves for supplies and where to put extra chairs for people waiting.

Shaking her head, Cheney retrieved the warm floor-length wool cloak, wrapped the shawl loosely around her head, and hurried back out to the stable. Her auburn hair curled about her face, her cheeks were pink with cold, and her green eyes sparkled. In spite of her misgivings about the people here, she was excited and eager to begin. *Shiloh said there were about two hundred people in these hills! How in the world have they been coping without a doctor?* she wondered. *And it's a full day's ride to Fort Smith! Surely, even if I am a woman, these people will be glad to have a doctor here!*

Stocking was saddled and hitched outside the stable. As Cheney hurried up, she stopped abruptly and stared.

Shiloh led Sock out of the stable and looked at her quizzically. "What's the matter, Doc?"

"But—but—" She pointed to Stocking and stammered, "that—that's—"

"A saddle," Shiloh offered helpfully.

"But it's a *western* saddle!" Cheney burst out. "Surely you don't expect me to sit astride that horse!"

Shiloh's face registered comic surprise, and it was his turn to stammer. "But—but—Doc—"

"Shiloh! Mother would kill me!"

"Rissy will kill *me*," Shiloh moaned. "But it just didn't occur to me! Come to think of it, I haven't seen any sidesaddles out here. I know there weren't any at the livery in Fort Smith where I got these. . . . I just bought some good, plain, sturdy saddles, and I didn't think. . . ."

Cheney's eyes flashed as she turned to him, her hands on her hips. "Have you forgotten that I'm not just 'the Doc,' I'm a woman, and I—"

"No," he interrupted her quietly, and stepped close to her. "I'll never forget that. Don't you remember we talked about that in Seattle, after I came back from the gold fields?"

Cheney did remember—and she also remembered the kiss that accompanied the conversation—and the memory flustered her. Stepping back a little, she looked up at him accusingly, "Don't change the subject! I was looking forward to riding, but now I guess I'll have to drive the wagon!"

"But," Shiloh answered, his eyes still warm on Cheney's face, "when DeSpain gave me directions, he warned me that we'd either have to walk or ride the last mile or so. The Carter place is on the other side of that mountain, about halfway up." He pointed to the group of hills looming over the valley to the north.

Cheney stalked to her gelding, tightened the girth, checked the bit, adjusted the blanket, slipped her fingers under the headpiece, and then went to the other side to go through the same routine.

Shiloh watched with amusement, noting the tiny lines between her eyebrows as she frowned darkly.

Finally she looked up and told Shiloh evenly, "I guess I can sit on this—this—monstrosity—sidesaddle. But let's take off this right stirrup. It'll drive Stocking crazy to have it flapping around."

"But how can you stay up without that little knob sticking out to hook your leg on?" Shiloh asked curiously.

"I'll just have to hold onto that thing." Cheney jabbed a forefinger impatiently at the saddle.

"Saddle horn," Shiloh volunteered. "And you're gonna look like a dude if you do."

"At least this way," Cheney snapped, "some people may realize I'm not a man!"

Soon the pair were riding in silence down the dirt street. Cheney was perched rather precariously on the big horse, her head held high. Shiloh gave her sidelong anxious looks.

Black Arrow was a small town indeed. On the left a few cabins huddled against the lake. One had the door standing open, and as Cheney and Shiloh passed, a small man with a gray beard appeared on the porch, drying his hands on his spotless white apron. A tiny faded sign above the door read "Sikes' General Store." The window displayed some canned goods and a bolt of cloth. The man watched them pass, and Cheney nodded pleasantly, but he didn't smile or nod back. The cabin seemed to be connected to an identical one by a curious open-ended hallway.

56

No sign was displayed, but three men lounged in a familiar manner on the porch. One of them leaned over and spat an amber stream as they passed.

"Is that a saloon?" Cheney asked curiously.

"Dunno," Shiloh shrugged.

"You mean you don't know yet," Cheney amended smartly.

"Mmm, maybe."

Cheney was a little surprised at the halfhearted response.

A few more buildings were scattered on their right, mostly cabins. Farther down a brand-new schoolhouse—painted red, with a bell tower—and a church, a white building with a small steeple, nestled against the low foothills, which DeSpain had called Wolf Run.

On the edge of town, by the river, was an imposing ranch-style house, conspicuous because of its size and the fact that it was of finished lumber, unlike the other rough-hewn lumber buildings or log cabins. Beside it was a long rectangular building, also of finished lumber.

"DeSpain's," Shiloh told her in a low voice, nodding toward it.

A few men trudged along the street, all of them stopping to watch the riders, the expressions on their faces ranging from curious to hostile. One buggy, pulled by a single horse and driven by a woman who kept her eyes straight ahead of her, passed them. No other horses were in sight, though there were a blacksmith shop and livery stable.

Cheney noticed that Shiloh was appraising her thoughtfully, then seemed to come to some decision. Tightening his jaw, he yanked his new black western hat lower over his eyes and stared straight ahead. "Doc, would you do me a favor?"

"Well, of course, if I can."

"Just—don't tell anyone that I used to be a fighter."

"All right." Cheney was surprised, and the two rode in silence for a few moments. She hoped he would say more, but he didn't, so finally she asked, "Can you tell me why, Shiloh?"

"Kinda hard," he muttered, and was silent again.

Cheney began to wonder if he would answer her—Shiloh wasn't shy, but he was extremely reserved when it came to personal matters. He never gossiped about other people, he expected the same courtesy to be extended toward him, and he didn't like to talk about himself any better than he liked telling tales on others.

At length he explained in a voice so low that Cheney had to strain to hear. "I'm tired of fighting. All I did before the war was fight. And the war—" He shrugged and made a helpless upturned-palm gesture, and Cheney recognized the same deep inner weariness that she had seen in her father since he had come home. "And the last couple of times I fought, I—didn't fight—*smart*; I was fighting *mad*. I don't want to do it anymore."

Cheney waited, then realized that he was finished. "I understand, and I think it's a good thing to do, Shiloh. Fighting—for money, or . . . you know. . . . People could get hurt."

"Yeah." He grinned. "Like me."

The tension eased in his face and the set of his jaw, and Cheney relaxed to enjoy the ride. They had reached the base of the mountain, and the wide road veered off to the left, but the two riders took a small cart track to the right and began to ascend. Soon they reached a ridge and followed it toward the second mountain in the range.

Cheney looked around with frank curiosity. She had never been in such deep, isolated woods. *So quiet,* she thought with wonder. *Hardly a sound! I guess if the wind were blowing . . . but I've never imagined silence like this.* Tucking the cloak more securely under her chin, she shivered slightly in the cold that seemed to be growing damp. The only sounds were the creaks of the saddles, the dull thumps of the horses' hooves, the calls and songs of birds, and occasional rustles in the underbrush. At first the mysterious crackles and sounds made Cheney uneasy, but eventually they saw three rabbits and several squirrels, and she realized that the sounds were surely made by the small animals.

Abruptly Shiloh reined in Sock and reached over to grab Stocking's bit and stop him.

"What—?" Cheney asked, startled.

"Quiet."

Obediently, her heart thumping, she remained quiet and still on the horse, whose ears pricked forward. She scanned the woods, the remoteness and silence weighing oppressively on her, and then glanced at Shiloh anxiously. He was motionless, vigilant and listening. Cheney didn't hear or see anything unusual. The same thick pines and cedars surrounded them, with the occasional bare oaks and maples, and the forest was as quiet as before.

They remained frozen and silent for long moments. Cheney noticed that the horses stood quietly, not fidgeting or stamping, obedient to the tightness on their reins. Shiloh pulled his long coat back from his right side, and she remembered the .44 from the train. She also noticed that her breath showed ragged gusts of steam on the air, while Shiloh's breathing was slow and even, long feathery plumes from his nostrils. Self-consciously Cheney steadied herself and determined to breathe normally.

Shiloh's eyes cut back and forth alertly across the limited view of the landscape, and then he loosened the reins and nudged Sock forward gently. Cheney did the same.

Quietly he told her, "I think there's someone here, close."

"But where? I don't see anything or hear anything."

"Neither do I—now." They went forward slowly over the rough track, both riders searching the woods on either side. After a while Shiloh seemed to relax, but Cheney felt the same uneasiness she had felt the day before. The landscape didn't look hostile—but somehow the silence seemed oppressive, as if the forest resented the intruders.

At the end of the ridge, the cart path forked three ways: one path went straight up the mountain in front of them, the right seemed to follow the gentle curve around to the other side of the mountain, and the left curved sharply down. Shiloh hesitated, turning in the saddle to look in all directions. The valley and Black Arrow had long since disappeared from their view; even though they were high up into the Moccasin Mountains, the timber was so thick that they could rarely see more than a few feet on either side.

"Guess it must be this way." Shiloh shrugged as he turned Sock down the path to their right. "DeSpain said the Carters lived on the north side of the mountains, and the other two don't look like they circle around."

Silently Cheney followed him, still nervously searching the woods and occasionally turning quickly to look behind. Once she thought she saw a movement in her peripheral vision behind and to the left, but when she focused on the spot, there was nothing.

"Path narrows up here." Shiloh pointed ahead. "We'll have to ride single file." He maneuvered Sock in front.

With a mutinous look on her face, Cheney sat up straighter and followed close behind.

The path was clear, because the pine trees on each side grew so close that the ground was carpeted with a thick pad of brown needles, and the sun didn't shine through enough to support thick undergrowth. The way grew dim and colder, and the quiet seemed completely unnatural to Cheney. Once she heard the distant high scream of a hawk, and it made her shiver.

Suddenly a loud crack split the silence of the forest, a telltale sound that even Cheney realized was a stick snapping from a heavy foot. The two riders pulled the horses up to a stop so abruptly that Stocking reared a little. Her eyes wide and startled, Cheney could feel herself losing her seat, and she desperately grabbed the saddle horn with both hands, fumbling so as not to drop the reins. Stocking settled down, and Cheney turned her head from side to side, trying to see whatever or whoever it was.

"Howdy," Shiloh said in a steady voice, and his right hand went to rest upon his thigh, close to the gun.

A man stepped onto the path directly in front of them from behind a tree, and Cheney drew in a sharp breath that sounded loud in the silence. Dressed in muted grays and browns, with a wide-brimmed hat pulled low over his face, he was carrying a worn double-barreled shotgun. Deliberately he planted his feet wide apart in the middle of the path and raised the gun slowly— three inches only—to point at Sock's chest—but he didn't put his eye down to the sight. His face was shadowed as he stood silent and still ten feet in front of Shiloh.

"Howdy," he answered in a voice as calm as Shiloh's. "Ya'll are lost."

5

ETIQUETTE OF HOSTILITIES

In the unearthly quiet of the forest the three froze in a motionless tableau. Stocking whisked his tail slightly, and to Cheney the swishing sound seemed very loud. Shiloh's back was ramrod-straight, and the stranger's posture looked equally as stubborn. *What do we do now?* Cheney wondered apprehensively. *Shoot it out?*

"We're going to visit a friend of mine. Her n-name is Sharon Bateman—I mean, Sharon Carter," Cheney offered hesitantly. "Do you know her?"

Still the stranger was silent and motionless, his face shadowed by the large-brimmed hat. Long moments passed. Finally he let the shotgun barrel drop a few meaningful inches toward the ground. Relaxing his watchful attitude, he reached up to remove his hat. "Like I said"—he nodded, dusting the hat against his breeches—"ya'll are lost. This here's Satterfield land. Carter land's on t'other side of the ridge."

Cheney was surprised at the appearance of the stranger, now that she could see his features. He was much younger than she had thought—about eighteen or nineteen—with a shock of thick straight black hair parted in the middle and wandering down over his collar. Sturdily built, of average height, he had wide shoulders and big, strong hands. As he glanced up from dusting his hat, Cheney saw that the expression in his dark eyes was almost shy. He was not a handsome young man, but his face was strong, with a prominent forehead, straight nose, and muscular jaw that made the hollows in his cheeks very pronounced.

"I'm Jimmy Dale Satterfield," he told them, "and if'n you wanna foller me, I'll take you to the Carter place. Y'all are lost," he said again. It seemed to be some sort of apology for his former hostile attitude.

"I'm Shiloh Irons, and this is Dr. Cheney Duvall," Shiloh replied evenly. "We'd appreciate your help."

With a meaningful glance at Shiloh's guarded face, Jimmy Dale walked carefully and deliberately between the two horses, giving them plenty of time to turn around so he wouldn't be at their backs.

Obviously my drawing room manners don't serve much purpose here, Cheney reflected as she noted the deliberation in the young man's words and movements, and Shiloh's wary, cautious reactions. *This—etiquette of hostilities—is all new to me, but I'll remember it. I'll learn!* she vowed to herself.

Jimmy Dale walked twenty feet in front of the two riders, and Cheney noticed that his steps made no sound. He was wearing knee-high moccasins, worn and plain. Cheney could barely see him as he moved against the muted winter colors of the woods. Pulling the gray cloak around her more tightly, she reflected that he looked much warmer than she, even though his clothing was worn and shiny.

"He must've stepped on that stick on purpose, to let us know he was there," Cheney whispered to Shiloh.

"I knew he was there," Shiloh muttered back, "and *he* knew I knew. But it's not a good idea to jump out in front of two riders like a haint. Good way to get shot up here."

"What on earth is a haint?" Cheney inquired.

"Well, they're not always *on* earth," Shiloh replied mysteriously. "You'll probably find out about 'em soon enough."

When they reached the fork again, Jimmy Dale took the left-hand path that led straight down the mountain. Shiloh hesitated slightly, his eyes narrowed. But Jimmy Dale never looked back as he trudged confidently down the track, and Cheney looked at Shiloh questioningly. Finally he nudged Sock, and the riders followed.

After a long, steep descent, the path led back upward and around the mountain, and Cheney realized that the deceptive downhill track followed the hollow between the two mountains, then threaded back up.

Half an hour passed, and the three made their way slowly upward. All sounds of their passing were hollow and muted in the deep woods, and when the music began, Cheney at first thought she was hearing things. Faint, mournful humming vibrated on the air, and she shook her head impatiently, thinking that her ears were ringing from the altitude. But as they made their way through the pine corridors, the notes crystallized into the music of some stringed instrument, tuned to a minor key, that somehow reminded Cheney of bagpipes. Then the singing began; a woman's voice, high and clear.

> *Alas, my love, you do me wrong,*
> *To cast me out discourteously!*
> *For I have loved you so long,*
> *Delighting in your company. . . .*
> *Greensleeves is my delight,*
> *Greensleeves is all my joy.*
> *Greensleeves is my heart of gold—*
> *And who, but my Lady Greensleeves?*

"Greensleeves" . . . Henry the Eighth wrote it. . . . Timeless hills and Tudor songs . . . It was an unearthly music, strange to Cheney's ears, but somehow fitting, and also unsettling. She glanced up at Shiloh, who nodded that he, too, heard it, and silently pointed up ahead. A slender thread of gray smoke was imprinted on the faded blue sky, and Cheney glimpsed a stone chimney outlined in the pines far above them.

The music grew somewhat louder. Without warning, Jimmy Dale disappeared—at first Cheney thought he had stepped into the woods—but then she realized he had turned a corner in the path. The music stopped abruptly as Cheney and Shiloh rounded the corner behind him.

Their guide was talking to a young girl who was sitting cross-legged beside the path on a large flat rock. On her lap was a stringed instrument quite unlike any Cheney had ever seen, and she was holding a large white feather. Even from a distance Cheney could see what a lovely young girl she was. About eighteen years old, she had thick golden hair, satiny against her shoulders and back, plainly dressed with a bit of light green ribbon.

"This here's some friends of Sharon's," Jimmy Dale was saying, nodding toward the two riders. "They got lost over on our land."

The girl looked up at Jimmy Dale, alarm evident in her unusual light green eyes, and he shook his head and made a negating gesture with his hand. Turning back to Cheney and Shiloh, she watched them with open curiosity as they rode toward her.

Cheney reflected upon the couple as she drew near. *Not touching, but close—tenderness in their eyes and in his gestures. She was waiting for him, I think.*

Shiloh stopped to dismount a few feet away from the rock where the girl sat and took off his hat. "I'm Shiloh Irons, ma'am," he told her, and gesturing to Cheney continued, "and this is Dr. Cheney Duvall."

"I'm Bobbie Jo Carter," the girl told them, staring with open curiosity at Cheney. "Sharon told us ya'll would be comin'."

Her words and gaze were neither hostile nor courteous, and Cheney was again a little unnerved at the evident lack of social niceties in these people, but she merely smiled and nodded pleasantly.

Jimmy Dale pointed up and to their left. "Josh and Sharon's is on up the path. Take the left fork at the stump. Right fork leads to Lige and Katie's."

"Thank you," Shiloh answered, and remounted.

"Mr. Irons," Jimmy Dale said in a low, intense voice as Shiloh turned Sock down the path, "you don't wanna go gittin' lost on Satterfield land agin. My daddy or my brother wouldn't be near as happy to see you as I were."

"Happy to see you, too, Jimmy Dale," Shiloh responded with a grin, which Jimmy Dale unexpectedly returned. "And call me Shiloh."

Bobbie Jo was still unabashedly staring at Cheney. Shiloh led the way up the path, and Cheney followed, smiling at Bobbie Jo and thanking Jimmy Dale as they passed. Both of them simply watched, neither smiling nor frowning, as she rode by.

When they were out of hearing distance Cheney muttered, "They don't waste your time with a lot of talking, do they?"

Without looking back Shiloh answered, "You're going to have to give them some time, Doc. You're a stranger, you know—"

"I know, you told me," Cheney sighed. "A strange, educated, Yankee, female doctor."

"Sittin' sideways on a horse," Shiloh added, "and holdin' onto the saddle horn for dear life."

Rebelliously, Cheney snatched her hand away from the saddle horn and, copying Shiloh, took both reins in her left hand. Then she didn't know what to do with her right hand, and, sighing again, she put it back on the saddle horn.

Soon they passed the fork in the path and came to a small log cabin perched on what seemed to be a ledge hewn out from the mountainside. Cedar shakes covered the roof, and smoke rose from the carefully laid natural stone chimney. Two rocking chairs sat companionably close on the front porch. On one side of the cabin was a large garden, with bright orange pumpkins cheerfully strewn along the ground. On the other side of the cabin a small stable huddled against the mountainside. Shiloh and Cheney reined up when they reached the porch, but he stopped her from dismounting with a commanding gesture.

"Hello!" he called loudly. "We're looking for the Carters!"

The heavy wooden door to the cabin swung open, and a woman came running out, skimming across the porch and flying down the steps. "Cheney! You're finally here!"

Cheney unceremoniously jumped down from Stocking and ran toward the girl. "Sharon!" They met at the bottom of the porch and embraced, patting each other on the back and talking at the same time. Shiloh watched with amusement, then dismounted and tied Sock and Stocking to the split-rail hitching post in front of the cabin.

"You look wonderful!"

"How marvelous! I've wondered and wondered when you'd be here—"

"How far along are you? Where's your husband?"

"Did you have any trouble? Did you get lost? I didn't know when to send to town for you—"

Arms around each other's waists, Cheney and Sharon forgot Shiloh completely and went into the cabin. He sat down on the steps, and his eyes fell on a small gray piece of stone lying at the base of one of the stripped pine saplings that supported the porch roof. Idly picking it up and running his fingers across the fine grit surface, his eyes lit with recognition. *Arkansas whetstone—supposed to be the best in the country.* Pulling a wicked-looking Bowie knife from the back of his belt, he spat on the stone and then began to carefully pull one side of the knife, then the other, along the flat gray surface of the whetstone.

Pretty girl—reminds me of a little kitten, he mused to himself. *But she doesn't look too good. Looks sickly. She can't be too far along, either—awful skinny—not showing at all.* Running the knife gently down his forearm, he nodded with satisfaction as it shaved the golden hair as neatly as a straight-razor. *Glad she's the doc, and I'm just the nurse. Sickly pregnant ladies make me nervous. . . .*

Inside the cabin, Sharon and Cheney chattered about Cheney's trip, the cabin, Black Arrow, the horses, Sharon's husband, and New York—all so eagerly that Cheney finally laughed and put up her hands in a gesture to stop the flow. "We've got so much to catch up on! I want to know so much about Black Arrow, and you, and this country—I can't wait to meet everyone!"

"Well, you'll have a chance to meet everyone tomorrow!" Sharon announced excitedly as she fixed them a cup of tea. "Mr. DeSpain has invited everyone for Thanksgiving dinner tomorrow at his new offices. Practically everyone in the county is going to be there—out of curiosity, if nothing else."

"Tomorrow's Thanksgiving?" Cheney asked, startled. "I've certainly lost track—anyway, that's wonderful. Considering the start Shiloh and I made today, it would take us forever to find our way to everyone's home! If it hadn't been for Jimmy Dale

Satterfield, we'd probably still be out wandering in the woods!"

"What?" The urgency of Sharon's tone instantly stopped Cheney's prattling. "Jimmy Dale Satterfield?"

"Why, yes. He brought us here, or rather down close to the fork."

"Cheney, there's so much to explain," Sharon began, and her voice suddenly was subdued. "These—these people are so *different*, you see?" Her eyes focused inwardly for a few moments. "Just don't mention to Josh that Jimmy Dale brought you here. I'll explain later, but for now, please don't mention it."

"Oh, all right, Sharon. Let's don't worry about all those man things right now," Cheney replied jauntily. "We can try to figure that out later. Right now I want to talk about the reason I came— you and the baby! How far along are you, and how are you?"

A shadow passed over Sharon's delicate face. "I'm a little over four months now, Cheney," she answered slowly, "and I'm—I've had some problems."

Cheney narrowed her eyes at Sharon's answer, and her gaze upon Sharon's slight form grew sharp and appraising. "You're very thin, Sharon—but then, you always were. What kind of problems are you having?"

Sharon wrapped a towel around her hands to pull the copper kettle from the glowing coals in the fireplace and pour hot water into two plain white mugs. A fragrance of herbs and citrus filled the tiny room, and Cheney inhaled gratefully as Sharon placed the cups on the small plank table and fetched honey, sugar, and thick cream.

Sitting down beside Cheney, Sharon poured honey into her cup and stirred it slowly and deliberately before answering. "I know you can see one problem. I'm certain I'm four months pregnant—but I'm hardly showing at all."

"Yes, that may be a problem. But it may not be anything serious," Cheney answered calmly as she put sugar and cream into her tea.

"The baby hasn't kicked yet. But I can feel something," Sharon told her, her fine brown eyes lighting up. "Just light

69

movements." Cheney nodded encouragingly, and Sharon went on quietly, "But I do seem to be so swollen. . . ."

Cheney appreciatively sipped the strong, sweet tea and unflinchingly met Sharon's anxious gaze. "Yes, I see, Sharon. It's probably much more noticeable because you're so slender."

Cheney's eyes fell to Sharon's hands, which were distended, the slender fingers and delicate wrists seemingly twice their normal size. Her face too, normally so fine-featured, was heavy and putty-colored, with dark shadows under her eyes.

"Is that all?" Cheney asked in a clinical voice.

"Well, there is just one more thing, I guess. A little thing . . ." Sharon ducked her head and fell into a brown study as she stirred her tea.

Cheney waited patiently, knowing that even for exceedingly intelligent people like Sharon the most fearful symptoms are the last thing they actually tell their doctor. On some deep primitive level patients often feel that, contrary to logic and reason, simply saying the worst out loud will make it more real, and therefore more frightening. *Like saying stomachache,* Cheney thought with an inward sigh, *because they can't say cancer.*

Finally Sharon took a deep breath and looked up at Cheney squarely. "A little thing," she repeated, as if to reassure herself. "Sometimes I just—my vision gets blurred. That's all."

"Yes?" Cheney looked up alertly. "Very blurred? Can you read when it does?"

"No."

"Does it happen very often?"

"It's only happened three times, and I was very tired each time, Cheney," Sharon said pleadingly.

Cheney sipped her tea in silence for a few moments, deep in thought. Then she raised her eyes to meet Sharon's. "Please don't worry, Sharon. I'd like to examine you and the baby, and then we'll see. All right?"

Sharon listened carefully, her face twisted with anxiety, then with an obvious effort smoothed her face and smiled at Cheney. "All right. I'm so glad you're here, Cheney. Thank you. Thank you so much for coming." She laid her hand affectionately on Cheney's arm.

Cheney returned the girl's smile warmly as she laid her hand over Sharon's. "I'm glad I'm here, too, Sharon. And you're very welcome."

Briskly Cheney stood up and surveyed the small one-room cabin. A beautifully pieced quilt hung over a doorway on the other side of the room, obviously partitioning off the bedroom. Cheney pointed to it. "If that's the bedroom, let's go in there and examine you right now. I'll get my medical bag—" Her mouth opened and she whirled to look at the stout oak door. "Goodness, I forgot about Shiloh!"

Sharon rose hastily, also looking remorseful. "Oh, dear! You mean that gentleman is a friend of yours, Cheney? I thought he was a guide or something! How terribly rude of me! And you!"

"Oh, well, he'll get over it." Cheney shrugged callously as she went to the door. "Besides, you've been more polite than the other people we've met—at least you didn't stand and gape at us open-mouthed—"

She flung open the door and stepped out on the porch, Sharon following close behind. "Shiloh—?"

"Here's my medical bag, Doc," he drawled, rising from the step and holding out a worn black leather bag to Cheney. "You can use it, since you forgot yours."

Cheney took the bag, giving Shiloh a dark look, but he doffed his hat to Sharon. "She also forgot to properly introduce us, ma'am," he went on airily. "My name's Shiloh Irons. I'm Dr. Duvall's nurse. But you can just forget I'm here if you want to. Everyone does," he added blandly, his startling blue eyes cutting to Cheney, whose face darkened even more.

Sharon laughed warmly. "No, I'll bring you a cup of tea first, and *then* I'll forget you're here." Shiloh returned her warm smile as she went on matter-of-factly, "My husband's not here, and Cheney's going to examine me. Would you mind staying out here on the porch?"

"Ma'am, it's a pleasure bein' on your porch." He waved his

hand at the view of the "holler" from the front of the Carters' cabin. "And when you two ladies are finished, would you join me? I'll save you two seats." He nodded toward the rocking chairs, and Sharon's eyes gleamed with appreciation.

"Let's go, Sharon," Cheney said absently as she rummaged through the bag. "There are several more questions I need to ask you, and I want to check you and the baby thoroughly. Shiloh, do you have any glycerin in this bag? It's such a mess . . . I can't find anything."

"Not geometrically arranged in cubicles like your bag," Shiloh pointedly observed.

Sharon smiled affectionately at Cheney, who was energetically mining into the depths of the large black bag. "You haven't changed, have you, Cheney?" She glanced mischievously up at Shiloh. "I asked Dev once if Cheney methodically arranged the rocks on the grounds at Duvall Court . . ." Her words trailed off as Shiloh's face lost some of its warmth at the mention of Devlin Buchanan's name.

Sharon's gentle brown eyes grew watchful as she prattled on cheerfully. "I hope she doesn't want to rearrange the boards more symmetrically in the cabin—"

Cheney pointedly ignored them. "I think I've found everything—and I'm going to straighten up this bag when we get back, in spite of what you two have to say. Come on, Sharon," she ordered, and the two women went back into the cabin.

Shiloh slumped back down on the step and looked out across the tops of the pines, dipping down below, and to the mountains rising on the far side of the ridge. From this height he could faintly see three more gray stains of smoke on the blue sky. His feet grew cold, and he got up to walk around for a few minutes, stamping to warm them.

Patting Sock and Stocking, he talked to them in a low voice. "Think I'll get me some of those moccasins, boys," he told them. "They look warm and comfortable—"

Click.

The unmistakable deadly sound of a rifle hammer being

pulled back sounded loud on the quiet hillside.

"—and they sure are quiet." Shiloh sighed as he slowly, with infinite care, turned to face behind and to his left, lifting his hands in the universal gesture of surrender. The barrel of the ancient Enfield muzzle-loader looked impossibly large and long from Shiloh's vantage point—which was about a foot from the business end of the barrel.

"Howdy." The man didn't move as he greeted Shiloh, and the gun didn't waver a centimeter.

"Howdy."

The man's unusually light green eyes narrowed as he studied Shiloh for what seemed like forever. Shiloh stood completely still, noting details of the man who pointed death at him. He was six feet tall, maybe twenty-four or twenty-five, with tousled sandy hair. His face was gaunt, rawboned, with a strong, wide mouth, now drawn taut under a thick blond mustache that grew down to either side of his chin. An angry red scar ran from his hairline down his face and disappeared into his collar.

Wonder if he got that in the war. Strange eyes, so light—green-glass color— With an effort Shiloh gathered his scattered thoughts and returned the man's gaze squarely.

"Who're you?" the man demanded.

"Name's Shiloh Irons. I came here with Dr. Cheney Duvall to see Mrs. Carter. She's in the cabin with her right now."

The man's eyes inadvertently darted toward the cabin, and the barrel of the gun drifted ever so slightly. Shiloh tensed, his mind filled with remembrance of the last time he'd stood quietly, his hands raised, facing down the barrel of an Enfield much like this one. *Kid behind it that time,* he remembered with a stab of mental pain. *Boy in blue . . . tunic too big for him. . . .*

Relentlessly the scene played out. Shiloh saw the boy's eyes dart to the left as a mortar went off near them; Shiloh grabbed the barrel of the rifle with one powerful hand, yanking down and to the left in a two-second swipe. *Finger bones cracked—odd how loud it sounded, and he opened his mouth to scream—and so afraid! So much fear in his eyes!* Shiloh saw the rifle stock smash against the boy's head, and crimson blood began to flow as he crumpled to the ground. *I was never that afraid,* he thought dully, *and I was never that young . . . and never again will I hurt someone like that. . . .*

Shiloh willed himself to relax his facial muscles, to ease his stance. In unconscious response, some of the fierceness in the rifleman's eyes faded. With great deliberation he lowered the rifle, and Shiloh let out a relieved breath.

"I'm Josh Carter, Sharon's husband. Didn't 'spect to see you here. How'd ya'll find the cabin?" he asked suspiciously, cradling the rifle in the crook of his left arm but keeping his hand near the trigger.

"Wasn't expecting to see you either, Mr. Carter. But I guess you could tell I was surprised," Shiloh answered lightly, eyeing the rifle pointedly as he lowered his hands. "And it wasn't easy, finding your cabin. We wandered over onto your neighbor's land, and Jimmy Dale took pity on us and brought us here—"

"Jimmy Dale Satterfield?" Carter's staccato words rang harshly in Shiloh's ears, and he tensed again. Carter raised the gun—a gesture more than a threat now—but when he spoke each word was weighted with vehemence. "Us Carters don't hold with no Satterfields, Mr. Irons. And you'd best know that afore you go makin' yourself free on a man's property!"

The cabin door opened, and women's soft voices drifted incongruously to the two men who faced each other warily. Abruptly Sharon's and Cheney's voices stopped—then, quietly and firmly, Sharon spoke to her husband. "Don't, Josh. They didn't understand, but now they do. Let it be—please."

Josh Carter slowly turned to look up at his wife. His face softened slightly, and once again he lowered the rifle. "All right, Sharon. If they're yore friends, then they'll be friends of the Carters." He turned back to Shiloh and continued in a courteous voice, "As long as you ain't Satterfields."

6

BLACK ARROW THANKSGIVING

"You sure look pretty, Doc," Shiloh remarked.

Cheney was dressed in a plain black taffeta dress, the severity softened only by a small onyx-and-ivory cameo pinned at the high neck. Gracefully draped around her arms was a soft white woolen shawl with a long fringe that dusted her hemline. Hesitantly she looked down at the rustling black fabric. "You don't think it's too—too—"

"Too too rich?" Shiloh countered. "Nope."

Cheney sighed in exasperation. *Typical Shiloh,* she thought wryly. *He knows what I'm thinking, he says it in three words, and then tells me what he's thinking in one word. So simple—so why is it so unsettling?*

"Thank you—I guess," she muttered. "Are we ready?"

The two left the cabin and walked up the dirt street to DeSpain's. Small carts and wagons with couples on the seats, and various numbers of children crowded in the back, cluttered the street. Some men rode horses, but Cheney saw no women riding.

"This must be a big event for Wolf County," Shiloh observed. "Bet there's never been this many people in one place at one time in Black Arrow."

"I'm glad we got here in time for this," Cheney mused. "This is the best way for me to meet these people and let them know they have a doctor now."

"Don't get your hopes up too much, Doc. It'll take a little while. Yesterday Carter let me know that he was glad Sharon was getting to visit with a friend, but he said there's a 'harb woman' who takes care of the people around here."

"What's a harb woman?"

"You say 'erb.' You know, like daffodils and tulips and rosemary and stuff."

Cheney laughed aloud, and Shiloh watched her appreciatively. Laughter lit her face and made her eyes seem greener. "Daffodils and tulips! Those are flowers!" Then she grew thoughtful and went on almost to herself, "Sharon mentioned a woman named Maeva Wilding who has advised her. I got the impression she was a midwife or something."

"That's the one, Doc. But she's a harb woman, and I'm not sure you can understand what that means to these people." Shiloh reflected on Cheney's background of quiet gentility and higher education. She had never brushed shoulders with the kind of people who were so insular, so backward, that they believed stomach cancer could be healed by drinking stump water that reflected a full moon; or that a woman could determine the sex of her unborn baby by drinking certain potions; or that it was better for a harb woman's spider webs to stop the bleeding of a deep wound than have a fancy doctor clean and bandage it.

Shaking his head slightly, he went on, "It's a little bit of faith healing, a little bit of potions, a sprinkle of tonics, a touch of superstition—and a lot of ignorance." Reflectively he watched the people threading down the street past them.

No hints of prosperity were in evidence here. The clothes were plain, mostly browns and grays, of rough woolen weave, sometimes shiny and patched. Although their faces were lit up with anticipation—even joy—at the coming festivities, both men and women looked weather-beaten and of indeterminate age. But the children were bright-eyed and red-cheeked and had glad voices. For them the grinding years of continual childbearing or farming the flinty, inhospitable hills still lay ahead.

Cheney considered Shiloh's words and saw his expression grow thoughtful as he watched the people of the hills making their way down the street. "Well, perhaps I'll get to meet Miss Wilding and we can somehow work together."

"Maybe . . ." Shiloh murmured, but he sounded doubtful.

As they neared Waylon DeSpain's sprawling house on the shore of Moccasin Lake, Cheney and Shiloh saw a sizable crowd milling around. Small logs piled up to eight feet high made two spectacular bonfires along the shore, for though it was high noon, the wind off the lake was biting cold. Between them a square of railroad ties had been laid and covered with thick canvas, drawn taut and tied down. Musicians crowded one corner of the square, and three couples were already dancing.

Closer to the house two fire pits had been dug, and two stout men continually turned loaded spits. DeSpain's fare for the festive occasion included a roasted pig and a steer, a dozen baked turkeys, a dozen fried chickens, and a dozen glazed hams—such largesse as Wolf County had never before witnessed. In addition, Mr. DeSpain had—through Ross Sikes, the general storekeeper—contracted the women of several families to prepare and bring bread, vegetables, beans, and desserts. And DeSpain had actually paid them for this!

Cheney found herself nearing the crowd with some trepidation. Most of the faces turned toward her burned with curiosity; some were dark with suspicion. *I know I'm supposed to be here*, she reassured herself. *I'm sure the Lord sent me here. No reason at all to be nervous . . .*

"Not nervous, are you, Doc?" Shiloh asked, offering her his arm. "I've already met some of these people, so why don't I introduce you until we find Miss Sharon?"

Gratefully taking Shiloh's arm, Cheney began nodding and smiling pleasantly as they reached the first wave of people. With ease Shiloh threaded his way through the groups, nodding and saying "Howdy" to the ones he didn't know and stopping to introduce Cheney to some he did. Their suspicious looks seemed to wane somewhat once she became a known quantity. Not a single person addressed her as "Doctor Duvall," but Cheney smiled slightly to herself, for without exception they pronounced her name "Miz DOO-vawl."

"Cheney!" Sharon broke away from a crowd standing by one

bonfire and hurried toward them. "Hello, you two! I was wondering when you'd get here!" Sharon hugged Cheney and smiled up at Shiloh. "Please come with me. I want you to meet my in-laws." The two women hurried back toward the group by the bonfire, Shiloh following close behind.

Studying Sharon critically, Cheney admonished her, "You look very tired, Sharon. Are you feeling all right?"

"Oh, I feel fine, Cheney."

"Good. I'd like to come visit you tomorrow and have a talk with you. Will that be all right?"

A hint of anxiety shadowed Sharon's delicate features, but it cleared almost immediately. "Well, of course! That's what you're here for, isn't it—to see me? Come any time; I'll be there all day."

They reached the group, who were watching their approach with undisguised curiosity. Sharon began the introductions.

"This is my friend from New York, everyone, Dr. Cheney Duvall. And this is her nurse, Mr. Shiloh Irons."

Muttered howdy's greeted them, and Sharon went on nervously, "This is my father-in-law, Lige Carter; my mother-in-law, Katie Carter; my brother-in-law Dane; my sister-in-law Glendean, my sister-in-law—oh, yes, you've met Bobbie Jo; and this is my aunt Mary, and her husband Deak, and this is my nephew David. . . ."

At varying times throughout the numerous introductions Cheney thought: *Must be more than two hundred people at this dinner—because there's at least one hundred Carters.*

All of them have those strange light green eyes! And all blonds, from yellow-gold to sandy! Except the little girl, what's her name? A man's name—ask Shiloh later.

How will I ever get all of these people straight—and whose children belong to whom?

Men all six feet tall—even the young one—Dane, that's right— barely a teenager—

Later Cheney, slightly breathless, found herself being led down to the lake by the little girl who was so noticeable because of her dark hair and eyes. *Can't remember her name. She's Josh's sister—so that makes her Sharon's sister-in-law!* Cheney shook her head slightly. *Hard to think of a sister-in-law only four feet tall!*

"I'm tired, Miss Cheney," the girl asserted firmly, pulling Cheney's hand with surprising strength. "Come sit with me for a minute, please?"

DeSpain had ordered large logs, suitable for seating, be placed strategically along the shore. Gratefully Cheney sank down on one, clutched her shawl tightly about her, and studied the child who scrambled to sit beside her. "I'm sorry," she said, "but I've forgotten your name."

"It's Glendean," the little girl announced matter-of-factly. "I'm named after my Oncle Glen, who you ain't met yet 'cause he ain't here yet, and my Grampa Dean, who you ain't met yet 'cause he's dead."

Cheney hid a smile. "Well, I certainly like that name, and I'm looking forward to meeting your uncle. Do you look like him?"

Bursts of giggles escaped from Glendean. "Oncle Glen looks like a bear!" she cried, crossing her small hands over her stomach. "When I was little, he tole me he *wuz* a bear! An' I b'lieved him!"

Sea green eyes sparkling, Cheney asked, "Well, is he?"

Glendean was overcome with delight at such a nonsensical conversation with an adult. Laughing fitfully, she cried, "Yes, ma'am, I'm pretty sure he is, but don't tell my mama or she won't let me play with him no more!"

Suddenly, to Cheney's consternation, Glendean began coughing hoarsely. At first Cheney thought she had choked from laughing too hard, but then the hacking deteriorated into painfully spasmodic coughing followed by a telltale crowing intake of breath. *Why, this child's got pertussis!* she thought in alarm. *I thought she was red-cheeked with cold, but now I can see how pale she is, with those two spots of red high on her cheeks!*

Instantly Cheney placed her hand on the child's forehead as she bent over, racked with coughing. Glendean's velvety dark eyes met hers, surprised but pleading, and Cheney's mouth tightened. "I'm going to get you some medicine, Glendean," she murmured, "and see if your mother might want to take you home. I believe you have a fever, and you should be in bed."

Slowly the coughing subsided as Glendean unconsciously leaned closer to Cheney. The implication took Cheney by surprise, and unnerved her. She hadn't been around children much, and she was rather unsure of how to talk to them or act toward them—or comfort them. But instinctively she put her arm around Glendean's thin shoulders, enveloping the little girl in her warm shawl.

Glendean nestled closer to her contentedly. "Mama'll give me some more of that ol' Maeva's stinkin' tonic," she mumbled weakly. "But it do make me stop coughing."

Cheney stiffened but merely told the breathless little girl, "I'll just go talk to your mother, Glendean. You stay here." Cheney rose from her seat on the log but Glendean pulled at her skirt in protest. "Here, would you please keep my shawl for me until I come back?" Cheney asked, draping the luxurious wrap about the girl, whose fever-dulled eyes lit up. "I've gotten rather warm, and I'd like for you to hold it for me. I'll be right back."

Cheney hurried back to the crowd surrounding one of the bonfires and found Glendean's mother. Katie Rawlins Carter was easily distinguished in the crowd of washed-out gray-clad women. She had blond hair—actually a bright corn yellow—wound around her head in a thick shiny braid. Light blue eyes sparkled with health and good humor in a fine-boned face made distinctively heart-shaped by a widow's peak and pointed chin. Unlike the other rather shapeless women Cheney saw, Katie Carter had borne only four children and still retained a robust hourglass figure at forty-five.

"Mrs. Carter," Cheney began, touching her on the shoulder as she was laughing at some murmured comment from her husband, Lige.

"Yes? Oh, Miss Duvall," she replied, turning around to smile warily at Cheney. "Call me Katie—Lige's mother's the onliest Miz Carter around here!"

"Yes, Katie, well," Cheney began again uncomfortably, nodding at Lige Carter, who was regarding her gravely. "I've just seen that Glendean is probably suffering from pertussis, and I'd like to go back to my cabin and get her some medicine. And she seems to have a slight fever, so I believe she'd be more comfortable resting in bed, don't you?"

Stone silence descended on the small group. Katie stiffened slightly, though her expression didn't change, and Lige Carter's light green eyes grew hard and suspicious. No word was spoken for what seemed a long, long time to Cheney. She could feel her cheeks begin to redden, but her gaze didn't waver.

"Miss Duvall—" Lige began.

"I am a doctor, you see, Mr. Carter," Cheney interrupted rather stiffly.

Lige Carter gave his wife a meaningful glance. He had a strong face, sandy hair, and a tall, sturdy frame. Cheney saw that Dane, Bobbie Jo, and Josh had all gotten their unusual light green eyes from their father. "Yes'm." He shrugged and turned to his wife. "Katie, you got that there tonic in your pocket, doncha? Thought such. We'll be thankin' you for your concern, Miss Duvall, but we already brought some medicine for Glendean. Where's she at?"

"She's sitting down by the lake, but—"

"Thank you, Miss Duvall." Katie nodded curtly, and the couple turned to head down to the lake.

"But I'd like to—"

Lige Carter stopped and turned back to Cheney. "Miss Duvall, Katie's a good mother, and Maeva Wilding's tonics have allus been good fer that there—whutever you called it. Us plain folk just call it whoopin' cough," he added dryly, the first hint of reproof Cheney had yet heard. "Now, we're all here to have some fun and eat somebody else's food and shuck work for a day—and give thanks to the Lord. So why don't we all just do that?" He nodded and slipped away.

Cheney put her hands on her hips and watched the tall form of Lige Carter amble unhurriedly off toward the lake. *Well, I've certainly been put in my proper place!* she thought with exasperation. *Rebuked, chastised, patted on the head, and summarily dismissed, without any doubt!*

"Dr. Duvall—?"

The cultured tone and use of her title startled Cheney out of her reverie. Hastily she turned to see a well-dressed man slightly behind her, smiling as he made a small bow. "Will you allow me to introduce myself?" he asked in a courtly manner. "I was going to get your nurse, Mr. Irons, to introduce us, but—" He waved an immaculate hand toward Shiloh, who stood at the edge of a group of young people, laughing down at a shapely young woman while she flirtatiously smiled up at him. "He's occupied at this moment, as you can see. I'm Waylon DeSpain."

Immediately Cheney relaxed. DeSpain's reddish-blond hair and mustache were meticulously groomed, his square hands manicured. His profile was clean and boyish, and he smiled at her with an easy yet not too familiar manner. He was the kind of man she was accustomed to meeting at social gatherings.

"Mr. DeSpain," Cheney smiled, "it's a pleasure to meet you. And since I'm in your debt, I hardly think it impertinent for you to introduce yourself."

Again DeSpain bowed slightly. "Why, you're not in my debt, Dr. Duvall, not at all. I believe we have a contract for you to provide certain medical services to DeSpain Timber Company in exchange for use of my cabin. So I believe that makes us even."

"Yes, Mr. DeSpain—if you still want me to serve as your company doctor," Cheney replied disparagingly, glancing in the direction that Lige Carter had disappeared.

DeSpain assessed Cheney knowingly as she glanced toward the lake. "You sound rather disheartened, Dr. Duvall. Would you prefer to make other arrangements?"

"Oh, no, Mr. DeSpain, I didn't mean to imply that I'm unhappy with our agreement," she amended hastily. "It's just that I know that when Shiloh spoke with you he omitted one small detail—my gender. I hope that doesn't make any difference to you, but if it does . . ." Cheney shrugged impatiently. ". . . I'll understand."

"As it happens, it does make a difference to me," DeSpain murmured, and Cheney's eyes narrowed sharply. "You're a beautiful woman—and if you're intelligent enough and dedicated enough to be a physician, I think it's outstanding."

His voice held a note of warmth and approval that Cheney was unaccustomed to hearing, and she immediately felt relieved and immensely gratified. "Thank you, Mr. DeSpain. In that case, please feel free to call upon me at any time, you or your men."

"Then I'm calling upon you now, to dance with me." Waylon DeSpain offered Cheney his arm. A full complement of musicians crowded one corner of the square: two fiddlers, one a man and one a woman; Bobbie Jo playing her dulcimer with the long white turkey feather; a banjo player; a man on harmonica; and one man expertly playing a flute. The music was a rousing jig, with lots of hand-clapping and stamping, and Cheney felt unsure of herself. But gamely she took Waylon DeSpain's arm and joined the crowd of couples nimbly moving 'round the floor in complicated, quick steps.

Squaring her jaw and lifting her chin stubbornly, Cheney covertly watched the other couples for the first few minutes and found that the dancing was simpler than it seemed at first glance. Most of it was quick, toe-tapping footwork, and the couples rarely joined except for an occasional locked-arm swing. Cheney lifted her skirts slightly and watched her feet austerely until she mastered the rhythm and some of the steps. Then she began to enjoy herself immensely. Waylon DeSpain was agile and quick, his steps light and clever. Her face glowed as she danced and basked in the look of pleased approval on his face.

The music never stopped completely, but flowed continuously from one tune to the next. Cheney found herself facing a new partner, a man of about twenty-eight or twenty-nine, with shaggy brown hair and brooding hazel eyes. Nodding curtly, he announced loudly, "I'm T. R.! Dance with me, Miss Duvall?" Without waiting for a reply, he simply began to step in time with the music in Cheney's general vicinity.

Cheney looked curiously at her new partner. Already she had noted that all of the Carters gathered around and near one of the bonfires; she had seen this man with the group of people gathered around the other fire. "I'm sorry, what did you say your name was?"

"T. R.," the young man nodded, clapping and stamping fiercely. "T. R. Satterfield. Over there's all my people." He pointed to the second bonfire, and Cheney realized that the segregation of the two fires must be both symbolic and purposeful: the Carters and the Satterfields.

"Is that your father?" she asked politely. A tall, fierce-looking man stood in the center of a large group of men, holding an unusual rifle, nodding and talking.

"Yes, ma'am," T. R. replied proudly. "He brung his rifle, an' ever'body allus wants to see it. He won't let no one touch it, not even me or my brothers."

Cheney and her partner separated for a moment, and she watched the group of men curiously. The rifle was unusual—it had an enormous bore and a long black cylinder mounted on the barrel. Catching sight of T. R. again—he seemed unconcerned that they were separated—she jigged over close to him. "That is a very unusual rifle," she nodded. "My father would be interested in it. What is it?"

"It's a Sharps fifty-two caliber, with a telescope," T. R. gasped. The dance was strenuous, and T. R.'s face was putty-colored. His breath smelled of whiskey, though he didn't appear to be drunk. "My pa, he took it away from one o' Berdan's Sharpshooters at Malvern Hill. Man had jis' shot me with it." Cheney's face grew stark with shock, which T. R. seemed to enjoy. "My pa charged him like a hungry wolf, yanked that there fancy shooter outta his shakin' hands, an' bashed him acrost the head. Smooth took it away from him. Won't let no one else shoot it or even touch it."

Waylon DeSpain had disappeared. Two more partners came and went, and Cheney was breathlessly about to attempt a graceful exit from the dance floor when a quiet voice sounded at her elbow.

"My dance, I believe." As she turned, Shiloh clasped her around the waist as the musicians quieted down to a sedate waltz.

Gratefully Cheney let Shiloh lead her around the floor in the graceful, flowing steps of the waltz as she caught her breath. When she was able to speak normally she began, "Glendean Carter has pertussis, and Katie and Lige wouldn't let me—"

"I know," he murmured. "We'll talk later, Cheney. Right now just dance with me."

Cheney caught her breath at his closeness and swallowed hard. Her thoughts tumbled in confusion, words fading away, blown into distant tatters by sensory images rushing in: Shiloh's nearness, his arm tightly encircling her waist, the rough skin of his hand engulfing hers, the clean smell of his linen shirt, the smoothly defined muscles of his shoulder. Dreamily Cheney closed her eyes. She loved the graceful circles of the waltz, and the music was familiar and soothing.

Abruptly the tempo changed into a lighthearted rhythm, and Cheney's eyes flew open. Stiffly pulling away from Shiloh, she muttered furiously, "What are you doing?"

With an exasperated sigh Shiloh retorted, "Why do you always say that when this happens? You always say that!"

"Say what?" Cheney snapped.

" 'What are you doing?' Like you just regained consciousness and found to your horror that I'm taking advantage of you!"

"Well, I think I know when someone's hugging me right in public!"

"And what do you call what you were doing to me?"

"Just dancing! Not hugging!"

Shiloh opened his mouth, his eyes glinting blue fire—then

he stopped to look around with caustic amusement. Men and women were dancing close around them, their steps automatic, their faces lit with interest at the heated conversation between the two newcomers posed stiffly in a waltzing position but unmoving on the crowded square.

"I'm going to get something to drink!" he growled to the crowd, then dropped his hold on Cheney and turned on his heel to stride off the dance floor.

Instantly Waylon DeSpain appeared in front of Cheney, his expression and voice carefully noncommittal. "Would you care for some refreshment, Dr. Duvall?"

Cheney, staring at Shiloh's tall form as the crowd parted wordlessly for his hasty exit, focused on DeSpain and made a deliberate effort to regain her composure as she took his arm. "Yes, thank you, I'm afraid I've gotten too warm."

"Yes, I see that," he nodded. Sharply Cheney searched his face but could find no hint of sarcasm there, so she allowed him to lead her through the crowd to his house.

★　★　★　★

No specific mealtime was signaled, so all Thanksgiving Day the DeSpain partygoers ate and drank, danced and laughed. Cheney wandered around, sometimes escorted, sometimes alone, as she found that the rules of this gathering were quite different from the choreographed parties she had always attended.

Twilight crept over Black Arrow. The pastel winter sun deepened into burnt orange as it dropped close over the western mountains, blackening them in relief, and fired a crimson path across Moccasin Lake. Cheney strolled down to the lake and saw with quiet enjoyment that the Evening Star capped the highest peak as a twinkling jewel.

"That's Maeva's Trace." She turned to find Lige Carter standing beside her, holding the shawl she had left with his daughter, his face lit by the last rays of the sun. He motioned toward the ragged peak lit by Venus riding low in the sky.

"Why is it called that?" Cheney asked softly.

"Long story..." Lige murmured. "My great-grandfather and Enoch Satterfield's great-grandfather fought there, for a woman named Maeva Randall. They fought, both of them got hurt, they separated. Maeva disappeared. No one ever seen her again...." His voice was sing-song, almost a chant. "Two nights later, lightning struck all around the highest peaks. The wolves howled and the coyotes screamed, and fire burned all over that mountain. Next day when folks went up there, lightning had burnt a three-foot swath to the biggest oak toppin' the mount, and split the oak into three splinters. You kin still see the path of the lightning up there. It's called Maeva's Trace, and the great oak lies in three pieces, pointin' south, east, and west, but not north."

Cheney shivered. Suddenly Lige Carter shook himself, smiled slightly at her, then wordlessly handed her the shawl.

"Is the old woman that—doctors you—" Cheney faltered. "Is she related to this Maeva Randall?"

"No connection, she says," Lige answered shortly, then moved away.

Cheney rejoined the crowd milling about the dance square. Across the group of dancers she spotted Shiloh moving along from the direction of DeSpain's house, holding two tin cups. Resolutely she decided to talk to him, and began to work her way toward him. As she neared him and the crowd parted, however, she stopped uncertainly. Shiloh was handing one of the cups to the girl she had seen earlier, a voluptuous young woman with glossy black hair, tall and shapely, with laughing eyes. She was one of the few women Cheney had seen who wore a dress of royal blue trimmed with black, instead of the uniform gray or brown. Tiny earrings of jet beads sparkled in her ears.

" ... I ain't gonna tell you if I have a boyfriend 'til you tell me if you got a girl friend, Mr. Irons," she was saying coquettishly.

"And I'm not going to tell you if I have a girl friend until you dance with me," Shiloh teased.

"If'n I *should* have a boyfriend," she replied saucily, staring up at Shiloh through thick black lashes, "he might not be likin' me dancin' with you."

Taking the empty cup from her, Shiloh grinned recklessly and thrust the two cups into the hands of a surprised young man standing near. "Miss Satterfield, if you had a boyfriend, he should know better than to leave you alone in this crowd of men!" he announced. Taking her by the arm, he led her to the platform. Clasping her small waist, he swung her energetically in a spirited dance resembling a polka.

Cheney was surprised at the strength of the resentment that swept over her as she watched the couple. Instantly she fought to stifle the unwelcome feelings and reprimanded herself severely. *What's the matter with you, Cheney? It's Shiloh! Stop acting like a—* The word "jealous" echoed dimly in her mind. Vehemently Cheney shoved it far away and blindly turned to go back down to the lake.

As she wheeled around a huge man brushed past her, almost knocking her down. Cheney's confused first impression of him was of flashing black eyes opened wide with rage, large white teeth, long thick black hair, and a bristling mustache and beard.

"Blast it to kingdom come, Lorine!" he shouted in a booming voice as he strode onto the dance floor. "I told you I'd be back in a minute! Cain't turn my back on you for an eye-blink, or you're slitherin' around with—with—who the devil are you?"

"Name's Shiloh Irons," Shiloh replied calmly, extending his hand. The great bear of a man blinked unbelievingly down at it, as if Shiloh had offered him a hissing viper.

"I'm Glen Rawlins, and that there's Lorine you're dancing with! And I don't like it!" he growled, thrusting his face ominously close to Shiloh's.

Shiloh shrugged, stuck his hands in his pockets, and took a small step backward. "Didn't mean anything by it, Mr. Rawlins. Sure isn't worth bustin' heads over."

Glen Rawlins made an outraged noise that Cheney admitted to herself did sound very much like a bear's growl. *Glendean may be right about her uncle's species*, she thought with dismay. *And Shiloh really is trying not to fight—thank the Lord.*

"Well, ain't you a yeller-bellied ninnyhammer!" Rawlins yelled, stepping close to Shiloh.

With growing dread, Cheney saw Shiloh's jaw clench and his nostrils flare, telltale signs that his temper was rising. His stance unobtrusively grew tense, though his position didn't change and he kept his hands in his pockets.

"I'm not chicken, Rawlins," he muttered in a low voice, "but I don't want to fight you."

T. R. Satterfield jumped up on the dance platform and shoved his way through the crowd to the two tall men squared off in the center. He was smaller than both Shiloh and Rawlins, but he was lean and wiry. His movements were sharp-edged and taut, like his voice. "You, Rawlins! Who do you think you are, lordin' it over my sister? She kin dance with whoever she wants to—and ain't no *Carter* gonna say naught about it!" He spat out the name as if it were a curse word.

Slowly Rawlins' enraged glare turned to the smaller man. "T. R., you just keep outta this! It ain't got nothin' to do with Carters and Satterfields! And I'm a Rawlins, and you know it. You must be drunk!"

"Your sister married a Carter," T. R. sneered, "and to my mind that makes you an Uncle Carter!"

"I'm a-warnin' you, T. R.!"

"Mebbe so, but it ain't scaring me!"

As Rawlins' menacing growls and T. R.'s cunning snarls increased in volume and heat, Shiloh smoothly edged away from them. Unobtrusively he moved toward Cheney, sliding quietly past the people surrounding the two shouting men. Finally he came to stand on Cheney's left and a little in front of her. With his eyes still on Rawlins and T. R., he muttered, "You better be clearing out, Doc. Looks like we're going to have a full-scale riot here."

"You think those two are going to fight?"

"I think everyone's going to fight."

89

Rawlins shouted, "I'm telling you for the last time, T. R., this here ain't got nothin' to do with you and your people! It's between me and this here feller— What? Where the devil—"

"Uh-oh," Shiloh muttered as Rawlins' great head swiveled around in a search. At six-four it was difficult for Shiloh to melt into a crowd.

But now T. R. Satterfield's stony hazel eyes glinted recklessly as Rawlins' eyes and attention turned away from him. With a quick, sharp movement, he sucker-punched Glen Rawlins on the side of the head. The bigger man's reflexes were slow, so the follow-through of the jab seemed to take a long time. Stunned, he shook his head like a wounded animal and glared at T. R. in disbelief. Then with an enraged roar, he clasped the smaller man in a bone-crushing bear hug. T. R.'s face grew red as he struggled, grunting piggishly.

Hoarse shouts rang out from the direction of the two bonfires, several men jumped up onto the dance square, and a woman began screaming loudly and incoherently. Suddenly the crowd seemed to take on an anger and hostility of its own. A woman cried out indignantly and shoved another woman; one man grabbed another's arms and held them while a third pummeled his stomach; the entire dance square turned into a stage of violence.

Cheney saw Dane Carter, only sixteen years old, tap Jimmy Dale Satterfield on the shoulder. When Jimmy Dale turned around, Dane soundly socked his jaw. Jimmy Dale fell. Dane, standing over him, almost grinned, but another brawler rammed into him from behind. Dane shot through the air and disappeared from Cheney's view into a confusing melee of men with fists flying.

Waylon DeSpain stood on the other side of the dance square. Cheney saw him signal to one side, then the other. Three hard-looking men waded into the fray, but instead of stopping it they were soon fighting as furiously as the people of Black Arrow.

"Can't you stop this?" Cheney demanded furiously.

"Oh, sure, Doc." Shiloh crossed his arms and shrugged.

"Who do you want me to shoot first?"

"Well, someone needs to go get the sheriff!" Cheney looked around helplessly.

"Black Arrow doesn't have a sheriff, never has," Shiloh replied, taking her arm and steering her away from the widening circles of the brawl. "But now they have a doctor—and it looks like you may have some patients when this is all over."

IN THE SHADOW

P·A·R·T T·W·O

OF HIS HAND

*. . . in the shadow of His hand
hath He hid me . . .*

Isaiah 49:2

7

BLOOD

Indian summer stealthily crept over Wolf County and lulled the people of the hills with its untimely warmth.

"What kinda stupid weather is this, anyway?" Gabe Stroud grumbled. "It's hot as Hades!" He was a lean whipcord of a man, with unkempt brown hair and close-set black eyes that darted unceasingly around the room. Nervously he crossed his arms, sat back in his chair, crossed his legs and uncrossed them, then leaned forward and clasped his hands together.

"Quit twitchin', Gabe," Tim Toney said with a grin. "It ain't that hot, you know. You're just scared 'cause the big boss wants to talk to us."

Stroud glared darkly at Toney's youthful face and jerked his head in the direction of the third man sitting across from them. Stroud attempted to make the signal unobtrusive, but one corner of Leslie Day's thin mouth twitched.

"Whatsa matter, Gabe?" Toney taunted him. "You think Mr. DeSpain don't know he's the big boss? And that Mr. Day might tell him I called him that behind his back?"

"Just leave me alone—Timmy," Stroud grunted, accenting the youthful name.

Tim Toney was only eighteen years old, with fiery red hair and brown eyes, already slightly crinkled at the corners with laugh lines. He was tall, thick, muscular, and intelligent, though unschooled.

"Now, Gabe." He reached over and punched Stroud on the upper arm. "You don't need me to remind you about the last fool that called me that, do ya?"

Leslie Day, Waylon DeSpain's lawyer, clinically observed the two men across the room from him. He found it extremely interesting that, although Tim Toney seemed jovial, Gabe Stroud noticeably flinched when Toney punched him playfully, and something flitted across Stroud's dark eyes.

Not fear exactly—wariness, Day observed meticulously. *Interesting. I'll have to remember to tell Mr. DeSpain.* He cleared his throat, a dry, artificial interjection, and the men looked up at him questioningly.

"To be precise," he began in a bloodless tone, "Mr. DeSpain is not *the* 'big boss,' as you say, Mr. Toney. Rather, he is one of the 'big bosses.' And that is, in fact, where he has been for the last week. Meeting with his financial backers—the other 'big bosses'—in St. Louis."

Day's long, thin nose wrinkled as he repeated the slang term, and Tim Toney watched with veiled enjoyment. Leslie Day reminded him of a strange cross between a weasel and a fish. His features were sharp and pointed, but he wore large round glasses that glinted continually as he spoke, giving his face a bizarre glassy-eyed effect. Even Tim treated him with a degree of respect, for Tim had observed that Leslie Day was the only person who dared disagree with Waylon DeSpain to his face.

The door opened, and Waylon DeSpain entered with his lieutenant, Bake Conroy. DeSpain amicably greeted the three men waiting in his office and unceremoniously threw himself into the wheeled chair behind his massive teak banker's desk.

Conroy, a hulking brute, crossed his arms and stood beside DeSpain's desk, his feet widespread. Curtly he nodded to Leslie Day and glared at Stroud and Toney. Gabe Stroud straightened in his chair, but Tim Toney casually lounged in his and stared back at Conroy with a hint of challenge in his eyes.

DeSpain made desultory small talk for a few minutes, then pulled a long slim cheroot out of his breast pocket. The room grew silent as he ran the brown cylinder appreciatively under his nose, kicked back his chair, propped two gleaming black boots on his desk, and magically produced a lit match between his left thumb and forefinger. With obvious enjoyment he blew a feathery stream of blue smoke toward the ceiling and regarded Stroud and Toney with steel blue eyes. "I've got me a new plan, boys," he told them with an expansive wave of the cigar, "and I want you to help me with it."

"I'll help, sure will, Mr. DeSpain, be glad to," Stroud declared, and Toney rolled his eyes with disgust.

"Thanks, Gabe," DeSpain replied with ill-concealed amusement, then went on soberly, "You're a good man, you proved that last summer in Missouri. You, too, Tim. Now, what we're going to do is a little tricky, but I know you can handle it."

Abruptly he slammed his feet to the floor and stood up. Stroud jumped and Toney smirked at him. With the lit cigar DeSpain pointed to the Wolf County map tacked up behind his desk.

"Maeva's Trace—Copperhead Gate—down to Hawk's Light—across Moccasin Lake to Blackcastle Springs—back up to Maeva's Trace." Deftly he traced a loose triangle on the map, then seated himself back in the chair and scrutinized the men before him with detachment. "Now I plan to own all that"—he pointed the cigar over his left shoulder without looking back—"come spring."

"But I thought that was the old plan, Mr. DeSpain," Stroud mumbled as he searched the map with bewilderment.

"Gabe, you wouldn't know a plan if it bit your horse on the—"

"Watch your smart mouth, Toney," Conroy growled.

"—hock," Toney finished with composure, and Bake Conroy's face darkened even more.

Waylon DeSpain ignored the exchange, though his eyes glinted with faint amusement at Tim Toney's impudence. The young man reminded him very much of himself at eighteen years of age. "You're right, Gabe," he nodded, and Stroud darted a triumphant look at Toney. "That was the old plan. The new plan is *how* we're going to do it. We've been here for four months, and I don't own one pine tree yet. I'm getting impatient—and so are the gentlemen that I do business with. And now that it looks like we're about to be in the middle of a blood feud, we're going to have to change our strategy."

Reflectively DeSpain ground out the cheroot in a cobalt blue glass ashtray on his desk, methodically reducing the ashes into uniform black powder. "Mr. Day," he murmured in a detached tone, "tell the men about the new plan."

Leslie Day fussily crossed his hands over one black wool-clad knee. "First of all, gentlemen," he began in a bland voice, devoid of inflection, "you may begin wearing your guns."

★ ★ ★ ★

"Shiloh, will you help me, please?"

Cheney's voice held a note that he had heard before, a note of uncertainty and doubt, and instantly he rose from his seat on the cabin steps and turned to the doorway. "Sure, Doc," he replied, his voice gentle. "What can I do?"

Cheney walked outside and motioned him to sit back down, and then she sank down tiredly beside him. "Read this and tell me what you think." Handing him a thick book, she opened it and pointed to a paragraph she had marked with an asterisk. Silently he began to read.

Cheney looked up the dusty street of Black Arrow. Two women were walking toward Sikes' General Store, three men lounged in front of the saloon, and a woman drove a buggy up the street toward Wolf Run. *Neva Sikes and Lorine Satterfield,* Cheney mentally named the women going into the store. *Enoch Satterfield, T. R. Satterfield, and Ross Lee Sikes in front of the Nameless Saloon. Leah Satterfield driving the buggy.*

We've been here ten days, Cheney thought ruefully, *and already I know almost everyone's name. First time in my life I've learned people's names so easily—and all for what? No social calls except for Sharon and Mr. DeSpain. And hardly any patients. DeSpain's men don't really count—or Sharon. The only hill people I've had are Booth Trask and Jimmy Dale, after that horrible Thanksgiving riot. Yesterday Katie Carter wouldn't even let me look at Glendean, just informed me courteously that she had gotten over the pertussis—or rather, the "whooping cough."*

Cheney sighed deeply, and Shiloh looked up questioningly. "Nothing," she murmured, and he bent his head to return to the book.

Her mind wandering as she sat limply beside Shiloh, Cheney marveled again at the strange weather that had begun the day after Thanksgiving. Thanksgiving Day had been classic autumn weather, cold and golden and crisp. The next morning Cheney awoke to temperatures that were more like June, and every day since then had been shirtsleeve weather. *So unsettling*, Cheney thought as she looked at the colorless landscape in the incongruous yellow sunshine. *Too bright, too warm for December. Seems artificial, unnatural. . . . Wonder if it's snowing in New York? Or in England . . . Dev . . .*

Closing the book, Shiloh looked up, his gaze unseeing.

Cheney looked at him expectantly, but he remained silent. Finally she asked, "Well? What do you think?"

"Do you have any more information about it?"

"No! And it's such a stupid, vicious, arbitrary—!" Noting the grim look on Shiloh's face, Cheney stopped abruptly and made herself speak more calmly. "The information is so horribly imprecise, you see. The cause is unknown, the symptoms are questionable, the treatment is guesswork—and the cure is nonexistent. That's why it's taken me so long to diagnose it."

"Yes, I can see that this doesn't fit into any of your little cubbyholes and compartments, Doc. But I think your diagnosis is probably right, if that's what you're fussin' about." Shiloh's tone of gentle teasing made Cheney smile slightly, and he went on, "Is that all?"

"It's all I know," Cheney sighed. "Except . . ."

Without turning to look at her, Shiloh reached over and took Cheney's hand, squeezed it lightly, and held it. Cheney's eyes were unfocused as she stared out across the Osage River to the bleak hills beyond. "There was a woman," she murmured, "at the hospital when I was in school who was diagnosed with it. She wasn't my patient, but Dr. Vallingham lectured us on the disease, or affliction, or whatever it is. We monitored her until the—until about—"

Cheney swallowed hard. Shiloh didn't speak, he merely caressed her hand lightly. Cheney's face was distant and expressionless, but when she spoke her voice trembled. "Until they died. She and the baby."

The two sat quietly for a while. A sullen breeze stirred Shiloh's hair, and Cheney lifted her face to it gratefully. Although it wasn't hot, the atmosphere was oppressive, similar to the heaviness before a severe thunderstorm. No clouds were in the blue sky, however, and the air was dry.

"You two goin' to see Miz Sharon, or ain't you?"

Rissy's deep voice from the cabin doorway startled Cheney, though Shiloh didn't react. Cheney jerked her hand away self-consciously and turned around. "Why, yes, Rissy, we are," Cheney answered. "Why?"

"I wuz just wonderin' if you was gonna go lak you said, or if'n you'd decided to sit out heah in public and hold onto Mistuh Shiloh's hand all day long in front of ever'body," Rissy sardonically retorted, hands on her hips.

"But, Rissy—" Cheney began, but she was protesting to an empty doorway.

Shiloh stood up, dusted off his breeches, and offered Cheney his hand. In abject embarrassment, Cheney rose hastily without help, stammering in confusion as she dropped her head and rubbed her hands on her skirt. "Rissy—I talked to her last night about Sharon, and what I'm going to do—and she—I mean, I guess she—but will you go with me?"

Shiloh looked amused at her agitation as he walked toward the stable. "I'll go with you, Doc, but you'll have to promise to try and control yourself and keep your hands off me."

Cheney's embarrassment evolved into indignation, and she sputtered, "You have such nerve, Shiloh—" But he had disappeared, so Cheney wheeled and stamped into the cabin.

Later, as they followed the now-familiar path up White Wolf Ridge to Sharon and Josh Carter's, Shiloh reached out and grabbed Stocking's bridle and brought both horses to an abrupt halt. "Howdy," he said politely to a large oak tree on his right.

"Howdy." Jimmy Dale Satterfield stepped out of the woods, grinning, his rifle carried at a comfortable angle. "Howdy, Miss Duvall. Reckon ya'll ain't lost today."

He turned and began to walk, and Shiloh pulled Sock up to a slow walk beside him. "Not yet, Jimmy Dale. You hunting?"

"Nope."

The three walked along in silence for a while. Jimmy Dale seemed deep in thought, frowning down at his worn moccasins as he soundlessly trudged between Shiloh and Cheney. He gave her an assessing glance, seemed to reach a conclusion, and turned back to Shiloh. "I reckon I'd best tell you, Shiloh. You orter be carryin' a gun when you and Miss Duvall's out and about."

Shiloh shrugged. "I've got my .44 in my saddlebag." He wasn't wearing his long coat that concealed the holster, and he had found it uncomfortably warm to wear it inside his shirt.

"That's a nice pistol," Jimmy Dale said rather wistfully. "Ain't nobody in these hills got a handgun. Just rifles."

"Let's go out and shoot it sometime," Shiloh offered. "It's a good pistol to learn on."

"I'd like that, sure would!"

Cheney spoke up. "I've noticed that since Thanksgiving, everyone's carrying their rifles everywhere! Why, church last Sunday looked more like a military muster, with all the rifles lined up along the pews!"

"Troubled times," Jimmy Dale said shortly.

"Has something happened? Besides the trouble at DeSpain's on Thanksgiving?"

Jimmy Dale looked around the woods, his eyes shadowed, his face close to sorrowful. "A whole lot's happened, Miss Duvall. Too much has happened 'tween us and the Carters." He spoke quietly, almost to himself, then his face cleared as he looked up at Cheney and answered her directly. "But no, ma'am, ain't nothin' happened." Turning his gaze straight ahead, he clenched his jaw and added so softly that Cheney almost missed it: "Yet."

Cheney and Shiloh exchanged meaningful glances over Jimmy Dale's head. Then Cheney went on gravely, "Jimmy Dale, I want to thank you for coming to me after the Thanksgiving riot. You had a bad black eye and cut lip, but I know you were just trying to—that your family, and with Miss Wilding, I think—well, I know it wasn't that bad—no, wait, that's not what I meant to say—"

Both Cheney and Jimmy Dale looked exceedingly uncomfortable, and Shiloh blew out an exasperated breath. "What the Doc's trying to say is that she knows you went to her instead of to Maeva Wilding, and she knows your family doesn't trust her, and she appreciates your confidence, and she thanks you for making a gesture that shows you believe in her."

"Yes," Cheney agreed with obvious relief.

"Well, Miss Duvall, that's a straight-talkin' speech for a woman," Jimmy Dale said with a perfectly straight face. "You're welcome. Am I the only patient you've had?"

"Not exactly," Cheney answered reluctantly. "DeSpain's men—Mr. Conroy, Mr. Stroud, and Mr. Toney—all had bumps and bruises. Ross Lee Sikes had a broken nose, and Booth Trask had a nasty cut on his forehead and a hairline fracture of the right wrist."

Jimmy Dale looked up in surprise. "Booth did? From the brawl at DeSpain's?"

"Yes. He came by that night, about nine o'clock."

"I didn't even know he were in town." He glanced slyly up at Shiloh, then turned to Cheney and said gravely, "He musta been really taken with you, Miss Duvall, to come to you. His daddy, Latham Trask, don't hold with strangers a-tall. And Maeva Wilding saved ol' Latham's life once. Yessirree, Booth must be right taken with you."

"Maybe," Cheney answered calmly. "And so, why did *you* come to me, Jimmy Dale?"

Jimmy Dale's head jerked up in surprise. Then Cheney and

Shiloh laughed, and he shook his head and grinned reluctantly. "Booth's my double-first cousin," he admitted, "and I thought I was gonna have somethin' to rile him about. Reckon I better keep my mouth shut, though, way it looks."

"What's a double-first cousin?" Cheney asked curiously.

"My daddy and his mama—no, that ain't right—his daddy and my daddy—no, that ain't right," Jimmy Dale wrinkled his brow and finally shrugged, "Niver mind. The Trasks and the Satterfields got lotsa family connections. My mama was a Trask—and somebody in Booth's family's a Satterfield. I think."

"I see," Cheney said, though she didn't. "But Jimmy Dale, can I ask you one thing?"

"Yes, ma'am."

"Since I'm friends with Sharon—a Carter—does that make it worse? I mean, for your family? I mean, for me to be your doctor, or their doctor, I guess is what I'm trying to—"

"What she's trying to say is—" Shiloh began with superiority.

"I'm purty sure I know how this goes now." Jimmy Dale winked at Shiloh, who grinned and motioned him to go on. Turning to Cheney, he grew serious. "No, ma'am. It don't make no difference about you bein' friends with Miss Sharon. 'Cause it's naught but blood, you see? Bad blood 'tween Carters and Satterfields, that's all. My people don't 'spect no one else to have the same bad blood. Nor do Carters."

Cheney tried to absorb this as they continued up Maeva's Trace. Before they came to the fork, the haunting strains of dulcimer music floated through the forest to their ears. Jimmy Dale turned, awkwardly pulled on the brim of his shapeless gray hat, then disappeared as quietly as he had come.

Cheney and Shiloh made their way slowly to Sharon's. When they reached the cabin, Shiloh shouted the familiar warning-greeting and Sharon came out on the porch, smiling and waving them to dismount.

After the initial hellos, Cheney glanced at Shiloh with veiled anxiety. Then she asked Sharon casually, "Would you mind sitting out on the porch today, since it's so warm?"

Sharon's eyes went back and forth from Cheney to Shiloh with sudden comprehension. "No, of course not, Cheney. It's nice out today. Might as well enjoy Indian summer while it lasts."

Cheney and Sharon settled themselves in the rocking chairs. Shiloh took his usual seat on the top step and picked up the whetstone that stayed on the front porch and began to sharpen his glittering knife. It was not an unpleasant sound, for Shiloh's strokes were strong and even, a low rasping rhythm.

As much trouble as Cheney had with expressing her emotions or conversing on a personal level, she was straightforward and direct when she talked to her patients. Without preamble she turned to Sharon and took her hand. It was cold.

"Sharon, dear," she said firmly, "I believe you have toxemia. Have you ever heard of it?"

After a sharp intake of breath, Sharon grasped Cheney's hand tightly. Then with a visible effort she smoothed the fear from her face and replied quietly, "No, I haven't, Cheney. Please tell me about it."

"It's a very serious condition, Sharon. But that's what it is— a condition, not a disease, and it's temporary. It chiefly affects young women in their first pregnancies and women who get pregnant after forty."

Cheney took a deep breath and her eyes involuntarily went to Shiloh's profile. His hands were steady, his eyes downcast, his movements methodical. Cheney was glad he was there.

"We don't know much about this problem, Sharon," she went on steadily, "but you're in the high-risk group—you're only twenty, and this is your first pregnancy. You have the classic symptoms associated with the condition: disproportionate edema—that's swelling—and blurred vision."

Sharon absently patted Cheney's hand, withdrew her hand, and began to rock. The rocking chair creaked slightly, and for long minutes the woody creak and the rasping of the Bowie knife on the whetstone were the only sounds on the porch.

"You're saying that you're not too certain I have this, aren't you?" Sharon asked.

"I'm saying that there's no way to be totally certain," Cheney declared.

"All right, I understand. So what is toxemia?"

Cheney steadied herself. It was hard for her to accept—and admit—ignorance, even though it was through no fault of her own. Shiloh glanced up at her, his eyes warm and sympathetic.

"We don't know what causes it, Sharon," Cheney finally answered. "We think it may be some substance in the mother's blood that unaccountably becomes detrimental both to the baby and to the mother herself during pregnancy."

Sharon's eyes went to the valley and far beyond. "Blood . . . cursed blood," she whispered hoarsely to herself. Then she seemed to steel herself and asked in a detached tone, "Detrimental how?"

"The swelling and even the blurred vision are not serious in themselves. The danger of toxemia is that sometimes the mother will have seizures. Convulsions." Cheney cautiously watched Sharon as she spoke, trying to gauge her reaction. She seemed to be calm and attentive, so Cheney continued. "The convulsions are extremely dangerous for two reasons: one is that they can occur so unexpectedly, without warning, and the mother may fall and hurt herself and the baby. The other is that the convulsions themselves may do harm to the mother and the baby."

Cheney waited, and Sharon rocked. Shiloh sharpened steadily.

Finally Sharon asked, "Does this condition always cause convulsions?"

"No."

"What is the treatment?"

"Complete bed rest," Cheney answered without hesitation but wincing inwardly. She had an idea what this meant for Sharon Carter.

"You mean—"

"I mean complete bed rest, Sharon. Twenty-four hours a day, every day. As little activity as humanly possible. Stay in bed, and don't move much."

"And that will cure this—this—horrible—" With an effort Sharon cleared her throat and unclenched her fists.

For the first time, Cheney looked down at her hands. They were clenched in her lap as tightly as Sharon's, and her neck hurt from tension. Shiloh quietly put down the whetstone, stuck the knife in the back of his belt, and looked out over the valley.

Cheney's voice was low and strained as she answered, "No, Sharon. There is no cure for toxemia. No medicine I can give you. The only thing I can give you is hope that bed rest will keep you and the baby safe; and I can give you a promise that I'll pray for you and the baby every single day. That's all I can do."

★ ★ ★ ★

What can wash away my sin?
Nothing but the blood of Jesus!
What can make me whole again?
Nothing but the blood of Jesus!
Oh, precious is the flow
That makes me white as snow . . .
No other fount I know;
Nothing but the blood of Jesus.

Bobbie Jo Carter sang quietly, but her clear voice carried far in the quiet woods on the mountain called Maeva's Trace. Idly she strummed the strings of her dulcimer with her fingers instead of with the turkey feather. The notes sounded hushed, muted, and again she sang her favorite church song, slowly and softly.

Jimmy Dale Satterfield followed the sweet music until he stood at the edge of a small clearing by a busy little stream. Bobbie Jo sat on an enormous rock that was almost three feet high. The top of it slanted downward at a steep angle, and Bobbie Jo perched on it with her legs bent gracefully to the side. Jimmy

Dale stopped and stood motionless as she finished the song. Bending over the dulcimer, her long shining hair brushed across the gleaming wood. She looked unreal, otherworldly, too gentle and sweet for the roughness surrounding her.

She sang the last notes of the song, and the vibration from the strings stayed in the air a few seconds after the music died. Jimmy Dale stepped forward. Bobbie Jo saw him, her face lit up, and he hurried to her before she could jump off the rock. Gently he bent and brushed her lips with his. "Howdy," he whispered.

"Howdy."

Bobbie Jo pulled her legs up close to her body and patted the rock. Jimmy Dale clambered up beside her, laying his rifle across his knees just as Bobbie Jo's dulcimer lay across hers. Taking her hand, he smiled down at her. "I like to come find you when you're singin', Bobbie Jo. It's—nice, someways, to foller that sweet music."

Nodding with understanding, Bobbie Jo asked tremulously, "Did you see or hear anybody?"

"Just Shiloh and Miss Duvall on their way to see Miss Sharon."

Bobbie Jo's face grew fearful. Jimmy Dale put his arm around her shoulders and laid his cheek against her hair. "Don't be scairt, Bobbie Jo. They ain't gonna say nothin' to nobody. Both of 'em minds their own business."

"I am scairt, though, Jimmy Dale." She maneuvered to sit closer to him, and his arm around her tightened. "Somethin' bad's gonna happen. . . . I can just feel it . . . and my daddy . . ."

"I know, darlin'," Jimmy Dale sighed. "My daddy too. And my brothers. They's all got fire in their eyes. And I don't know who T. R. would shoot first—you or me."

"Why does it have to be now?" Bobbie Jo cried mournfully. "Now, just when I found you! For so long the Carters and the Satterfields been just ignorin' one 'nother and grousin' about t'other! And then we finally wake up and see how much we love each other, and all of a sudden our daddies decide we better start shootin'!"

"I know, I know," Jimmy Dale murmured comfortingly against her hair. "Don't be afraid, Bobbie Jo. I'll take care of you, I swear." Turning her face up to his, Jimmy Dale kissed her gently, and Bobbie Jo put her warm hand on the side of his face and caressed it. For long moments they kissed, then Jimmy Dale straightened and put his arm protectively around her shoulders again. "Just think about Christmas, Bobbie Jo. Daddy promised me them forty acres north o' Maeva's Trace. By New Year's we'll be married and moved to the farrest end, I swear." Bobbie Jo sighed softly and nestled closer to him. The two sat close together, contented in the quiet and the peace and in each other's company.

A crow called hoarsely, far off, and Bobbie Jo stirred uneasily. "My daddy said something to Josh last night I wasn't s'posed to hear, Jimmy Dale," she murmured uncertainly. Looking down, her hair fell across her shoulder and hid her face. Lightly she strummed the strings of the dulcimer, and the drone notes sounded haunting in the stillness. "He said we's all cursed."

Suddenly Jimmy Dale savagely shoved Bobbie Jo off the rock.

She fell behind it, into a small cleft formed by a ring of rocks similar to the one they had been sitting on but smaller. Landing on her side against a sharp edge, Bobbie Jo's breath whooshed out of her lungs forcibly. Hot tears rolled down her face. Her mind screamed, "What? Why?" but she could make no sound, or even raise her head to look up at Jimmy Dale.

Loud cracks seemed to split the very air of the woods. Gunfire. Someone was shooting at them.

Loud zinging noises sounded, and tiny sharp pieces of rock exploded all around Bobbie Jo.

Still unable to take a breath, she managed to raise her eyes to the rock that was now sheltering her. Jimmy Dale was nowhere to be seen. Another loud whining zing sounded. Bobbie Jo thought something stung her on the forehead—and in a single instant the world turned black.

8

TRAPS

"Thou shalt not be afraid for the terror by night; nor for the arrow that flieth by day; nor for the pestilence that walketh in darkness; nor for the destruction that wasteth at noonday."

By the yellow light of the flickering candle Cheney spoke the words of the beloved psalm aloud, and was comforted.

All night she had been tormented by nightmares. Long before dawn she had awakened filled with fear for a nameless, faceless terror that she could neither fully recall nor completely forget. After almost an hour of lying stiffly prostrate, eyes determinedly closed and jaw clenched, willing herself to go back to sleep, the absurdity of her posture had finally occurred to her. Resignedly she had gotten up, dressed, lit a single candle, and read the Bible.

Now she looked out the tiny window that faced the west. No eastern glow warmed the river and hills yet, but she could begin to make out details of the landscape in the neutral grayness that is neither dark nor dawn.

Tiny, careful noises came from the back door and the kitchen. *Shiloh building the fire*, Cheney thought. *Might as well go down*. Stiffly she rose and stretched. She felt sluggish and rather cross, but the paralyzing fear of the night had long dissipated from her mind.

In the dimness she made her way carefully down the stairs and to the kitchen. Shiloh knelt in front of the squatty black stove with his back to her, carefully laying in kindling.

"Morning, Doc," he greeted her without turning around. "Couldn't sleep?"

"No. You couldn't either?"

Striking a match, he coaxed the sticks into a busy blaze and piled in some small logs cut exactly the right size for the stove's potbelly. "I slept just fine." Securely slamming the door of the stove, he walked to the deep sink and began to pump. With two or three cranks, a small trickle of water began and Shiloh washed his hands thoroughly. "I always get up this early." He smiled over his shoulder at her.

"Whatever for?" Cheney asked with disgust. She was a defiant late sleeper whenever possible.

"I go to Sikes' Store and get Rissy's fresh milk and eggs, and take a bath and shave. Then I come back here and build the fire, make the coffee, tend the horses, and clean the stable."

"All before breakfast?" Cheney protested. "I had no idea so much industry was going on before I ever opened my eyes!"

Shiloh put the tin coffeepot on the stove, then busied himself pouring two cups of creamy milk from a huge earthenware jug.

"Wait a minute," Cheney yawned. "Did you say you go to Sikes' to take a bath?"

Setting the two cups of foamy milk on the table, Shiloh seated himself close beside her and thirstily emptied his cup. "Yeah," he replied. "Ross had a big idea once of opening a barber parlor in a little back room of the store, with baths and shaves and haircuts. But somehow it didn't go over too good. I think I'm his only patron."

Cheney sipped the cool milk and studied him over the rim of the cup. *He is always so clean,* she thought. *It never even occurred to me to wonder how he manages, living in the stable. . . .*

He was sitting at the head of the table, very close to her. Her eyes went from his tousled blond hair to the V-scar beneath his eye and his smoothly shaven jaw. His plain white shirt gleamed, his hands were spotless, the short square-cut nails clean. Unconsciously Cheney breathed deeply of his scent. He smelled of soap and the cleanness of outdoors. *Spicy, woodsy smell,* she reflected. *What is it—pine? Cedar? Must be the pine sticks he gathers for the fire.*

"I like pine for the fires, don't you?" he asked innocently, his expression amused at Cheney's perusal. "Smells good."

An exaggerated sigh escaped from Cheney. Looking away from him, she drained the cup of milk and gave the coffeepot a longing glance.

Rissy appeared, soundless and silent as her mother, Dally, always was. "Coffee," she grumbled. Normally she, too, was a late riser, and it took a while before she was her usual voluble self. Busily she fixed three cups of coffee and began to prepare breakfast with one hand, sipping noisily from the cup she held in the other.

Cheney had a uniform white stripe across her top lip. Shiloh leaned close to her and gently wiped her lip and the corner of her mouth. "I was talking to Ross Lee this morning," he said conversationally. Ross Lee was Ross and Neva Sikes' eighteen-year-old son.

"Milk mustache?" Cheney murmured, sitting very still.

Rissy turned around and almost dropped her coffee and the bowl she held in the other hand.

"Hmm-hmm," Shiloh answered absently. "Ross Lee said T. R. Satterfield got drunk last night at the Nameless Saloon and started talking. Too much."

"What did he say?" Cheney licked her top lip carefully and then looked at him questioningly.

Nodding with approval at her now-clean face, Shiloh replied, "T. R. says Bobbie Jo Carter got shot yesterday while she was wandering around in the woods."

"What!" Cheney banged down her coffee cup, and the scalding liquid splashed messily all over the table, but she didn't notice. "Those shots we heard yesterday—" she muttered anxiously.

Shiloh cautioned her, "Now don't get all wrought up, Doc. There's been lots of rumors flying around about the feud since Thanksgiving, and so far there hasn't been anything to them. And Ross Lee didn't say anything about Jimmy Dale—and you know he was with her up on Maeva's Trace."

With vigorous strokes Rissy mopped up the table and nod-ded, "Dat's right. I hears all kinds of stuff when I goes to Mistuh Sikes' store. So you jest calm down. You kin check on Miz Bob-bie Jo when we goes to Miz Sharon's."

"We?" Cheney repeated. "You mean you want to go, Rissy?"

"Well, I better! Since you done got big for yo' britches and tole Miz Sharon you'd help tend to her house if'n she'd stay in bed!" Rissy straightened and put her hands on her hips.

"I had to, Rissy," Cheney argued. "The Carters aren't going to like it if Sharon stays in bed all the time—they're going to think that I'm just a fancy doctor putting on airs! And Sharon, too! They won't help her. Besides, I can do all those things."

"All dem things," Rissy mocked. "Yes, ma'am! You done spent so much time larnin' how to git firewood and kindlin' and tend the fires and cook and clean and wash clothes and mend 'em and tend the garden and the chickens and the dogs. Why, you cain't even wash yo' own face! Mistuh Shiloh's gotta wash you like a mama cat!"

"Rissy!" Cheney snapped, appalled.

Shiloh laughed and shook his head. "This is going to be an interesting day, I can tell," he chuckled. "Rissy, are you going to ride to the Carters'? If you want to, you can ride Stocking, and Doc, you can ride with me."

"I ain't ridin' on top of no hoss," Rissy sniffed. "I'm a-walkin'. And don't tell me I cain't, neither, 'cause I kin, and I'm gwine to."

Cheney felt relief out of all proportion. The thought of cling-ing to Shiloh all the way to Sharon's had disturbed her greatly.

Shiloh shrugged and said, "All right, Rissy. After breakfast I'll saddle up Stocking for the doc, and I'll walk, too. Be good for me."

Rissy looked rebellious and opened her mouth to say some-thing, but a shriek from outside stopped her.

"Doctor Cheney! Doctor Cheney! Are you here? I need help!"

Shiloh and Cheney jumped up and ran to the front door

with Rissy gliding silently behind them. Shiloh threw open the door.

Glendean—Josh Carter's eight-year-old sister—was outside mounted on a prancing, snorting horse. The horse looked enormous with little Glendean astride it, bareback.

"Doctor Cheney!" she shrieked again. "Beauregard's done tromped on one of T. R.'s stinkin' wolf traps! His leg's prob'ly broke and he's prob'ly dead from bleedin' by now anyways, so you gotta hurry! Please!" Tears were streaming down her face.

"I'll get my bag. Just a minute, Glendean, I'm coming." Cheney disappeared inside, Rissy right behind her, while Shiloh ran toward the stable.

Glendean remained on the horse, fidgeting and muttering, "Hurry, hurry, hurry, please . . ."

Within ten minutes Cheney hurried out of the house. Shiloh rode around from the stable and tossed Stocking's reins to her. To his surprise Cheney mounted astride Stocking, her wide skirts billowing out and completely covering the saddle. Seeing his glance she blushed deeply but ordered Glendean, "Let's go, Glendean! You lead!"

Glendean's horse reared, and Cheney was frightened for the girl for a moment. But Glendean clung tightly as the horse turned and galloped wildly back up the street. Cheney and Shiloh followed.

They were about halfway up Wolf Run when Shiloh noticed a rider coming through Copperhead Gate to the east. He was shouting something, and Shiloh reined up to shade his eyes to look and try to hear.

"Miss Duvall!"

Shiloh heard faintly the rider's call, so he called sharply to Cheney to stop. Farther up the hill, Glendean stopped and looked back impatiently. Cheney rode back to Shiloh to wait for the rider to reach them.

It was Booth Trask. "Miss Duvall, I'm glad I caught you," he gasped as he reined up his horse close to them. "My little sister's sick, and I was hoping you could come."

Cheney looked anxiously at Shiloh, then back at Glendean, who was calling in a high voice, "Please, Doctor Cheney! Please hurry!"

"Will you go with Booth, Shiloh?" Cheney asked.

"I don't want to leave you two out here," was Shiloh's troubled answer.

"I don't want you to leave me," Cheney murmured, her eyes on Glendean's small form. "But I think I'd better go see about this Beauregard. Glendean's really scared, and it sounds serious."

Booth Trask was a rather shy young man of eighteen who was somewhat enamored of Cheney. The bandage that Cheney had put on the cut on his forehead was dirty, and even as distracted as she was, she reminded herself that she needed to change the bandage and check the two stitches.

Booth listened carefully to the conversation, his own face distraught. "Mr. Irons? I know you was a medical corpsman in the war. Please, if Miss Duvall cain't come, will you? My sister's real sick."

"All right," Shiloh relented, then turned to Cheney, who was already riding toward Glendean. "You be careful, Doc! I'll meet you back at the cabin later! Don't dawdle!"

"Yes, Rissy!" Cheney called sarcastically over her shoulder.

"Female doctors," Shiloh muttered darkly.

Turning back to Copperhead Gate, Booth Trask spurred his horse into a fast trot. "You sound jis' like my pa did," he told Shiloh with a shy grin, "when he told me to go fetch Maeva Wilding."

★ ★ ★ ★

Cheney had grown up riding spirited Arabian stallions, and was quite a good rider. But never in her life had she imagined a ride such as the one she took now; and not in her wildest dreams had she ever seen herself riding a horse astride. Her cheeks burned as she thought of it; to her, it was vulgar and common, not at all something that a lady would do. *Nothing*

114

else for it, she comforted herself. *I sure couldn't daintily mince along riding sidesaddle and keep up with that child!*

Glendean rode headlong up the hills and around the curves of the narrow path with no apparent fear. Her thin little legs stuck out from under her skirt, kicking wildly, and Cheney was certain that the horse never felt a tap from her small bare feet. *She doesn't even have a headpiece or bridle,* Cheney thought. *Just that silly piece of rope knotted about that huge horse's neck.* But Glendean and the horse flew as one through the deep woods.

Abruptly, Glendean's horse slowed almost to a stop, and Glendean slid off and ran off the path to the right. Breathlessly Cheney dismounted, grabbed her medical bag, and followed.

"He's this way, Miss Cheney! Hurry!" Glendean plunged into the woods.

Cheney followed with some difficulty. Glendean was surefooted and quick, but Cheney had some trouble with the underbrush and low-hanging branches.

They went farther up Maeva's Trace, through a thick grove of trees, and abruptly came out into a small clearing. A stream gurgled quietly by several huge, lichen-covered rocks. In front of the rocks stood Glen Rawlins, patting an enormous horse.

Cheney stopped short and took in the scene.

Glendean ran to the horse and reached up to stroke his nose, which had a white blaze. " 'S'awright, Beauregard," she crooned, "Doctor Cheney's here now."

With disbelief and open mouth, Cheney looked the horse—and then Glen Rawlins—up and down accusingly. "Do you mean to tell me that Beauregard is a *horse?*" she stormed.

Glendean's and Glen Rawlins' faces were identically distraught. "B-but, Doctor Cheney," Glendean said in a small woebegone voice, "he's hurt. . . ." She knelt by the horse's right foreleg, and tears began to roll down her face.

Glen Rawlins walked to Cheney, his shoulders bent. His black eyes were haunted and his gait was shambling. Removing his wide-brimmed black hat, he looked down at it and fidgeted with it nervously as he spoke.

"Miss Duvall," he muttered in a thick voice, "Beauregard carried me fer four years through the worst hell I never thought of. Never did I git a scratch—and I'll allus believe 'twas because of that horse holdin' me safe. Now he's done got his laig all tore up in that there cursed trap, and I'm askin' you, please—" He raised his great grizzly head, and his mournful dark eyes filled with tears. "Please, see if you can do something fer him. Please."

Cheney's heart softened. She knew what it was like to have a beloved horse hurt, and she could see that Glen Rawlins, great bear of a man that he was, wasn't the least bit embarrassed to cry for his Beauregard. "All right," she said softly and smiled. "I've never doctored a horse before, Mr. Rawlins, but I'll do my best."

"Thank you, ma'am," he answered humbly, and wiped his eyes with an enormous square of red flannel he pulled from his pocket.

Briskly Cheney walked to the horse, who was sweating and shivering and showing the whites of his eyes. Cheney was doubtful about Glendean flitting around him in the nervous state he was in, but the horse seemed to be watching the little girl and listening carefully to her prattling.

Glendean popped up from where she was kneeling. "Now Beauregard, I know you're scairt, 'cause me and Oncle Glen are scairt, too. This here's Doctor Cheney and she's gonna fix your leg. But you gotta be nice and not kick her nor nothin'." The horse steadily gazed at Glendean as she patted the white blaze on his nose with one tiny dirty hand. He even seemed to relax a little.

Cheney decided to analyze it later and just do whatever seemed necessary to make the big horse happy.

"You keep talking to him, Glendean," she ordered, "while I look at his leg. Just pet him softly and speak in a quiet tone."

"I know what to do, Doctor Cheney," Glendean assured her. "Beauregard's my horse Murdoch's brother, so I know him pretty good."

Glen Rawlins stood a little behind Cheney, still fiddling with his hat and looking helpless. Cheney knelt in front of the horse, who started nervously.

Glendean murmured, "Now jis' a dadblamed minute, Beau. You gotta quit stompin' around like that! She's gonna have to look at it, you know, and touch it, too, so you might as well jis' git ready."

Cheney stayed very still and watched to see if the horse would allow her to look at the injured leg. To her wonder, his ears pricked forward as Glendean rebuked him, and he seemed to settle down resignedly. Cheney bent forward and looked closely at the leg.

The trap had locked just above the fetlock, on the cannon bone. Cheney glanced about questioningly, for the trap was not still on the horse's leg. With amazement she saw a rusty saw-toothed trap lying to one side. It was about a foot long, rather crudely fashioned of iron—but now it was in three pieces. Involuntarily her awed gaze went to Glen Rawlins.

"I hadda git it off'n him, Miss Duvall," he explained, looking rather embarrassed.

"Yes, well, that's—good, Mr. Rawlins," Cheney finally stammered. She couldn't imagine the kind of strength—or rage—it took to literally tear a wolf trap to pieces.

Again she bent close to study Beauregard's leg. Glendean chirped and chattered and the horse remained still, though he shivered occasionally. The tear went to the bone, front and back, and was already hideously swollen.

Thank you, Lord, that this bone isn't fractured, Cheney gratefully prayed. She knew that the horse would have to be put down if it had a broken leg—and she was pretty certain who would have to do the shooting. Miraculously, the two strong cords of the tendons in Beauregard's leg had not been cut. Evidently the teeth of the trap had gone deep into the bone on either side of both of them.

Cheney sat back and looked around her appraisingly. "Where does that stream come from? What's the source?"

"Nowhere. Hit's jist here," was Rawlins' childlike answer.

"Can Beauregard walk?"

"I don't know," he replied, so distraught he could barely make sense of Cheney's questions.

"Beauregard, can you walk?" Glendean asked the horse earnestly. Then she looked down at Cheney and nodded, "He'll walk."

Cheney thought ruefully, *I should have thought to have Glendean ask Beauregard.* "All right, Glendean, let's get him to go stand in that stream."

Without hesitation Glendean put her hand under the horse's chin and said in a no-nonsense tone, "You heard her. C'mon, we gotta go over there." She pointed. Cheney glanced at Rawlins, but the absurdity of the gesture didn't seem to make an impression on him. He merely watched the horse and Glendean gravely.

In the next moment it was Cheney who felt rather absurd, because Glendean started walking slowly to the stream, her hand lightly on the horse's side—and Beauregard limped pitifully along beside her. Glendean stopped at the bank and wordlessly pointed to the water. Cheney could have sworn that the horse sighed; then he tossed his head slightly, stepped into the stream and waded out. When he reached the middle Glendean said, "That's good, Beau." The stream bubbled noisily about Beauregard's knees.

"Let the cool water run over it for a few minutes," Cheney instructed. Beauregard looked mournful, but he stood still. Cheney was certain the cool water felt soothing to the swollen leg. *And the swelling will go down, and it'll clean it out at the same time,* she thought with satisfaction as she went to organize the supplies she'd need. *Carbolic acid . . . bandage it. Beau'll have to stay off it for a few days . . . then mild exercise. Check it next Wednesday.* Busily she planned and rehearsed the instructions she would give Glendean, so the little girl could in turn tell the horse.

★ ★ ★ ★

"Where in the world did you get fresh grapes?" Cheney asked with delight.

Beauregard was happily snuffling and rolling in the cool green moss a few feet away. His leg was clean and bandaged, and Cheney, Glen, and Glendean had all rubbed him down and babied him after Cheney had finished dressing his wounds.

Rawlins had unsaddled Stocking, and he and Murdoch wandered lazily around the clearing. Glendean had produced a sackful of round red grapes, and had proceeded to feed the horses so many that Cheney had finally made her stop.

"They ain't grapes," Glendean scoffed. "They's muskydines. Ol' Maeva give 'em to me—sorta." She popped one in her mouth and looked at Cheney shrewdly. "You hungry, Doctor Cheney?"

"Why, yes, I am," Cheney said, sinking to the ground beside Glendean, who had plopped down underneath a huge pine tree on a deep, fragrant bed of brown needles. "I just realized that I missed breakfast."

Glendean pointed to the sack of muscadines, and Cheney eagerly grabbed a handful.

Glen Rawlins turned and went to his saddle, which lay in a heap beside the wolf trap. Rummaging about, he produced a small brown paper bundle. Then he went to the stream and pulled out a small jug that was lying in the shallows. Strolling back, he sank to the ground with curious grace to sit cross-legged beside Glendean. He offered Cheney the jug, but she eyed it suspiciously.

"Hit's only apple cider, Miss Duvall," he said with a grin. His teeth looked very white and even in the jungle of his black beard and mustache.

Holding the jug with both hands, Cheney turned it up and drank thirstily. The cider was sweet, with a hint of spice, and wonderfully cool. "Mmm, thank you. Doctoring horses is thirsty work."

"I cain't thank you 'nuff, ma'am," Rawlins said as he unwrapped the bundle. It was thick slabs of ham, and Cheney eyed

119

them hungrily. He held out the bundle to her, and she greedily picked two of the biggest.

"You're welcome, Mr. Rawlins. I was happy to do it." She took a huge bite of the juicy, salty meat. It had a distinct smoky flavor that Cheney had never tasted before, and she liked it very much.

"I'm so glad you was here, Doctor Cheney," Glendean declared. "That ol' witch Maeva won't doctor no animals a-tall." She sniffed disparagingly.

"Now, Glendean," Rawlins grunted, "you know she ain't no witch. She's busy with your sister, anyways."

"What?" Cheney demanded alertly. "Bobbie Jo? We heard in town that she'd been shot—is it true?"

"Naw," Glendean scoffed. "But some gol-derned fool was huntin' up here yesterday, and Bobbie Jo hadda hide behind them rocks to keep from gittin' shot." Popping a muscadine in her mouth, she nodded toward the huge rocks hunched by the stream. "Gol-derned fool shot them rocks," she summarized, "and the rocks hit Bobbie Jo in the head."

"You quit cussin' like that, Glendean," Rawlins growled. "Yore mama hears you, and she'll make us both sorry."

Cheney delicately placed a muscadine on her tongue and popped the sweet fruit out of the skin, then chewed with enjoyment. She had been troubled by the seeds, but finally she just spit them out as Rawlins and Glendean did. "But is Bobbie Jo all right?"

"Oh, sure," Glendean answered. "Ol' Maeva put some mud on her head, and she was just a-fussin' about it when me and Oncle Glen left." She giggled and continued slyly, "That's where I heard that new cuss word."

Rawlins moodily tore apart a thick slab of ham. "Decided to come up here and have a look around," he told Cheney. "Found more'n I wanted to know about." He eyed Beauregard regretfully.

"Was—did—was Bobbie Jo. . . . Did she see anyone?" Cheney asked with difficulty. She knew Jimmy Dale Satterfield had probably been with her, but she didn't know if anyone else knew. Cheney never repeated tales; much like Shiloh, she firmly believed in people minding their own business.

Rawlins looked up sharply to search Cheney's face, then glanced furtively at Glendean. "Reckon Bobbie Jo saw someone," he replied rather obliquely. He chewed carefully and went on, "I was up to the Satterfields' this mornin' and talked to Jimmy Dale. T. R.'s out huntin'. Been out since yestiddy."

"Do you think maybe . . ." Cheney began hesitantly, also conscious of speaking too freely in front of Glendean.

But their careful intimations were wasted. Glendean spoke up in the offhand manner of a child. "Mebbe T. R. shot at Bobbie Jo 'cause nobody wants her and Jimmy Dale to be together. Or mebbe it was a haint thet did it, on account of we's all cursed, you know." Mischievously she held up two muscadines to her eyes and looked through them at Cheney, who managed a half-hearted smile.

"Now, Glendean, I done tole you ain't nobody cursed!" Glen snapped. "And ain't no sucha thing as real haints, no more'n I'm a real bear!"

"Well, my daddy was talkin' to Josh 'bout bein' cursed and all," Glendean argued. "An' as far as you bein' a real bear—" She shot a sly look at Cheney, who smiled sincerely now.

"Glendean," Rawlins said with exasperation, "why don't you run on over and check on Beauregard and git to know Miss Cheney's horse."

"His name's Stocking, and I'm sure he'd like you a lot, Glendean," Cheney added.

Glendean's face lit up and, grabbing the leftover muscadines, she jumped up and ran toward the three horses, who were nibbling idly at the edge of the clearing twenty feet away.

As soon as the child was out of earshot, Cheney demanded, "What in the world is that horrible talk about a curse?"

Shaking his head regretfully, Glen explained, "I dunno who got that started. Sounds like some of Leah Satterfield's notions—but there, I jist dunno." He looked around the quiet clearing with a hint of sadness. "The feud seems like it skips from father to son. These Satterfields and Carters—the kids, y'know—is the accursed ones."

"I don't understand! Why should they be the ones who are cursed?"

"They jist are, Doctor Cheney," Glen replied soberly. "See, it all started with Enoch's and Lige's great-grandfathers—and them two got hurt, almost to the death. Then it skipped the grandfathers. Then Enoch's uncle got kilt, and Lige's daddy and his uncle. Then Enoch and Lige has been all right. So the feud burns to every other son—and blood's spilt. So these sons are sons of the curse."

"Nonsense!" Cheney snapped. "Each one of them makes his own decision each day, just as we all do! And we don't—" She broke off her vehement words when she realized that Glen was watching her with regretful agreement. "Anyway, to get back to Bobbie Jo—and Jimmy Dale—do you think T. R. actually shot at her?"

"I dunno, Doctor Cheney," Glen shrugged. "He's ornery enuff to. But then agin, it'd be more like him to bust in on them two and beat the tar outta Jimmy Dale, an' then drag him home an' let Enoch beat on him fer a while." He spoke with something akin to exasperated affection, which surprised Cheney.

"I thought you and the Satterfields were—probably not friends. At least, not on terms of knowing family problems."

"I ain't got no quarrels with the Satterfields. Them and the Carters, they got bad blood 'tween 'em. I'm a Rawlins."

"I guess I just don't quite understand this feuding business," Cheney sighed. "I especially thought—since the dinner at DeSpain's on Thanksgiving, you and T. R. Satterfield—"

Like a guilty young boy, Rawlins dropped his shaggy head. "Aw, me an' T. R. was drunk. T. R. allus wants to fight when he's hittin' the jug, and I was already mad 'cause Lorine makes me plumb crazy sometimes." His head jerked up, sudden remorse in his eyes. "Oh, no! That big boy that Lorine was flirtin' with— I forgot! He's your friend!"

"Yes," Cheney answered dryly, "and my nurse. He's a good one, too—and a good man."

"I'm sorry, Miss Duvall," he said with genuine regret. "I owe you more than money for savin' Beauregard. And I'm sorry I took on such to your friend. I'll make it up to both of you, I swear."

Cheney eyed Rawlins for a long moment. She had never met a man so rough, so crude looking, so like a wild animal—but also so tenderhearted as Glen Rawlins. He met her assessing gaze unflinchingly. Cheney smiled at him, and his eyes lit up as if she'd given him a great gift. "I'm just glad to have you for a friend, Mr. Rawlins. And I'm sure Shiloh will feel the same."

9

MAEVA

"Dorcas! Dorcas! Wake up, child!"

Sluggishly, Dorcas Trask rolled over and opened her eyes. It took several seconds for her to focus on Maeva Wilding standing by her bed. Dully her gaze went to the giant who entered her bedroom and lounged against the wall by the door. The sight of the stranger kindled no flicker of interest or curiosity, for she was certain that he was another of the creatures she had been seeing since her fever had gone so high. She had had many visions: people, animals, fictional creatures, nameless shapes and shadows. The tall, broad-shouldered blond man was simply another one of these.

Maeva leaned over to place a cool, long-fingered hand on her patient's forehead, then smoothed back her lank hair. Briskly but gently she picked up the top quilt from Dorcas' bed and folded it precisely. She did the same with the second and third quilt, leaving Dorcas with only a sheet and light cotton coverlet.

"I'm cold, Miss Maeva," Dorcas protested weakly.

"I know," Maeva replied, "and I'm sorry." Her voice was a deep alto, throaty and earthy and sensuous.

She's ... not beautiful, Shiloh thought, *but ... something ... what? Dunno.* Smiling foolishly to himself, Shiloh realized he was so surprised that he still wasn't quite thinking clearly.

Maeva Wilding did not even remotely match his expectations. Shiloh had known two "harb women" in his life: one in South Carolina and one in Alabama. Both were old, shapeless, toothless, mumbling women who smelled like garlic, and both had eyes that saw too much about people and their weaknesses and fears.

Harb woman—not hardly. Need to call her "earth woman," Shiloh decided as he watched and listened to Maeva.

She was only five feet tall, but she had a presence, an aura of quiet strength and self-confidence that made her seem more powerful than her small frame would suggest. Her tiny waist accentuated an hourglass figure . . . a woman in full bloom. Shiloh supposed that Cheney and most New York ladies like her would be horrified at Maeva Wilding, for she was suntanned a dark bronze color, obviously uncaring of the lily-white-skinned fashion of the day.

Her hands fascinated him. She had long fingers, slender and sensitive, and long nails, perfect ovals, with very white tips and cuticle half-moons. Her long, straight black hair was pulled back from her face and tied with a leather thong. Her eyes were a deep blue, and at that moment they were looking Shiloh up and down disdainfully.

"Where's Judith?" she asked curtly.

Shiloh shrugged and fleetingly hoped he didn't look or sound as foolish as he felt. "Not sure. Booth brought me here and then disappeared. I never saw Mr. or Mrs. Trask."

Maeva wasted no time on idle speculation or questions. "Go get me some water," she ordered, "and I don't mean none of that lukewarm water from the pump. Go down to the stream and fill two buckets. Bring me one and put one on to boil."

"Yes, ma'am," Shiloh answered and left the room.

Maeva turned back to Dorcas, who was looking at the doorway with faint surprise. "He's real? That big tall man?"

"Yes, child, he's real." Maeva gently pulled Dorcas to an upright position and took the two pillows off the bed to lay them aside.

"I thought I was dreamin' him," Dorcas murmured, then shivered hard, a chill that shook her whole body.

"He's pretty enough to be a dream, ain't he?" Maeva helped Dorcas to lie back flat on the bed.

"Yes, ma'am," Dorcas answered listlessly. She was fifteen years old—quite old enough to see that Shiloh was a handsome man—but she didn't care because she was convinced she was going to die soon.

"Now listen, Dorcas," Maeva said sternly, and obediently Dorcas roused a bit. "I have to listen to your insides while you breathe real deep. So I'm gonna get real close and hug you, and you breathe for me. Don't talk."

"Yes, ma'am."

Maeva pulled the covers down and put her ear against Dorcas' thin chest. "Breathe deep, Dorcas. Again. Again."

A bucket of water appeared by Maeva's foot. Soundlessly Shiloh moved back close to the door and took up his stance, leaning against the wall with his arms crossed.

"Turn over, Dorcas, and put your arms above your head." Maeva helped the weak girl turn over to lie flat on her stomach and put her arms up. Then she put her own arms securely on either side of Dorcas' thin body and laid her head down between Dorcas' shoulders. "Breathe. Again. Again. Again." Maeva frowned with concentration.

Maeva lifted her head and helped Dorcas turn back over. Then she took the two pillows and propped her in an upright position. Her movements were strong and sure, with no wasted motions.

"First I'm gonna bathe you with this cool water, Dorcas," Maeva told the girl. "It's gonna be miserable for you at first, but in just a little bit you'll feel better. Then I'm gonna fix a little bag of medicine. We're gonna throw it in the water that's boilin', and you're gonna sit up and breathe it in. You understand what I'm tellin' you?"

"Yes, ma'am."

"Do you got any questions?"

"Yes, ma'am."

Maeva waited for a moment, then with a half-smile said, "Well, go ahead, Dorcas. What is it?"

"I have two."

"That's all right." Maeva nodded patiently. She was accustomed to people treating her with a mixture of awe and fear.

"What's his name?"

"Shiloh Irons," Maeva replied, to Shiloh's surprise. "What's your other question, Dorcas?"

"Am I going to die?" she whispered.

Unmistakable pain marred Maeva's smooth features, but her voice was direct and clinical. "No, Dorcas. I'd tell you if you were." She looked back at Shiloh, and for some reason unknown to him her eyes held a clear challenge.

Maeva began preparations to give Dorcas a cool sponge bath, so Shiloh left and went out on the front porch. Booth had watered Sock, unsaddled him, and was now brushing him down. The ride to the Trasks' had been hard and long, and Sock was dirty and sweating.

"Appreciate you taking care of Sock for me, Booth," Shiloh said.

"Appreciate you coming to see about my sister."

Shiloh shrugged ruefully. "I don't mind, but it looks like I wasn't really needed. Miss Wilding seems to have it under control."

"Yeah," Booth muttered, "she surely does. T. R. come by after I left. Maeva were at Uncle Enoch's, so he fetched her."

A thought occurred to Shiloh. "Where's Miss Wilding's horse?"

Booth snorted, "She ain't got one, ain't never had one. Seems like she don't like horses much." Under his breath he added, "And they don't care for the likes of her much, neither."

"Why don't you like her, Booth?" Shiloh asked curiously.

"Ain't a question of like or don't like," Booth answered. His youthful face grew troubled, and his brush strokes on Sock's flank grew vehement. "Reckon she scares me a little."

Shiloh muttered, "Know what you mean. She scares me a little too."

Booth gave him a puzzled look, but at that moment Latham Trask came out on the porch. Shiloh had only spoken briefly to

Booth's mother and father in the kitchen when he went to find buckets to fetch the springwater. Now Trask came to stand by Shiloh and address him, though his ill-humored gaze was on Booth.

"Mr. Irons, I ain't got no quarrel with you fer bein' here," he stated in a no-nonsense tone, " 'cause my son fetched you. And we done had a talk on that subject," Trask added dryly. "But Maeva Wilding's allus took keer of me and mine, and that's the way it's gonna be fer the Trasks. You're welcome to water and rest your horse and yourself. Then I know you'll wanna go on about your business."

"Mr. Trask, Miss Wilding's going to be here for a while," Shiloh told the taciturn man. "Probably until late this afternoon. That'll put her walking home late. I'd like to stay until she's finished and escort her home."

"She tell you she's going to be here that long?" Trask demanded, turning his startled gaze to Shiloh.

"No, sir," Shiloh replied, "and I could be wrong. How many days has Dorcas been sick?"

"This here's the sixth day."

"Then Miss Wilding may have to stay until tomorrow," Shiloh murmured, his brow furrowed.

Latham and Booth Trask looked completely mystified, and Shiloh shrugged. "But I'd like to stay and see, anyhow. If that's all right with you, Mr. Trask."

Trask allowed his straight, thin mouth to curve upwards in a grim smile. "Boy," he grunted, "you're sure askin' the wrong person about all them plans. I ain't sayin' naught for Maeva— ain't nobody but Maeva does that."

"Then I'll ask her, Mr. Trask," Shiloh said firmly.

Latham Trask studied Shiloh with hard blue eyes. "If'n you got a mind to do that, an' Maeva says it's all right with her, then you might as well be makin' yourself useful. Go on back in there and ask Maeva do she want some help." He looked meaningfully at Booth and crossed his arms. "His mama's useless when

Maeva's here. Got it in her empty head that Maeva's got the evil eye or some such nonsense."

"Yes, sir," Shiloh said, and went back into the cabin.

★ ★ ★ ★

"If we ride, I can get you home before dark," Shiloh urged.

"I don't like horses," Maeva stated matter-of-factly. "And they don't like me."

"Are you afraid?" Shiloh asked.

Maeva glanced sharply up at him, but his face showed only genuine concern. "No," she answered simply.

"Then let's go."

The two walked off the Trasks' porch toward Sock. To Shiloh's surprise, Sock began snorting and prancing nervously as they neared. "Whoa, boy," he murmured reassuringly, and began to stroke the horse's neck.

Maeva stopped a few feet away from the horse to watch expressionlessly. "I told you."

"He'll be all right," Shiloh insisted. *Must be her scent—it's gotta be*, he told himself. *She smells good to me—some kind of herbs, I guess. Might be a flower—but none I ever smelled before.*

After a few minutes of stroking the nervous horse and speaking softly to him, Shiloh calmed Sock down. Then he motioned to Maeva.

With obvious distaste, but no sign of fear, she walked to the horse and allowed Shiloh to lift her up behind the saddle. Her skirt hitched up to her knee, and Shiloh couldn't help but notice that she wore pretty white knee-high moccasins with intricate beading on the sides. Her knees and thighs were the same smooth bronze hue as her face.

With an effort Shiloh tore his gaze away to watch Sock's reaction to the rider. Now that Maeva was mounted, Sock seemed to be fine, so Shiloh swung up into the saddle and the two rode off at a slow pace.

"I don't even know where you live." Shiloh smiled over his shoulder.

"Go due south, through Copperhead Gate, acrost Wolf Run, up behind the lake," Maeva instructed. "I live close to Blackcastle Springs."

"Heard of it, but I've never been up there."

"You haven't? You oughta see it."

"What is it?" Shiloh asked curiously.

"Hit's a black castle," Maeva replied with a smile in her voice, "with a spring."

"I see," Shiloh grinned. "Another legend."

"No."

Maeva's conversation was so definite, so matter-of-fact, that Shiloh was a little disconcerted. It never occurred to him that it was this particular quality about himself that unsettled many people, particularly Cheney. "You can't mean it's a real castle," he argued. "It's got to be a symbolic name, like everything's named around here."

"I don't know what that means," Maeva stated without rancor or embarrassment.

"Like Hawk's Light and Hangman's Pass and White Wolf Ridge," Shiloh explained. "They're named after legends. Stories people tell."

"No. They're named after real things, just like Blackcastle Springs. Just like Maeva's Trace is named after Maeva Randall. Just like the Moccasin Mountains is named after moccasins."

"Oh, I see what you're saying," Shiloh said triumphantly. "The Moccasin Mountains are named after the Indians that were here. But they're gone—there sure aren't any moccasins up there anymore."

"There sure are," Maeva countered. "The Moccasin Mountains and Moccasin Lake are named after water moccasins, Mr. Irons. Snakes."

"What?" Shiloh exploded and jerked around to face Maeva. "Snakes!"

Shrewdly her deep blue eyes searched his distraught face. "Yes, snakes." She shrugged. "I'm surprised you ain't seen 'em. They been stirrin' agin since this accursed Indian summer." Shi-

131

loh turned back around. His shoulders were taut, and she could see that the muscles of his neck were tense from the set of his head. "Don't worry," she said quietly, and clasped him tighter around the waist. "I kin see you're scairt of snakes. But I ain't."

Maeva seemed so capable, so practical, that somehow her words made Shiloh feel a little better. He had almost died from snakebite when he was a child, and since then the fear of them ran deep and uncontrollable in him. Most of the time he was a little ashamed of being so horribly frightened, but somehow he didn't mind this woman knowing.

The late afternoon was warm and pleasant, as all the days had been since Thanksgiving. Maeva and Shiloh had stayed at the Trasks' for several hours waiting for Dorcas' stubbornly high fever to break. Finally the girl had fallen into a peaceful, exhausted sleep. Maeva had consented to Shiloh's escort home as impassively as she had accepted his offer of assistance. But now, as they rode and talked, her manner toward him was warm and friendly.

When they came out of the mountains into the lowlands leading to Copperhead Gate, just before evening, Shiloh urged Sock into a faster gait. Maeva seemed to be riding easily. As Sock broke into a steady trot, Maeva moved closer to Shiloh and clasped him about the waist tightly. He was very conscious of her body pressed against his back, and he was certain that Maeva was not only aware of the effect it had on him, but that she was deliberately making the contact between them into an embrace.

For a long time, they rode in silence. Occasionally Shiloh reached down and touched her hands on his waist; it fascinated him that, in spite of the warmth of the day, her hands were so cool.

They kept a good pace through Copperhead Gate and Wolf Run. The sun was nearing the western mountains, so they stopped only briefly to rest at the river. They began the steep ascent up the mountain where Maeva's cabin was, and again she clung tightly to him. By now, however, it seemed natural to Shiloh, and he kept one hand on hers as they rode.

"You're a good doctor," she said in a low voice. She was pressed close against him, her cheek laid against his back.

"I'm not a doctor," he corrected her. "I'm just a nurse."

"So—nurse," she said mockingly, "did you know what I was doin' with Dorcas?"

"I think so."

"Tell me then."

Her voice was gentle, half-joking. But Shiloh knew this was a test, and he considered carefully before answering. "You listened to her heart, to make sure it was strong. Then you listened to her lungs, to see if there was fluid in them. There was—which told you she had pneumonia. The fever from pneumonia usually breaks on the sixth or seventh day—if it breaks at all—and you knew that bundling up someone with a high fever in a bunch of blankets only makes it worse. So you gave her cool baths, which finally broke the fever. Then you told her to breathe in the steam from the hot water, with the stuff you put in it."

He stopped and looked back over his shoulder, but she made no comment, so he went on, "And I think you know that just the breathing exercises are going to help clear up the pneumonia, without the potion."

Again he stopped, but she was silent. Then slowly and deliberately her hands traced the muscles of his stomach, then moved up to lightly rub his chest. Shiloh decided that he had passed whatever test she had set for him in her mind.

The light in the deep woods began to fade, and Shiloh looked around him carefully, trying to imprint landmarks on his mind. The path was very narrow, almost disappearing at times, and he was rather uncertain about finding his way back down in the dark. Then he realized that all he'd have to do is go down and stop to find the lake whenever he had a clear view of the valley. That happened often, for this mountain was less wooded and more rocky than the others.

"We's almost there," Maeva finally said, "but I want to look at somethin' over here for a minute. Would you mind stoppin'?"

"No, of course not. What is it?" Shiloh reined up and dismounted, then lifted Maeva off. He was again surprised at how small and light she was. His hands lingered on her waist, and she let her hands slip down from his shoulders to his chest.

Looking up into his face, her blue eyes dark and unreadable, she replied, "Witch hazel." Then she stepped close to him and turned her face upward in an unmistakable invitation. He kissed her, his mouth gentle on hers. She slid her hands up his back and caressed him, pressing her body against his, and the kiss grew more urgent.

Finally, as if by a signal they both heard, they ended the kiss and drew back. Shiloh searched her face, unsure of what he wanted or hoped to see. She met his gaze directly, unflinching and unashamed.

Not bold, he thought. *Just sure of herself and comfortable with herself. And me*, he mentally added.

He smiled at the thought, and Maeva smiled back. "That was nice," she said, her voice low and slightly husky. "I really like kissing you, Shiloh."

Again her forthrightness rather confused him, but he decided that it was one of the things about Maeva that fascinated him. Finally he managed to say, "Thank you, Maeva. I liked kissing you, too, very much."

He pulled her close again, but she looked up at him and said quietly, "No. It's going to be dark soon, and I need to get some of that witch hazel." She didn't struggle or push him away as she spoke, only gazed up at him with a certainty that he would do as she wished. So he let her go, and she turned and pointed to the left. "They's an ol' witch hazel bush over there," she explained. "Since this Indian summer come along and fooled everything, it's tryin' to bloom agin. I need some of it when it does." She began to pick her way across the rocky ground, and Shiloh followed.

"What do you use it for?" he asked.

"If I woulda had some of it today, poor little Dorcas' fever woulda broke a lot sooner."

They were heading for a grove of trees, and the ground became softer. Scrub bushes were dotted here and there, and the underbrush was thick, though it was dead and crackly. Shiloh could hear a stream gurgling close-by.

Maeva pointed just ahead. "Good, it's bloomed out. See it? That bush with the little yeller flowers?"

Shiloh headed for the bush, holding Maeva's hand to help her through the knee-high brush.

He reached the little bush, Maeva close behind him. Bending over it in the growing darkness, he reached out to pick some of the flowers. Maeva's hand suddenly shot out and gripped his arm, her long fingers tightening into a vise. "Don't move," she whispered, her voice low and vibrating with tension.

Instinctively he froze but looked around to see what had happened. "What?"

"Snake," she breathed.

Instantly Shiloh yanked his arm away from her and straightened his body with a jerk, his head whipping back and forth frantically. Maeva was furiously whispering in a guttural tone, but he paid no attention.

In a time-frozen instant, his eyes focused unbelievingly on a black snake literally hanging on a small sickly-looking shrub close by his right leg. It was neatly draped into uniform folds up and down over a branch that looked much too skinny to hold its weight. Somehow his mind registered that the snake was moving, unfolding itself, but sluggishly.

Shiloh was terrified. He wanted to run, but his legs seemed to be numb, ignoring the signals his brain was frantically sending, and he stumbled—directly against the snake. He felt a sharp pain on his right thigh, and he almost fainted from terror.

"Shiloh!" Maeva shouted. "Be still!" She was at his left side, desperately trying to maneuver around him.

But Shiloh felt as if he were in a nightmare, and now his movements were instinctive and had nothing to do with logic and method. He swept his left arm out in a purely animal move of defense, and knocked Maeva sprawling backward. His teeth bared and his breath raggedly tearing in and out of his throat, he reached down and plucked the long black snake from his leg, then literally tore it into two pieces.

Maeva jumped up and ran.

Shiloh stood motionless, his eyes wide and staring, then he began to moan in a mindless repetition that he couldn't seem to stop. His hands were gripped about the two pieces of the snake so tightly that his nails, short as they were, cut into his palms, and they began to bleed. His leg throbbed, and one part of his mind announced quietly, *I'm going to die, and she ran away.*

He was still standing there, holding the torn snake and staring down at his leg, when Maeva ran back up to him. His blow had knocked the breath out of her, and she was still gasping. Brusquely she pushed something against his lips and panted, "Drink!" He was motionless, uncomprehending. "Drink!" she shrieked.

His dull eyes focused on her, and he opened his mouth slightly. Burning liquid coursed down his throat and into his belly. Immediately his mind was dulled, and the terror subsided. His hands grew heavy and he dropped the pieces of the snake. Like a great tree almost felled, his shoulders dropped and his knees began to buckle.

Maeva stepped under his arm and clasped him around the waist. Her features were slightly blurred, but he could see her eyes glinting furiously in the semidarkness, and he concentrated on looking deep into them.

"You listen to me, Shiloh," she said hoarsely. "I kin help you, do you hear? But I have to get you to my cabin! And I cain't— I cain't get you on that horse by myself! Now you jis' git yourself together, right now, and come git on that horse! Now!" Her voice rose into a rough scream as he sank down, and she fought madly to hold him upright.

Something touched him; whether it was her eyes or her voice or the sense of her words, he never knew. But somehow he began to stumble toward the path where Sock waited. He leaned on

136

Maeva heavily, and she was moaning rather than breathing after a few feet. But she held him with an almost superhuman strength, and after an eternity of stupidly willing one foot to go in front of the other, Shiloh found himself grabbing onto Sock. Pulling with all of his strength he managed to get up into the saddle. Gratefully he fell forward onto Sock's muscular neck, put his arms around it, and fell into a dark, cold, deathlike sleep.

★ ★ ★ ★

The fire glowed red and yellow in a massive fireplace cunningly made of stones fitted together as if they had been created with angles to interlock.

That fire looks so warm in that place, Shiloh thought despairingly. *I wish I was there instead of here, in this cold place. This cold and thirsty place,* he added laboriously. The heavy shutters of his eyelids slammed down again, and he worked very hard to lick his lips. He was surprised that they felt so hot, since he was so cold.

Something soft and cool touched his lips, and it took a great effort to open his eyes. Maeva's dark face swam tantalizingly before him, then came closer. Her fingers brushed against his mouth, and they felt cool and wet. Gladly he parted his lips, and a bitter taste invaded his mouth. Instantly he began to feel as if he were falling backward again.

"Am I going to die?" he whispered.

Pain shadowed Maeva's face, and again her fingers brushed his lips. "No," she whispered raggedly. "I'd tell you if you were."

10

HUNTING

Reverend Charles Scott watched the two women curiously as he greeted the members of his congregation. He was a slender young man, thin-faced and earnest, and his innocent blue eyes were mystified at the sight of Dr. Cheney Duvall and her companion Rissy standing by the street in front of the church. They had been there when he arrived to take his position on the church steps. Now it was almost time for the service to begin, and still the two women stood unspeaking and unmoving, watching the arriving families intently.

Reverend Scott pulled nervously on his black waistcoat, ran one hand through his curly brown hair, and decided to go speak to them. But even as the last family filed in the door of the church, the two women turned away and walked down the street. *I suppose they'd ask if they needed help,* he thought indecisively. *Dr. Duvall is such a capable woman, and proud. I hate to intrude. . . .* He turned, entered his church, and shut the door.

"I still think you oughta jest go ast," Rissy grumbled as they made their way back down the one street of Black Arrow toward the cabin. "Cain't hurt to ast."

"No," Cheney retorted stubbornly. "Those people aren't interested in helping me find Shiloh. They don't care, any of them!"

"You jist upset 'cause Miss Sharon were at church," Rissy snapped. Then in a subdued tone she added, "And it does be a cryin' shame."

Rissy had walked to Sharon's by herself the previous day, when Shiloh and Cheney had left with Glendean. All day she had done things for Sharon, who was embarrassingly grateful.

139

But when Josh Carter had come home, he had coldly thanked Rissy and told her that neither she nor Dr. Duvall need come by tomorrow, since it was Sunday. He could attend to his own wife, thank you. Rissy had walked home alone and hadn't mentioned the conversation to Cheney . . . especially as the hours wore on, Shiloh didn't return, and Cheney paced the floor and grew paler and quieter.

"Yes, it is a shame," Cheney echoed bitterly. Then she lifted her chin defiantly and declared, "I'm going to go find Shiloh, Rissy. I don't need these people's help."

"Well, I wisht them Trasks had come to church," Rissy grumbled. She pronounced the name "Trask-is." "They mighta tole you what Shiloh thought he was doin' when he left they house yestiddy."

"They might've," Cheney said bitterly, "or they might've been suddenly struck dumb. That seems to happen to these people a lot."

They were passing Sikes' General Store and the Nameless Saloon. The store had originally been Ross Sikes' cabin. He had begun bartering out of it with a few of the families of Wolf County, and business had been quite good. So he added onto the original two-room cabin and made a dogtrot house, with the open hallway connecting to another two-room cabin.

Then Ross Lee had come along—their only child—and Sikes had built a roomy house across the street. Slowly the second cabin connected to the store by the dogtrot had become a meeting place for the men of Black Arrow to talk, smoke, play cards—and eventually drink the whiskey that Ross Sikes never advertised but kept fully stocked and tidily stored under a counter.

As they passed, Cheney noticed that the store seemed to be closed up tight, but the door to the Nameless Saloon stood open, and a man lounged in the doorway. Rissy sniffed with disdain and walked faster.

Cheney stopped abruptly in the middle of the street, then turned and began to walk toward the saloon. Rissy's mouth flew open and she almost yelled, but she had been taught that ladies never called to anyone on the street. With a snap she shut her mouth tightly and glided silently behind Cheney with surprising speed.

"You ain't goin' in that there hellhole!" she hissed furiously.

"Yes I am," Cheney argued. "That was Bake Conroy standing in the doorway a minute ago. I forgot about Mr. DeSpain! He'll help me, I know!"

"Mebbe he will, an' mebbe he won't," Rissy muttered dourly.

Cheney paid no attention as she bounded up on the porch and stood in the doorway of the saloon. She stopped abruptly to let her eyes adjust to the darkness, and Rissy cannoned into her from behind. So Cheney made an unexpected, stumbling entrance into the saloon, with Rissy practically walking on the hem of her dress.

"Mr. Conroy?" Cheney said tentatively into the sudden silence. She blinked several times, and faces began to materialize in the dimness. Bake Conroy sat at a table close to her, with Tim Toney and Gabe Stroud. All of them were wearing guns. More men were at two other tables and leaning against the small, plain wooden bar. Fleetingly she thought, *Horrors! So early on a Sunday morning!* The room was filled with smoke and the sour smell of whiskey.

Bake Conroy's fleshy face slowly creased into a sly smile. "Well, well! If it ain't the pretty lady doctor!" He elbowed Gabe Stroud, who was staring in shock at Cheney and Rissy, and almost jumped out of his chair at Bake's rough punch. "Pull up a chair—Cheney."

Rissy looked murderous. Hastily Cheney stepped closer to the table and said in a low voice, "Thank you, but no, Mr. Conroy. I was just wondering if Mr. DeSpain might be here."

"Naw, him and Mr. Day went to Little Rock yesterday," Bake shrugged. "But I'm here," he added, his rough voice echoing in the silent room. Slowly he unfolded from his chair and came to stand too close to Cheney. His black eyes crawled over her inch by inch.

Cheney's jaw was clenched in anger, but she merely stood straighter and said calmly, "Thank you, Mr. Conroy. Goodbye."

But Bake Conroy's huge hand shot out to grab Cheney's arm. "Just a minute—what do you want, Cheney? I take care of things when Mr. DeSpain ain't here."

"Let go of me!" Cheney snapped. She tried to jerk her arm away, but Conroy's grip was like an iron band. Her struggle seemed to amuse him.

Rissy stepped forward and started to say something, and Tim Toney stood up with a threatening look on his face. Cheney never knew whether Tim was going to stop Rissy from interfering with his boss or if he was going to try to help her, because at that moment a voice, gruff but calm, sounded behind Conroy. "You don't wanna do that, Mr. Conroy. Let her go."

Conroy kept his grip on Cheney's arm, but whirled around to come eye-to-eye with Glen Rawlins. Conroy's hand went to the gun at his side, but Rawlins was unarmed, standing casually behind Conroy with his arms crossed. Everyone froze mid-gesture. Conroy measured Rawlins; they were the same height and of much the same build, with muscular hands and arms and barrel chests. Conroy's body tensed, and his meaty hand tightened into a fist.

Glen Rawlins grinned like a hungry wolf. "Same difference to me, Conroy," he growled. "You'll hafta let her go either way."

Long moments passed, and finally Cheney felt the iron grip on her arm suddenly relax. She pulled her arm free and rubbed it. Later she would have blue and purple marks of four fingers and a thumb on her forearm. "Th-thank you, Glen." She nodded stiffly, gave Bake Conroy a black look, and turned. "C'mon, Rissy, let's go."

"Jest a minute," Rissy grunted, to Cheney's shock. Sweeping her skirts aside from Bake Conroy disdainfully, she stalked past him and deliberately took a stance between him and Glen Rawlins, turning her back on Conroy pointedly. "Mistuh Rawlins, would you be kind enuf to step outside fo' a minute? They's somethin' Doctah Duvall needs to ast you."

Turning, she faced Conroy directly, and her expression was very much like when she found beetles in the flour sack. Conroy ungraciously moved aside, his hard black eyes narrowed and glinting as Rissy sailed majestically past. Glen Rawlins followed her and Cheney out the door, his lobo's grin intact.

"I'm not gonna forget this, Rawlins," Conroy snarled.

Tim Toney, still standing by the table, sank back into his chair, crossed his arms, and grinned slyly up at Conroy. "Y'know, Bake," he said conversationally, "if I were you, I'd make sure I forgot this."

"Whaddya mean by that?" Conroy grunted.

"He let you off pretty easy this time," Tim replied, "but you just let Glen Rawlins find out about you botherin' Maeva Wilding. Or Lorine Satterfield." He shrugged, still grinning. "That man'll kill you dead, Bake."

Cheney didn't waste any time on social amenities when she and Rissy got Glen Rawlins outside of the saloon. ". . . so I went to church to see if the Trasks were here, to ask them where he was going when he left their house yesterday. But they didn't come to church." Cheney's face was pale, with dark smudges under her green eyes.

Glen Rawlins crossed his muscular arms, narrowed his eyes, and sucked on his teeth thoughtfully. He glanced up the street toward the church and asked, "Is Enoch and Leah Satterfield at church?"

"I don't think so. Why do you ask?"

" 'Cause the Satterfields prob'ly know 'bout Mr. Irons goin' out there. Their land borders the Trasks'—they's double in-laws, you know."

"No, and I don't want to know," Cheney snapped. "I just want to find Shiloh, and I don't want to go trying to talk to any of those people! Are you going to help me, or not?"

"Jest 'cause we's in a saloon, beggin' help from a man what gits up early 'nuf to drink and gamble on a Sunday mawnin' 'stead of goin' to church," Rissy declared pointedly, "don't mean you s'posed to be orderin' folks aroun' and fussin' like some saloon girl trash, Miss Cheney!"

"We're not in the saloon, Rissy," Cheney argued. "We're on the porch!"

"I didn't get up this early to come down here!" Glen protested with a hurt look on his face. "We been playin' poker all night!"

"First time I've ever wished Shiloh had been doing that," Cheney muttered.

"Amen, Lawd!" Rissy fervently agreed.

★ ★ ★ ★

Within an hour Cheney and Glen Rawlins were riding up Maeva's Trace. When they came to the familiar three-way fork, Rawlins took the right one that wound around the Trace, down, over to the next hill, and then the next. They kept a fast pace, and Cheney determined that she wouldn't complain at the hard ride. Glen had insisted that they go first to Enoch Satterfield's, to see if T. R. had seen or heard anything of Shiloh since he'd been out hunting the last two days. If not, they'd ride on to Latham Trask's.

The path widened into a respectable cart track on the mountain where the Satterfields' home was, although the ascent was steeper. Soon Cheney could see buildings ahead. About halfway up the mountain on a roomy shelf was a large cabin, two smaller ones, a good-sized barn, and two smaller sheds.

When they were still quite a distance from the cabins, Rawlins pulled Murdoch up and signaled Cheney to stop. *I'm sure I know what this means*, Cheney thought wryly. As she suspected, Rawlins spoke to an unseen observer by the side of the road.

"Howdy, Jimmy Dale. C'mon out. Hit's jis' me and Doctor Cheney."

Jimmy Dale suddenly became visible at the edge of the woods by the track, loosely cradling a rifle. "Howdy, Glen. Howdy, Miss Duvall."

"Doctor Cheney's done misplaced her friend Mr. Irons,"

Glen said mischievously. "You seen him?"

"No, sir," Jimmy Dale replied with a grin. "Ya'll get lost agin, Miss Duvall?"

"Not me," Cheney replied shortly. "Just him." At that moment she hated men!

Glen glanced back at her and sobered quickly. "Sorry, Doctor Cheney. It ain't funny to git lost in these here hills." He turned back to Jimmy Dale, who also looked repentant, to ask quietly, "T. R. in from huntin' yet?"

"Yes, sir. Come in early this mornin'. He's been out for two days. Might be he saw somethin'."

Glen nodded, then became very still and seemed to be weighing something in his mind. Jimmy Dale met his gaze unflinchingly. Finally Glen murmured in a deceptively casual tone, "Beauregard got tangled up in a trap yesterday. Up on Maeva's Trace. Me'n Glendean was up there lookin' around where Bobbie Jo got shot at. Reckon T. R. might know somethin' 'bout that?"

"I don't know, sir," Jimmy Dale answered steadily. "You'd best ask T. R. I'm sorry about Beauregard."

"Doctor Cheney here fixed him up," Glen replied gravely. "But I still wanna find out whose trap were up there on the Trace." His voice was mild, but Cheney felt sorry for the fool whose trap had closed on Glen Rawlins' horse.

"Yes, sir," Jimmy Dale agreed. "I'm kinda interested in who's been huntin' and trappin' on the Trace myself. I'll for certain tell you if'n I find out something—and I'd thank you to do the same, sir."

A meaningful look passed between the two men. Jimmy Dale nodded courteously to Cheney, then melted back into the forest. Glen and Cheney rode on toward the Satterfields' home.

Cheney was burning with curiosity. "I know Jimmy Dale's a little younger than you, but not that much, Glen."

"You mean 'cause he yessirs me?" Rawlins shrugged carelessly. "Reckon it's jis' habit. We was in the same outfit in the war—most all the men around here. Third Arkansas, Wolf

Company. Mustered from Wolf County, and I ended up bein' the lieutenant." He spoke in an offhand tone. They were nearing the main cabin, and a dog began to bark. "Carters and the Satterfields fought together then. Fought hard and true, all of 'em. But that's all over now. . . ."

They reached the house and stopped in front of a hand-carved post of oak that had an iron ring hammered into it. Several dogs were barking now, and as Cheney looked to her right, a pack of about eight mongrels rounded the corner of the barn, barking and snarling viciously.

The door to the cabin opened, and Enoch Satterfield stepped out, a huge shambling man with shaggy black hair and a drooping mustache. Behind him came his wife, Leah. Cheney had met her at church last week, and she felt sorry for Leah Satterfield. She was tall, thin, and stoop-shouldered. Her form had long ago become shapeless with childbearing. Cheney thought that at one time her hair was probably a glossy black mane like Lorine's, but now it was a lifeless gray.

With a shock, Cheney now saw that both Enoch's and Leah's hands were covered with blood, and Leah's white apron was smeared a gory red.

The dogs ran circles around the horses, snapping at them and growling and barking sharply. Rawlins snapped, "You, Reb! You, Blackie! Whatsa matter with ya'll!"

Instantly every dog froze and stared upward. Then they began to circle Murdoch, yipping and yapping with recognition. Rawlins dismounted and patted every single dog and called them by name, and they made fools of themselves over him.

Enoch Satterfield watched Glen Rawlins with something akin to affection, but when he focused on Cheney—still mounted on Stocking, watching the dogs doubtfully—his hazel eyes hardened. "Glen, quit actin' sillier than them dogs," he grunted. "Miss Duvall's scairt to get off'n her horse, an' I cain't blame her. She might git slobbered to death."

Regretfully Glen straightened and growled, "Here, now! You dogs git! Go on, now!" Both large and small dogs ran off as urgently and busily as they came, barking importantly, and disappeared back around the corner of the barn. Glen helped Cheney dismount, and the two walked up to the porch.

"Me'n Miss Duvall's lookin' for her friend Mr. Irons," Glen told the couple. "Decided to come ask T. R. if he seed anythin' of him in the last coupla days."

"He's down to the shed skinnin' out the deers he kilt," Enoch informed Glen. "I'll go with you." Without a second look at Cheney, Enoch stepped off the porch and left with Glen.

Leah eyed Cheney expressionlessly, and an uncomfortable silence ensued. Finally Cheney said, "Mrs. Satterfield, if you're busy, I'll be glad to wait out here."

"I'm busy butcherin'," was Leah's begrudging response. "Hit's nasty work."

"Mrs. Satterfield, I am a doctor," Cheney smiled.

"So thet means you're use ta butcherin', do it?" The words were said so mildly that Cheney hardly knew how to react. "Reckon you kin come in an' have some cider. You look hot and thirsty." She disappeared through the cabin door.

Cheney followed her, and was astounded at the inside of the roomy cabin. It was spotlessly clean, with handmade quilts and doilies and pillows everywhere. Full, ruffled yellow curtains covered the front windows. The floors were covered with the same type of rugs as were in Cheney's cabin, with lemon yellow woven in through the white. The room, which Cheney had pictured as tired and colorless as Leah Satterfield, was sunny and cheery.

"Back here," came a weary call through a door along the back wall. Loud, resounding thumps sounded, and curiously Cheney entered the kitchen. It, too, was bright. The dark wooden walls and floor were whitewashed. An enormous table was covered with a yellow checked tablecloth, and a bowl of polished red apples gleamed in the center.

At the end of the table sat a young girl. A pile of bloody red meat was on a wooden butcher slab in front of her. To the side, Leah Satterfield stood at a butcher block counter with a cleaver held high. As Cheney entered the room, the bloodstained cleaver fell in an arc, and bright red blood spattered from an unrecognizable hunk of meat, now split in two.

"H-hello," Cheney said to the young girl, who was salting the pieces of raw meat on both sides and repeatedly stabbing holes in them with a large butcher knife.

"That there's my daughter Caroline," Leah said without looking up. Again the cleaver fell, and more blood colored Leah's apron. "Miss Cheney Duvall."

Caroline was a slightly younger, subtler version of her sister Lorine. She had dark brown hair, a rich chestnut color, with a delicate nose and wide red mouth. When she finally looked up, Cheney saw she had hazel green eyes like her father's, but they were mild instead of sharp. "Howdy," she almost whispered, and shyly looked back down to return to her work.

"Well, it's very nice to meet you, Caroline," Cheney said warmly. "I thought I had met the entire family at church last week."

"Caroline don't go to church," Leah interjected sharply. *Thump!* "And naught of us went today, 'cause T. R. got three deer, and in this weather we gotta git 'em smoked in a hurry."

"Y-yes, I'm sure," Cheney uncertainly agreed. "I suppose it's a lot of work when you have three deer to—to—smoke." Neither Caroline nor Leah commented, and the silence made Cheney uncomfortable. "And this is such strange weather," she added lamely.

"Bodes a hard winter, Indian summer do," Leah muttered ominously. "A white wolf winter. Thass why Enoch done tole T. R. to git the smokehouse filled up."

"What?" Cheney asked in confusion. "A what winter?"

Caroline spoke up in a singsong voice:

Thanksgiving gold
'Til Christmas snow,
Certain winter mercies.
Indian summer
'Twixt gold and snow,
White Wolf winter lurking.

The cleaver's *thump!* was a dark ending punctuation to the melodramatic verse, and Cheney jumped.

Caroline finished salting the gory pile of meat in front of her. She stood up and stretched, then began placing the red lumps in her apron. "I'm gonna take this down to the smokehouse, Mama," she said quietly. "An' I'll take some cider down to T. R. and Daddy."

"Glen Rawlins is down there too. Take enough."

"He is?" The words seemed to burst from Caroline before she could stop them. Cheney saw Caroline's face light up, and two spots of pink appeared high on her pronounced cheekbones. *Oh, dear,* Cheney thought with dismay. *She's in love with Glen. And Glen is—whatever he is with her sister—*

Caroline turned toward the back door and began to make her way across the large kitchen. Cheney's heart lurched, because Caroline had a terrible limp. With narrowed eyes Cheney studied the line of Caroline's slender back. *No spinal deformation,* she thought clinically. *Clubfoot, maybe? Can't see her legs or feet—*

Suddenly Caroline glanced back at Cheney, to see if she was watching, and Cheney's cheeks flushed crimson. But Caroline merely smiled with understanding, turned, and made her slow way through the open back door without comment.

Somehow Caroline's grave smile made Cheney determined to talk to Leah Satterfield—though she had a good idea how her offer of help would be received. Nevertheless she steeled herself and spoke softly. "You know, Mrs. Satterfield, some problems that cause a limp can be corrected."

"No, ma'am, *Miss Duvall,*" she retorted sarcastically, "I didn't know that."

"Will you at least tell me why she limps?"

Savagely Leah slammed the cleaver down into the chopping block, threw two pieces of meat to the side, and turned to Cheney, cleaver in hand. "I'll tell you why she limps! She limps 'cause she's a Satterfield—and 'cause she's my daughter!"

"I don't understand—"

"No, you don't!" Leah muttered as she turned back. "You, a fancy woman from New York! Come down here with your darkie servant an' your sweet-talkin' stable boy to tell us what's wrong with us! Tell us things we know, things we've b'lieved in fer a hunnerd years, is all wrong 'cause you're a doctor and you kin save us!"

"Mrs. Satterfield, the only reason I'm here is to help." Cheney shook her head helplessly. "That's all. Just to help whomever I can."

Leah pulled herself up to her full height, and her dark eyes raked Cheney with scorn. "You cain't help Caroline, you cain't help the Satterfields—and for all your fancy book-learnin', you ain't gonna help Sharon Carter!"

"I'm sorry you feel that way, Mrs. Satterfield—"

"Cain't you see? It's right there fer ever'body to see!" Leah's voice rose high with near-hysteria. "They's cursed! My kids, all of 'em!" She broke off abruptly, and her face flushed as she went on. "And Katie Carter thinks her kids is so perfect, so good, so healthy! Hit don't matter none! They's children of the curse, too—and that includes their families! And ain't nobody on this earth can help naught of 'em!"

Cheney shook her head resignedly, then looked up to meet Leah's distraught gaze with warm sympathy in her eyes. "You may be right, Mrs. Satterfield," she replied gently. "Maybe no one on this earth can help you. But you know that Jesus can."

The fire in Leah Satterfield's eyes died. Her shoulders sagged, and once more she was a weary, stooped woman who looked much older than her years. Turning back to her bloody chore she muttered, "Cider's in that there pitcher an' cups is in the cupboard. Help yourself."

Not another word passed between the women until Glen Rawlins burst through the back door. "T. R. says he was huntin' far north and met up with Booth yestiddy evenin'. Last they saw of Shiloh he was ridin' off with Maeva."

"What?" Cheney burst out. "Riding off with whom?"

"Maeva. He were takin' Maeva Wilding home."

150

* * * *

"That's it?" Cheney demanded.

"Yep. That's Maeva's place."

The small log cabin was nestled in a dark grove of tall trees that grew right up against the walls. Dried herbs and flowers hung upside down from the outside eaves. A wolf skin was stretched over the wooden door. The cabin looked dark and shuttered and private.

Glen Rawlins seemed to feel none of the reluctance that Cheney felt. He dismounted, looped Murdoch's reins around a tree, strode up to Maeva's door, and knocked twice. "Maeva? It's Glen."

Cheney saw the ghostly white sheer curtains covering one of the small windows move slightly. Hastily she dismounted and walked up to stand at the doorway with Glen. The door opened a tiny crack, and Cheney saw very little in the semidarkness inside. Suddenly the door opened wider. A woman stepped outside and quietly closed the door behind her.

When Cheney saw Maeva Wilding, the first thought that flitted through her mind was, *I'm hot and dirty and smell like a horse.* "You're—you're Maeva Wilding?" she stammered.

"Yes. And you're Cheney Duvall." The woman's voice was low-pitched, as rich as black earth by a river. Her hair was loose, falling in an ebony cascade over one shoulder and down to her waist. Tiny brown feet peeped out from her blue skirt. Her tanned face was expressionless as she addressed Cheney.

"Is—Do you know where—I'm looking for my nurse, Shiloh Irons." Cheney hated herself for her awkwardness, while Maeva Wilding seemed so cool and self-possessed. *It should be the other way around,* she furiously chided herself. *And she's so cool and clean and smells like sandalwood! How can this woman afford sandalwood? And why am I so tall and gangly?* Desperately Cheney tried to get her thoughts under control.

"Yes," Maeva said slowly, "Shiloh's here."

"What? He is?" Eagerly Cheney took a step toward the door.

151

Without actually moving to block her way, Maeva stopped her. "You cain't see him right now. He's sleepin'."

Cheney stepped backward and looked Maeva up and down with astonishment. "I can't—what? You said he's what?"

"Reckon I'll go water them horses," Glen mumbled, trying to be inconspicuous. He moved off with surprising haste for his size.

Maeva watched Glen grab the horses' reins and lead them around the corner of the cabin. Cheney felt slightly numb, and found that her mind refused to frame sentences and questions correctly. Maeva waited patiently for Glen to disappear, then turned back to Cheney, crossed her arms, and repeated slowly, with peculiar emphasis, "I said you cain't see him. He's sleepin'."

"But—but—" Cheney shook her head in bewilderment. "He didn't come home last night!"

The corners of Maeva's full mouth turned up in a sleepy smile. "Yes. I know."

Cheney made a funny, squeaky noise in her throat, and Maeva's eyes sparkled. " 'Course, if'n you wanna say truth, Miss Duvall," she went on in a lazy drawl, "it ain't that Shiloh didn't come *home* 'zackly. He jist didn't sleep in your stable last night. Ain't that what you meant to say?"

Cheney opened her mouth for a stinging retort, but the horrid squeak came out again. Her cheeks burning, she cleared her throat and began again. "I suppose so," she muttered through clenched teeth. "But I've been v-very worried about him. I d-didn't know he—I didn't know you—"

Maeva was obviously enjoying Cheney's discomfort. "You know, Miss Duvall," she murmured, "I could give you some special stones to put in your mouth that might help that there stutter. Four or five of 'em would do it, I reckon."

"S-stop it!" Cheney snapped. "Since Shiloh is obviously all right, Miss Wilding, I'll leave now!"

But Maeva was a woman who instinctively recognized boundaries, so reluctantly she murmured, "He's all right—*now*. I been taking good keer o' him."

152

Cheney had already turned to go somewhere—anywhere—but she whirled and demanded sharply. "Now? What do you mean? What happened to him?"

The door behind Maeva opened again, creaking slightly, and Shiloh stepped out. He was pale and his eyes were heavy-lidded. He wore no shirt, and he, too, was barefoot. Blinking several times, he ran his hand through his tousled blond hair and mumbled, "Doc? What—when did you get here?"

"I was jis' tellin' Miss Duvall that you got snakebit," Maeva said softly, her eyes fixed on Cheney. "And that I been takin' good keer o' you."

"You got what!" Cheney almost shrieked.

"Snakebit, Doc," Shiloh said wearily.

Cheney's flashing green eyes went from Shiloh's face to Maeva Wilding's. Maeva lowered her head slightly, smiled at Cheney, and imperceptibly moved backward to stand very close to Shiloh.

"Good!" Cheney shouted. Then she whirled and stalked off into the woods.

11

KNIVES

". . . so there he was, all sleepy and tousled and shirtless—"

"—and snakebit," Rissy interrupted Cheney with a snort.

"—and innocent and—and—barefoot!" Cheney finished, determinedly ignoring Rissy. "Can you imagine—I have never been so horribly embarrassed in my life!"

"Oh, poor Cheney," Sharon murmured sympathetically, hiding a smile.

"Oh, poor Cheney," Rissy echoed sarcastically. "A respectable man woulda been daid on the side o' the road wif his boots on!"

Cheney gave Rissy a withering glance, which had absolutely no effect on the black woman's serenity as she rocked and mended one of Josh Carter's shirts. Cheney, Sharon, and Rissy were sitting on Sharon's front porch, enjoying the late afternoon sunshine and the fact that chores were finally done. Cheney had reluctantly allowed Sharon to get out of bed, suspecting that Sharon did it anyway when Cheney wasn't there.

Although the snakebite incident had occurred a week ago, Cheney hadn't told anyone about it or about her meeting with Maeva Wilding. But when Sharon expressed concern about Shiloh, who was still looking a little pale, Cheney found herself pouring out the entire story.

"So, Cheney," Sharon asked in a too-casual tone, "what did Maeva do for Shiloh's snakebite?"

"She gave him mandrake root mixed with laudanum! And it's a wonder that *it* didn't kill him if the snakebite didn't!" Cheney snapped. "Then she cut him with a knife—which was probably dirty—and actually bled him! Cupped him! Like some medieval torturer or something! And then stuck some kind of evil-smelling weeds all over his leg!"

"An' he got well," Rissy added under her breath.

Suddenly the fire in Cheney's green eyes faded, and she looked down at the embroidery she held. "Oh, yes," she muttered, "he's fine. Maeva saved his life. And now they're such good . . . friends."

Shiloh had brought Cheney and Rissy to Sharon's, as he did every morning. After gathering the kindling and splitting wood, he had told the women he'd be back for them that afternoon and had ridden off to the south.

Cheney had grown strangely sullen, Sharon had noticed at the time. Now, searching Cheney's downcast face and shoulders bent with discouragement, Sharon decided that the less said about Maeva Wilding and Shiloh, the better.

Gently Sharon began to rock and hum. Rissy sewed, and Cheney stabbed vengefully at her embroidery. Suddenly a strange popping sound came to their ears from the east. Sharon sat up tensely, and Cheney threw her an anxious look.

"That's rifle fire! Sounds like it's from Maeva's Trace!" Sharon's voice trembled.

"Sharon, if you don't calm down, I'm going to put you back into bed right now," Cheney ordered. "You know that both your family and the Satterfields hunt all the time. It must be that."

Sharon shook her head fearfully. "No one is supposed to hunt on Maeva's Trace—us or the Satterfields. It's supposed to be neutral ground!"

Cheney gave Rissy a meaningful look, and wordlessly Rissy got up and went inside the cabin. Cheney dropped her sewing to kneel by Sharon's chair. "Sharon, you cannot get overwrought every time you hear a gunshot in these hills! Please, please listen to me! I know you don't—you haven't—that it's hard for you to believe that I know what I'm talking about, but I swear, you must stay calm and quiet!"

Sharon listened to Cheney, a distraught expression on her delicate features. Slowly she drew a deep breath and smiled tremulously. "I'm sorry, Cheney dear," she murmured, patting Cheney's hand.

Her eyes were still fixed on the peaks of the Trace, but Cheney saw that her respiration was slowing down, and surreptitiously she took Sharon's pulse as they held hands.

Sharon sighed and went on, "It's just that . . . I seem to be doing so much better. I've gained weight, I have my appetite back, I'm actually showing the way I'm supposed to."

"Yes," Cheney agreed quietly. Sharon's pulse was too fast, but it was slowing down.

"Cheney, I don't feel sick at all, much less dangerously ill. So it's hard . . . hard for me"—Sharon's voice dropped—"and hard for Josh."

Cheney searched her features appraisingly, then rose to sink back into her rocking chair. "I understand, Sharon," she sighed. "Especially, I guess I can see how hard it must be for your family. I know that you trust in me—and I know it's hard even for you."

"Yes," Sharon nodded, "but I promise I'll be good, Cheney. Please don't be angry or upset with me."

"Nonsense," Cheney countered with some discomfort. "You know I love you, Sharon. Now, then, suppose you tell me some more about Maeva's Trace. Who owns it, anyway?"

"Lige says he does, and Enoch Satterfield says he does," Sharon sighed. "Just like their fathers, and their fathers before them—back to their great-grandfathers."

"So that's how this silly feud got started," Cheney grumbled.

"Well, it's odd," Sharon replied in a dreamy voice. "I've never been able to understand whether the feud started over the Trace—or over Maeva Randall. It doesn't really matter now, anyway, because they've all gotten so caught up with legends and curses and dark beliefs." Sharon shrugged wearily, and her eyes went to the remote heights of Maeva's Trace. The highest of the Moccasin Mountains, its brooding peaks were always visible to the people who lived in Black Arrow and the surrounding hills.

Cheney's eyes followed Sharon's gaze and she resignedly laid her sewing down again and began to rock slowly. In the quiet, more ominous crackling sounded from the direction of the Trace, and Cheney turned to glance at Sharon with warning in her eyes. "We don't know, Sharon," she said in a voice of deliberate calm. "It could just be the boys out target shooting. Shiloh told me he's going to take me up on the Trace and teach me how to shoot," she prattled on, "and I told him certainly I'd like to go—his head looked like a good target to me—"

Rissy came back out carrying a tray with three cups of milk, some cookies, and a bowl of bright red apples. Cheney put the small table in front of them, between hers and Sharon's rocker, and the three women settled down for a snack.

"I know, Cheney, but it's hard for me not to worry," Sharon continued the conversation as she obediently drank her milk and ate a crispy apple. "You see, Josh and Dane and Enoch have been clearing off forty acres at the foot of the Trace for farming in the spring. Last Monday someone shot at them twice. They're sure it was one of the Satterfields."

"Was anyone hurt?" Cheney demanded.

"No." Sharon shook her head. "But someone is going to be soon. Now one of them guards while the other two work. Josh shot at someone in the woods yesterday. So whenever I hear gunshots—" Her voice broke off and she bit her lip hard.

"It'll be all right, Sharon," Cheney said firmly. "We'll stay here until Josh comes home. I'm sure he'll be here soon."

"Cheney, I'm so glad you're here," Sharon said, and reached over to pat Cheney's hand. "I really am."

"Me too." Cheney smiled warmly, while a nasty little voice inside her spoke up with unashamed rebelliousness. *That's a lie, a big black lie! You wish you'd never come here—and especially you wish Shiloh never had!* Quickly Cheney began to embroider, hiding her face from Sharon. Rissy shot Cheney an all-knowing glance, but said nothing.

I guess I'm glad Glen asked Shiloh to stay with him, Cheney tried to rebuke herself. *He couldn't stay in that stable forever—especially with winter coming on. At least, I suppose winter's coming on someday.* Indian summer had dulled Cheney's sense of the time of year; in fact, the sullenly warm weather seemed to make her sluggish and cross and dull. *Today's December twelfth,* she thought with a jolt. *Only thirteen more days until Christmas?* Then her thoughts began to drift longingly: *New York . . . Father and Mother . . . snow . . . Dev . . .*

The three women rocked, sometimes talking, sometimes quiet, as the afternoon wore on to evening. Cheney knew that Josh had left at dawn and wouldn't return until the light failed, and she was truly confident that nothing had happened to him. *Everyone here lives with the sound of gunfire all around them,* she thought bitterly. *It's a way of life.*

They heard horses galloping recklessly fast up the track toward the cabin. With a grim look on her face, Sharon picked up the rifle that leaned up against the cabin wall and began to rise. Cheney snapped, "Don't be a fool, Sharon! Put that back and sit down!"

With a stubbornness and rebelliousness totally unlike her, Sharon argued, "You may be the fool, Cheney!"

Cheney jumped out of her chair, snatched the rifle from Sharon's hands, and almost pushed her back in the chair. "If it will make you feel better, I'll hold this! But you sit down and stay calm!" Cheney turned to face the approaching horses, the gun held loosely cradled in her arms, pointing at the ground. Two riders appeared, and immediately she slowly, with exaggerated care, leaned the rifle back up against the wall. "It's just Shiloh," she murmured to Sharon, who still looked frightened. "Be calm."

Shiloh rode Sock hard, right up to the cabin porch, and wasted no time on greetings or explanations. "Booth Trask brought Wanda Jo Satterfield to Maeva's. Wanda Jo's little brother Isaac is real sick—Wanda Jo says he's dying. We've got to go, Doc! I'll saddle up Stocking."

He wheeled Sock around, but Cheney's sharp voice stopped him. "Me! Run to the Satterfields!" she scoffed. "I'm certain they'd be so glad to see me—especially when they sent for the marvelous Maeva Wilding! Why isn't she riding to the rescue with you?"

Rissy jumped up and hissed, "Miss Cheney Duvall!"

Sharon looked sorrowfully at Cheney and then at Shiloh, but the two seemed to have forgotten that anyone else was there.

Shiloh looked incredulous; then anger washed over his face and he snapped bitterly, "She's not there, Cheney. I don't know where she is. Isaac Satterfield is Levi Satterfield's only son—he's eight years old. Are you coming or not?"

Cheney still looked rebellious. Putting her hands on her hips, she snapped, "If they want me, why didn't Booth come get me? Everyone knows I'm here at Sharon's every day!"

"Yes, they know you're at the Carters', Cheney!" Shiloh countered. "And they're Satterfields!" He and Cheney held each other in a bitter gaze.

Then Sharon's soft whisper broke the silence. "Oh, Cheney, this isn't like you."

As if she had been rudely awakened, Cheney jumped slightly and stared at Sharon. "I—I have to go," she declared in a normal tone. "Rissy, can you—"

"I'll make it home by myself jest fine. You go on and tend to dat boy," Rissy ordered, flapping her hands at Cheney in a shooing motion. "An' quit talkin' like you ain't got no sense, even if you ain't!"

Wordlessly Cheney fled toward the stables, and Shiloh followed her with a look of weary relief on his face.

★ ★ ★ ★

Booth Trask and Wanda Jo Satterfield waited on the first gentle rise of Wolf Run. Wanda Jo was eighteen years old but still lived with her parents, Levi and Ruthie. No one had ever courted her; she was colorless and plain and bookish. When she reached her eighteenth birthday she determined not to think any longer about getting married and having a family of her own, so she had dedicated herself to raising and teaching her younger sisters, Eulalie and Shirl, and especially her little brother, Isaac. Tears rolling down her sharp face, she sat astride a tired gray mare and waited.

"I'm glad at least we found Mr. Shiloh," she told Booth mournfully. "Isaac's so sick! I'm so scairt!"

"But Shiloh was there with Maeva day before yesterday, and they didn't do Isaac no good," Booth argued unfeelingly. "You better be glad we found Doctor Cheney!"

Wanda Jo dropped her head. Her limp brown hair covered her face, but a stifled sob escaped. "I'll be glad—I'll be so thankful to God—if she kin help Isaac," she managed to get out in a strangled voice.

"She kin help him." Booth nodded with certainty. "But you're gonna hafta talk to your ma and pa and Grandma Trask. Make 'em let Doctor Cheney do what she has to do!"

Wanda Jo straightened her shoulders and pushed her hair back from her eyes. "They'll listen to me," she cried, "or else some Satterfields is gonna be feudin' amongst theirselves!"

Booth nodded his approval, and Wanda Jo wiped the tears from her eyes to watch the small valley below for the first sign of Shiloh and Cheney. Soon two riders came into view, riding two huge horses, almost identical. Cheney's hair had come loose and flowed like a red pennant in the wind behind her, and Shiloh's face was grim as he rode, broad-shouldered and tall.

"Golly Molly," Wanda Jo breathed. "A Viking and a Valkyrie!"

Booth Trask had no earthly idea what those might be, but he sighed knowingly anyway. "More like Death and Destruction," he muttered, "when Grandma Trask sees Doctor Cheney."

When the riders neared Booth and Wanda Jo, Shiloh shouted, "Ride on!" Without stopping to chat, the two turned and galloped across Wolf Run toward Copperhead Gate, with Shiloh and Cheney flying close behind.

Two hours of hard riding without stopping brought them to Levi Satterfield's cabin. Booth Trask decided to ride on to his aunt and uncle's instead of cutting off and going home. Levi and Ruthie weren't exactly favorites of his, but his Grandma Trask lived with them. Booth visited his grandmother often because, aside from his cousin Isaac, he was her favorite, and she babied and spoiled him shamelessly.

No one hailed them as they approached the cabin. In the growing darkness, light shone from every window.

"That's not good," Shiloh muttered grimly to Cheney. "These people don't waste candles or kerosene." They rode right up to the Satterfields' porch. Wordlessly Booth dismounted, took the reins of all four horses, and led them away. When the sound of the horses' hooves ceased, they could hear wailing coming from inside the house.

Wanda Jo ran up the porch, wrenched open the door, and cried, "Ma! Pa! I brung a doctor! Is Isaac—"

Cheney and Shiloh followed her up on the porch and waited. From inside the cabin a dull voice called, "Come on in, Wanda Jo. Who you got with you? Where's Maeva?"

Cheney pushed her way past Wanda Jo, who was standing in the doorway and staring up a flight of stairs. The wailing was coming from the second floor. "My name is Dr. Cheney Duvall. Please let me see your son."

Levi Satterfield sat on a settee by a sobbing woman, staring into an empty fireplace. Two girls, younger than Wanda Jo, hugged each other and cried as they sat on the cold hearth. His eyes vacant, Levi glanced up at Cheney, then returned to his desolate contemplation. He was Enoch Satterfield's youngest brother; he had the same shaggy brown hair and hazel eyes, but there the resemblance ended. He was smaller than Enoch, plump, and almost jolly at times. But now he looked pale and leaden, and his voice was colorless. His wife, a crumpled heap on the settee beside him, had her face buried in her hands and never looked up.

Cheney's shoulders slumped as she whispered in a stricken voice, "Is he dead?"

"Not yit," he replied in a hopeless voice.

Cheney's head jerked up sharply to look upward at the sounds of the hysterical keening. "Do you mean to tell me that the child's not dead, and that awful—" she protested. Shiloh's hand, warm and gentle on her shoulder, stopped her.

"Then, Mr. Satterfield," he said quietly, "me and the Doc here will just go take a look at him. All right?"

"Hmm? You again?" Satterfield's face momentarily looked bewildered. "Where's Maeva?"

Cheney glanced at Shiloh with instant accusation, then she merely dropped her head and sighed.

"Wanda Jo and Booth and I couldn't find her," Shiloh answered, with a single worried glance up the stairs. "So please, let Dr. Duvall go see if she can help."

"Guess it don't make no never-mind now," Satterfield murmured absently, and turned his blank gaze back to the fireplace.

"C'mon! Hurry!" Wanda Jo hissed from the foot of the stairs.

Shiloh and Cheney hastily followed her upstairs to a small bedroom under the eaves, much like Cheney's own. A small boy lay on a bunk with his eyes closed. Even by the single candle Cheney could see his sickly yellow color, the deep purple shadows under his eyes, and the beads of sweat on his forehead. An old woman sat by his bedside, crying out loudly and automatically, with tears rolling down her face. Her eyes were closed and she rocked back and forth, hugging herself with clawlike hands.

"Who is this woman?" Cheney demanded.

"That's my Grandma Trask," Wanda Jo replied softly. "She lives with us."

"Get her out of here and tell her to stop that caterwauling," Cheney ordered sternly. "The boy's still alive!"

The woman's eyes flew open and she stopped screeching, though she still rocked back and forth. "He's on the brink o' death! My baby Isaac!" Her faded blue eyes were unfocused and panicky.

"Shut up!" Cheney snapped furiously. "I tell you, he's still alive—unless he hears you and just decides he might as well go on and die!"

With a jolt the old woman snapped up straight, and her

163

faded blue eyes raked Cheney up and down with ugly suspicion. "Who are you? Get out!"

"No, you get out!" Cheney retorted. "Now!"

"Mrs. Trask, come now, let Wanda Jo take you down and fix you a nice cup of tea." Shiloh bent to take the old woman's arm and lead her out of the room with gentle insistence, talking in a low, soothing murmur. "Dr. Duvall is going to help Isaac, and he's going to be all right."

Surprisingly, the old woman allowed Shiloh to lead her out of the room, looking up into his face with a glimmer of recognition. "Mr. Irons? You say Isaac ... but where's Maeva?" Abruptly, suspiciously, she jerked her arm out of Shiloh's grasp and wheeled back toward the door. "Where's Maeva? Who are you?" she screeched.

Again Shiloh took her arm and spoke in an undertone, and the woman seemed to calm down. After a few moments she allowed Shiloh to lead her away.

Cheney sat by Isaac's bedside and desperately peered into her black bag, barely able to see by the dim candlelight. She found her stethoscope, pulled the covers down, and opened the boy's nightshirt. At her touch his eyes opened and met her gaze uncomprehendingly.

"Hello, Isaac." Cheney smiled as she placed the stethoscope on his chest.

"Howdy," he whispered. Though his eyes were dull with pain, he watched her with interest. In a voice so weak it was almost inaudible he spoke conversationally. "My grandma jis' tole me I wuz daid. Are you an angel?"

"Not hardly," a deep voice answered behind her, and Cheney shot Shiloh a withering glance. Smiling at both her and the boy, he went on, "But she does look like one, doesn't she?"

"Howdy, Mr. Shiloh," he breathed. "I dunno. I niver saw an angel with their hair like that. All dark and on fire at the same time."

Shiloh glanced at Cheney. Her hair curled riotously around her head and down her shoulders to her waist. By the candle's glow it had depths of black, with the auburn highlights glowing an aura of red. "That is a problem," Shiloh teased. "She does go galloping around with her hair on fire sometimes."

Cheney was blushing furiously and hoping it didn't show in the dark room. Pointedly ignoring Shiloh, she answered the boy, "No, Isaac, I'm not an angel, and you're certainly not dead. I'm a doctor, and I'm going to examine you. Is that all right?"

"Yes'm," he replied wearily, and closed his eyes. "I'm awful tired, and I hurt."

Silently Shiloh went to a small washstand at the far end of the room, poured some water out of a pitcher into a basin, and wet a white cloth. Like a benevolent shadow he stooped almost double beneath the sloping eaves to return to Isaac's side. Gently he sponged the boy's forehead with the cool cloth, then his neck and chest. Isaac seemed not to notice Shiloh's ministrations, but his taut body relaxed slightly.

Cheney marveled again, as she had so often, at what a good nurse Shiloh was. *He moves quietly, doesn't bang and bump around,* she thought as she listened carefully to the erratic beat of Isaac's heart. *He has such a gentle touch, probably more so than mine.*

Cheney sat up and laid her hand on Isaac's stomach. Probing lightly and casually, she asked, "Can you tell me where it hurts, Isaac?"

"On my side."

Cheney's hand moved lightly over the boy's body.

Suddenly his eyes flew open, his body stiffened, and he screamed.

Wanda Jo, standing silently behind Cheney, stuck her fist in her mouth, and again tears boiled out of her eyes and down her cheeks. From downstairs, the mindless wailing resumed.

The animal scream, high-pitched and shocking, stopped as abruptly as it began. Isaac's body relaxed somewhat, and he lay limply gasping and crying. Neither Cheney nor Shiloh had jumped at Isaac's sudden cry of pain; their eyes met gravely over the boy's arched body.

Shiloh smoothed the cool cloth across the boy's forehead and told him quietly, "We're going to step outside the room, Isaac. We'll be back in just a minute."

Isaac replied trustingly, "Awright, Mister Shiloh."

Together they rose and led Wanda Jo outside the room. Cheney took both of her hands and searched her face. Wanda Jo looked frightened, but Cheney thought she looked strong and seemed to trust her. "Wanda Jo, Isaac has appendicitis."

"I read about that once, in a book the schoolteacher give me," Wanda Jo replied fearfully. "Can you help him?"

Cheney's eyes met Shiloh's over Wanda Jo's head. He smiled down at her, and his eyes lit with warmth. "You can do it, Doc."

"We can do it, Shiloh." She nodded and looked back down at Wanda Jo. "I'm going to have to operate on Isaac."

Fear flamed in the young woman's eyes, and Cheney could see her fight to control her panic. When she finally spoke, her voice was rough but determined. "I'll have to try to explain to my ma and pa. And," she sighed, "my grandma."

Cheney had an idea what a difficult task this would be. She knew that these people only knew of surgery for a wound or an amputation. Preventive or corrective surgery was unheard of; she doubted that anyone in these hills had ever even heard of an appendix. "Shiloh, will you go with her and try to help her?" Cheney asked.

"Sure I will," he drawled softly.

"Then let's git it over," Wanda Jo said stoutly. "And then I kin help you, Doctor Cheney. Find stuff and fetch stuff, mebbe. I ain't scairt."

"Good," Cheney smiled. "I can use the help, and I can see you're very smart and very courageous. Now go talk to your grandma. And Shiloh, give her some laudanum if she'll take it," adding under her breath, "Please, Lord."

Shiloh and Wanda Jo turned toward the stairs. As they left Cheney heard Wanda Jo mutter, "Ain't no need for no laudanum, Shiloh. I'll jis' tell Grandma that she's overwrought and needs some of her tonic what's in the brown jug. She'll quieten down. . . ."

Cheney slipped back into Isaac's bedroom. He lay on his side, his body drawn up taut with pain. "Don't worry, Isaac," Cheney whispered, leaning over to lay her hand on his forehead. "You're going to be all right."

The boy's eyes fluttered open and wandered over Cheney's face and hair. A long, curly lock fell over her shoulder and lay on the bed beside him. Weakly he touched it, rubbed it between his fingers, and finally dropped it, exhausted. Cheney's eyes stung as he muttered, "Went to heaven . . . angels . . . with their . . . hair on fire . . ."

12

BALEFIRE

"Where are we going?" Cheney asked.

"Up here to a sandstone cliff," Shiloh answered. "We can shoot into it without having to worry about killing somebody's cow a mile away."

They rode up a nameless mountain directly across the river from Cheney's cabin. Soon they came to a small shelf, almost devoid of the usual brown vegetation and shrubs, facing a sandy red wall. They dismounted, and Shiloh unsaddled Sock and Stocking. He turned to Cheney as the two horses began to amble off the way they had come.

"Shiloh, the horses!" Cheney cried. "Shouldn't you tie them up?"

"Nah," Shiloh shrugged. "They won't go far. There's a stream over there, with a little grass. Sock'll come back when I call."

"I hope you know what you're doing," Cheney responded. "I don't want to walk home."

"Don't worry," Shiloh reassured her. Bending down to his saddlebag, he pulled out his holster, buckled it on, and pulled out the gun. "Let's get down to business."

"Let's do. I want to learn how to do this, even though I have no intention of shooting anyone."

"Just because you learn how to use a gun doesn't mean you have to shoot people, Doc." He walked to a point about twenty feet away from the cliff and held the gun up, pointing to the sky. "This is a Colt revolver, caliber .44, six-shot, single-action, front-loading—"

"Is it loaded?" Cheney asked impatiently. Striding up to him, she reached for the gun, but Shiloh held it high out of her reach.

169

"Now wait a minute, Doc! Lemme explain it to you!"

Cheney glanced up at him mischievously. "I already know what all that means. All I need to do now is shoot it."

"Huh? You do? But I thought you didn't know how to shoot!"

"I don't," she shrugged, "but I can read, can't I? It's made by the Samuel Colt Firearms Company, it fires a bullet that is forty-four one-hundredths of an inch in diameter, and there are six of them in the revolving chamber, which turns when you cock the hammer and fires when you pull the trigger!" Triumphantly she held out her hand, and Shiloh placed the gun in it, grinning.

"I can't believe how well Isaac is doing, after only two days," she said conversationally as she felt the weight of the pistol, passing it from one hand to the other.

Shiloh stepped forward and squinted at the cliff rising up about twenty feet from them, trying to find a target.

Cheney went on, "Neva Sikes asked me all kinds of questions about the operation." Lifting the gun with both hands, she pulled back the hammer. "I refused to discuss it with her"—*Bang!*—"but I figure she probably heard about Grandma Trask screeching that I'd split Isaac"—again she cocked the hammer—"open like a"—*Bang!*—"watermelon!"

Shiloh didn't exactly throw himself prone on the ground, but on the first shot he jumped and on the second he fell to one knee and ducked his head.

Cheney frowned and waved the gun expressively in large circles. "This is no good!" she grumbled. "Isn't there something I can shoot at?" She turned and with astonishment pointed at him—gun in hand—and asked, "What are you doing down there?"

Shiloh threw himself flat on the ground and rolled a safe six feet away. Slowly he rose, removed his hat, dusted off his breeches, replaced his hat, and looked at her warily. Cheney half turned to watch, and he threw up his hands in surrender. "Now,

Doc," he said, speaking with infinite care, "just give me the gun. Please?"

Timidly he held out his hand, and Cheney blew out an exasperated breath and slammed it into his palm. "I thought you wanted me to learn to shoot!"

"I do, Doc," he breathed a loud sigh of relief, "but I didn't mean at me!"

"I didn't shoot at you! What's the matter?"

"Let's start all over again, all right? I'll go find something for you to shoot at. No, I'll hold the gun while I do it! You're wavin' a loaded gun around like it's a little ivory fan or something!"

"Oh." Cheney shrugged again. "Well, I didn't have that little knob pulled back, so I didn't think it would shoot. Just calm down. All you have to do is tell me, you know."

"Sometimes that's not so easy," he muttered, and wandered off into the nearby brush. Cheney heard him crashing around in the trees, and she looked around idly. *What's that?* she wondered. The mountain that rose a little higher to her right seemed to be steaming. Shading her eyes, she squinted up at the thin white wisps that drifted up into the deep blue sky and then dissipated almost before they could be seen. *Not smoke from a fire . . . it really does look like steam!*

Shiloh returned holding an armload of small logs. The sandstone cliff had small shelves and niches, and he stuck the logs along it at various heights, nodding with satisfaction.

"Is that smoke over there?" Cheney asked, still searching the sky. The small white puffs were so thin, she still wasn't certain she was really seeing them.

"Blackcastle Springs," Shiloh replied without looking.

"What's that?"

A distant smile crossed Shiloh's face as he tucked one of the logs neatly into the crumbly red shelf. "It's a black castle, with a spring." Cheney turned to give him a withering look. "It's a hot spring," he continued. "Guess since the air's cooler today, it's steaming a little."

"Can we go up there? I'd like to see it! I've heard of hot

springs, but I've never seen one. And what did you say about a castle?"

"Not today, Doc." Shiloh didn't meet her eyes, and his voice was aloof. "Maybe some other time." He stepped back and surveyed the targets with satisfaction.

Maeva Wilding, she thought bitterly. *When he looks like that and sounds like that—like a stranger—it's something to do with Maeva.* With an effort she made herself smile. "Can I shoot some more now?"

Shiloh covered the gun in his holster with one hand and held the other up in a cautious gesture. "If you'll just listen to me for a minute first! There are still four cartridges in this gun—just the amount of arms and legs I have—and I kinda wanted to keep 'em in one piece!" His face was youthful and boyish again, his voice playful, and Cheney determined that nothing would spoil this time she had with Shiloh. Lately their times together had been scarce.

Putting her hands on her hips, she cocked her head and looked up at him jauntily. "You think I'm going to be that good a shot?"

"I imagine," he sighed, pulling the gun out and again pointing it to the sky. "If you're as cool with a gun as you are with a scalpel. Just remember, Doc: any time you pick up a gun, just go ahead and assume that it's gonna shoot, no matter what! Whether it's loaded or not, or whether it's cocked or not, or even if you're just moving it out of the way to dust under it! All right?"

"All right," Cheney muttered, "but it certainly seems like you have to go to a lot more trouble than that to actually get it to shoot—and then hit something. Good enough to stop anything, I mean."

"Doc, you just point this thing in the general direction and pull the trigger." Shiloh grinned. "Anything that's comin' will stop, I promise." Gingerly he gave the gun to Cheney, who made a little face at him but handled it more carefully than before.

"Now, aim at any one—" Shiloh pointed, but again Cheney

raised the gun and shot. Then again she cocked the hammer back, stuck her tongue out of the side of her mouth with concentration and squinted through the sight.

"Doc," Shiloh said helplessly.

Another explosion split the air.

"Doc!" Shiloh yelled.

"What!" she snapped. "I didn't wave it around, did I?"

Shiloh blew out an exasperated breath and again settled his hat on his head more firmly. "No, but would you just kinda take it slow, and let me know what you're doing?"

"You sure are nervous," Cheney teased.

"Yes, I am," Shiloh grunted, "and I wish you were."

"You know I don't get nervous around you," Cheney said casually. Shiloh looked at her curiously, but she went on, "I'll do what you say, Teacher." Raising the gun with both hands, she said in a monotone, "I am now pointing the gun." With both thumbs she pulled back the hammer. "I am now cocking the hammer of the gun." Closing one eye, she intoned, "I am now sighting down the barrel of the gun. I am now—"

"I'm not sure this was such a good idea," Shiloh grumbled.

Cheney shot and Shiloh jumped. "I have now shot the gun," she announced with a grin, "and I am now out of bullets."

Cheney and Shiloh shot the revolver for two hours, using up all the cartridges that Shiloh had made up. Cheney proved to be a passable shot, and, to her surprise, she enjoyed target shooting. She wheedled Shiloh into teaching her how to pack the cartridges with the primer—fulminate of mercury—and the ball, and how to insert the cartridges and place the percussion cap over the nipples on each of the chambers. Then she insisted that he teach her how to take the revolver apart and clean it. Her questions were so persistent he finally had to explain the entire chemical reaction of percussion firing to her.

"Now, tell me again about centerfire and rimfire," she began, holding up the metal cap that formed the base of a cartridge, and squinting at it. "What's the difference in the cartridges— wait a minute, I can't see—"

Both Shiloh and Cheney looked around in surprise. Soft gray twilight surrounded them. They couldn't even see the cliff from where they sat thirty feet away. "Guess we can't see, since it's dark," Shiloh said unnecessarily, rising and giving Cheney a hand up.

As she rose, they stood close together for a moment, and Shiloh looked down at her upturned face. She caught her breath, but he merely smiled politely, stepped back, and turned toward the woods below them. Cheney felt a depth of disappointment that she refused to explore or even acknowledge, and with a small sigh she gathered up the gun and empty cartridges. Shiloh turned away and whistled shrilly, then muttered, "Hope Sock remembers his part of the bargain."

Immediately they heard a crashing in the underbrush, and both horses loped into the clearing. Shiloh took something from his pocket and gave it to Sock, who smacked noisily. Impatiently Stocking nosed him and soon was making enthusiastic sounds.

"What's that?" Cheney asked curiously. In the semidarkness she couldn't see what he had given the horses.

"Muscadines. They love 'em, and they only get them when I whistle. See?"

"Yes, but wherever do you get them this time of year?"

Shiloh didn't say anything for a moment as he busily saddled Stocking. Finally he answered evenly, "Maeva."

★　★　★　★

Rissy and Cheney rocked and gazed at the cold, distant full moon that floated above the dark peaks of the Moccasin Mountains. No lantern or candle was lit in Black Arrow, and the sterile moonlight transformed the valley and mountains beyond into thick geometric lines of black and gray and navy blue. Shiloh sat on the porch steps, silent and remote as the impersonal white globe staring down from millions of miles away. In spite of herself, Cheney wondered if his thoughts were of Maeva Wilding. Bleakly she stared at the jagged black outline of Maeva's Trace and thought about the woman who was the namesake of a mountain.

"That sure was a good dinner, Rissy." Shiloh turned to smile at the two women. "Sure a lot better than what Glen and me usually eat."

"I'm glad it worked out for you to stay with Glen," Cheney murmured. "I like him."

"Well, he sure likes you, Doc. You're his hero since you fixed up Beauregard." He turned back, and his face grew somber. "And Glen Rawlins is a good man to have for a friend. He's the kind that'll do anything for you, you know, no matter what. He'll be there."

Cheney looked at his profile with doubt clouding her face. *I used to think that of you, Shiloh . . . now I'm not so sure.*

"And I'll always be here for you, Doc," he finished quietly.

Rissy stood up and walked to the steps to search the full panorama of the sky. Leaning against one of the porch supports, she yawned, then stood up straighter. Narrowing her eyes, she looked hard up the street toward Maeva's Trace. "What's dat?"

Her voice was sharp, and Cheney rose and walked to the steps. "What? I don't see anything."

"I see people comin' down thet hill," Rissy retorted impatiently. Pointing to Maeva's Trace, she insisted, "Looky there— you see? Peoples movin' down to dem foothills!"

"Rissy, you're not seeing people," Cheney argued, craning her neck to look around Shiloh, who had risen to stand in front of her. "It must just be the trees, or the moonlight, or shadows."

"It ain't no tree, an' it ain't no moonshine," Rissy snapped.

"I dunno," Shiloh muttered. "It does seem like there's something."

For a few minutes the three stood motionless, their eyes searching the bewildering shadow-play of moonlight on the foothills to the north. Cheney thought she saw movement, but she was straining so hard she couldn't tell if there really was something or if her eyes were playing tricks. Then a white spark glinted and grew into the glare of a flame. Then there were two, then four, and more. Finally twelve distant torches burned across the top of Wolf Run. The middle dot of flame moved, and slowly the other flames fell into a snaky line behind. Men were coming down from the mountains.

"Rissy, go get that pouch I brought from Maeva's," Shiloh muttered. Wordlessly Rissy slipped into the dark house.

"What? What is going on?" Cheney demanded.

"I'm not sure, Doc," he answered, "but I got a bad feeling about this." Standing on the bottom of the porch steps, he stared uneasily at the line of approaching torches.

Cheney, standing behind and above him on the porch, reached down and tapped him on the shoulder impatiently. "No, I mean what does this have to do with Maeva Wilding? What did you send Rissy for, some eye of newt and toe of toad? Those people don't have anything to do with us, whatever they're doing!"

"Maybe not," Shiloh snapped, "but it still looks like trouble."

Hastily he stalked to the side of the porch. About ten feet away from the house on either side was a neatly folded tarpaulin covering a pile of small sticks and logs split into large splinters. Cheney had vaguely wondered what Glen and Shiloh were doing when they had made the two piles of wood, but she had never thought to question them. Now Shiloh uncovered a pile, lit a match, and set fire to the dry wood, then went to the other side of the house and did the same. The two small bonfires burned brightly, sending bright, white sparks upward.

"What in the world is that for?" Cheney demanded as Shiloh returned to his stance on the porch steps.

"Balefire," Shiloh muttered. "To call Glen."

Rissy came out of the cabin and glided across the porch. A tall, silent shadow, she passed by Shiloh and went toward the bonfire on the far side of the cabin.

Shiloh glanced apprehensively up the street. The torches were even with DeSpain's now. Some of the men carrying them were on horseback, some were on foot. Leading them was a tall man holding a torch and riding a pale, dappled gray horse.

Shiloh ordered in a low voice, "Rissy, get back up here. I'll do that."

From the darkness on the far side of the house, Cheney heard an indignant, "Hmph! I ain't a-scairt of these here little fireballs!" Suddenly the bonfire exploded into a bright white and yellow glow, and loud pops and crackles sounded like gunfire in the quiet night. Rissy's sturdy frame was outlined against a ten-foot aura of white.

Holding her apron up in a pouch, Rissy trudged by the porch grumbling, "Miss Maeva Wilding might fool some folks into thinkin' these here leetle puffballs is some kinda magic, but I done set fire to a bunch of 'em when I were a chile wid no good sense!"

The procession reached the cabin, and Cheney saw that Enoch Satterfield was the grim-faced leader on the pale horse. Behind him rode his son T. R. on a dark horse, his features shadowed by a black hat. The rest of the men gathered close behind, and Cheney recognized most of them as Enoch Satterfield's brothers and their sons. Latham Trask was there, his gaze remote but with a hint of regret as he stared at Shiloh. Cheney realized gratefully that Jimmy Dale was not in the group, nor was Booth Trask.

Enoch reined his horse in at the first bonfire to stare at Rissy. With a look of defiance she reached in her apron and tossed several round balls into the fire. Satterfield didn't flinch, but his horse reared at the blinding light and loud cracks from the fire, and behind him T. R.'s horse screamed and pawed the air. Some of the men shaded their eyes, and the rest of the horses tossed their heads and stamped nervously. Calmly Rissy returned to the porch to stand by Cheney.

Satterfield got his horse under control and rode close in front of the porch. His face was ugly with hostility, and when he spoke, his voice was ragged and strained. "I ain't no man of words," he told Shiloh. "So I'm jist gonna keep it simple." Turning to the men who had closed in close behind him, he ordered, "Jude, D. K. Go hitch up thet wagon."

The two young men walked around the corner of the cabin. Enoch Satterfield turned back to Shiloh, Cheney, and Rissy. "You're all leavin'. Go git whutever you kin git in ten minutes, 'cause thet's all the time I'm figgerin' it'll take them boys to hitch up."

"What?" Cheney cried. "What—Why are you here? Why are you d-doing this?"

"Woman, be silent!" Satterfield snarled. "Reason I'm even doin' any talkin' a-tall is 'cause of your boy, there! He acks like he might have one hairsbreadth of sense, even if he do go with you on yore butcherin' raids! But I ain't gonna dignify this here conversation talkin' to the likes of a murderin' woman like you!"

Even though his words and accusations were senseless and untrue, Cheney felt dread, and even shame, for some reason she could not fathom. Dropping her eyes, she moved closer to Rissy. The strong, stolid black woman slid a muscular arm about Cheney's waist and hugged her close.

"Mr. Satterfield, I have an idea what this is about," Shiloh said in a voice that sounded wonderfully calm and soothing after Enoch Satterfield's hoarse ranting. "And you should at least give us one chance to explain. Any judge would do that much."

Satterfield's eyes glinted malevolently by the flames surrounding him. Pulling himself stiffly upright in the saddle, he thrust the torch up higher in an unmistakable signal of danger. "What kinda explanation is they for a woman who goes about cuttin' up babies? Bible talks about people like that! And runnin' 'em outta town—with they arms an' laigs an' head still attached—is goin' easy on her, I says!"

Dark mutterings of agreement sounded from T. R. and the other men gathered behind Enoch Satterfield.

Distraught, confused, and overwhelmed, Cheney lifted her gaze to search the faces of the men before her. "But I n-never— Who could ever say such a h-horrible th-thing? I n-never—"

T. R. pointed at her accusingly. "Ever'body knows about you, woman! Bake Conroy said he heard you split open my nephew like a ripe watermelon!"

"But . . . please . . . you don't understand!" Cheney pleaded, and the words began to tumble out with helpless confusion. "He had appendicitis!" The men's faces reflected disbelief and disgust, and Cheney struggled to explain in words they could understand. "He . . . There was a small . . . growth inside him, very small, kind of like a . . . worm, because it grew . . . putrid, and he would have—"

With a frightening intensity, Satterfield shook his head violently from side to side with each word Cheney spoke. When her words faltered and stopped, he again lifted his torch high and turned to gaze at the men gathered with him. "This woman says that baby had a poison worm inside of him, so she hadda cut it out with a knife!" He turned and pointed the flaring torch at Cheney, and she threw up her hands and flinched. "You got nerve to call Maeva Wilding a witch! Maeva Wilding don't kill babies!"

"Enoch!" Shiloh grabbed the torch just below the flame and pushed hard. Enoch relented, raising it high as his gaze went reluctantly to Shiloh. "Isaac isn't dead, Enoch," Shiloh muttered in a low voice. "He's fine! He's well because Dr. Duvall operated on him!"

"He's lyin' for that woman, Pa!" T. R. shouted. "I swear!"

"Boy, you shut up and let me think!" Enoch growled, his eyes burning on Shiloh's face.

The torches hissed, and the balefires crackled in the silent moments that followed. The men were so still that their flames burned bright and high and didn't waver so much as an inch. Cheney felt as if her mind were filled with gray cotton-wool, and her mouth tasted brassy. Dully she thought, *They thought Isaac died—but he didn't—and now it seems like that doesn't even matter. It's just me. They just hate me.*

Enoch Satterfield's face suddenly took on a look of violent distaste, almost a sickened look, and he pulled his horse to back it away from the porch as if it were poisoned ground. "You lie," he muttered to Shiloh. He turned to the men backing up slowly behind him. "Burn it," he ordered in a hoarse whisper.

T. R. immediately jumped off his horse and started toward the cabin with his torch held in front of him like a shield. Shiloh turned and grabbed Cheney and Rissy, yanked them off the porch, and pulled them along to the street, farther up from the men who crowded about Satterfield.

"No!" Cheney screamed. "No! I haven't done anything wrong!"

Shiloh enveloped her in his arms. She fought him for a moment, beating on him futilely, but he only clasped her tighter and murmured softly. Finally she quieted down, and he spoke against the fragrant cloud of her hair. "Cheney, it's not worth dying for. But if you think it's worth fighting for, I'll fight. Maybe I can stop them."

Cheney grew very still in his arms, then buried her face against him and whispered brokenly, "No . . . the house doesn't matter, and the only thing that does matter we can't win by fighting."

"Stop! Enoch, stop it!" The faint call was one of desperate warning, and T. R. pulled back his torch and looked at Enoch Satterfield uncertainly. Enoch turned to face the approaching riders, and the men around him scattered as the galloping hoof beats drew near.

Cheney, Shiloh, and Rissy had heard the sound of more horses coming. But with sinking hearts they had realized the riders were coming from the north—not from Hawk's Light, where Glen Rawlins' cabin stood. They had all assumed that more Satterfields were joining Enoch, but now they craned their necks to see.

Bursting into the lurid light, Booth Trask and Levi Satterfield thundered up to Enoch's mount, their horses screaming and rearing as their riders pulled them up sharply.

"Enoch! For God's sake, what're you doing?" Levi cried.

"What're *you* doing, brother?" Enoch thundered, pointing his torch at the smaller man much as he had thrust it accusingly at Cheney. "That witch kilt your only son—and you cain't see what I'm doing?"

"Enoch, no! Isaac's fine! Thank God, the boy's strong and well! She saved his life!" Levi cried, his face twisted with both joy and dread. Enoch Satterfield was the oldest son, Levi the youngest. The other four brothers—Noah, Ben, Hiram, and Caleb—were all there, crowded around Enoch. Not one of his five younger brothers had ever in their lives disobeyed Enoch or even questioned him. Enoch's face grew even darker, and all five of his brothers looked fearful.

Enoch's eyes glinted as they raked over his youngest brother. Levi looked small and weak under the scorching disdain of his older brother. "Now you listen to me, Levi," Enoch said in a voice of anger with only a thin veneer of reason. "I say that woman's gotta go. Now, I'm glad Isaac's well"—he turned to shoot a murderous glance at Cheney—"but I say it's only a miracle of God he's alive, after that heathernish woman cut on him!"

Slowly Levi Satterfield's rounded shoulders straightened, and his head lifted proudly. With deliberate movements he pulled a long-barreled, worn muzzle-loader from the sheath on his saddle. Ignoring his brother's growing fury, he dismounted, walked to the porch of Cheney's cabin, and pointed his rifle straight at Enoch's chest. "Doctor Duvall," he called in a clear voice. "You kin come on home now."

Cheney hesitantly took a step forward, then another. Shiloh took her arm in a warm grasp, and Rissy took her other arm. Together the three walked back to the porch. Shiloh stood by Levi Satterfield, his tall, lean frame towering over the shorter man. Booth Trask scrambled off his horse and ducked under Levi's rifle to stand on his other side. Cheney and Rissy stood behind the three men. Though he was shorter and slightly chubby, Levi stood firm, holding the gun to his eye with deadly seriousness.

"Levi!" Enoch shouted hoarsely. "You ain't goin' agin your own blood! You cain't!"

"It were my son's blood that were spilt, Enoch," Levi answered somberly, "and it were my son's blood she saved. Satterfield blood, 'twas, that she saved. Mine—and yourn."

It seemed like hours that the two brothers stared at each other with the deadly black cylinder in between them. With a muttered oath, Enoch Satterfield threw his torch into the dying bonfire close-by. He neither spoke nor looked to the right or the left as he turned his horse and disappeared into the night.

MAKE THY SHADOW
P·A·R·T · T·H·R·E·E
AS THE NIGHT

*Take counsel, execute judgment;
make thy shadow as the night
in the midst of the noonday . . .*

Isaiah 16:3

13

ANCIENT OF DAYS

Between the darkening of one day and the dawning of another, Indian summer departed from the Moccasin Mountains as enigmatically as it had come. The morning of December 23 was jarringly cold after the sultry weather since Thanksgiving. Rumpled gray clouds stole over Maeva's Trace to blanket the sun and sky. Some of the people of Wolf County muttered dourly of Christmas snow after Indian summer, referring to the ominous verse Caroline Satterfield had quoted to Cheney. Most, however, looked toward the sky with furtive hope, for who does not have a childlike wish for snow on Christmas Eve?

Early that morning Glen Rawlins pulled smartly up to the church in a wagon piled with one-by-fours, two-by-fours, chicken wire, and hay bales. Without saying a word to anyone, he proceeded to build an open shed in back of the church.

He built the two sides to angle out from the back wall, so as to give plenty of room for all participants, human and animal. He laid chicken wire across the top of the three-sided structure and thatched it with hay. Carefully he covered the ground with the hay, making sure it was a uniform five inches thick. Frowning, he picked out all of the burrs and rough sticks.

Then he constructed simple hitching posts of the two-by-fours to fit diagonally across the corners of the shed, and measured the angle from the crosspieces to the corners to make certain that there was enough room for a horse and a cow.

A small wooden manger he placed exactly in the center; it was a true manger, the sides made of rough wooden X's, joined by a single wooden piece at the center of each X. It took him a long time to get the hay in the manger arranged to his satisfaction; Neva Sikes later swore that "he fooled with that manger fer two hours!" Finally he stepped back and dusted off his hands with satisfaction. The hay was thick and secure and had a perfect little depression in the center.

Lastly he nailed up an intricately carved and lovingly polished wooden star in the center of the roof crosspiece, right over the small manger.

★ ★ ★ ★

"I love Christmas," Sharon breathed. "Thank you so much for—everything, Cheney!"

A reprimand almost burst from Cheney's lips, but with an effort she reminded herself that rebuking Sharon for not staying in bed would only hurt both Sharon and herself. So she merely smiled. "Stop thanking me, Sharon! You're getting as bad as Glen Rawlins and Levi Satterfield!"

An inexplicably heavy silence followed Cheney's teasing words. Cheney realized that she had never told Sharon about her successful operation on little Isaac Satterfield, or about the dismal night exactly one week ago, when Enoch Satterfield and his brothers had stood in front of her home, their menacing visages lit by torches and balefire. She had never mentioned that night to anyone, although she was well aware that everyone in Wolf County had talked ceaselessly of it all week.

Now Cheney sighed and went on in a low voice, "I suppose you've heard about Isaac Satterfield—and Enoch and his brothers."

"Yes, I have," Sharon replied, her voice roughened by the hurt she felt for Cheney. "But Levi stood up for you, didn't he? Even against Enoch? That's a miracle, Cheney—a miracle for you."

"Yes, it is," Cheney admitted. "It's also a miracle that no one got hurt. Shiloh set signal fires, and Glen Rawlins came down from his cabin to a ledge on the mountain that overlooks my house. He watched the whole thing through his rifle sight. And Jimmy Dale Satterfield was with him."

"You mean—Jimmy Dale would've—?"

Cheney shook her head. "No, of course not. But Glen said Jimmy Dale's such a good shot, he could've sat up there all night and shot the torches out of those men's hands."

Sharon looked across the valley toward the distant blue peaks of the Satterfields' land. "The Satterfields' smokehouse burned down that night," she whispered.

Cheney's cheeks burned because for a few moments she felt a fierce gladness, and it shamed her. When she realized the implications of Sharon's words, however, the self-righteous feeling dissolved into concern and regret. The Satterfields were hunters and trappers, not farmers. Leah Satterfield had a garden and put up some vegetables for winter, but Cheney knew that most of the family's winter food had been in that smokehouse. With distress she thought of the children. Besides the grown Satterfield children—T. R., Jimmy Dale, Lorine, and Caroline—there were Abe, Frannie, Prince, and four-year-old Cassia. "How did it happen?" Cheney asked.

Sharon didn't answer for a long time. "I don't know." She frowned. "Josh just mentioned it to me in passing the next day." At the look on Cheney's face, Sharon hastily amended, "I mean, he wasn't there. That is, he was at Lige and Katie's 'til late, talking about some land sales to DeSpain."

Obviously Sharon was distraught over the incident; she seemed to be afraid that her husband knew more about the fire at the Satterfields' than he had told her.

In spite of the fact that Cheney was bothered about the incident—and Josh Carter's possible involvement—her primary concern was for Sharon's well-being. "Let's not talk about anything serious anymore!" she demanded. "Let's just have fun today!"

"Oh, yes, let's!" Sharon breathed a sigh of relief and beamed at Cheney. "I do love Christmas!"

Sharon and Cheney were sitting on the Carters' porch watching expectantly for the arrival of Josh and his family. It was Christmas Eve, and they were all going to church. Sharon was now five months pregnant and was beginning to look bulky and awkward, though it was more because of her small frame than because she had gained an inordinate amount of weight. Josh Carter had never accepted Cheney's diagnosis of toxemia and her insistence upon complete bed rest for Sharon. He had, however, reluctantly indulged his wife to a certain extent—except when it came to going to church.

"But Josh," Sharon had protested at first, "Cheney said complete bed rest, twenty-four hours a day, every day. I'm not sure—"

"God ain't gonna strike you down with no fits when you're a-goin' to church, Sharon," he had countered firmly. "I'll 'low Miss Duvall an' all them to come up here an' do your chores, even though it do seem to me to be takin' charity. But Carters go to church."

Sharon knew that such a compromise was, in Josh's mind, very generous and she didn't want to press the issue further. So she went to church, praying fervently each moment that Cheney was wrong and Josh was right.

In what Cheney viewed as at least a partial acknowledgment of the delicacy of Sharon's condition, Josh had finally widened the narrow horse track from their cabin down to Wolf Ridge. With some measure of relief, Cheney had asked Josh if Sharon could ride in her wagon to the Christmas Eve festivities. To her surprise, he readily agreed.

Early that morning Shiloh had come to Cheney's house for breakfast and had hitched Stocking up to the roomy wagon.

"Can he pull this alone?" Cheney had asked anxiously.

"If it's just you and Miss Sharon. Any more than that, and you'd better double-team one of the Carters' horses." Shiloh had slapped Stocking's muscular flank and then mounted Sock. "I'll see you later, Doc."

"You will?" Cheney burst out, hating herself for sounding so desperate.

"Sure!" He had grinned. "It's Christmas Eve!" With that he had ridden off across the river toward Maeva's house, and Cheney and Rissy had gone to the Carters' alone.

Now, in spite of Cheney's determined cheerfulness, Sharon could see a hint of sadness in her friend's countenance. Sharon didn't know exactly why Cheney was upset; she hoped her friend would talk to her about it or at least give her some hint. But Cheney steered the conversation to lighter matters, and Sharon was reluctant to intrude on her privacy by asking personal questions.

Glendean came tripping down the footpath from Lige and Katie's carrying a box that must have been heavy for her. "Howdy, ya'll!" she cried in an excited little-girl voice. "Howdy, Doctor Cheney! Kin I use your waggin?"

"Use it?" Cheney repeated cautiously, and Glendean held up the box. "Oh, you mean put something in it? Of course! In fact, if you want, you can ride with us."

"Oh, yes, I want to!" she exclaimed. Running to the wagon, she carefully placed the box in the back, then turned and ran back toward her house.

"She's going to be Mary in the pageant, you know," Sharon told Cheney proudly. "Reverend Scott said she was a good actress."

Cheney observed Sharon's pride in her diminutive sister-in-law with affection. "You're going to be a wonderful mother, Sharon."

"And Josh is going to be a wonderful father," she sighed. "Cheney, I'm so happy."

"You are?" Cheney didn't mean to sound quite so astonished, but Sharon merely giggled a little.

"Yes, I am. Oh, don't look so repentant, Cheney. Do you think I don't know you've wondered about Josh and me?"

"Well, um, yes, I suppose . . ."

Sharon had been attending the New York Academy of Arts and Letters when Cheney had met her. Immediately Cheney had realized that Sharon was brilliant, sensitive, and creative, and had made an effort to make friends with this rather shy woman from Virginia. Since she had come to Black Arrow, Cheney had reflected many times that Sharon had buried herself alive in these hills with a taciturn, ignorant man.

"I know what you think about us, Cheney," Sharon said lightly. "But you see, Josh loves me very much."

"Well, of course he does—"

"No, Cheney," Sharon uncharacteristically interrupted, shaking her head. "You don't understand. But after you've been around us awhile—and Lige and Katie—I think you'll see why I'm so happy. And lucky."

Cheney felt a surge of impatience at Sharon's cryptic words, but she merely smiled an understanding she didn't feel.

Glendean appeared again, shouting with excitement and leading a small goat by a rope around its neck. "Ma says I kin ride with you—and says fer me to ast can she and Pa put some of their stuff in your waggin, and kin they ride too? And she says Murdoch can help pull that waggin, even if he is lazy as a summer slug—" She reached the wagon hitched in front of the porch, expertly tethered the goat to the back, and then hopped from one foot to the other with impatience. "Kin we, Doctor Cheney?"

"Well—well—of course!" Cheney stammered, and again Glendean sped up the footpath. Cheney had not been around Kate and Lige Carter much. They had never acknowledged her as a doctor and still staunchly believed in Maeva Wilding. But they seemed to be good-natured people, and their attitude toward Cheney was fairly congenial as long as the conversation wasn't about her profession.

"Oh, that'll be fun, Cheney! We'll put a big pile of bearskins in the back, and it'll be almost like a sleigh ride! Oh, if it would only snow!" Sharon looked longingly at the high, dirty cotton-wool clouds.

"Bearskins?" Cheney repeated automatically. "Yes, of course. Maybe it'll snow." Visions of smelly rugs with huge snarling bear heads and long deadly claws distracted Cheney for a moment, but the festive air of the day was beginning to cheer her up.

Doubtfully eyeing the small white goat with its one-inch horns, Cheney asked, "What is that?"

"It's a goat."

"Well, I suspected that, Sharon!"

"Oh! Well, Glendean offered to bring all the animals for the manger scene."

"This," Cheney muttered, "is going to be an interesting ride."

The narrow cart path from Katie and Lige Carter's cabin had not been widened, so Cheney could not drive the wagon up to their home. A footpath through the woods that led from Katie's kitchen door straight down the mountain to Josh and Sharon's cabin was the oft-used shortcut. Down this path came what Cheney and Sharon laughingly dubbed "The Carter Christmas Procession."

For the next hour Lige, Josh, Bobbie Jo, and Dane Carter trudged through the woods carrying boxes, piles of brightly-colored quilts, deep stewpots that steamed in the cold, the ever-present rifles and pouches of powder, and the promised bear-skins. To Cheney's delight, they had no facial features or digits still attached. Though the fur was rather coarse, the hides had been combed and worked until they were as flexible and cozy as Cheney's ermine cloak (which she refused to wear in Black Arrow). So she and Sharon hugged bear rugs close around their laps and shoulders and were quite warm and comfortable, though the temperature seemed to be dropping.

Glendean made five trips to the wagon with her precious cargo. She brought one box with the cat Notta and her four six-week-old kittens; one box with two brown rabbits, as yet un-named; a large reddish dog named Roamin' or Roman, Cheney could not be sure which; two bored sheep named Dawdle and Don't; and a raccoon called Jim-Jim that constantly skittered around Glendean's shoulders and head, his beady black eyes watching everyone and everything.

Finally Lige and Katie came down the path leading Glen-dean's horse, Murdoch. As Lige led the horse around and began hitching him to the wagon, he said stridently to Katie, "Ain't no coon niver been in no manger! You ort not let the child bring that there coon!"

" 'Twas either Jim-Jim or No-No, Lige," Katie laughed. "An' you know that blamed fox bites ever'body. 'Sides, I didn't hear you 'zackly dressin' Glendean down, now did I?"

Lige Carter glanced up from the harness to grin at his wife, his light green eyes teasing. "I jist didn't wanna argue with you, wife. You know you love that silly varmint."

Katie stood on tiptoe and whispered something in Lige's ear. He threw back his head and laughed. "Thought such!" Then to Cheney's astonishment, he grabbed his wife around the waist and lifted her off her feet. "I got the best one, boys!" he called. "You best pay attention, Dane, like your brother Josh, an' git you a wife jist like your ma!"

"Aw, Pa," sixteen-year-old Dane grunted with some embarrassment, "right here in front o' Miss Duvall an' everthin'—!"

"What I wanna know is," said a disgruntled voice from behind Cheney's rocking chair, "where you'uns is plannin' to put all dis here stuff in dis here house. I gotta whole kitchen of vittles in there, an' some Crissus boxes o' Miz Sharon's, and dey's Mistuh Josh's gun and what-not, and—"

"We need a bigger waggin," Lige groaned.

"What we need's a mule train," Josh muttered under his breath. The terrible red scar on his face contrasted oddly with the lightness in his voice and eyes.

"Look!" Sharon cried. "It's snowing!" Her eyes bright and her face lit with joy, she pointed.

A hush fell over the rowdy group, and everyone's face turned toward the sky. A large flake fell on Lige Carter's nose, and his smile was as delighted as a small child's. Glendean slowly raised her tiny hand, and a flake settled on it as lightly as a moth's wing. Then another fell, and another, and another.

Josh Carter hurried to the porch, swept up his wife in his arms, and took the four porch steps in two strides. "Here," he said, smiling down at her upturned face. "This here first snow-fall is for you."

★　★　★　★

Black Arrow's Christmas pageant mirrored the souls of the people who partook in it. Some elements of the presentation were as traditional as the dawn of day and the fall of night. But unexpected remembrances of the meaning of Jesus' life and death, on this eve of His birth, were also offered. These men and women and children, who walked each day both on high places and in valleys, acknowledged birth and death as equals.

Glendean made a lovely Mary, wrapped in Cheney's gray cashmere cloak with the graceful hood that Rissy had cut down to size. Her face was heart-shaped, with a widow's peak inherited from her mother, and she looked like a somber woods elf swathed in the soft gray folds. Cheney was delighted that the pageant provided a good excuse to donate the warm robe to the child.

Prince Satterfield, ten years old, was a grave and sober Joseph. He and Glendean knelt on either side of the manger, which held a live baby who slept peacefully through the entire pageant. Of course there were wise men, shepherds, and lots of angels. Carter children, Satterfields, Trasks, Sikeses, Booths, Smiths, Rawlinses—all together, there were over forty children in the pageant, all under ten years of age.

Their procession from the back of the church to the manger was dignified and orderly, with a minimum of fidgeting and whispering. Murdoch the horse watched the procession with equine gravity, Junie Moon the milch cow chewed respectfully. The sheep, Dawdle and Don't, posed peacefully, their tiny hooves tucked neatly under them. The box containing Notta and her kittens, and the other box with the duplicate rabbits, were displayed to one side. From time to time Jim-Jim's pirate face peeped watchfully around the star on the roof.

As the children's procession from the church started, a discreet quartet at one side of the crowd began to sing. Instead of a traditional Christmas carol, Cheney recognized Haydn's majestic high-church music with delight, and listened carefully to lyrics unfamiliar but fitting.

> O Worship the King, all glorious above,
> And gratefully sing His pow'r and His love;
> Our Shield and Defender, the Ancient of Days,
> Pavilioned in splendor and girded with praise.
> Thy bountiful care what tongue can recite?
> It breathes in the air, it shines in the light;
> It streams from the hills, it descends to the plain,
> And sweetly distills in the snow and the rain!

The children settled into their places. Out of the snow-streaked darkness Bobbie Jo Carter and Jimmy Dale Satterfield appeared on each side of the manger scene, each dressed in solid black and holding an unlit torch. Wordlessly, Reverend Scott came forward and lit both of their torches, then again took his place as one of the crowd.

Bobbie Jo held her torch high. The Carter family stood on the right and the Satterfield family on the left, just as they sat in church. Bobbie Jo's light green eyes mysteriously reflected the torchlight as she paused for a moment to search the divided families. Then her face grew still and peaceful as she began, "My soul doth magnify the Lord! And my spirit hath rejoiced in God my Saviour! For he hath regarded the low estate of his hand-maiden: for, behold, from henceforth all generations shall call me blessed. For he that is mighty hath done to me great things; and holy is his name!"

Jimmy Dale lifted his torch high and called in a strong baritone, "Blessed be the Lord God of Israel; for he hath visited and redeemed his people, and hath raised up an horn of salvation for us in the house of his servant David."

Bobbie Jo continued Mary's Magnificat: "His mercy is on them that fear him from generation to generation. He hath shewed strength with his arm; he hath scattered the proud in the imagination of their hearts. He hath put down the mighty from their seats, and exalted them of low degree. He hath filled the hungry with good things; and the rich he hath sent empty away!"

Jimmy Dale continued with Zacharias's prophecy: "That we should be saved from our enemies, and from the hand of all that hate us; to perform the mercy promised to our fathers. . . . That he would grant unto us, that we being delivered out of the hand of our enemies might serve him without fear, in holiness and righteousness before him, all the days of our life!"

Reverend Scott stepped forward and faced the crowd, his face shadowed, a two-dimensional figure outlined in the flickering torches behind him. He spoke very quietly, but in the peculiar hush of snowfall his clear tenor voice could be heard by each of the two hundred people standing before him. "Through the tender mercy of our God, whereby the Dayspring from on High hath visited us—to give light to them that sit in darkness and in the shadow of death. . . ."

Raising his face toward the darkened sky, smiling a little at the soft snowflakes that fell steadily and melted as soon as they touched the warmth of earth, he finished, ". . . To guide our feet into the way of peace."

★   ★   ★   ★

It was almost midnight when Rissy and Cheney trudged wearily down the street from the church to the cabin. The festivities of eating, singing, merrymaking, and gift-giving had lasted long hours.

As they neared her home, Cheney looked up in surprise. "It looks like a painting," she murmured. Snow still floated steadily earthward, and the ground was beginning to take on a translucent silver sheen. The tiny cabin seemed to nestle contentedly at the foot of the darkened mountains, and yellow light-squares made each of the windows a glow of welcome warmth.

"A Crissus painting," Rissy said softly.

Shiloh waited for them on the front porch. "Merry Christmas!"

"Merry Crissus!" Rissy called.

"Merry Christmas Eve!" Cheney laughed, her heart suddenly light. The two women hurried inside. A roaring fire greeted them in the sitting room, and Shiloh had piled fragrant pine and cedar branches and cones on the mantle. The spicy smell of hot apple cider wafted throughout the house. "How wonderful, Shiloh!" Cheney breathed. "It's cold! It's snowing!"

Sniffing loudly with appreciation, Rissy promptly disappeared into the kitchen. Cheney threw off her gray wool mantle and hurried to the fire. Shiloh moved to stand close beside her.

"I know," he responded in a deep voice. "But it's warm here, Doc." His face was lit by the yellow and white flames that burned high and bright in the massive fireplace. "I got you a present, Cheney."

"You did? I got you something, too, but I was going to give it to you tomorrow morning!" she replied excitedly. His face grew still and remote, and she continued haltingly, "You'll—be here for Christmas breakfast, won't you? Rissy's going to fix everything you like."

Staring down into the fire, he shook his head from side to side twice with precise movements.

Cheney's face fell, in spite of her effort to remain unmoved. "Maeva," she muttered.

"She doesn't have anyone, Cheney. No family, and no real friends," Shiloh said gently. "And it's Christmas."

To her profound dismay, Cheney's eyes filled with tears. Quickly she turned away and tried to blink them back, but they scalded her eyes and spilled down her cheeks in a ruinous stream. Furtively she wiped her eyes and cheeks and straightened her shoulders. As her vision cleared, she suddenly saw in the far corner of the room a high wooden stand made of three smooth oak boards to form a sturdy triangle. On the stand was a saddle—an English saddle, small, with delicate lines and no pommel. A lady's sidesaddle.

"Oh, Shiloh," she murmured quietly, her eyes filling with tears again, "it's beautiful!" She turned to run to him.

But she was alone.

14

FAIRY TALES

"Jimmy Dale," a soft voice said at his elbow.

Defensively, he spun around to see only his sister Caroline smiling gravely up at him. "How'd you git in here 'thout me hearin' you, girl?" he gasped. He was in the barn saddling his horse, Brand, and had heard no sound.

"I dunno," she answered honestly, "but I ain't gonna do it no more. If'n you'd been holdin' onto somethin' I reckon you woulda knocked me acrost the room."

"Sorry," he murmured absently.

She saw his eyes searching her face with some fierceness she didn't understand. "Why are you lookin' at me like that, Jimmy Dale?"

"Uh—no reason." He shrugged, then smiled a little. "I was jis' thinkin' how pretty you look today, with that red thing on yore head."

She looked slightly amused at Jimmy Dale's words, and refused to countenance his compliment. "Hit's called a scarf."

"Yep. Bobbie—" he began, then stopped and frowned. "Anyways, you do look pretty. Whatcha doin' out here in the cold an' all?"

"I'm a-goin' to the springs." Though the words were factual, she looked up at him with wordless pleading.

"Caroline," he began with exaggerated patience, "there's two foot of snow on the ground. Hit's cold. Blackcastle Springs is dangerous." Her face took on the merest hint of reproof, but he refused to let it stop his steady argument. "Yep, I know you know that better'n anyone. But it's even more dangerous when there's snow on the ground."

Caroline wasn't the type of girl to shake her head impatiently, but her mouth compressed into a straight red line and her hazel eyes grew hard. Her unemotional tone matched Jimmy Dale's cold logic. "Hit'll be warm at the springs. And there won't be no snow there—only on the way. And you know, Jimmy Dale, that it ain't dangerous for me no more. Goes t'other way, in fact."

"I ain't too sure 'bout that, Caroline," he sighed, but she could see him relenting. He slapped Brand on the flank, muttering, "But I reckon me and Brand could ride up that way."

"Thank you," she said formally, and stood without moving as he finished saddling up. Caroline made no wasted movements or elaborate gestures, and the result was that a strange stillness seemed to surround her.

Her way of not drawin' attention to herself, Jimmy Dale thought. *An' it works—shame, though, 'cause it don't just hide her limp, it hides all of her.*

"Ready?" he asked. "You tell somebody you're goin'?"

"Yes," she answered without nodding, "I told Daddy." Caroline was the only Satterfield child who called Enoch "Daddy" instead of "Pa." When she did, Enoch Satterfield's expression was as close as it ever would be to gentle.

She mounted by herself, for it was her right leg that was crippled, but it was strong enough for her to throw it over the horse. Wordlessly Jimmy Dale went to Brand's right side to shorten the stirrup to fit Caroline's leg; she wasn't strong enough to grip a seat with her legs from behind the saddle. Then he swung up behind her, and Brand slowly began his walk down the road in the brilliant snow.

They went around and then down Maeva's Trace to White Wolf Ridge, then down to Wolf Run. Instead of going across the foothills, however, Jimmy Dale turned Brand straight down toward Black Arrow.

"I—I don't wanna go into town, Jimmy Dale," Caroline whispered. "You know that."

"We cain't cut acrost no more, Caroline," he said shortly. "And you know that."

For ten years, Caroline had made this pilgrimage almost every week, accompanied by either T. R. or Jimmy Dale. Ordinarily they went across Wolf Run, forded the river where it narrowed going around the Trace, and then followed it along the west side to the foot of Blackcastle Springs Mountain. But going that way meant that they would cross a corner of Carter land, so on this day Caroline said nothing more. But as they went down the street, she pulled her crimson woolen scarf around to cover her face, and dropped her head. Gently Jimmy Dale reached around to take the reins from her lifeless hands, and gave her a quick hug.

"It's all right, Caroline," he whispered fiercely. "I ain't gonna let nothin' bad happen to you! I swear to you! Ain't nobody never gonna hurt you!"

Dully she thought, *Already the bad thing's happened to me . . . and already somebody's hurt me. You're too late, brother dear. . . .*

Riding in silence, looking to neither the right or the left, they went down the street at a quick trot, past the lake and the church and the school. The town was clean and white and quiet, with blue smoke glistening skyward from every chimney. Jimmy Dale turned Brand at Black King's Ford, where the river narrowed down to a bubbly stream at the foot of Blackcastle Springs Mountain before it widened as it wandered into Cougar's Way.

As soon as they rose above the timberline—out of sight of the town—Caroline straightened in the saddle, pulled her scarf back from her face, and looked around with interest. Her home and this mountain were the only two places on earth she knew well, and the mountain shone new in her eyes with its snow cloak.

Blackcastle Springs Mountain, in contrast to the rest of the Moccasin Mountains, was a series of steep ascents to small flat plateaus, until one reached the plateau called Blackcastle Springs. Behind the springs the mountain thinned and narrowed into a naked peak that thrust sharply up into the sky.

The mountain's terrain from a distance was deceiving, for the pines that grew thick and tall on its sides dulled and softened the outline. Ascending it could be treacherous. The ground was made up of small, sharp rocks mixed with black sandy dirt. Only the hardy pines seemed to find fingerholds in it, and they thrived thick and green, as though to spite the inhospitable mountain.

Brand negotiated his footing carefully. Jimmy Dale let him find his own way up to the third shelf, and then the ascent grew steeper. He slid off the back of the horse and led him the rest of the way to the plateau they sought. Finally Brand went up the last gentle circle around an outcropping of rock, and they entered the courtyard of the castle.

Twenty feet in front of them glittered a wall of black glass. The wall was loosely shaped like a triangle, with the two sides rising to form a sharp peak in the middle. The steep peak of the mountain rose above and behind it, the virgin snow-covering contrasting sharply with the hard black angles of the many-faceted "castle" wall.

They stood on a flat plateau of the same black glass. To their right was a terrace, slightly raised above the floor of the shelf. In the hush they could hear the spring bubbling inside the terrace, which actually was a rounded enclosure, shallow all around but dropping steeply in the middle and deepening to where the mineral waters bubbled up from a fissure in the rock wall. Clouds of steam rose from the natural pool, and wisps floated along the floor of the shelf, curling around Brand's hooves and Jimmy Dale's boots and Caroline's skirt, then dissolving when it rose a few inches above the shiny black floor.

"First time I saw this place was when snow was on the ground," Caroline said in a hushed tone usually reserved for churches and funerals. "I thought it looked like God had took a knife and cut out this here mountain's heart, and jis' left this black mirror instead."

Fragrant pines grew thick to the right and the left of this

dark cleft called Blackcastle Springs, forming a living wall and insulator. Standing on the edge of the shelf, they felt cold air biting their backs and tropic warmth on their faces. Brand shifted uneasily, the smooth surface obviously feeling strange under his hooves.

Caroline turned and looked up at Jimmy Dale, her hazel eyes calm and serene. "I'm a-gonna bathe my leg, and rest and warm up fer a spell."

Jimmy Dale knew she wanted him to go. She always wanted to be alone at Blackcastle Springs, and she never seemed ready to leave. Apprehensively he looked around. This place was alien, remote, inexplicable. Somehow Jimmy Dale was always conscious of oldness—of the mountains, the streams, the rivers, the land itself—when he came here. Today his senses seemed heightened, more sensitive and more troubling, and he didn't want to leave Caroline alone.

Caroline spoke again in a low voice without inflection, but she moved one hand in the slightest of pleading gestures. For Caroline it was tantamount to falling to her knees and begging. "Please," she said.

Jimmy Dale searched the brooding smoky walls with exasperation. "How long?"

"You know."

"Aw, Caroline—"

"Jimmy Dale, it takes a long time to git here. Might as well stay. I brung a book, an' I wanna bathe my leg real good, two-three times."

"All right," he reluctantly assented. "I'm a-goin' back to Wolf Run." He swung up into the saddle. Brand turned around and started back down the path before Jimmy Dale pulled the reins or tapped his sides. Just before they disappeared behind the rock sheltering the entrance, Jimmy Dale looked back over his shoulder at his sister. She stood in the same position, her eyes roving over the castle wall in front of her, clutching the crimson shawl around her shoulders. "I'll be back in a coupla hours."

"Take yore time, Jimmy Dale," Caroline said softly without turning. "She'll be glad to see you."

Jimmy Dale sighed as he rounded the jutting black rock. *Caroline knows 'bout Bobbie Jo; Glendean knows 'bout me. Plumb foolish, it's gittin' to be, sneakin' an' hidin' like this.* But as he turned Brand to the north and his narrowed eyes searched the gentle slopes of the Carters' land, Jimmy Dale Satterfield's face looked anything but foolish.

★ ★ ★ ★

Shiloh supposed that Glen Rawlins was the only person in Wolf County who had what might be termed a normal friendship with Maeva Wilding. He added a cautious mental footnote, *If anyone has an ordinary relationship with Maeva.*

Thwack! The round oak log divided into two precise halves beneath the heavy maul and tumbled off the leveled stump. Shiloh picked up another log, set it atop the stump, and split it cleanly. Wiping a light sheen of sweat from his forehead, he looked around with satisfaction. *Looks like I'm posing for a picture-book illustration of "The Woodcutter's Cottage,"* he decided with a half-smile. Then his thoughts ambled a bit. *What made me think of such a thing, I wonder. Picture book at the orphanage, maybe, when I was real young? Kinda fuzzy, but I can see it . . . "The Woodcutter's Cottage" . . .*

Growing up in the crowded orphanage in Charleston, South Carolina, had not really been too bad, Shiloh had long ago decided. It was clean; the food was nutritious and plentiful, if not exactly delicious; and the stolid German women who ran it believed that educating the orphans was as important as providing a roof over their heads and food for their bodies.

But Shiloh had no one to reinforce and solidify his childhood, to make it stay real to him as he grew, and adult thoughts crowded out remembrances of the child. No stories of his childhood experiences were repeated over and over by proud parents, no brother or sister teased or taunted him with stories of when he was little. So when wisps of memories such as this came to him, he tried very hard to capture them and hold them. But mostly they were so vague and uncertain that he simply let the layers of years cover them again, instead of allowing the visions and smells and touches of a small boy to sharpen his sense of loss.

Now, as Maeva Wilding and Glen Rawlins rounded the corner of Maeva's cabin, talking and laughing, Shiloh pushed away the bit of childhood to smile at the two.

"That's enough, Shiloh," Maeva commanded, nodding at the full cord of wood stacked against the wall of her cabin. "I thank you both." Shiloh and Glen had come to Maeva's mountain at dawn that morning to gather and split wood for her.

"You're welcome, Maeva," Glen replied. "An' I think you orter lemme have some more o' that molasses fer my trouble."

Shiloh had taught them to make candy by drizzling warm molasses on clean snow. He was surprised that the two had never done this, but they were as absorbed and delighted as children as he showed them how to make the crunchy sweet.

"No," Maeva told Glen flatly. "You've et enough o' that candy. So have I. An' them horses is gonna be colicky if'n you keep givin' it to 'em."

"But they like it so good," Glen objected, then added slyly, "An' they ain't had no muskydines lately. They miss them somethin' awful!"

"Especially Sock," Shiloh grunted. "I've never seen a horse so sad as when I ran out of them. Kept roughing up my saddlebags so bad hunting for them, I had to quit hanging them up by his stall!"

"Yeah, but you was smart, keepin' 'em in yore saddlebags," Glen said mournfully. "I kept 'em in a little pouch inside my shirt."

Shiloh and Maeva laughed, for they had seen Beauregard almost knock Glen down trying to check him for muscadine stashes. Then Maeva's eyes went to Shiloh thoughtfully, and her face became still and composed, as it always did when she was considering something.

He noticed the intensity of her scrutiny and started to tease her about it, but he was momentarily distracted. Everything around Maeva on this day seemed to emphasize her exotic good looks. The titanium white of the landscape contrasted sharply with her bronzed face and made her blue eyes deepen into sapphire. Sun brilliance made her smooth hair glimmer with bluish-black highlights. She wore a simple woolen dress of dark gray with a high, modest neckline, although the heady scent she wore was an unspoken denial of the severity of her clothing.

But the cape thrown carelessly about her shoulders was what distracted Shiloh. Full-length, cleverly tailored, with a hood now thrown back to make a high imperial collar around her neck, it was made entirely of white fur. The combination of the dramatic cloak and Maeva's primitive beauty made Shiloh's mind again wander over forgotten bits of fairy tales.

Shiloh and Maeva both came out of their momentary reveries. "I wanna take you up to Blackcastle Springs today, Shiloh," Maeva said decisively.

"Finally!" he grinned. "I was beginning to think maybe that place hid a dark secret of yours—or maybe you just imagined it!"

"Kin I come?" Glen asked. "I ain't been up there in a long time. Bet it's somethin' to see in snow."

Now Maeva considered Glen with deliberation. He, too, was accustomed to Maeva's ways, and bore her scrutiny patiently. "Yes," she finally said, then turned to go back to the front of the cabin, the cape swirling in white waves behind her. "Wait for me."

Glen turned back to Shiloh to ask in a slightly furtive, hasty tone, "What's it like in there?"

"You mean in her cabin?" Shiloh asked in confusion.

"Yeah," he nodded anxiously. "I ain't niver been in there. Don't reckon no one has I know of, 'cept you."

Shiloh was shocked. Glen had been friends with Maeva since childhood. For years he had been keeping her supplied with wood in winter, sharing his game with her, making certain she had food staples, taking her to far-off calls of distress and escorting her home. The thought that he had never been in Maeva's cabin seemed unthinkable to Shiloh, for he knew that Maeva liked Glen Rawlins very much; more importantly she seemed to trust him implicitly. Shiloh had taken Maeva's invitations to come inside on his visits for granted, but now he realized that what had seemed like simple etiquette to him might be something very different to Maeva.

"It's just a cabin," he replied lightly. "Not much different from yours, except for the plants."

"Plants!" Glen exclaimed. "You mean growin' inside the house?" From his astounded expression, Shiloh saw that Glen probably pictured a dirt floor with grass and weeds and flowers growing right up to the windowsills.

"In pots and things," Shiloh tried to explain. "You know, like some people have nice big plants to decorate their houses. But Maeva's aren't exactly like that, either—most of 'em are little, in little boxes or something—but she does have some big ones, too."

Glen's dark eyes grew round above his bushy beard. "Are you a-tellin' me," he demanded in a voice raw with disbelief, "that you really know peoples that bring dirt *inside their house*—on purpose? In pots! An' then try to grow stuff—*inside their house?*"

Shiloh rubbed the distinctive "V" scar beneath his eye and muttered, "Never thought of it exactly like that. . . ."

Glen shook his head and made funny little grunting sounds. "Mm, mm, mm! If that don't beat the fur off'n all I ever heard!"

"Did you give her that cape?" Shiloh asked abruptly.

"What? Oh, no. She's had it for a coupla-three winters now." He hesitated, then went on uncertainly, "I think T. R. Satterfield give the skins to her, an' she made the cape. Drives me crazy, 'cause she's got some kinda way to soften hides an' preserve 'em, an' she won't tell nobody 'bout it." He went on chattily for a few moments, casting sidelong glances at Shiloh to try and gauge his reaction. But Shiloh's face looked only mildly thoughtful.

"What kind of fur is it?" he asked finally. This morning had been the first time Shiloh had seen her wear the cloak. When she had come outside to greet them in the dim pre-dawn, he had, quite without intending to, reached out to stroke the fur, and Maeva had grown still and smiled up at him as he did. The coat was rather coarse on top, but fine underneath, and the hide seemed to be very resilient.

"You don't know?" Glen asked with surprise. "Why, it's white wolf."

"I'm ready," Maeva announced as she rounded the corner. "Let's go." She was carrying a large leather pouch that looked about half full.

"Here, let me put that in the saddlebag," Shiloh offered, reaching for the pouch.

"No. We're walkin', Shiloh. An' don't you fuss, with them long legs of yourn!" They entered the quiet woods surrounding Maeva's cabin and began a slow ascent. "An' no hollerin' about snakes, neither, cold as it is!"

"You mean this place doesn't have snow snakes?" Shiloh half joked. Snakes still frightened him. "Sure seems to have every other kind!"

Glen and Maeva chuckled.

The three climbed steadily upward to a ridge connecting Maeva's mountain with Blackcastle Springs Mountain. Although it was cold, the vigorous climb and the quick pace set by Maeva kept them warm. Shiloh's and Glen's boots were wet, but they kept them so well-oiled that it didn't penetrate to their thick woolen socks. Maeva wore her knee-high moccasins, and Shiloh worried that they weren't warm enough for her. He also noticed that because of the lightness of her step and the softness of her footwear, she left almost no visible tracks except where the snow was deep.

They dipped down between the mountains, then began to climb again. The woods on this slope were almost all pine, with an occasional stunted cedar. The ascent was gentler, Shiloh noticed, but it was harder walking because of the rough, rocky ground under the snow covering. Once Shiloh had to lift Maeva up onto a flat shelf that rose abruptly waist-high in front of them.

Then it looked to Shiloh as if Maeva walked into a rock; but of course, she had made a turn into a narrow rock hallway that wound and twisted around strange, jutting black rocks that stuck out of the mountainside at sharp angles. Warm drafts trickled by them, touching their cold cheeks with invisible fingers. The bizarre pathway opened out onto Blackcastle Springs, and at last Maeva stepped through the opening, with Shiloh and Glen close behind her.

To Shiloh, Blackcastle Springs instantly struck him as a place not made for man's footsteps. The look of the place was dark and brooding, the coppery smell of the water made his nostrils flare, the illogical heat of the place disturbed him on a deep level. Unconsciously he stepped closer to Maeva.

★　★　★　★

To Caroline it seemed that Maeva and the two men suddenly materialized out of the solid rock wall behind the pool where she was wading in the steaming, uneasy waters. She screamed, a sharp cut-off shriek of panic as she stuck her fist in her mouth to stifle it, and then began to scramble toward the low side of the enclosure.

"Be still, child," Maeva said briskly, walking toward the pool. "I reckon you scairt me as bad as I scairt you."

"No—I—go away—!" Caroline panted hysterically, struggling painfully to untie her two petticoats and wool skirt from around her hips as she fought her way through the knee-high waters.

"Caroline!" Maeva called sharply. "Be still! Yore jist stirrin' the pool up worst, an' you might fall!"

But Caroline still fought the waters and her clothes, her eyes darting to Glen Rawlins' huge form as he hurried to the side of the pool. Stepping up onto the narrow ledge, he held out his hand to her and said in a gentle baritone, "Hit's all right, Caroline. You jis' take yore time an' let me help you. You step right up here now, afore you let yore skirts git in the water. You know you cain't leave outen here in wet clothes." His voice was low and soothing, as if he were trying to gentle a wild horse.

Abruptly Caroline stopped struggling and thrashing and stood still in the pool for a moment, her head bowed. She took a deep breath, then reached out to take Glen's outstretched hand, though she did not look up to meet his eyes. Slowly she waded to the side, the water bubbling just above her knees, and stepped up onto the flat-topped rock where Glen stood. Immediately she snatched her hand back, pulled on the hem of her skirts where they were tucked into the waistband, and smoothed them down with a shaking hand.

In that brief instant she stood on the rock, Shiloh couldn't help but see the misshapen right leg. Between her ankle and knee was an angle where none should be, and an uneven lump grew in the corner of the angle. *Compound fracture of the tibia*, he analyzed, *and set improperly. Must have happened some time ago—looks like some calcification. . . .*

Glen stepped off the rock, then turned to pick Caroline up as if she were a small child and set her down beside him. Her head was lowered, but Shiloh could see the high color on her cheeks.

"Caroline, I didn't think 'bout you bein' here, sweetie," Maeva said for an apology. "But I'm glad you are. This here's Shiloh Irons. Shiloh, this here's Caroline Satterfield."

Shiloh snatched off his black hat. "Howdy, ma'am. I'm pleased to finally meet you, since Jimmy Dale's told me about you."

Caroline raised her head for the first time, and Shiloh was surprised at the clearness of her hazel eyes and her expression, now calm and still. "Howdy, Mr. Irons. You know Jimmy Dale?"

"Yep," Shiloh nodded. "Count him as a friend."

"He told you about me?" Caroline asked carefully.

Shiloh realized that her question implied, *He told you about his crippled sister?* so he smiled warmly at her and answered, "He

208

told me he had another sister, prettier even than Lorine."

In no way did Shiloh anticipate the devastation his light but truthful answer would cause Caroline. Her face crumpled, her eyes immediately filled with tears, and again she dropped her head. "I need to git my shoes on," she muttered painfully. "I feel like a idiot standin' here in my bare feet."

"Too bad," Glen said heartily, maneuvering to block Caroline as she took a halting step toward her shoes lying a small distance away. " 'Cause I'm gonna wade in that there pool, an' you're a-comin' back in with me. My feet are cold, and that steamy water looks pretty good right now." He sank down to the rock and began to tug at one knee-high boot, grunting with the effort. "C'mon, Caroline, don't jis' stand there laughin'! Gimme a hand!"

Caroline seemed far from laughter. Her face had darkened with doubt at Glen's words, and she watched him dumbly as he yanked on the stubborn boot. Suddenly she straightened, swiped her hand across her eyes as if removing a veil, and a small smile transformed her face. "But I'll—I ain't sure if I kin do that, Glen," she whispered. "I dunno if I'm strong enough."

"Well, fer cryin' out loud, Caroline!" Glen gasped. "I'm strong enough, but it don't seem to be doin' me no good! You jis' c'mere and help me, and then we'll wade 'til our feets wrinkles up like raisins!"

Shiloh grinned as Caroline limped slowly to grab Glen's enormous boot. "Maeva, let's go wading—" he began, but there was no sign of Maeva on the plateau. "She got away again," he muttered. "Have the hardest time keeping up with that woman!"

"Don't envy you that chore none," Glen muttered, twisting and turning his leg. Caroline was working on the other boot now, her eyes shining with shy merriment as she glanced up at Glen.

Shiloh almost made a disparaging remark about Lorine Satterfield leading Glen a merry chase, but the vision of Caroline's stricken face rose up in his mind. *Uh-oh*, he thought, *that's it.*

Caroline's in love with Glen—and he's like a blind, deaf, and dumb man over Lorine, her sister! Uh-oh. "Gonna go find Maeva," he mumbled, and disappeared back into the narrow entrance of the pathway.

Finally Caroline managed to yank Glen's other boot off, and he rolled up his denim breeches to his knees. Blushing hotly, Caroline again bent to pull up her skirts and tuck them into her waistband as Glen jumped into the spring. Then he held out his arms to her, and she allowed him to pick her up by the waist and set her into the pool. *He niver looks at my leg, or seems like he notices I'm crippled,* she thought. *Even when peoples is good at hidin' it, you kin allus see the shadows behind their eyes. 'Cept Glen.*

"You know Miss Duvall pretty good, doncha?" she asked with studied carelessness. Stopping to look down, she wiggled her toes in the warmth that was almost hot.

"Doctor Cheney? Guess so." Glen shrugged.

They walked in slow circles, the steaming water bubbling gently above Caroline's knees and below Glen's. Finally Caroline said in a low voice, "You reckon she's a good doctor?"

"Yep."

Again there was a long silence, but it was a comfortable silence, for though Caroline felt awkward about the intensity of her feelings for Glen, she had known him since she was born. When she was unguarded they lapsed into a lifetime's familiarity. "You think she could help me?" Caroline asked humbly.

"Dunno, Caroline," he answered matter-of-factly. "She's onliest one can answer that. Or Shiloh might know."

"No!" Caroline exclaimed. "He's—I ain't sure—I mean, I don't want—"

Glen stopped wading to look up at Caroline curiously. At the sight of her stricken face, he moved close and put his great arms around her small shoulders. "Now, don't you worry, little girl. I unnerstan'. You don't want Maeva to know, do you?" He sighed, and the great breath he took made Caroline cling hard to him, her heart beating too fast. "I ain't sayin' nothin' to nobody 'bout your business. An' neither will Doctor Cheney." To himself he reflected, *Maeva ain't the problem, little girl, and you know it. Ain't no tellin' what "Daddy" would do if'n he found out you went to the lady doctor. Reckon I better stick close to Doctor Cheney, and Shiloh, too. . . .*

Caroline made herself forget that Glen had called her "little girl" as he did his sisters. She erased Lorine's beautiful, sultry face from her mind. She ignored the weakness in her right leg as the water swirled around it. Her small hands were at Glen's sides, and her head rested against his chest. His heartbeat, a strong, regular rhythm, warmed her in the enclosure of his great arms. They stood motionless for long moments in the troubled pool of Blackcastle Springs.

★   ★   ★   ★

Shiloh was only about halfway down the rock hallway when Maeva materialized in front of him, and he jumped with shock. "How'd you do that?" he snapped.

Maeva put her hands around his neck and looked up at him slyly. "How do you think I done it? Rode my broom down from the top?"

"Maybe," he grinned, then bent and brushed her lips lightly. "Where'd you go?"

She let go of him and swept by to lead him back toward the springs. "Hadda go git some things," she answered vaguely, as she so often did.

He questioned her no more, but his face looked troubled. So she patted her now-bulging pouch and explained, "I went to git some muskydines fer them fool horses! And I hadda git some things I need fer Eula Ray Trask. She's a-gonna have some stomach trouble."

Now Shiloh gave her an incredulous look. "Going to have?"

Maeva laughed, and the sound echoed eerily in the black crystal hallway they traveled. "Oh, Shiloh! Don't tell me you're startin' to b'lieve everthin' you hear 'bout me! Eula Ray allus has stomach trouble 'zackly four days after Christmas—so poor little Wanda Jo Satterfield will be knockin' on my door come mornin'!" Eula Ray Trask was Levi Satterfield's mother-in-law, the old woman who had screamed most of the night when Shiloh and Cheney operated on Isaac.

Shiloh struggled to stay expressionless as Maeva spoke, for he suspected that from now on Levi Satterfield's family would be knocking on Cheney's door instead of Maeva's. Shiloh flatly refused to discuss Maeva's business with Cheney, and was just as determined never to discuss Cheney with Maeva. *But Maeva never asks,* he thought in spite of a sneaking feeling of disloyalty to Cheney. Hastily he said, "Tell me about Caroline."

Maeva walked slowly upward, her face lifted toward the bleak rock face rising in front of them. "She fell ten years ago this New Year. From up there." Her slender finger with the perfect oval nail pointed to the peak of the castle wall just ahead. "She were only nine then. Broke her laig somethin' awful, an' she were by herself."

"What?" Shiloh exclaimed with dread. "Alone? What . . . how . . . who found her?"

"After two days," Maeva whispered, "I did."

15

SONS ACCURSED

Each man present in Waylon DeSpain's office was well aware that Mr. DeSpain was not happy. His clothing and hair and hands were, as usual, immaculate and tastefully done. But his normal expression of smooth congeniality had changed to cold anger as soon as he came through the office door.

"Sit down, Bake!" DeSpain barked as Conroy took his usual crossed-arm stance by his desk. "Quit standing over me like I need a bodyguard or something!"

Conroy moved clumsily and slowly to pull up a chair, his face distorted with impotent anger. He looked and moved like a wounded bear. Four angry red gashes ran from his forehead down to below his jawline. One scratch had slashed right down his swollen left eye, and the white of the eye was a painful blood-red.

Tim Toney and Gabe Stroud exchanged meaningful glances as Conroy took his seat by Leslie Day. Conroy seemed to be falling out of favor with DeSpain, and it had all begun with Conroy's coarse treatment of Dr. Cheney Duvall at the saloon. Tim Toney had spent long hours speculating on that event, and Mr. DeSpain's reaction to it. But he suspected—quite rightly—that no one except Leslie Day completely understood all of Waylon DeSpain's actions and reactions.

Now, however, Tim Toney came out of his reverie to pay close attention as DeSpain addressed them in a voice of tightly reined fury. "You men listen to me. We've got several problems here, and I'm losing my patience. I considered calling in some outside—assistance," he pronounced sarcastically, "but Mr. Day has convinced me that my best bet is to stick with you."

Stroud, Toney, and Conroy looked at Leslie Day with ill-concealed surprise. Day, who looked like an undertaker in solid black except for the two starched white points of his collar, remained impassive. He sat still, the large round circles of glass covering his eyes glinting eerily as he watched the boss.

DeSpain yanked open the top drawer of his desk, snatched up a cigar, stuck it in his mouth, and violently snapped the top of a match with his thumbnail. Inhaling deeply, he blew out a straight plume of thin gray smoke. "So I'm going to stick with you all right—and I'm sure you're going to stick with me. Never mind, Stroud," he grunted rudely as Gabe opened his mouth for his usual fervent declaration of loyalty. "Just listen, all of you. I'm going to talk straight, I'm going to say this once, and I expect you all to understand what I want."

"Whatever you want," Gabe could not help but saying.

"I want some coffee, Gabe," Toney remarked brightly.

"Tim," was all DeSpain said, but Tim Toney sat up straighter and turned back to face his boss. DeSpain's iron eyes searched the faces of Stroud, Toney, and Conroy, and then he gave an imperceptible nod to Day as he continued, "I got a verbal contract with Jimmy Dale Satterfield yesterday to buy forty acres north of Maeva's Trace, at two dollars an acre."

"Well, heck-fire, Mr. DeSpain, thass good!" Conroy ventured. Gabe's head bobbed enthusiastically, but Tim Toney's expression remained grave.

"That's nothing," DeSpain countered in a tight voice. Conroy's grin was erased instantly, and Gabe's head jerked to a stop. "I should own about three thousand acres by now, but counting that forty acres, I now own around six hundred."

"Six hundred eighteen," Mr. Day hummed.

"Thank you," DeSpain nodded curtly.

"That's some real good timberland, Mr. DeSpain," Tim said thoughtfully. "Ol' Enoch wouldn't sell it to you, but his son did?"

"That's right, Tim." DeSpain nodded approvingly. "And it may have been because of you." Bake Conroy's frown deepened and the scratches became a fiery red. DeSpain went on, "Jimmy Dale didn't make any small talk about selling, so it may have been because of your idea about burning the smokehouse. So you did good, Tim—but we're going to have to do better."

"What else do you want us to do, Mr. DeSpain?" Gabe asked eagerly. "We been poppin' a shot or two at them Carters every day they're down there clearin' at the foot of the Trace, just like you told us. We scared them two kids good, too, that day Tim shot all around 'em like there was three, four gunmen there!"

"Yes, Gabe," DeSpain nodded wearily, "but what good has it all done? You can't shoot at people—especially marksmen like Jimmy Dale Satterfield—for long, just for fun, because they're not going to understand that we're just trying to make them mad! They're going to jump up and shoot back, eventually! Like the Carters have been doing, when you're out there waving your pistols and shooting in the air like drunk cowboys!"

"You're sure right about that, Mr. DeSpain," Gabe agreed enthusiastically. "It ain't doin' no good, is what I say!"

"Gabe," Tim sighed, "you're scaring me."

"Huh? I thought you weren't scared of nothin'!" was Stroud's astonished reply.

But Tim ignored him and turned back to Waylon DeSpain. "But I thought that was what you wanted, Mr. DeSpain. For them to start shooting."

"Yes, Tim," DeSpain said indulgently, "but not at you. At each other. And that's the problem, you see. We want Wolf County to be such a hellhole that both Enoch Satterfield and Lige Carter will jump at the chance to sell their land—and we want them to sell it to us. Not shoot us."

"Ohhh," Gabe breathed with sudden revelation.

Leslie Day nodded, a slight, taut gesture, and Tim's eyes narrowed thoughtfully. But Bake Conroy's wide forehead furrowed with incomprehension. He didn't understand politics, he didn't understand why Mr. DeSpain was angry with him, and his face hurt.

DeSpain watched his men's reactions, and again he and Leslie Day exchanged a look of mutual assent as they saw Bake Conroy's blank expression. "Now we're going to take each problem one at a time, and I'm going to tell you exactly what I want you to do," DeSpain said tightly. "First of all, I need some quick money. My investors are choking up because this is taking so much longer than I thought. Now, I've come up with a way to get it." He paused for emphasis, and the room was still and quiet. "Blackcastle Springs," he said.

"That worthless piece of rock?" Gabe exclaimed.

DeSpain nodded to Leslie Day and stuck the stub of the cigar in his mouth with an impatient gesture. Day said in his precise voice, "That rock is called obsidian. Originally it was only used by the Indians to make arrowheads, I believe. But now it is classified as a semiprecious stone and is currently enjoying a wide sweep of popularity as ornamentation of ladies' fashions."

"Wait a minute," Conroy growled, his patience wearing even thinner as the conversation seemed to be turning to women's fripperies. "You said that rock's enjoyin' what?"

"Bake, it's called 'jet,'" DeSpain interpreted impatiently. "They're small black beads that trim ladies' hats, reticules, sometimes skirts and shawls. Just take my word for it. Right now I've found—excuse me, *Mr. Day* has found a buyer, a Frenchman, who'll take all of it we can haul to Fort Smith. We won't even have to mine Blackcastle Springs, we can get tons of it with a pickax right now. Then we can blast the whole accursed mountain and pick the stuff up off the ground."

Tim Toney said shrewdly, "I know you wanted to buy Blackcastle Springs anyways, Mr. DeSpain, because it's in a line of hills with good timber. I suppose it's not in the six hundred"—he stopped to wink impudently at Leslie Day—"and eighteen acres you own?"

"No, it's not, and that's the first big problem," DeSpain replied with exasperation. "When Mr. Day and I went to Little Rock to check the state surveyor's maps and try to find out who owns what around here, I found out that Maeva Wilding, of all people, owns Blackcastle Springs!"

Stunned silence greeted this revelation. DeSpain allowed it to sink in, then said in a businesslike tone, "So I need to buy it from her. And of course she doesn't know anything about obsidian, so I can make her a respectable offer that will still make me some money. And Tim, I've decided to give you a little more responsibility, so I want you to go talk to her. Tell her that we'll build her a little cabin here in town, where she can be closer to all of her patients, or whatever she calls 'em. And tell her that we'll supply her with firewood for the next five years. In addition to the money, of course."

Bake Conroy's anger at DeSpain's words was obvious. His breathing, erratic and loud, sounded like a bull's outraged snort in the quiet room, and he clenched and opened his fists several times.

But Tim Toney merely settled back in his chair, crossed one booted ankle over one knee, and idly spun his silver spur. "Mr. DeSpain," he said evenly, though his brown eyes were fixed steadily on Bake Conroy, "I guess I better tell you right now that Maeva Wilding ain't gonna be too happy to see any DeSpain men."

DeSpain followed the direction of Tim's gaze, and blue steel glints shone in his eyes. "Bake," he said in an ominously low voice, "don't tell me you've been bothering Maeva Wilding! I've told you over and over again to leave these women alone, you fool! First place, I just don't like men that treat women bad! Never have! And even if my wishes don't mean anything to you"—his voice dripped with venomous sarcasm—"you better know right now that running over Maeva Wilding will get every muzzle-loader in the country trained right square on us!"

Bake dropped his head to stare at the floor, his shoulders hunched defensively, and said nothing. In a telling gesture, one meaty hand went up to lightly trace the wide scratches on his face. DeSpain jumped up and slammed both hands down on his desk. "Do you mean to tell me that Maeva did that? You stupid—!"

DeSpain threw himself back down to sprawl in his chair and

wheeled it around, away from the men, to face out the window. The room was silent for long moments. Leslie Day, his detached expression intact, had not moved; Gabe Stroud looked positively frightened; Tim spun his silver spur, which made no sound; and Bake Conroy hunched over, shame evident in the sagging line of his shoulders.

DeSpain turned back around, his face drawn into tight lines of deliberate control. "All I'm going to say, Bake, is you'd better do what I say or you are going to regret it, I promise you." Somehow the careful pronunciation and deliberate spacing between the words sounded more threatening than his former anger.

"Yes, sir," Conroy muttered almost inaudibly.

DeSpain began again. "Now, let me tell you a couple of things very clearly and slowly, since some of you don't seem to understand anything about what I want!" His voice rose scathingly, and he shook his head with frustration, trying to remain calm and impassive.

"May I?" Day asked ironically, and DeSpain nodded savagely.

"You must understand two things," Day declared in his headmaster's voice. "One is that, in order to facilitate—that is," he amended dryly with an oblique glance at Conroy, "to make it easy for Mr. DeSpain to buy these people's land, we have to make them fight each other. That way, they will no longer want to live here, and they will no longer want their children to be raised here. Do you understand?" He glanced at each man in turn for affirmation, and the three nodded obediently.

"Now the second thing that you must understand," he went on pedantically, "is that there are two people who could possibly unite the people of Wolf County. Bring them together," he added with a another fishlike glance at Conroy, "and end the feud. One of them is Maeva Wilding, and the other is Glen Rawlins."

"So?" Bake dared to growl, his head still down.

"So," Day said patiently, "if you cannot be friends with them, then stay away from them, so as not to give them any cause to take a stand. So far neither of them has shown any wish to interfere with the Satterfields and the Carters. They are neutral observers, if you will."

"Don't even ask, Bake," DeSpain grunted. "Just stay away from them. Especially Maeva!"

"So that's why you didn't plan to buy any of Rawlins' land," Tim said thoughtfully. "You just didn't want to stir him up. But what about Blackcastle Springs?"

"I guess I'll have to go talk to Maeva myself," DeSpain snapped, "and apologize to her! That is not something that I really care to do, but it looks like it's the only way, thanks to you!" His disgusted gaze raked up and down the defeated Conroy. "I don't know why you want to mess around with that woman anyway, Bake! She is trouble, any fool could see that! Serve you right if those nails of hers were poisoned!"

"Yep," Toney agreed cheerfully, "and you sure couldn't go see Dr. Duvall, even if you was turnin' all green and slimy and the rest of your hair fell out and you was gurglin' your last breath from poison, could you, Bake?"

"Loathsome," Day commented fussily.

"Wouldn't be anyone's fault but your own, Bake," DeSpain grunted. "I'm sending you to Fort Smith for supplies. Get you out of here—and away from me—for a couple of days."

"Yes, sir," Conroy muttered.

DeSpain turned to Tim and Gabe. "One thing I'm sending Bake to Fort Smith for is to buy some Enfields for you men. Like I said, shooting pistol shots in the air hasn't done much good so far; but if we can really make it look like Carters are shooting Satterfields and Satterfields are shooting Carters, I have a feeling that pretty soon I'll be able to buy all the land I want. So for now, I want you to step up the gunplay; hit the Carters in the fields, and start watching for the Satterfields out hunting. But I want you to be farther away from them, and more accurate. Make 'em dance. You understand?"

"Yes, sir," Tim nodded.

"I'm a real good shot with a rifle," Gabe bragged.

"Hope so," Tim commented, "since you couldn't hit a buffalo you were riding bareback, with a pistol."

DeSpain grinned faintly, and even though it was at his expense, Gabe felt relieved. "And springing the Satterfields' traps was a good idea, Tim," DeSpain went on expansively. "Keep it up. The hungrier they are, the more land they'll sell."

Tim looked puzzled, then sighed. "Well, Mr. DeSpain, I ain't never been a man to take credit if it ain't due. Me and Gabe ain't been out springing their traps."

"But we sure will now, Mr. DeSpain, sure will," Gabe added.

"You haven't?" DeSpain exclaimed, then glanced at Conroy, who shrugged moodily. A light came over Waylon DeSpain's smooth features, and his smile became wide with pleasure. "Then, Tim, I don't guess it'll be necessary for you to start springing them. It seems that our friends the Carters must be doing that little chore all by themselves."

★ ★ ★ ★

"I ain't no man fer makin' long speeches. But the time's here when I got some things that need sayin' to you two." With grim deliberation, Enoch Satterfield ran the oiled cloth down the long barrel of his Sharps rifle. Squinting down at it with one hazel eye shut, he moved the rag in meticulous circles, polishing an imaginary smudge.

Enoch, T. R., and Jimmy Dale sat at one end of the long table in the Satterfields' incongruously cheerful kitchen. The yellow tablecloth glowed benevolently, the whitewashed walls and floors were spotless, and outside the two windows the white winter sun glittered on a snow blanket that softened all the harshness of the view. But the faces of the men were drawn and grim, and Enoch's voice rasped low with strain.

"I let the babies have Christmas 'thout stirrin' nothin' up. But now Christmas is four days gone, an' it's time fer the Satterfields to take an accountin'.'" He dropped the block with an ominous crack, blew into the breech, and peered down the wide tunnel of the barrel. Daubing at the mortises in the receiver walls with the rag he continued, "We're lookin' at a long, lean

220

winter." With another businesslike snap he slammed together the stock and barrel. "So we're gonna hunt, and we're gonna protect our family."

Enoch laid his gun across his lap, leaned back in his chair, crossed his muscular arms across his chest, and searched his sons' faces with a dark gaze. "Carters started by inchin' up the east side o' Maeva's Trace, takin' one step an' then 'nother on land that orter belong to us. Carters shot at you, Jimmy Dale, jist fer bein' on Maeva's Trace."

Jimmy Dale's eyes flickered and his hands, clasped together on the table, jerked convulsively, but Enoch seemed not to notice.

"Then they started springin' T. R.'s traps." Enoch's hazel eyes narrowed and beneath the drooping mustache, his jaw tightened into a hard, unforgiving line. "But that weren't enough! They hadda come burn down my smokehouse! That I ain't gonna forgive—nor forget!"

"Let's ride tonight, Pa!" T. R. snarled as he slammed his palm on the table. "Ain't a man in this county what'll say us wrong! Let's burn 'em!"

"No!" Jimmy Dale shouted.

Enoch Satterfield's burning gaze raked over his younger son. "You, boy," he spat, "seems like all you keer about is dreamin' or singin' or pickin' flowers! Yore the bestest shot in miles, you kin hunt better'n a hungry wolf—but yore so took up with whatever fool dreams is crowdin' yore head that you cain't take keer o' yore own!"

T. R. snorted derisively, and Enoch's fiery gaze turned on him. "And you! You got too much hot blood in yore head an' not enough brains! An' too much corn whisky in your veins. But both of you is gonna shut up an' listen to me!"

Jimmy Dale's face was pale and strained, but he met Enoch's eyes steadily. T. R. looked cowed and ducked his head.

Enoch went on in a tightly controlled voice, "You two boys are my eldest sons, an' you both been good boys in yore own ways. T. R., you allus done ever'thin' I ever tole you. Jimmy

221

Dale—" He paused for a moment, and seemed to gather and weigh his thoughts. "Son, I know yore an honorable man, an' a good fightin' man. Learnt that of both of ye for the first time at Pea Ridge."

His deep, raw voice grew thicker, and he nodded his head with a touch of sorrow in the gesture. "I knows yore different from me an' T. R., Jimmy Dale. I ain't in the way of unnerstandin' 'zackly what kinda man you've growed to be—but I know yore a man. I even allowed fer you bein' different, like that night I didn't make you ride with us to that doctor woman's, on account o' you tellin' me respectful-like that you couldn't do it."

Only now did Jimmy Dale's eyes drop to the table. With an effort he kept his clasped hands still. *Smokehouse burned while I was lookin' down a rifle sight at my own pa*, his mind agonized for the thousandth time. *Feels like the Gates o' Hell opened right up in my insides. Worst part is, he ain't niver ast me nothin' about that night . . .'cause he trusts me . . . worst part . . .* A sickening, raw lump in his throat made him keep silent.

Enoch sighed, a small, broken sound. Then he seemed to shake off his sorrow. His eyes began to burn as if he had fever, and when he spoke, Jimmy Dale thought it sounded like a bear growling in its throat just before it opens its maw. "They took meat outta my babies' mouths! Night-sneakin' and slitherin' to wage war on women and children! I say now, they better git ready to stand up like men and fight!" Enoch jumped up, and the chair smashed against the floor. His knuckles were bloodless as he gripped his rifle and shook it over his son's heads. "My sons might be cursed—but ain't none o' my children gonna be blooded without a fight!"

The roar of his voice seemed to echo in the kitchen, as if the three men were in an airless chamber. T. R. jumped up and grabbed the barrel of Enoch's rifle, and his father clasped a raw-boned hand over his.

Slowly Jimmy Dale looked up, and his eyes burned a steady flame of anger. Then he stood, and with a deliberate gesture, clasped his hand over those of his father and his brother.

★ ★ ★ ★

Lige Carter shook his head firmly and repeated in a louder voice, "I said, we ain't a-gonna go work down by Maeva's Trace no more today! I'm tired o' duckin' shots fer one day!"

Josh and Dane Carter glanced at each other as they followed their father's stiff figure up the mountain. It was the highest peak in the Moccasin Mountains, except for Maeva's Trace. The Carters had never named this mountain, mostly because they had never been on it much, except when they all wandered it as children. It huddled up to the gentle hill where they had built their cabins, overshadowing the smaller one, but the Carters had for generations preferred kinder slopes and mountain meadows.

The three men climbed steadily to the top, and Josh noted with affectionate amusement that he and Dane were breathing heavily but Lige was not. Their father pumped his long legs in a steady, relaxed rhythm and kept his upper body loose, not fighting the mountain, simply making his stride fit the terrain.

They climbed for two hours, and soon they stood on an enormous rock ledge that afforded a breathtaking view of the valley below and Maeva's Trace beyond. Lige crossed his arms, and his unusual green eyes lit up with warmth as his gaze swept the land below him. Josh stood on one side, studying the snow-covered terrain with a more proprietary and assessing gaze than his father. Dane looked puzzled, even a little worried, as he watched Lige and Josh. At sixteen, he did not yet see the land his family had owned for generations as his history, his heritage, the very breath of his life; to him it was still simply property.

"I didn't bring you boys up here to gawk at the view," Lige murmured, "even if 'tis awful pretty." He turned to Josh, whose eyes lingered on the mountain meadows that his father had given him when he married Sharon. "Josh," Lige went on in a gentle tone, "this land is yourn now. But I don't want you jist to look at yore land. I want you to see Carter land. Do you un-nerstan' what that means?"

"Yes, sir," Josh nodded firmly. "I surely do. I been thinkin' a lot about what that means to our fambly—to me, to Sharon, to my baby . . . an' to his babies." He turned back to stare across the gently rolling valley.

A small frown of pain crossed Lige Carter's face as the angry scar on Josh's face was colored scarlet by the cold winter sun. Then he turned to his younger son. "Dane, most men don't even try to explain to their sons what the land means. Not until it's time for their sons to have land of their own. But 'cause of— who you are, and—what you are—" Lige choked slightly, the words thick in his throat.

"It's all right, Pa," Dane said quietly. "I think I know what you're tryin' to say. It's cause we's Carters, ain't it? An' me an' Josh, we're the ones who's gonna hafta fight for it. For bein' Carters, I think, an' for the land, too." He turned and pointed past Maeva's Trace to the blue-gray outline of Satterfield hills behind. "Us, an' T. R. and Jimmy Dale—we're all the sons of the curse."

"Good Lord have mercy," Lige groaned. "This is a hard thing to say to you two. I've knowed it all my life, o' course, an' yore ma has too, but we hoped—" He shrugged and turned his face back to the hills, his strong profile weakened with sorrow. "Then, when we all went to fight in the war . . . all of us . . . Josh an' T. R. was the onliest ones who got hurt. Outen all of us, only Josh an' T. R.," he repeated in a voice of sad wonder. "So then we knew."

"That's when you an' Ma knew the curse was true, an' it was gonna be on us?" Josh asked curiously.

Lige Carter shook his head. "No, son," he said sadly, "that's when me and Enoch Satterfield knew. We knew that each of us was the ones who'd lived in a time of peace, even though we had bad blood 'tween us. And we knew thet it wouldn't be that way fer our sons."

16

DELICATE OPERATIONS

Cheney sat at the large desk in the front room of her cabin, ostensibly writing a letter to Dev. But her eyes had wandered to the snowy view outside the window, and the long slender turkey quill in her hand was idle.

Christmas seemed to be a signal or something, she reflected idly. *Hardly anyone darkened my door before then, but now! Colds, sniffles, earaches—and lots of stomach upsets! That's because they all ate way too much, for days! Of course,* she sighed to herself, *almost all the gifts they exchanged were food.*

Again she envisioned the festivities on Christmas Eve at the church, knowing that Christmas goodwill was not the only reason for her sudden popularity. Levi and Ruthie Satterfield had brought Isaac to the pageant, bundled up until he was as round as a ball of twine, his pale face beaming out from the layers of clothes and homemade quilts.

Cheney had sternly checked him over after the pageant—it had not quite been two weeks since his surgery—but his incision was healing very quickly, almost miraculously, as often happened with children. Levi and Ruthie had showered her again with humble gratitude, Levi had tried to give her more of his hard-earned money, and Cheney had finally extricated herself with some embarrassment.

All Christmas Eve people had "viewed" Isaac Satterfield. Shifting crowds gathered around Ruthie and Isaac as they sat on a pew, and over and over again Isaac proudly showed them the lurid red scar running down his right side. Some people stepped backward hastily, their eyes invariably seeking out Cheney with shocked wonder; some people softly touched Isaac's taut little

225

tummy; some people frowned and hurried off, muttering ominously to themselves and shooting horrified glances at Cheney from the corners of their eyes. Since that night, however, Cheney had had a steady stream of patients.

Her reverie was interrupted by a knock at the door, which proved to be Ross Lee Sikes fetching a headache remedy for his mother.

Three more patients came early that morning, but the afternoon was quiet. It was almost dark when another soft knock sounded.

"Don't you git that there do'!" Rissy warned from the kitchen. "You the doctor, you ain't s'posed to be gittin' yo' own do'!"

"Rissy, I'm standing right here!" Cheney called with amusement as she threw open the heavy oak door.

Jimmy Dale and Caroline Satterfield stood on the front porch, Jimmy Dale close behind his sister as if to shield her from prying eyes. Caroline's smooth face was outlined by the crimson shawl as she stared up at Cheney and asked politely, "Please, kin we come in?"

"Certainly," Cheney answered, and stepped back for the two to enter. Jimmy Dale stepped in close behind Caroline, and in spite of herself Cheney glanced up and down the street cautiously before slamming the door and leaning against it.

"Thank you, Miss Duvall," Caroline said. "I mean, Dr. Duvall. I know you prob'ly niver wanted to see a Satterfield on yore porch agin." Tentatively she smiled at Cheney, and her clear hazel eyes held a plea that no doctor could mistake.

Cheney stood straighter, took Caroline's arm, and led her to the fire. Caroline followed obediently at her painfully uneven gait. "No, Caroline," Cheney replied in a determined voice. "I know why you're here, and I'm very glad you are. Jimmy Dale, why don't you go into the kitchen and ask Rissy for some hot tea or coffee. Sit down," she ordered Caroline, "and I'll examine you. Then we'll talk."

★ ★ ★ ★

First light, first day of 1866, Shiloh and Glen reined up in front of Cheney's small stable and led their steaming horses inside. Stocking whinnied happily as they entered. Shiloh led Sock into the open stall next to Stocking, and Glen led Beauregard into the next one.

Quickly they unsaddled the horses. When Shiloh finished, he slung the saddlebags over his shoulder and tried to hurry outside with them. But Sock lifted his head, sniffed accusingly, and took one nimble step forward. The big gelding clamped his strong jaw on the pouch hanging down Shiloh's back and gave a mighty jerk. Shiloh's feet almost flew out from under him, but instinctively he let go of the leather bags instead of yanking back. Wheeling around, he watched as his noble steed dropped his prize to the floor and maneuvered his entire snout inside the saddlebag as if it were a feed sack. Muffled smacking noises followed.

"Muskydines in there, huh?" Glen remarked idly as he watched Sock.

"How could you tell?" Shiloh replied caustically.

"Where does Maeva git them things?" Glen asked curiously. "Even with two foot o' snow on the ground, she conjures up them fresh grapes!"

"I don't know." Shiloh knelt and began to wrestle the saddlebags away from Sock, who fought back by clamping down on the flopped-open top of the bag. "She doesn't exactly flood me with information, you know." A tug-of-war ensued, and when Sock loosened his grip momentarily to try to get a better one, Shiloh yanked the saddlebags loose and tossed them out the shed door. Sock laid back his ears, snorted loudly, and stamped one hoof impatiently. "That's it, Sock!" Shiloh declared. "Those were supposed to be for Stocking anyway!"

Glen began to brush down Beauregard, who sniffed around his shirt just in case. Shiloh began cleaning up the soiled hay of the stable and dumping it into a small homemade wheelbarrow.

Shoveling and raking energetically, he wiped his forehead and removed his long canvas coat. Called a "fishskin" because it was oiled lightly to be waterproof, the coat was not particularly warm of itself, but was an excellent insulator if one wore enough layers underneath. It had originated in the West with men who lived on horseback. The back of the coat had a high slit, with a triangular piece sewn into the top of the slit, which fit neatly over the back ridge of the saddle as further protection against rain. Glen eyed it enviously. He had a heavy buffalo-skin great-coat for the cold weather, but it was bulky and too hot except for the dead of winter.

Glen hummed softly to himself for a while, currying his horse in time to the song. Then he stopped and said casually, "My pa give them two mountains to Maeva's ma, you know."

"What!" Shiloh's head jerked up. Then he slowly emptied the soiled hay into the wheelbarrow and leaned on the upright shovel. "Your father . . . and Maeva's mother . . ."

"Dunno nothin' more about it," Glen said lightly. "All's my pa tole me was that he give them two mountains outta my parcel to Justine Wilding when I was jist a little boy. They was hers, and passed to Maeva. Belongs to the Wildings as long as they live."

Shiloh's eyes narrowed as he searched Glen Rawlins' features. *The dark, straight hair, the long nose, wide nostrils, strong teeth . . . even the throaty, almost hoarse voice . . . must be true . . .*

"Me an' Maeva ain't never talked about it, Shiloh," Glen went on conversationally. "But I know she knows it. My daddy deeded that land over to Justine proper. Registered it in Little Rock, he did, an' give the deed to her."

"I see," Shiloh nodded. "I wouldn't say anything to her, you know."

"Yep."

Shiloh resumed mucking out, his thoughts busy on this revelation. It was another facet of Maeva Wilding revealed, another piece of the puzzle, another stroke of the brush. He had spent a lot of time lately trying to understand this woman, but the fact that she was such a mystery didn't frustrate him. Quite the opposite, in fact.

The shed door creaked open, and Rissy came in holding a steaming coffeepot with a thick towel wrapped around the handle, and two plain white mugs. Her eyes were heavy-lidded and her voice raspy. "Reckon you two needs some hot coffee," she muttered. "If ennybody kin see good enough in the middle o' the night to get the cup to they mouths. An' if it ain't froze on the way out heah."

"Why, it's not even got real cold yet, Miss Rissy!" Glen teased. "When it gits real cold, the words freeze comin' outta yore mouth, an' you gotta read what folks says instead o' hearin' it!"

"Then I reckon," Rissy snapped, "onliest word peoples have to be able to read when they's talkin' to you is 'foolishness'!"

Glen grinned and shook his head. "I ain't even gonna try to best you no more, Miss Rissy!"

"Speaking of cold and early—you mean the Doc's up this time of the morning?" Shiloh demanded.

"Yas, suh, an' she says would somebody please saddle up her hoss an' she's gwine to see Miss Sharon," Rissy muttered as she made her way out the shed door.

Shiloh called after her, "Figured she was. Tell her I'm going with her."

"I'm comin' too," Glen declared.

Shiloh turned to Glen with a slight smile. "We don't need a bodyguard, you know, Glen. Enoch Satterfield's got other problems now, besides the Doc."

"Yep. But from what I've seed and heard lately, seems to me like you two need somebody to protect you from one-nother," Glen muttered with ill-humor.

Trudging over to the triangular saddle stand against the stable wall, Glen crossed his arms over his chest and looked doubtfully at the saddle mounted on it. Compared to a Western saddle, Cheney's sidesaddle was a study in minimalism with its simple lines. The leg grip sticking out of the side looked absurd to Glen, as if someone walking by the saddle had stuck a knob on it for lack of anything better to do; and the single stirrup made the entire saddle look unfinished. "This is Doctor Cheney's new saddle, huh?" he asked tentatively.

"Yep."

"The one you special-ordered, and then had to go to Fort Smith to pick up? This here saddle right here?"

"She can ride as good and as fast as you or me with it too. You oughta see her, when she's in that get-up—what do you call it?—riding habit. She's something to behold."

Glen shook his head with the familiar triple grunt. "Mm, mm, mm. Well, settin' on that there saddle," he said, nodding thoughtfully, "I kin see how a woman would git up some bad ridin' habits."

★ ★ ★ ★

"Katie and Bobbie Jo have been so good to Sharon," Cheney said enthusiastically. "It seems as though since Christmas everything has been going so well. I've had lots of patients, so it's been a real relief for me to know that Sharon's being taken care of. It's been a relief for Rissy, too, since she hasn't had to go back and forth to the Carters' to help Sharon," she added with a sidelong look at Shiloh, who was riding by her side. "Since she's been helping me so much at the office."

Shiloh dropped back a little, as they were reaching the narrow path leading up to the summit of White Wolf Ridge. Glen rode behind him, looking from side to side and up and down, trying to look like he wasn't listening.

"I've been busy, Doc," Shiloh muttered. "And you don't need my help to give out medicines for stomachaches and sniffles."

Cheney turned easily in her sidesaddle to face backward. "But I do need your help with Caroline Satterfield!" she burst out. "If you could tear yourself away from—" Abruptly she cut off the words, her face became smooth and bland, and she turned to face front.

"Wait a minute!" Shiloh demanded. He nudged Sock up

alongside Stocking and reached out to yank on Cheney's reins. Both horses stopped abruptly, and Glen stopped a few feet back with a deliberately nonchalant look on his face. Shiloh continued, "What do you mean, you need my help with Caroline Satterfield? You asked my opinion, and I gave it to you! Which was a waste of your time and my breath, since there's not much anyone can do for her, anyway! What do you need my help for?"

Cheney looked up at him with a pleading expression, but said nothing. Shiloh searched her face intently, but to his vague surprise, he simply didn't know what she wanted of him. Dropping Stocking's reins, he nodded curtly up the path. "Go on," he muttered, "no sense in this wagon train standing out here in the snow all day."

Cheney touched Stocking's side, and he obediently started up the path again. Shiloh dropped slightly behind, but Cheney could sense that he kept Sock close. "You didn't even give me a chance to talk to you about it, Shiloh," she said in a low, pained voice without looking back. "Before I could even tell you about it, you just shrugged and said that I'd be crazy to treat Caroline."

"But, Doc," Shiloh argued, "I think my reasoning was pretty obvious, don't you?"

"No."

Shiloh sighed loudly, and again pulled Sock up to stop Cheney. "All right, then, I'll lay it out for you, if that's what you're asking! In the first place, I've seen Caroline's leg, and I'm pretty sure I know what's wrong with it. So I know, Doc, that there's nothing much you can do! Face it," he insisted with a trace of anger, "Maeva's done the best anyone could do for her! Just the exercise of going back and forth all the way to the springs has kept her leg stronger than it should be! And the hot springs do seem to do some good, you know—"

"Shiloh!" Cheney snapped, her eyes flashing green glints. "Are you telling me that you believe that—that—ignorant mixture of hydrotherapy and homeopathy! You can't possibly!" Shaking her head, she went on mockingly, "Take the waters, they cure everything! And 'like cures like'—since Caroline broke her leg at Blackcastle Springs, making her go back there year after year is supposed to make her better! Such drivel!"

Shiloh's face closed, and he drawled in a monotone, "Doesn't matter what you call it or if you cuss it. Caroline's doing all right—and you can't do better."

"I can, too!" Cheney retorted hotly. "I can fix her l-leg! But I need your help to do it, and you're—you're— You won't help me!" she finished with a wail. Then she kicked Stocking soundly, and he bounded up the path at a fast clip.

"Wait, Cheney!" Shiloh called, and nudged Sock ahead to catch up to her.

Glen followed cautiously. Walking, galloping, and stopping from minute to minute unsettled both him and Beauregard. Under his breath he told the horse, "Yep, this here's some bad ridin' habits Doctor Cheney's got, fer sure."

"Wait a minute!" Shiloh called again. "I didn't know. . . . Will you just pull up and wait a minute!"

Finally reining Stocking to a stop, Cheney sat motionless, waiting for Shiloh to catch up. She sagged in the saddle, her shoulders hunched wearily, her head down. When Shiloh came up alongside, he reached out to tilt her head up with one finger so he could look directly into her eyes. "I didn't know, Doc, that you meant you needed my help for some kind of treatment for Caroline," he explained slowly.

Cheney's woebegone face slowly lit up as she spoke. "It's not a treatment, Shiloh, it's an operation. There's an operation I can do—I mean, we can do—to correct the problem with her leg!"

"What? What are you talking about? There's nothing anyone can do for a leg that was set wrong nine years ago!"

"Yes, there is!" Cheney insisted. "Dev and I have talked about it. There have been several successful ones on broken fingers, wrists, arms, legs—"

"In England, you mean."

"Well, yes," Cheney answered reluctantly, "but I can do it! I know I can! That is," her voice dropped and became uncertain, "w-with your help, I mean. I d-don't think I can do it w-without you." The halting words and telltale stutter sounded hateful to Cheney's ears. Cheney despised the stutter, and despised herself for the weakness it showed.

Shiloh shook his head regretfully. "Doc, I wish you knew what a good doctor you are. You don't need to feel so—unsure of yourself like this!"

"It's not just that, you see." Again Cheney's head dropped and her voice was so low Shiloh could barely hear it. "It's that— I'm not certain that I'm strong enough. Not me—inside—but my hands. I'm not sure my hands are strong enough."

"What are you talking about?" Shiloh asked in a bewildered tone.

Cheney took a deep breath, her shoulders heaving. "I'm not sure I'm strong enough," she muttered, "to break her leg."

Beauregard had wandered close enough to Sock and Stocking for Glen to hear Cheney's words, and before he could stop himself, Glen yelped two picturesque oaths. Then he tried to control himself, but intermittent sputterings and grunts seemed to jump out of his powerful lungs. "Mm, mm—Great—frogs! Jumpin'—horned—vipers! Great blitherin'—snow snakes!"

Shiloh's cornflower blue eyes grew wide, and his jaw tightened. His startled gaze locked with Cheney's, and they ignored Glen's sputterings. He muttered through clenched teeth, "Let me get this straight! You want to operate on Caroline Satterfield. Enoch Satterfield's daughter!"

"Yes."

"You want me to tell you it's all right!"

"Yes, and—"

Shiloh shook his head and made a chopping gesture with one hand. "Let me just take this in step by step! You want me to assist you in this operation—that I never heard of!"

"Y-yes."

"And last of all," he enunciated very slowly, "you want me to break her leg."

"That's a pretty good summary," Cheney said timidly.

Glen grew quiet, and he took out a piece of red flannel to

wipe his forehead, shaking his head as if he'd recovered from some sort of spasm.

Shiloh looked up the path to the distant snowy peak of Maeva's Trace. Cheney watched him carefully, her eyes pleading again, but without glancing back at her he murmured, "I'll do it."

"Whew!" Glen exclaimed, mopping his face steadily.

Shiloh looked back at him with an amused expression. "What's the matter with you, Rawlins? You'd think the Doc was asking *you* to do it!"

"You think I couldn't see who was the next car on that track, Irons?" Glen snapped, and Cheney laughed, but Glen went on almost to himself, " 'Course, it ain't like I ain't gonna git to break nobody's laig—'cause I'll prob'ly hafta break both of Enoch Satterfield's to keep him away from you two!"

After two more hours of riding, or more correctly, walking and stopping—for Cheney kept stopping to talk excitedly to Shiloh about the operation—they finally reached Josh and Sharon Carter's.

"Our wagon's here," Cheney observed. "They must be clearing instead of hauling wood today."

On Christmas Eve, Cheney had begged and pleaded enough that Josh had finally consented to keeping the large, roomy wagon for a while. Cheney had been triumphant, because she knew that it would mean Sharon could ride to church in the back of the wagon, resting. Josh and Lige Carter had been grateful for it, too, as they had found they could haul wood from the fields at the foot of Maeva's Trace, where they were clearing, back to the two cabins. Lige didn't like to cut too many trees from the gentle mountain that housed the two Carter families.

"Guess I'll ride down and see what Josh needs, then," Shiloh told Cheney. "I was going to cut firewood, but it looks like they're pretty well stocked up."

"Reckon I'll come with you," Glen nodded. "You foller me, Shiloh. I know how to cut down the mountain to the foot of the Trace without havin' to go back around to the road. Snow ain't gonna bother Beau and Sock." The two rode off into the woods, and Cheney went on up to Sharon's cabin.

Bobbie Jo waited for her on the front porch. "C'mon in, Doctor Cheney," she called. "Sharon said ya'll would prob'ly show up today."

Cheney dismounted and went inside with Bobbie Jo, noting that the girl looked pale and wan. *These days have been hard on everyone,* she thought, *but especially on Bobbie Jo and Jimmy Dale....*

Katie was cooking, Sharon was sitting up in bed under piles of quilts reading *Ivanhoe* by Sir Walter Scott, and Bobbie Jo was cleaning. Cheney checked Sharon and the baby carefully. *It's a miracle,* she thought gratefully. *Thank you, Lord, that Sharon and the baby are doing so well . . . with all this fighting and burning and shooting going on.*

The four women visited, calling back and forth to each other in the tiny cabin. Katie was cooking an enormous pot of hot, thick vegetable soup, and baking bread, biscuits, and cornbread. The delicious smells filled the cabin, and Cheney saw that Sharon's cheeks were pink and her eyes sparkled as she joked about being too hungry to wait for the men. Her fingers, wrists, and ankles were still swollen, and Cheney thought that her vision might still blur sometimes. *She's been reading* Ivanhoe *for the past two weeks,* she worried, *and I know Sharon normally devours that kind of book in two days. Odd that she's reading a romance like* Ivanhoe *anyway . . . she used to read things like* On the Origin of the Species *or* War and Peace. But Cheney said nothing, as Sharon did seem to be following Cheney's orders as much as she could under the circumstances.

Neatly repacking her medical bag, Cheney asked casually, "Sharon, can I ask you something?"

"Of course you can."

Cheney shut the black leather bag with a snap and sat down on the side of Sharon's bed, holding it stiffly in her lap as if to shield herself with it. "This is rather difficult, Sharon," she said hesitantly. "You're much younger than I am, you see. . . ."

Sharon searched Cheney's face, and in a moment her puzzled expression cleared. "You want to ask me about being married, don't you?" she asked gently.

Cheney didn't speak. Dropping her eyes, she began to fiddle nervously with the brass clasp of the bag. Finally she said, "I've been wondering about it a lot lately, it seems. You and Josh are so different, but you seem very happy. Isn't it—hasn't it been hard?"

Sharon leaned back on her pile of pillows with a faraway look in her eyes. When she spoke, her voice was soft and dreamy. "Yes, of course it's been hard. It's been hard for both Josh and me. But we promised each other that we'd work at being happy; I suppose that sounds rather strange, but it's true. I've worked at being happy in this place, with these people, so I can be happy with Josh."

"And what has Josh worked at?" Cheney asked rather shortly.

Sharon smiled and waved her book. "At this," she replied. Cheney looked puzzled, and Sharon went on. "No, I haven't gotten him to read *Ivanhoe* yet . . . and I'm not quite certain that I'll put him through that anyway." She went into a deep reverie for a few moments, gathering her thoughts. "Just as I promised him I'd make him happy, he promised me he'd do things to make me happy. We started by reading the Bible. It was familiar to him and"—Sharon laughed—"it was a revelation to him that he was reading Middle English. So from there we went on to Shakespeare. He likes some of the sonnets and all of the historical plays. We spend long hours reading out loud to each other and discussing the difficult parts."

"Yes, I see." Cheney nodded thoughtfully. "You work at it, but . . ."

"Then it's not work!" Sharon finished the thought. "And there's something else, Cheney, something that I tried to tell you at Christmas. It's so simple. Josh loves me, and he respects me. In this world, that's saying a lot. So many men treat their wives badly, or indifferently, or with barely contained impatience.

Josh doesn't mind—no, that's not right—he insists on openly showing his love and respect for me. You understand. You've seen it."

"Yes, I have." Cheney nodded. "But I never realized how important that must be to a woman."

"It is important. It's your life," Sharon said simply. Eyeing Cheney, who sat with face averted, fingering her medical bag, Sharon asked gently, "Does that help you understand a little better?"

"I suppose so," Cheney said in a muffled voice. After a long hesitation she added, "Dev asked me to marry him, you know."

"No, I didn't." Sharon smiled. Cheney had not mentioned Devlin Buchanan since she had arrived in Black Arrow. "But I'm not surprised."

"You're not?" Cheney asked in astonishment. "Well—well— I certainly was!"

"That doesn't surprise me either, Cheney dear," Sharon replied. "You never seem to understand how people feel about you."

Denial sprang into Cheney's mind, but suddenly she wondered if Sharon's simple words might not be true. Her thoughts began to scatter, and with an effort she attempted to organize them again. "But that's not the issue here," she declared flatly. "I just . . . have been thinking a lot lately . . . about Dev . . . and . . . things."

"What things, Cheney dear?"

"I suppose . . . about being . . . lonely."

Sharon's brown eyes softened, and she laid her hand on Cheney's. Cheney stopped playing with the clasp of her medical bag and looked up at Sharon as she spoke. "I know you must get lonely sometimes, Cheney. And all I can tell you is that sometimes being married can be lonely, too, even if you are blessed enough to be married to the right man."

"Are you saying that you don't think Dev is the right man for me, Sharon?"

"Cheney, dear," Sharon said and smiled a little wistfully, "I'd give anything if I did know the answer to that question, for your sake. But I don't. Only God knows that—and you."

17

SONS OF GOD

Glen and Shiloh came out of the tree line at the foot of the Carters' mountain. A high plain cradled by White Wolf Ridge to the south and Maeva's Trace to the north stretched before them. The field lay quiet and peaceful, as all the land seemed to be since it had been blanketed by Christmas snow.

Glen pointed, and Shiloh followed his gaze. In about the middle of the field they saw Lige and Josh Carter using a cross-cut saw on one of the big oak trees that dotted the plain. Farther to the south they saw a small figure on horseback, slowly tracing the base of White Wolf Ridge. Against the snowy background Shiloh could see the thin pencil line of a rifle held upright by the rider.

Dane riding shotgun, he sighed to himself. The sight of the slim, solitary figure bundled in dreary muted colors reminded him of fifteen- and sixteen-year-olds in gray and butternut walking a perimeter on a field that once might have looked like this one, but in Shiloh's mind was stained crimson. Resolutely he blotted the picture from his mind and touched his boots to Sock's sides to follow Glen toward the two men.

"Howdy!" Glen called cautiously as they approached.

Josh and Lige had left the crosscut buried halfway in the great oak to bend and pick up rifles. "It's Rawlins and Irons, Josh!" The two men lowered their rifles.

At the sound of Glen's call, Dane had turned and immediately begun a fast gallop toward his father and brother. Shiloh and Glen reined up at the oak tree, and Shiloh muttered, "Look at that young 'un coming across that field! Hope he can stop that horse!"

"Horse'll stop," Lige said sagely, shading his eyes to watch the big horse thundering toward them. "Young'un prob'ly will. Dane, he's been practicin' that part."

"That's Murdoch," Glen told Shiloh proudly. "Beauregard's little brother. I give him to Lige when we got back from the war."

"Jist don't say that in front o' Glendean," Lige grinned, then shrugged. "Katie won't let me ride 'im anyways."

The horse stretched out full speed, his hooves kicking up spouts of snow a foot high. The line of his neck was even with his back, and he seemed to be carefully aiming for the oak tree where the men stood in a loose circle. "Think we might better move aside?" Shiloh inquired casually.

"Horse'll stop," Lige repeated patiently.

Murdoch didn't slow to a stop. He galloped so close to the men that they could hear the air pounding out of his lungs when his front hooves touched the earth. Straight arrows of steam flew from his nostrils, turning to puffy clouds and disappearing in the heat of his run. Six feet from the men, he reared straight up to the sky, tossing his long mane and baring his teeth. Dane looked small on the horse's bare back, bent low over the glistening neck, clinging to the single rope that served as reins and bridle. But he kept his seat, grinning foolishly as the horse stood still, sweating and rolling his eyes.

"Boy, I orter shoot you fer ridin' thet horse thet-a-ways!" Lige grunted, but his light green eyes sparkled with pride.

A loud explosion sounded from a peak on Maeva's Trace.

Shiloh, Glen, Josh, and Lige immediately flattened to the ground. Glen and Josh threw themselves on their bellies with their rifles pointed toward the Trace, and Glen's sharp eyes picked out a faint puff of dirty gray smoke about halfway up the mountain.

Unlike the three men who responded to the ominous crack of rifle fire as they had in the recent war, to Dane Carter the sound registered as commonplace in this land of hunters. Murdoch stood quietly, his ears pricked forward slightly at the sight of the men who lay flat on the ground at his feet. Dane's green eyes were wide with bewilderment as he looked down at his father and brother. Then his mind slowly registered that something was wrong. *Red, Pa ain't wearin' no red. Whassat red on the snow?*

"Pa!" Dane screamed, and Murdoch started, his hooves flailing the air.

Shiloh jumped up and ran to the still form of Lige Carter. He glanced down for a split second, then looked up at Dane, his eyes dark and somber. "Go get Cheney! She's with Sharon. Hurry! Ride!"

Murdoch hit the ground already at half-stride. Tears began to roll down Dane Carter's face, but now he looked like a grim warrior instead of a crying boy. The roar of Murdoch's hoofbeats faded, and there was only the sound of Shiloh's voice in the snow-silent field.

"No, Josh! Don't turn him over yet!" Shiloh jumped up, stripped off his fishskin, and laid it out beside the wounded man. Lige Carter's face was turned to the side, half-buried in the snow.

Josh bent close over him and murmured, "Just a minute, Pa. You're gonna be all right. Hold on, we'll git you turned over and warm." The sound of his father's weak, erratic breathing frightened him, and his eyes sought Shiloh's with a desperate plea.

Lige was wearing a red flannel undershirt, two overshirts, and a canvas jacket. From a telltale black hole in the back of his jacket, bright red blood bubbled up, then began to spread a ragged circle of black around the deadly bull's-eye center. Shiloh stripped off his flannel shirt, eyeing with dread the scarlet stain on the clean snow underneath Lige Carter.

"Cold . . ." Lige mumbled into the snow.

Josh's eyes filled with pain, then he jumped up and began peeling off his long woolen coat.

"Josh!" Shiloh barked. "Wait! Go over there and get a handful of that clean snow! Where we haven't been stepping on it, and with no wood shavings or dirt in it! You hear me?"

Glen was still on his belly, sighting down his rifle with a

241

darkly murderous eye at the spot where he had seen the puff of smoke. He knew it was way out of range of his Enfield, so he didn't return fire. Still he watched. But no other shot sounded, and he saw nothing on the far slopes of Maeva's Trace. Now he jumped up with an oath and ran to Shiloh, who was struggling to get his white cotton undershirt over his head. Josh half stood, half knelt, staring up at Shiloh, his face white and vacant with shock, the long scar standing out in painful relief.

"Josh!" Glen roared as he reached over with one hand to literally tear Shiloh's shirt off into two pieces. "Git over there an' git some clean snow! Now!" Methodically he handed one half of Shiloh's shirt back to him, and tore a long strip, then another, from the half he held.

"Yes, sir!" Josh ran a few feet away and began skimming clean snow from a powdery drift. The left arm and side of his coat flapped behind him.

Shiloh and Glen tore the shirt into long strips about six inches wide. "Hurry!" Glen ordered Josh.

Josh turned around, his hands red against the white snow. Holding it as carefully as if it were a baby, he half turned to run back, but Shiloh yelled, "No! Pack it! Pack it hard!" Then he knelt down, pulled out his Bowie knife from the back of his pants, and split open all the layers of Lige Carter's clothing to lay his back bare. Strangely youthful muscles and tendons were knotted against the white skin, and in the center of Lige Carter's back was a neat hole about a half-inch in diameter. Blood still seeped out of it, but it did not bubble as it had before.

Glen laid the strips of Shiloh's shirt across Shiloh's bare shoulder so he could reach them easily, then he stripped off his great fur overcoat. Kneeling on Lige's other side, he began to arrange it under Shiloh's waterproof fishskin. His dark eyes met Shiloh's blue ones as they exchanged glances tinged with dread.

"Can't feel my legs . . ." Lige moaned. "Prob'ly . . . a . . . good thing . . ."

Josh slid up to his father's side on his knees, his hands held out. A ball of snow packed so tightly it was almost ice lay in the center of his palms, and he held it up to Shiloh as if it were an offering.

Wordlessly Shiloh shoved the knife into the sheath at his back and began to pack around the wound with the strips of white cotton that fluttered from his shoulder. Folding it into six-inch-squares, he made several layers then muttered, "Hold that snow over this. Keep it right over the wound. Me and Glen will turn him over."

With his son holding the snow securely over the white squares, Shiloh and Glen expertly rolled Lige over onto Shiloh's fishskin. Lige whispered, "Josh? You here, son?"

"I'm right here, Pa." Josh scrambled up into his father's line of vision, then bent over him and began to clean the snow from his face.

Shiloh and Glen once again met each other's gaze over Lige Carter's body. His entire midsection was black, but the snow where he had fallen was a wide circle of dark red. The bullet had gone through the man's midsection and exited just below his rib cage. "You find the bullet," Shiloh ordered. "I can do this." Glen jumped up, his eyes as cold as an eagle's, and his gaze traced an invisible line from Maeva's Trace to Lige Carter's position. He stalked off ten feet away, his head bent. Then he fell to his knees beside a small round hole in the snow.

Shiloh cut the clothing from Lige's body. His chest barely rose and fell, and his skin was beginning to look death white instead of winter white. Again Shiloh folded the strips of clean cloth and laid them against the wound, but this time he noted grimly that he had to fold them in larger squares. The exit wound was much messier than where the bullet had entered. Losing velocity as it tore through his body, it ripped rather than cut as it came out. Shiloh saw glimpses of white rib in the mass of red. He packed it as quickly as he could, but still the cloth instantly transformed into scarlet as he put the last strip on top. Then he jumped up and ran for some more clean snow, un-mindful of the cold, even though he was shirtless.

"Son," Lige muttered with difficulty, "I . . . I reckon I need to tell you . . . a coupla things."

"No!" Josh shouted, then stuck one arm under his father's shoulders and struggled to lift him. "I'm a-gonna carry you home, an' you're gonna be fine!"

"No!" Shiloh shouted from ten feet away, already starting to run. "Don't move him! Wait for Cheney!"

Josh felt Glen's hand on his shoulder. "Josh, don't you do it. You do like Shiloh says."

Josh dropped to his knees beside his father once again.

Weakly Lige Carter patted his son's hand, his green eyes darkened by pain. "Think I'll . . . rest . . . fer a minute," he murmured with some effort, then closed his eyes. Quickly Shiloh knelt by him, grabbing his wrist.

Josh's eyes were mirrors of his father's as he watched. "He's . . . not . . ." he began to ask fearfully.

Shiloh shook his head. "Bleeding's stopped, but he's going into shock. We have to warm him up. Let's cover his arms and legs, and I'm going to massage his feet. Josh, you rub his hands and arms, keep them warm. Glen, you keep fresh-packed snow on that wound. In a few minutes we'll check his back. . . ."

So began the dreary task of keeping Lige Carter alive. He slipped in and out of consciousness, occasionally looking up with a faintly surprised expression on his face, and then the fatal knowledge would set in. He spoke little. Shiloh had seen many men with serious, painful wounds such as this. *All of them are different*, he thought grimly as he worked. *Lige seems to be calm, peaceful—making an effort to save his strength. So much better than the ones who fight and scream and are so afraid.*

With determination Shiloh pushed away the dreadful memories and methodically began to review every possible thing he could do for Lige until Cheney arrived. *Glad she's here*, he reflected. *Whatever scares her about herself disappears when she's The Doctor. I've seen lots of men like Lige. Some live, some die. I can't tell. But Cheney will be able to.*

Glen's thoughts were dark and doubtful. During the war, he

had been able almost to sense life dissolving and death looming, especially in men he knew well. He had known Lige Carter for many years, and though he didn't allow his mind to form the words, already he had begun to grieve for this strong, proud man. His shirt pocket was weighted down with the mangled bullet he had found still steaming in the snow.

Some bull-killer this bullet is. His mind gritted over and over the thoughts as he paced up and down, occasionally packing snow into hard crystal to put on Lige's chest. *Even at two hundred yards! Gotta be a fifty-two caliber . . . gotta go up on the Trace and find the cartridge . . .* In his mind, he saw Enoch Satterfield's Sharps rifle with the telescope, mounted proudly over his mantle, the bore larger than any rifle's in Wolf County. *Only uses those fancy Winchester cartridges with the "H" stamped on the case head*, Glen reflected grimly. *Shot probably woulda mangled the case too bad to see . . .* In a way, Glen hoped this might be true . . . assuming he even found the cartridge. But the singular weight of the ball of metal in his pocket served to remind him that no one else he knew of, besides Enoch Satterfield, had a firearm that fired a .52 bullet.

Josh Carter had no thoughts. His mind was filled with images, some dark and shadowy and confused, some stark and black-and-white. Impotent anger made his hands tremble, and sharp thrusts of pain from the war bullet that had grazed his jawbone shot all the way up the side of his face and seemed to scrape his skull. His voice was hoarse, and he panted wet clouds of steam. "Pa," he gasped over and over. "Pa . . . Pa . . ."

Lige Carter opened his eyes. His face was a sickly gray against the innocent white snow, and his lips were blue. He looked up into Josh's face, and almost a smile drifted over his countenance. "Josh . . ." he whispered, "I . . . love you, son. Ain't . . . said . . . thet too many times. I . . . love you . . . a lot."

"I know, Pa," Josh replied huskily. "I . . . love you, too. A lot."

"You tell your ma . . ." Lige began with difficulty, then his face cracked into lines of pain, and he coughed twice. The men around him could not imagine the agony those coughs must have cost Lige, and all of them cursed their own helplessness as they watched. Lige gasped unevenly, raggedly for long moments. Then his face settled into familiar lines, and again he struggled to speak.

"No!" Josh croaked harshly. "Don't talk!"

Lige licked his lips. "Water . . ."

Josh jumped up, and Shiloh jumped up with him to place two hands on his shoulders across his father's body. "No, Josh. He's got a gut wound. He can't have any water."

"God in heaven!" Josh cried in anguish. Then he threw himself down to his father's side again. Grabbing a handful of snow, he rubbed his hands together hard and fast. Melted snow was on his fingers, and as he wet his father's lips, his hands were almost as red as the blood that seemed to be everywhere around them. They stepped in it, knelt in it, his father was clothed in it. Josh's hands shook visibly. "Pa . . . please . . ." He didn't know what he was pleading for.

Gratefully Lige licked his lips, then swallowed with an effort. "You tell Katie," he said with ragged determination, "thet I promised to love her . . .'til the day . . . I die. . . . And I did . . ." Turning his head slightly to the side, he appeared to drift off into sleep. Shiloh grabbed his wrist and after a moment nodded reassuringly to Josh. Lige's heart still beat a weak, erratic rhythm.

The men continued doing their frustratingly inadequate chores: packing snow, massaging Lige's arms, legs, hands, and feet, adjusting coats and shirts and red rags. Once Shiloh stood, stretching his back and rubbing his eyes. Glen came close to him, unbuttoning the rough woolen shirt he wore over a red flannel undershirt. "Here. Put this on. You're cold."

With surprise Shiloh looked down at himself. He had forgotten that he was naked from the waist up. Now he realized he was half-frozen. Gratefully he put on Glen's scratchy shirt and looked around in confusion. He pulled a heavy gold pocket watch out of his pants pocket and snapped open the plain cover.

Plaintively the tune chimed, an alien sound in the heavy silence. *When Johnny comes marching home again, Hurrah! Hurrah!*

Inside, in block letters, was his name: SHILOH IRONS. *No nonsense, no airs, just solid gold and block letters,* his mind meandered. *Nice Christmas gift from the Doc . . . just like her . . . expensive, useful, not fussy, not frilly.* With concentration he squinted at the time. *Nine-eighteen. In the morning.* Snapping the cover shut with irritation, he pocketed the watch. *Doesn't help much, since I don't know what time Lige got shot or what time Dane rode out.* Sighing, he began again to work over Lige Carter, murmuring empty comforts to Josh.

It seemed like hours, days, before approaching horses, moving fast, broke the silence. Lige stirred a little.

"Doc's comin', Lige," Glen said kindly. "You jis' hang on now, you hear?"

Stocking led Murdoch across the plain; Murdoch was tired, Stocking fresh. Cheney's hair shone in the bright sunlight, and she seemed to be one with the horse, even as he flashed over the snow at an impossibly fast pace. She sat straight, her face intent, holding her medical bag with one hand and the reins with the other. She and Dane rode dangerously close to the men huddled around Lige, and together they dismounted to kneel beside him.

"Where's Katie?" Lige asked weakly.

"She's bringing the wagon," Cheney answered, her hands busy over Lige's body. "It'll be just a few minutes. You're going to be fine, Mr. Carter, now just relax. Shiloh, this is good, you've done very well. Get the laudanum out of my bag."

"Miss . . . Duvall," Lige gasped weakly, and slowly reached up with one arm to lay it heavily on Cheney's. "Now . . . I want you to . . . look at me."

Cheney's busy hands grew still. She sat back on her heels, took a deep breath, and met Lige's knowing eyes. He stared at her for a moment, then nodded as if she had spoken. "Miss Duvall, I'm beholden . . . to you fer rushin' out here . . . an' all." His voice was thick with pain, and Cheney bent close to hear. "But . . . right now . . . I need you to . . . answer me a question."

"Yes, Mr. Carter. Go ahead."

"Do you think . . . you kin . . . keep me alive?"

A silence fell. All eyes were on Cheney. "No, sir, Mr. Carter. I don't think so," she whispered. "I'm sorry."

Lige Carter's eyes flickered, and he drew a shuddering breath. Josh's big red hands fluttered helplessly over his father for a moment, a curiously light, graceful movement. Dane's head dropped to his chest, his shoulders sagged, and one sharp, choked sound escaped from his throat.

"Thought . . . such," Lige finally muttered. A slight moan escaped as he drew a deep breath, but somehow he seemed to be marshaling his ebbing strength. "So thank ye . . . agin, Miss Duvall, but I think I better talk to . . . my boys now. Then you . . . kin do yore . . . doctorin'."

Every fiber in Cheney's body fought against her stillness and self-imposed calm. She wanted to hurry, to move fast, to find something else white to rip into pieces for new bandages. She wanted to give this man something to ease the stabs of pain that marred his face, she wanted to scream orders to Shiloh—she wanted to do anything but sit here and watch Lige Carter bleed. Her face paled, she bit her lower lip until it turned scarlet, and her nostrils flared.

A strong hand slid under her elbow, and in her ear she heard Shiloh's soothing voice. "C'mon, Doc. Let go, and let him rest."

Slowly she allowed Shiloh to raise her to a standing position. Without thinking she put both arms around his waist and leaned against him. He held her as they looked down at Lige Carter.

"Josh, you listen to yore pa now." Lige, with great difficulty, turned his head to his elder son. "You an' me . . . we allus been God-fearin' men, an' called ourselfs . . . Christians. Reckon I am, at that . . . 'cause I ast the Lord Jesus to come into my heart when I was a boy . . . 'bout Glendean's age . . . an' I know fer sure . . . He ain't never left me."

Lige coughed, and blood bubbled up around his mouth and spilled down his chin. Dane looked up and with the tenderest of touches wiped it away with a corner of his shirttail. Lige's green eyes smiled as he struggled to breathe. Cheney could hear slight gurgling sounds in his throat. Lige closed his eyes, and Josh's face blanched, but Lige's face grew still and composed, and he managed to draw an even breath before he opened his eyes to look back up at his sons.

"See, boys . . . you ain't heard me talk much 'bout Jesus. An' the reason for that is . . . most o' the stuff I been talkin' about to you . . . like who's a Carter an' who ain't . . . bad blood . . . vengeance . . . curses . . . seems like . . . somehow you jis' couldn't fit that . . . Name into the same sentences I was sayin'. Don't fit, do it? Jesus . . ." He raised his hands slightly, and the blood flowed anew from the wound in his chest. Josh grabbed one of his father's hand with both of his, and Dane grabbed the other. Dane had rivers of tears running down his face and falling to the crimson snow at his knees. Josh's entire body was strained with grief, and his sharply outlined features looked skeletal.

Lige looked up to the naked branches of the tree above him, up to the cheerful blue sky. "I cain't see Him yit," Lige rasped, "but I will. An' I know one thing . . . I gotta tell you afore I do. All this hatin' an' talk of blood . . . curses on our heads . . . it's gotta stop here!" Suddenly his eyes shone with the last light of life, and his voice grew strong. "Yore both men, you make yore choices as men—God-fearin' men, with the light of Jesus in yore hearts!"

Even at this moment, the faintest flicker of rebellion lurked behind Josh's eyes, and recognition shadowed his father's face. "I know, son, what I've told you. But just think about it . . . cain't be no curse, you know . . ." His voice fell to a whisper, and Josh and Dane leaned close over him so they could hear. "Ain't no man niver wanted to outlive his sons, an' that were the worst part of it. . . . So now, I'm glad I'm the one who's goin' home, boys. Now we know you ain't sons of the curse. . . . All we are is sons of God . . . and His mercy . . . in Christ . . . Jesus."

Lige Carter sighed, closed his eyes, and died.

18

SUFFICIENT UNTO THE DAY

"Heah's tea," Rissy said brusquely as she set the tray on the plain wooden table in front of the settee. "If you cain't eat, you kin drink." She began to fix a mug of steaming tea. Glancing sidelong at Cheney's pale face, she added more sugar than usual and a thick dollop of Rissy's Double Cream.

Cheney rocked steadily as she stared into the fire. Her thoughts were not sharply defined and clearly delineated as they normally were. Instead she let her mind take almost a liquid form. When she bumped into solid reality or uncomfortable pictures, her thoughts would roll over it or split into two paths as a stream splits around a big rock. She was too weary to discipline her thoughts, and too dispirited to care.

Her mouth set in a determined line, Rissy held out the steaming mug. Absently Cheney took it and sipped the scalding liquid. "Rissy, will you have a cup with me?" she asked quietly. "Will you sit with me until it's time to go?"

Crossing her arms, Rissy considered Cheney thoughtfully. She was not uncertain or doubtful because of Cheney's unusual request; her relationship with Cheney had never been the standard mistress-servant type. Rissy simply doubted that she could help Cheney, and wished that Shiloh were here. But he wasn't, so Rissy fixed herself a cup of tea, sat in the rocking chair across from Cheney, and began to rock.

"Yo upset 'bout Mistuh Lige," she stated.

"Hmm? Oh . . . yes . . . I guess I am," Cheney answered in a distant voice. Most of the night she had gone over and over the events of the previous day, picturing each moment that passed after she knelt by Lige Carter's bleeding body. Relentlessly her mind had envisioned every medical technique, every possible treatment, every move she might have made. Each time Lige Carter died. Now Cheney was exhausted, and finally had let her mind get a semblance of rest in vagueness and lack of concentration.

Rissy regarded the vacant expression on Cheney's face. The absence of intensity and fire made Cheney almost unrecognizable. Rissy pitied Cheney for her heavy burden, but she was not unduly concerned. *Miss Cheney, she a strong woman*, Rissy thought, sipping her tea and rocking in companionable silence.

The only sounds in the room were the muted crackle of the fire and an occasional hiss from the low flames. The sitting room was dim, even though it was ten o'clock in the morning. Outside the light was indifferent, the sky neutral gray. *Gonna snow agin*, Rissy decided. *Nice to hev Mistuh Glen and Mistuh Shiloh to keep us in kindlin' an' firewood. I could do it, but it ain't my most favorite chore. . . .*

A sturdy knock sounded, three slow raps against the heavy oak. Cheney stirred slightly in her chair, and Rissy rose and glided to the door. She opened it to face Caroline Satterfield and her mother, Leah. "Yes'm?" she asked, her voice courteous but stern.

"Kin we see Miz—I mean, Dr. Duvall, please?" Leah asked, her tone as determined as Rissy's.

Wordlessly Rissy glanced over her shoulder. Cheney rose and came to the door, her face surprised. "Of course. Come in, Mrs. Satterfield, Caroline," she said.

Rissy decided that, for good or ill, the appearance of Caroline and her mother had brought Cheney out of her weary apathy. So she fetched the tray and disappeared into the kitchen to make more tea.

"Please sit down." Cheney resumed her seat in the rocking chair and watched Caroline and Leah warily.

They sat together on the settee. Caroline settled in comfortably, but Leah perched stiffly on the edge, her back a straight, taut line, and watchfully regarded Cheney. She wasted no time. "Caroline's tole me what you said 'bout her laig." Leah waited until Cheney acknowledged her with a cautious nod, then continued matter-of-factly, "So we want you to fix it."

Cheney's sharp intake of breath sounded loud in the quiet sitting room. "You . . . do? Who is 'we'? You can't mean—"

The faintest light of stubbornness came into Leah Satterfield's eyes, and she shook her head very slightly. "No, Enoch don't know nothin' 'bout it. He sent me an' the young'uns in to town yesterday, to stay fer a few days." She paused, visibly defensive, waiting for Cheney's reaction.

"I see," Cheney replied with intentional mildness. "Well . . . as I told Caroline when she came to see me last week, she's nineteen years old, and in my mind that makes her an adult. She has the right to make this decision for herself."

"Thet may be true, Miz—Dr. Duvall," Leah nodded, "but she wouldn't be able to do it 'thouten my help. An' Jimmy Dale's," she amended with a glance at Caroline. Reaching into a worn black reticule clutched tensely in her lap, she pulled out two folded bills, laid them on the table in front of the settee, smoothed them carefully flat, and looked back up at Cheney with determination. "Here's the forty dollars fer the operation, Dr. Duvall."

Cheney eyed the bills regretfully. Jimmy Dale had insisted that Cheney tell him how much Caroline's operation would cost. Cheney had tried to minimize the money in every way she could think of. She tried to shrug it off completely, but neither Jimmy Dale nor Caroline would hear of it. She had suggested that Caroline pay her by weaving more beautiful rugs such as those she had seen in the Satterfields' home; Caroline smiled, glanced around the room, and mutely shook her head. Mr. DeSpain had contracted her only months before to make all the rugs in Cheney's cabin.

Cheney had then relented and told them that the operation would probably cost around forty dollars, and she would be more than happy to put it on an account that Caroline could pay off at her convenience. But as soon as she had mentioned the amount, Jimmy Dale had nodded thoughtfully, thanked her, and the two had left.

Now Cheney made a last attempt to avoid having to accept the Satterfields' money. "Mrs. Satterfield, please don't worry about that right now. I-I have money. My family, you see . . . it's really not necessary. . . ."

Leah's dull eyes warmed into a glow, and her lips turned very slightly upward. "I unnerstand thet, Dr. Duvall. Hit ain't nothin' to be ashamed of, you know. But we'uns don't take no charity, so if'n you'll do this here operation, you'll hafta take the money."

"You can pay me anytime," Cheney argued. "I know the situation your family is in, and it's painful for me to accept money from you right now."

"Hit shouldn't never be painful fer nobody to accept money they've earned right and fair," Leah stated briskly. "Ain't no use in arguin' with me 'bout it noways. It were Jimmy Dale's money, an' now it's yourn. If you'll do this here operation, that is."

"All right," Cheney agreed reluctantly. "But I do have some conditions that you, Mrs. Satterfield, must agree to first. And there are some things that Caroline must understand about this operation and agree to before I'll do it."

"Go ahead," Leah said stoutly.

"You have to let me treat Caroline after the operation is over," Cheney stated firmly. "She'll need special care, and even if you—or Maeva Wilding—disagree with it, you must promise that Caroline will be taken care of *exactly* as I say."

"Dr. Duvall, did you know Isaac's my favorite nephew?" Leah remarked, tenderness smoothing the sharp edge of her voice. "I might be old an' ignorant, but I ain't too old to change my mind, nor too ignorant to learn. I believe in you, Dr. Duvall, and from now on I'll stand by you."

"Why—thank you, Mrs. Satterfield!" At best Cheney had expected resigned agreement from Leah, not this sturdy pledge. The shadowy fog that had enveloped Cheney's mind since yesterday afternoon seemed to dissipate in sudden warmth.

Turning to Caroline, she continued gravely, "Now, Caroline, I want you to understand exactly what I'm going to do. There are risks I want you to think about. And it could be that this isn't going to work. I have to tell you all of these things, and make sure that you understand everything before you make up your mind."

No doubt marred Caroline's smooth countenance. "Yes, I want to know all about it, Dr. Duvall. But I ain't gonna change my mind."

"Good." Cheney nodded with encouragement. "So when do you want to do this?"

"Now," Caroline answered calmly.

Startled, Cheney glanced from Caroline to her mother. Both women looked quietly determined and unafraid. "Well," Cheney said hesitantly, "I'm sorry, but I can't do it right now. I must go to Lige Carter's funeral. And Shiloh isn't here."

Cheney paused, expecting that Caroline and Leah would respond by making alternate suggestions or asking questions, but both of them simply watched her and waited.

Only then did Cheney realize that, for them, this was not the beginning of a frightening experience, but the end of a journey. They had somehow drawn strength from each other and had found their way here, to her. Now they simply waited—for her.

"I'll go to the funeral," Cheney declared, "and Shiloh will be there. We'll be back at about two o'clock. Caroline, you rest here until then. Mrs. Satterfield, please stay with her. We'll operate at about three o'clock this afternoon."

★ ★ ★ ★

Lige Carter's funeral was conducted in the same manner he had lived his life: with simple, quiet dignity. His coffin was a pine box built by his sons, and he was laid to rest on one of the high peaks of the nameless mountain that shadowed his family's home. Reverend Scott read the Twenty-third Psalm. A woman sang the first and last verse of "Amazing Grace" in a strong, mournful, slightly off-key voice that befit both the Moccasin

Mountains and the man for whom they all grieved.

Over one hundred men, women, and children gathered on the snowy hillside by the shocking rectangular wound in the white ground. Nearly everyone from Black Arrow was in attendance. Waylon DeSpain stood alone, slightly apart, his men conspicuously absent. Flave and Deak Carter, Lige's brothers, stood with their families, living remembrances of Lige Carter when he was younger. Katie Carter, Josh and Sharon, Dane, Bobbie Jo, and Glendean huddled close together, surrounded by dozens of Carters who loved them, but tragically set apart by their special grief. Glen Rawlins stood slightly apart from the crowd, alone, crying unashamedly, his final tribute to this man he had called a friend.

Although Cheney had tried to prepare herself for it, she still felt desperately alone and lonely as she took her place, facing the dark black hole in the ground. Across from her Shiloh stood with Maeva Wilding. They were not touching, or standing particularly close together. Even Cheney, however, who had never been very observant of people and their personal relationships, could see that they were *together*. They exchanged intimate glances of understanding and support. Once Maeva reached out and lightly touched Shiloh's sleeve, a seemingly unconscious gesture of reassurance both given and received. Cheney felt like an intruder, and wished fervently she had not come.

As soon as the last notes of the woman's sorrowful voice died, Katie Carter threw a handful of dirt on the pine box that already lay at the bottom of the grave, turned, and walked away. Two teenage boys—Carters, by the look of them—picked up shovels and began to cover Lige Carter with earth.

Cheney steeled herself and walked over to where Shiloh and Maeva stood quietly talking. "Please excuse me," she said, and to her disgust her voice sounded weak and petulant. Straightening her shoulders and lifting her chin, she continued in a businesslike manner, "Shiloh, may I speak to you for a moment?"

"Sure, Doc," he replied easily. Maeva turned around gracefully to face Cheney, her eyes dark cobalt blue, her expression immutable.

Uncertainly Cheney greeted her, nodding stiffly. "Miss Wilding."

"Miss Duvall."

An uncomfortable silence ensued. Even Shiloh seemed ill-at-ease, his eyes darting back and forth between the two women. "What can I do for you, Doc?"

Cheney was reluctant to discuss Caroline Satterfield in front of Maeva Wilding, but she was also loath to ask to speak to Shiloh in private. She was certain that no matter how she worded it, it would sound like a curt dismissal of Maeva, and worst of all, she wasn't sure Shiloh would go along with it. Despising the situation, and her ineptness, she finally looked up at him and spoke stiffly and too formally. "I have scheduled an operation at three o'clock. Will you be available to assist me?"

Shiloh took his watch out of his pocket and studied it. At the sight of the heavy gold watch Maeva's eyes seemed to glint and her white teeth gnawed at her bottom lip for a moment. "Operation?" she asked Cheney with an air of innocent curiosity. "On who?"

Cheney weighed the implications of discussing this with Maeva, but found herself too weary and impatient to be politic. "Caroline Satterfield," she replied shortly and turned back to Shiloh. "She's already at the cabin, so as soon as you can get there . . ."

Shiloh closed the cover of his watch with a snap and replaced it in his pocket with finality. "It's twelve-thirty-two now, Doc. I'll take Maeva home and be back at the cabin as soon as I can."

Maeva turned to him, softly laying her tanned hand with the long fingers and white nails on his arm. "But, Shiloh, did you fergit? You promised to go with me out to the Wilkeses'. Little Joanie's so sick, an' I'm gonna need you to take me out there an' help me." Her lips curved upward in a smile of gentle rebuke. "Little Joanie needs me, an' I need you."

Cheney's temper rose right along with the blood that rushed

257

hotly to her cheeks. In a few seconds her emotions plummeted to familiar hated feelings of awkwardness, childish rudeness, and being embarrassingly out of place. Then her mind sharpened to focus on one point: *What will Shiloh do?* Instantly her gaze went up to his face.

Shiloh remained very still, his brow furrowed with thought as he considered Maeva. She was relaxed, the feline half-smile in place, with no sign of doubt as she waited for Shiloh's words. Every nerve in Cheney's body seemed to strain toward him, but she remained stiff and mute, unable to say a word.

"I—" he began.

"Perhaps I may be of some assistance," a voice sounded behind Cheney. Waylon DeSpain appeared beside her with an apologetic look on his face. "I was waiting to speak with Miss Wilding, and I couldn't help but overhear. Dr. Duvall, Mr. Irons, if you are needed back in town, perhaps I might escort Miss Wilding home. I need to talk to her anyway."

"No," Shiloh said curtly.

"Shiloh, please—" Cheney began.

"But, Mr. Irons, didn't I hear Dr. Duvall say that she is operating on Caroline Satterfield this afternoon?" DeSpain asked, his face smooth and bland. "Surely she would need you to go back to the office with her now, if Caroline and Mrs. Satterfield are waiting?"

Cheney had been vaguely aware of people standing around them in close groups, talking in hushed voices and only glancing at the four with casual curiosity. Now, however, they suddenly seemed pressed in by a large circle of people, their faces as gray and grim as the sky. Instinctively Cheney turned to see Sharon at her elbow, her face ashen and stricken. Evidently she had come up to speak to Cheney, and her family had followed. Josh stood by her side, the scar on his face a jagged rope of red.

The realization that they had heard DeSpain's words wrenched Cheney, almost with physical pain. *Just today . . . just for now . . . no Satterfield name should have been mentioned. It's my fault . . . my fault . . .*

"Cheney, I—" Sharon whispered.

Josh stepped forward almost as if to shelter Sharon from Cheney. "So you're a-gonna fix Caroline Satterfield's pore little laig today, are you?" he grated. "Too bad you couldn't do none o' thet fancy doctorin' on my pa!"

Waves of regret washed over Cheney. Unable to speak, she dropped her head and felt hot tears burn her eyes for the first time since Lige Carter had died.

"That's not right, and you know it, Josh," Shiloh said in a voice gentle but firm. "All of us, including Dr. Duvall, are here to honor your father, and to grieve for him. There was nothing anyone could do."

Incoherently Cheney thought, *I wish he'd called me Cheney. . . . He never seems to say my name anymore.*

"Looks to me like Miss Duvall's doctorin' is a lot more use to Satterfields than Carters," Josh rasped in an undertone that somehow sounded much more vicious than if he'd raised his voice. "So she better go sharpen her accursed blades, 'cause when I git through with those—those—Satterfield mongrels thet kilt my pa, she's gonna hev some doctorin' to do!"

For some reason Cheney's eyes fell on Maeva Wilding as Josh Carter railed. Maeva's face stayed unreadable, perfectly expressionless. Her eyes met Cheney's wounded glance with no trace of compassion, but also with no triumph or glee. It was as if she were watching a play.

"Oh, Josh, no! Please—" Sharon gasped.

Josh ignored her, ignored everyone surrounding him. His green eyes glared as he raked Cheney's pale face. "All I know you've done is scare my wife with tales of women havin' fits and stillborn babies, and then you stood by watchin' while my pa died! You hear me, Miss Duvall! You stay away from my family!"

Shiloh's face grew still, but a muscle in his jaw clenched repeatedly. He stepped forward, unconsciously taking the same protective stance in front of Cheney that Josh had done with Sharon. "Carter, you're too wrought up right now," he muttered in a tone less gentle than before. "Looks to me like you're making a whole lot of mistakes right here in a row. Why don't you take your family home and get your grieving done before you say and do some things you might regret?" Shiloh's hands hung loosely at his sides, but his shoulders were set in a tense line that Cheney recognized.

"Can't you do something, Glen?" she pleaded.

Glen stood apart, watching with dark eyes that still held sorrow. "I won't," he answered in a voice devoid of inflection. "I'm sorry Lige is gone. But he weren't my blood."

"We all have the same blood!" Cheney burst out, her voice high and cracking with tension. "Believe me, when it's spilled, Enoch Satterfield's is going to look just like Lige Carter's!" She turned to Josh Carter and faced him squarely for the first time. "And the blood on your hands will be just as sinful as the blood on the hands of the man who shot your father!"

"That man were Enoch Satterfield," Josh replied in a dead tone. "And he ain't gonna live while I walk this earth!"

★ ★ ★ ★

Shiloh's face was remote, his eyes unfocused as he rode beside Cheney.

He's thinking about her. Resolutely Cheney ignored the nagging worry the thought caused her.

Maeva Wilding had finally spoken up, a sane, cool voice of reason in the midst of a maelstrom. "Glen, come on now an' take me out to LaMar Wilkes' house. Mr. DeSpain, you kin ride along fer a spell if'n you wanna talk to me. Shiloh, you go on with her." As if they were orders that could not be disobeyed, the mourners of Lige Carter had cut off all conversation and gone their separate ways.

"Shiloh," Cheney said softly.

"Hmm?"

"Let's talk about this operation."

"Hmm?"

"We need to talk about this operation," Cheney repeated patiently.

"Oh! I'm sorry, Doc. I guess I was wandering around in my head." Shiloh shrugged. Grasping Sock's reins more firmly, he searched the silent woods surrounding them. "Yes. This is good. You tell me now and make sure I know what to do. Then we'll be ready as soon as we get home."

Home . . . Cheney's mind echoed hopefully, but she thrust it aside and pictured Caroline Satterfield's twisted leg in her mind. "You'll administer chloroform. We'll have to be very careful because she ate an apple for breakfast."

"Yes."

"Good. Then we'll secure her leg tightly at the thigh and above the knee and at her ankle. I want you to make sure she's under deep, so you can help me tie off. You're as good at knotting catgut as I am. I'm going to have to make a long incision all the way from the knee to the ankle."

"You are? I thought all I had to do was re-break the leg." Shiloh's voice was calm and certain, and Cheney felt some of the tension in her shoulders and neck relax.

"There's some calcification where the original break mended," Cheney replied. "I think even a little lump of bone would show, right on her shin. Besides, this is going to have to be a full compound fracture, you know."

"I know."

"So I want to open it up and make sure no bone splinters b-break off, and—and—" Cheney hesitated and searched Shiloh's face.

He nodded encouragingly at her. "Go ahead. I understand."

With a slight sigh of relief, Cheney continued, "It's very likely that the bone will protrude through the skin anyway, when you break it. So we might as well open it up cleanly. Then we can scrape off that excess bone growth at the same time."

"Yes, I see. You're right."

"Shiloh?"

"Yes?"

"Do you think you can do it? Break the bone . . . with your hands?"

Shiloh met Cheney's anxious gaze squarely. "I think so," he replied calmly. "I guess you could say I've had some experience."

"Oh, that's good," Cheney said with satisfaction, then her face twisted as she realized the implications of what Shiloh had said.

Shiloh chuckled, deep in his throat. "No, Doc," he replied, "you're good."

★ ★ ★ ★

Cheney wearily wiped sweat from her forehead and sank lifelessly into her favorite rocker. "How long did that take? About three or four days?"

Shiloh threw himself down on the spare settee in front of the fireplace. His long legs sprawled ridiculously over one rickety arm, but he seemed to lounge comfortably. Reaching over to the table in front of the settee, he picked up his watch. The burnished gold gleamed richly in the firelight. The cover popped open, and the first few notes of the song rang clear and high in the room. "It's seven-eighteen," he yawned.

"You tell time funny," Cheney said with a smile.

"What does that mean?"

"It's never 'six-fifteen' or 'about six-twenty.' It's always 'four-oh-seven,' or 'eleven-thirty-nine.' "

"First watch I've ever had," he shrugged. "Takes practice to learn how to use one right."

Cheney leaned her head back and closed her eyes, the smile lingering on her lips.

Shiloh watched her. *She looks relaxed, almost happy. Not completely happy, but almost. Closer to it than any time since we got here.* "I thought it went pretty well," he said. "Am I right?"

Cheney rocked, tiny little back-and-forth movements she tightly controlled with her toes. The jerky movements contrasted oddly with her languid face. "To be perfectly honest, it went much better than I expected."

"Then what's wrong, Doc?"

With an effort, Cheney raised her head and opened her eyes.

"It's just that the next two days are so crucial. If her leg gets gangrenous . . . or if it doesn't heal straight. . . . It'll be at least two weeks before we can see."

Shiloh held up his hand, not imperatively, but in a gesture of reassurance. "Isn't there some Bible verse . . . something about this day having enough trouble of its own?"

" 'Sufficient unto the day is the evil thereof,' " Cheney quoted softly. " 'Take therefore no thought for the morrow: for the morrow shall take thought for the things of itself.' "

"There, I told you," Shiloh said smugly.

Cheney smiled and shook her head. "Shiloh?"

"Hmm?"

"You're good."

19

COPPERHEAD GATE

Lige Carter had taught his son Josh well. Among men who viewed stoicism as an admirable quality, Lige had cherished his wife unstintingly and visibly. His children and kin he had loved and honored. Josh Carter had seen this true charity in his home, and he had grown to be a man who, like his father, understood and revered the power of love.

And I loved him so much, Josh thought bleakly. *He were the best friend I ever had, besides Sharon.*

His glass-green eyes, now clouded with pain, swept over the valley below his home, sterile and colorless in the muted afternoon light. Beneath him his horse, Blackjack, stirred restlessly, shifting back and forth and tossing his head. The jingling harness and bridle and the leather creaks of the saddle were comforting, familiar sounds to Josh.

"Jis' wait, boy," he muttered absently. "We're gonna ride agin here in a bit, like before. You kin smell it, cain't you?"

Blackjack had been Josh's faithful mount during the three years Josh had been in the war. The black horse had carried him like a shadow-mount in the night for three hours at Brandy Station, Josh slumped over the saddle like a dead man, his face a river of blood. Josh loved this horse almost as much as he loved his brother and sisters.

If only . . . Josh saw the slow-motion review of the day before in his mind, his gaze unseeing on the glowering sky over Maeva's Trace. He saw a high plain with a towering oak tree almost in the center, a crosscut saw buried forever in its heart. *If I jis' woulda stepped two feet closer, it woulda been me instead of him! It shoulda been me . . . I'm the son of the curse!*

His uncles Flave and Deak led their horses around to the front of the cabin from the stables. "We're 'bout ready to ride, Josh," Flave grunted. "Dane and the rest of the boys are almost saddled up."

Josh regarded his uncles with pain evident on his twisted face. *Guess I'll feel a shock every time I see 'em,* he thought. *Uncle Deak and Uncle Flave look so much like him, it hurts.* Josh remembered the jolt he had received when he shaved that morning. His father's eyes had stared back at him from the mysterious depths of the smoky old mirror.

"Josh . . ." The soft voice of his wife made Josh jump and turn around in his saddle to face the front porch of the cabin.

"Get back inside and stay there, Sharon," he ordered curtly. "Hit's cold."

"Josh, please don't. Don't do this." She clutched her black woolen shawl closer, and her pale, swollen face rebuked him. He was suddenly very conscious of the dark shadows under her eyes; her thin shoulders and frame emphasized the round swell of her belly.

His face closed, his jaw tightened. "This ain't none of your concern, Sharon," he muttered with the merest hint of remorse.

"None of my concern! Josh, you're my husband!" Her voice shook and rose to an unnaturally high pitch.

Katie Carter came out on the porch. All joy seemed to have been wiped from her face, and now all traces of weeping had disappeared. "Come in, Sharon," she said, putting her arm around Sharon's waist. "You don't have no business out here. Josh has to do what he sees is right."

"But, Katie! No! Someone has to—" Sharon was nearing hysteria. Shaking off Katie's encircling arm, Sharon stumbled toward the steps.

Josh turned his back on her.

Sharon stopped short, drawing a deep, trembling breath. Her eyes opened wide with incomprehension, and big tears ran down her face. One deep, wrenching sob escaped from her lips as her husband's mother led her firmly back inside.

Josh flinched very slightly, but his face remained set in deep granite lines as he searched the eastern mountains. *What I see is right*, he repeated to himself. *He was the best pa a man could ever have, and I was a good son. I allus honored him, allus obeyed him. . . .*

Somewhere inside his wounded mind a quietly reasonable voice shouldered aside the fury in Josh's thoughts of revenge. *Always obeyed him? What about his last words to you? Were they demands of vengeance, cursing, and reviling bad blood?*

Relentlessly Josh shut out the voice, but unbidden and unwelcome, a vision of Caroline Satterfield rose up in his mind. Young, pretty, and cruelly flawed. Would she feel grief such as he did when she lost *her* father? Would she, given the choice, gladly step in front of Enoch, painfully pull herself up straight, and look down the barrel of Josh's rifle?

"It don't matter," Josh said too loudly. The stark croak of his voice startled his uncles. Uneasily they watched him as he turned, and the desolate look in Josh's face made them drop their eyes. "I'm gonna kill Enoch Satterfield today!" he growled. "Ya'll jis' make sure I stay alive long enough to do it!"

★　★　★　★

"They'll be a-comin', most likely today," Enoch stated flatly. "Mebbe tomorrow. But most likely today."

"Most likely," T. R. agreed absently. His dark eyes, normally red-rimmed and bleary, were sharp and feral as he scanned White Wolf Ridge below.

Jimmy Dale sighted down the telescope mounted on his father's Sharps rifle once again and settled more comfortably in the cleft behind and under an outcropping of lichen-gray rocks. *Today?* he wondered. *With their pa barely in the ground?*

With a mental shrug, he dismissed all uncertainty and doubt to ready himself. With a coldly disciplined gaze he searched the mountain directly to the west from his sniper's eyrie on Maeva's Trace. Memorizing the landscape, the undulations of the terrain, the play of dark and semidark of trees and rocks and shadows, he reassured himself that he would see men moving down the mountain. Even in the dimness of the afternoon, in the twilight, or in the dark of night.

"I won't be able to see 'em if it snows, Pa," he said.

"You'll hear 'em," Enoch shrugged. "And you do jis' like I say, Jimmy Dale. Send T. R. back to the foot of the mountain. Somebody'll be there, waitin', an' they'll ride up to the cabin to let us know."

Jimmy Dale reflected on the unique position he was in, waiting for the Carters to come for his father. Was he the sentinel, the picket? Or was he the first line of defense? *Them's jis' war words*, he thought grimly. *What I'm really wonderin' is, what do I do then? Pick 'em off one by one? Or sneak back to the cabin and wait 'til Josh Carter is aimin' at my pa from six feet away?*

"Pa . . ." he began, his voice tentative.

Enoch laid a heavy hand on his son's shoulder. "Yore a good boy, Jimmy Dale. Allus have been. You do what you see is right." Enoch turned and walked back to his horse, his shoulders slumped, his outline weary and suddenly old.

★ ★ ★ ★

They finally appeared with the bleak light that comes over the land just after sunset but before true dark. The lowering clouds remained, sullen with snow. They would smother the moon and stars as they had blocked all cheer of the sun that day.

Josh Carter was no military tactician, and had no thought of quiet or stealth. Eight torches were lit, then the riders began to move in a ragged wedge down the mountains toward White Wolf Ridge. No word was needed between the two brothers who waited above, hidden on Maeva's Trace, their hands and feet wooden and their faces stiff with cold. Silently T. R. melted into the woods behind Jimmy Dale.

Seen 'em comin' an hour away, he thought almost with regret. *At least I won't have to make no decisions about killin'—not by myself, anyways. Pa an' them'll have time to git here, prob'ly before the Carters do.*

Jimmy Dale sighted down his rifle, drew a deep, calming breath, and waited.

Forty minutes later, moving in the direct line of Jimmy Dale Satterfield's sight, Josh Carter rode Blackjack unhurriedly up the first foothill of White Wolf Ridge. His mind was now calm, unrippled, almost numb, much as it had been before every battle he had faced. Holding the torch high, he led his brother, his uncles, and his cousins toward the Satterfields' land.

He heard the faint pop almost as soon as he felt the finger-numbing jerk of the torch. "What the devil!" he swore.

Three more pops sounded, and three torches flew out of the hands of the men directly behind him—Dane, Flave, and Deak. Yelps and curses split the air, and confused voices rang out.

"It's gotta be Jimmy Dale!" Josh called out harshly.

"What're we gonna do?" Dane cried. "He kin pick ever one of us off—where's he at? How kin we—" He sounded very young and very scared.

"He cain't shoot all of us!" Josh growled. "Put all of them torches out, now! Grind 'em in the snow! Ride across the ridge, hard and fast, to Copperhead Gate!"

The men behind him were still swearing and calling out questions as they dismounted to put out the targets they carried, when Josh kicked Blackjack hard. The dark horse reared, then galloped across the low foothills, a black stain melting into the night. Soon the seven men followed, the sound of hoofbeats muted but still ominous.

Far above them, Enoch Satterfield and his thirteen kinsmen heard the distant sound of men riding across the Ridge. Instantly he realized that they wouldn't try to charge up the Trace, with Jimmy Dale's rifle an invisible long-distance menace directly above them. Quickly he turned his men, leading them with a hoarse shout, back to the far end of White Wolf Ridge. Almost blind in the thick darkness, he grimly prayed that they wouldn't all—men and horses both—die in the headlong race to the vantage point above the narrow valley that was Copperhead Gate. One horse did stumble and go down, and another man was brutally swept off by a low-hanging branch. Still the Satterfields rode hard, and reached the sharp-peaked mountain overlooking the narrow gorge only minutes before Josh Carter rode headlong into the Gate.

The Satterfields dismounted and ran to the edge of the precipice. Each man had a muzzle-loader, already loaded, and they fired fast and blind down into the gorge. Josh Carter already had taken a semblance of cover in a skinny cleft in the rock side of the canyon. Seven horses shot through the Gate minutes behind him, their riders already throwing themselves belly-down and desperately trying to aim above their heads. The Satterfields, after raining down a volley of useless shots, had to stand up to reload, and even in the shadows of the night they made clear targets.

Only seven minutes after Enoch Satterfield fired the first shot at Josh Carter, Copperhead Gate was silent except for groans of wounded men. Latham Trask and Levi Satterfield lay side by side on the hill overlooking the gate. Booth Trask, kneeling between them, desperately fumbled to try to find how and where his father was injured. Two other Satterfield men groaned and called out weakly. T. R. sat up against a tree, holding his side, his face white and shocked, cursing loudly.

Below them, Josh Carter stood tense over Dane's still body, crumpled and small at his feet. Josh aimed up the hill, tears rolling down his cheeks unheeded and incongruous with the deadly determination on his face. Flave Carter looked wearily down at his blood-soaked right arm. Close beside him, his brother Deak lay face down, and blood ran from under him to form an ugly black stain on the snowy ground.

Until the Day Break,

PART FOUR

and the Shadows Flee Away

Until the day break,
and the shadows flee away,
turn, my beloved. . . .

Song of Solomon 2:17

20

COPPERHEAD GATE: AFTERMATH

"Dane took a shot in the hip. He ain't doin' too good." Josh's voice was harsh with weariness and fear. "Uncle Flave took a hit in the arm, up here"—jerkily he brushed the upper part of his right shoulder with his hat—"an' I think he's a-gonna be all right. Uncle Deak got shot twice."

He stopped to swallow hard before continuing. His mouth was parched, his throat raspy, but he knew better than to ask a drink from Maeva. "One bullet hit him in the right side. Went right through, but it cracked a rib. Reckon he was spinnin' from thet shot when a bullet grazed him longways across the chest. Burnt a swath from arm to arm." Crushing his hat mercilessly between his hands, his troubled green eyes implored Maeva. "He's hurtin' something awful, but he's gonna be all right, I reckon. Hit's mostly Dane I'm troubled about."

Maeva stood in the doorway of her cabin, silent and motionless. Josh tried to keep himself from fidgeting or pleading or panicking as he waited. He must have waked her—it was not yet dawn—but her eyes were clear, her face smooth, her hair shiny and not tousled. Her white cape was carelessly thrown about her shoulders. Underneath she had on a plain white cotton nightgown, and her feet were bare. In Josh's mind, she looked like a dark angel in a shimmer of white, and he thought of her hands. *Hands full of grace, so sure, so quick. Feel so cool on yore forehead when you're sick*, he thought awkwardly. *Healing hands . . .*

"I'll come," Maeva said evenly and shut the cabin door, leaving Josh in the dark and the cold to wait. It began to snow.

★ ★ ★ ★

Sharon, sitting by Dane's bedside, felt stinging in her eyes that blurred her vision even more. After staying at Dane's side almost constantly for the last three days with her husband and with Maeva, she was utterly exhausted. At times she thought she was asleep and dreaming that she sat at Dane's bedside; then she would become confused and disoriented because she was actually sitting by Dane's bed—wasn't she? But was she awake or asleep?

Wearily she tried to concentrate on what Maeva and Josh were saying, even though she could hardly hear them. They seemed to be farther away from her than just across the room.

"I sent Bobbie Jo for Shiloh, Josh," Maeva was saying evenly. "I gotta go back to my cabin and git some more medicines for Dane."

Josh looked rebellious for a moment, but then his shoulders sagged and his face lost its strength.

"There are streaks of red around the wound," Maeva continued. "I need to go git some oak galls and charcoal and flaxseed fer a poultice to pull the pizen out."

Wearily Josh rubbed up and down the scar on his face. "All right," he muttered, "all right. What kin I do?"

"You and Sharon keep on bathin' him ever thirty minutes with that willow bark tea," Maeva instructed. "Keep on tryin' to git him to drink all the water he can, and then all the lukewarm tea he can. You got any honey? Mix it with the tea. Make him drink at least a cup every hour."

Josh's eye roved over the form of his brother as he lay in the narrow bunk. He seemed smaller, wasted somehow, and his skin was an oddly colored gray. Dane either slept or was unconscious, but periodically a shiver would wrack his body. Josh could hardly bear to look at him, much less bathe him and try to bully him into drinking anything. *Sharon'll help*, he thought desperately. *She's been a godsend these last three accursed days. She's tired, I'm tired, Dane looks like a sickly ghost. May be a good thing Irons is comin'.*

As if she were about to ask a question, Sharon murmured softly, "Josh . . ."

Instantly her body whipped into a ruler-straight line, her head against the wall, her feet on the floor. For a moment she formed a right triangle with the wall and floor. Sluggishly Josh was filled first with amazement, then with choking fear.

Maeva was already at her side, pulling the straight chair out from behind her, desperately trying to lay her down flat. "Josh!" she barked. "Git a wooden spoon! Now!"

Josh turned on his heel and ran.

Sharon's face grew beet red, and only white showed beneath half-closed eyelids. Seemingly she picked herself up, her body rigidly straight, and threw herself down on the floor. Maeva tried to shove her hand beneath the crown of her head, but only managed to cradle her neck. Josh ran back in the room with a flat wooden spoon, his face stark with shock. Maeva snatched the spoon from his limp hand and managed to work it into Sharon's mouth just before her jaws clamped shut with such force that Maeva was afraid she might bite the spoon in two. Then with horrifying force, in a deadly rhythm, Sharon's head, arms, and legs began to beat the floor.

"Pillow!" Maeva almost screamed, trying to cradle Sharon's head with her hands.

Josh looked around the room helplessly, his body jerking first toward Dane's bed, then toward the door, his eyes wild, uncomprehending. Shiloh burst through the door and rushed to Dane's bedside. He managed to lift Dane's head, slide his pillow out, lay Dane's head back down, and move to Sharon's side to put the pillow under her helplessly pounding head, all of his movements quick but gentle.

"What kin I do?" Maeva yelled. The flailing of Sharon's body on the wooden floor was loud.

"Nothing!" Shiloh called back. "Don't try to hold her! Just wait!"

Josh stood helpless, thoughtless, horrified as Sharon convulsed. It seemed to go on and on, but actually the convulsions lasted less than a minute. As abruptly as she had stiffened up, Sharon's body suddenly went limp. She opened her eyes for a moment, moaned softly, then seemed to go to sleep.

"Josh!" Shiloh ordered. "Let's get her to bed!"

Josh flinched and staggered a half-step backward. Then he rushed to gather Sharon's still form up in his arms and carried her out of the room.

"What kin we do now?" Maeva asked. Her voice was steady and calm, but Shiloh noted that this time she had said "we" instead of "I." The thought would have warmed him if he hadn't been so filled with dread for Sharon and her baby.

"She's probably unconscious right now," he answered in a low voice, "so we wait. Let her come to naturally. Keep her absolutely quiet and still. From now on, Maeva! You tell Josh!"

Maeva nodded, her white teeth worrying her bottom lip. "And the baby?"

"I have a stethoscope in my bag," Shiloh replied evenly. "We'll have to see if the baby's heart is still beating." His eyes met Maeva's cool blue gaze as he gravely added, "If you're a praying woman, you might want to put in a little time right now."

Maeva's mouth twisted slightly, and her usual steady tone was somewhat roughened. "Niver have been before," she shrugged, "but then, I niver was a-scairt of tryin' somethin' new."

★ ★ ★ ★

"T.R.?" Enoch demanded.

"Bullet hit his ribs an' bounced off," Noah said wearily. He was Enoch's next younger brother. Smaller of frame, quieter, less severe than his five brothers, Noah had helped tend the wounded in the last days of the war as the Confederacy waned, and doctors and medical corpsmen were scarce or simply unavailable. Now he was again tending wounded men, although his medical training was woefully inadequate. He felt lost and afraid, but Enoch had told him to do it. Now he shook his head and muttered with wonder, "Same place T. R. got hit at Malvern Hill. Very same place, same rib nicked. When you took away the Sharpshooter's rifle."

"Wisht I coulda took every Carter rifle an' burnt 'em," Enoch rasped, "along with their owners. What about Levi?"

Noah frowned and shook his head. "He got bashed on the head when he run into that big oak branch. He ain't shot, Enoch, but he's out. Ain't moved nor waked up nor blinked nor nothin'.'"

"What does that mean?" Enoch demanded harshly.

"I—I dunno, Enoch," Noah faltered. "I jis' don't know. All I know to do is set with him, be there if'n he tries to wake up."

"*When* he wakes up," Enoch corrected him. "Go on."

"Caleb hurt his ankle when his horse went down. Think it's broke."

Enoch's head jerked up and his eyes burned. "No!"

Noah added hastily, "Not like Caroline's—I think it's jis' cracked a little. Swollen, an' he'll have to stay off it awhile. But I don't even think it'll have to be splinted." Enoch visibly relaxed, and Noah felt some of the constriction in his throat loosen as he went on, "and Will's rifle misfired, burnt both his hands pretty bad. Leastways, he'd already lowered the rifle when it fired the next chamber. He coulda been blinded—or worse."

Enoch nodded and asked, "Latham all right? He jis' got thet one bullet through his hand?"

"Yep. He's all right. Dunno about the hand."

"What? What about it?"

"Enoch, there's lots of little bones in a hand. I dunno if'n it's gonna work right."

"Seems like there's lots of things you don't know," Enoch muttered, but now his voice held no anger or reproach. Suddenly he sounded very tired. "Reckon we better send Jimmy Dale after Maeva."

Noah nodded with relief, but neither man moved. Their shadowed eyes turned toward the kitchen window. Morning had brought no light of dawn, merely a lessening of the dark. The brothers could see that it was beginning to snow.

★ ★ ★ ★

Before Jimmy Dale finished knocking, Cheney threw open the door. Her face was white and strained. Immense relief transformed her for a moment, but almost instantly she looked crestfallen and her eyes dulled. "Oh, hello, Jimmy Dale," she sighed. "I suppose you've come to see Caroline. Your mother's down at the Sikes', having lunch with your brothers and sisters. Caroline's asleep, but you can see her. Come in, please."

Cheney had insisted that Caroline not be moved for a week after the operation, so she and her mother had remained at Cheney's cabin. Shiloh had converted the homemade operating table into a bed for Caroline, somehow managing to put a feather mattress under her, and a clean cotton sheet, while hardly moving her at all. Then he had fixed a cot for Leah and put up a curtain across the back of the sitting room.

Jimmy Dale entered the cabin, eyeing Cheney with doubt. "Um, yes'm, I surely want to see Caroline. I saw my ma down at Sikes'. But thet ain't the only reason I'm here." Hesitantly he asked, "You was expectin' somebody else, maybe?"

Cheney smiled wearily and shook her head. "For three days, I've been waiting—hoping—for someone." Glancing at his chastened face, she hurriedly added, "Not just a Carter, either, Jimmy Dale. I know there must be both Carters and Satterfields who need my help. Of course everyone knows about all the shooting at Copperhead Gate three days ago." With a small helpless gesture she added in a low voice, "But no one's come."

"Well, now I'm here, Doctor Cheney," Jimmy Dale said stoutly. "We had some men hurt. Seems like ever'body was a-gonna be all right—'til today. My uncle Latham, he jis' got shot through the hand. Didn't seem like much. But this mornin' it looked like a red streak was beginnin' to run up his arm." Uneasily Jimmy Dale added a footnote. "My pa's out, been out checkin' traps all day. Reckon he might be out all night, too, if'n he decides to go up to the north huntin' cabin."

"So you mean he doesn't know you're asking me to come?" Cheney asked.

"No, ma'am. But my ma does, an' she's all fer it." Cheney looked doubtful, and Jimmy Dale added somewhat reluctantly, "Glen brung us some deer meat this mornin'. He took Pa aside an' tole him thet Caroline was here, an' thet you'd done fixed her laig."

"What did he say?"

"Nothin'." Jimmy Dale seemed to grope for words and finally added, "But he didn't go gunnin' fer you, did he?"

"No," Cheney muttered dourly, "and that's so reassuring." Unconsciously she pleated her dress between her fingers, then released it, then pleated it again. Jimmy Dale waited patiently.

"I'll come," Cheney finally said. Jimmy Dale looked so grateful, Cheney was slightly ashamed of her hesitation. But still she added uncertainly, "Shiloh isn't here, Jimmy Dale. He left before I got up this morning."

"I know," Jimmy Dale nodded.

"You do? Have you seen him? Do you know where he went?"

"Why—yes, ma'am." Jimmy Dale was obviously loath to answer Cheney's frustrated questions. "I—I saw Bobbie Jo, at the place where we—well, that don't matter," he faltered, "but she were on her way to fetch Shiloh."

Cheney was puzzled. "But—no one—Josh didn't—"

"No, ma'am," Jimmy Dale muttered uncomfortably, then dropped his eyes. "Miss Maeva sent fer him."

Cheney felt resentment and anger rising up in her, a bitter flood tide. *Let it go*, she thought desperately. *You have to let it go. At least be glad that Shiloh can check on Sharon.* Straightening her aching shoulders, she told Josh, "I'll go change and get my medical bag packed."

"Thank you, Doctor Cheney," he murmured. "Thank you very much. I swear the Lord'll bless you fer comin'!"

"Jimmy Dale? Is thet you?" Caroline's voice sounded from behind the curtain, clearer and much stronger than he had expected. "Come back here an' see my new leg! Hurry up!"

Jimmy Dale's hazel eyes lit up, reminding Cheney with a jolt that he was only eighteen years old. He seemed so much older than that most of the time. "She sounds good," he said hopefully. "Is she all right?"

"She's fine," Cheney reassured him. "The operation went well. Caroline is so determined, she'll probably regain her strength very quickly."

"Jimmy Dale!" Caroline called. "If'n you don't come here, I swear I'll jump up an' run in there!"

Grinning foolishly, he turned to go back to the curtained-off cubicle, but Cheney put her hand on his arm. "Jimmy Dale," she said softly, "I just want you to know that I'm not afraid . . . because of your father, or . . . or anything. I trust you just as much as you trust me."

"Doctor Cheney," he said simply, tightly clasping her hand with both of his, "I count it an honor to be yore friend."

★ ★ ★ ★

Enoch Satterfield trudged up the old path from his home that led around to the south side of Maeva's Trace. He wanted to look out over White Wolf Ridge and Black Arrow and Copperhead Gate, and think about the bloodshed of three days ago. For the first time in four days he was alone, and it was a great relief to him. He needed to breathe some free air, some clean mountain air that held no tension or smells of blood or sounds of men in pain. He needed to think.

Cradling his treasured Sharps rifle closer to his side, he negotiated a tree that had fallen over the path. With a trace of amusement he noted that there actually was no visible path; yesterday's snow had layered it even with the surrounding forest floor. Enoch knew the way, however, and reflected idly that he probably could shut his eyes and unerringly negotiate any path on Maeva's Trace.

Seems like I orter be able to see the right path, he thought bitterly. *But it appears I been wrong about two-three things here lately.* His nostrils flared as puffs of steam arose from them. *No* use in strainin' to look over your shoulder, though. Man's gotta figger out how to fix his wrongs, not cry about 'em.

Dispassionately Enoch considered an offensive against the Carters. *Jis' me an' Jimmy Dale, and Noah. Me an' Noah down at the tree line, an' Jimmy Dale halfway up the Ridge. Wait for 'em to come ridin' down agin—only this time, they won't even git off Carter's mountain. An' this time won't be a man of 'em ridin' back home!*

Bitterness rose up in him, sour and painful, as he thought of T. R.'s white face and shredded left side. *Reckon I know jis' how cold the blood is in Miss Maeva's veins,* he railed to himself. *Niver thought I'd see the day that she couldn't git away from the Carters long enough to doctor my people! But there's thet fancy woman I almost burnt at the stake—fixin' my baby Caroline's laig, an' all! With a knife!* He shook his head in wonder at a vision of Caroline walking tall and strong.

As Enoch slowly ascended Maeva's Trace, his thoughts turned to the injured men in his family. *Mighta been my fault they're hurt,* he thought stonily, *but I vow, right here and now, ain't gonna be another drop o' blood shed unless it's my own—or Carters' black blood!*

Enoch veered off the path toward one of the hundreds of streams that trickled down Maeva's Trace to flow into Moccasin Lake. *Think Ben said he set the first trap up here,* he decided, *by thet there little pool. Wouldn't mind havin' a brace o' rabbits fer supper. Shore takes a passel of meat to feed all them men.*

The jaws of the trap were snapped shut, tightly clenched on air, on top of the fresh snow.

Enoch had never said a curse word in his life—a legacy from his stern father. Now he rebelliously thought one but said nothing. Expertly, he reset the trap and returned to the path with long, angry strides. *Winter stores burnt to the ground, men ridin' after me like a hangin' posse, traps sprung! Curse this country, and curse them Carters! Soon as Josh Carter's dead, Waylon DeSpain's gonna git himself all the Satterfield land he wants, cheap!*

Abruptly, Enoch halted in the middle of the path, his mouth

slightly open, his eyes dark with frustration. *Trap was on top o' the snow!* he thought furiously. *On top o' this snow . . . fresh-fallen this mornin'! Gotta be tracks—maybe only a few minutes old! An' here I am like a tom-fool chargin' bull, stompin' all over!*

His sharp hazel eyes searched the line of the invisible path. No tracks were visible; the snow lay completely undisturbed. *Ol' fool!* he chided himself. *Coulda gone off in any direction from that there trap! Whoever it is might not be able to follow the path, like you do.* Cautiously, but quickly, Enoch began to walk again. *Hurry an' check the rest o' the traps . . . jis' might catch thet thievin' varmint! Bound to be a Carter—Lord rest his soul!*

Enoch thought he spotted tracks just ahead, veering off the path to the right. Hurrying to stoop over the marks, he studied them carefully, but they were a mystery. Undoubtedly they were some sort of track, but exactly what kind he couldn't imagine. Some indistinguishable deep marks, quite small, were regularly spaced out in the snow; but the trail Enoch had spotted were wide, shallow brush marks. It almost looked as if a soft broom had been swept along the snow.

Enoch stood, his sharp gaze following the trail where it disappeared into a thicket, naked sticks pointing skyward. *Goin' to the next trap, all right,* he decided. *Up there by them rocks, where somebody took them shots at Jimmy Dale. An' I ain't a-gonna blunder in there this time. . . .* Checking the load of his rifle, he held it in a ready position across his body and made his quiet way through the woods.

The snow crunching beneath his boots was the only sound, and Enoch distributed his weight evenly with each step to mute even that. Within minutes he was at the tree line that surrounded the small glade with the huge rocks, now white with powdery snow instead of lichen gray. He saw no one; but even as he brought his rifle up to firing position, he heard the unmistakable snap! of a trap springing shut. *Behind the rocks,* he thought.

Silently he crept around the ring of rocks. A figure clad in gray stood over the sprung trap. *Kneeling? A man? Small . . .*

Fragments of thoughts flew around Enoch's mind as he pulled the rifle up to his shoulder and growled, "Turn around! Slow!"

The figure seemed to jump straight up, then whirled, then fell sprawling. Enoch, who had been expecting a man to throw down a gun and throw up his hands, jumped too. Then he froze in shock.

Glendean Carter's white, scared face stared up at him from where she had fallen. "Oh, no!" she gulped. "Are you—are you gonna shoot me, Mr. Satterfield?"

Enoch Satterfield suddenly found that his body seemed to be paralyzed as his mind took a visual step back to imprint the scene in his mind forever. He saw not a Carter child, with black blood and hate in her heart, but a small girl, a baby almost. Her dark eyes were huge, filled with terror. From beneath a billowing gray hood a lock of rich brown hair stuck wetly to one cheek. Her feet were bundled in soft moccasins that were obviously secondhand and too big for her.

And with loathing he saw himself: a huge, shambling man with shaggy brown hair, glaring hazel eyes, and a fearsome mustache, pointing a .52 caliber Sharps rifle down at a small child lying in the snow.

Enoch's hands began to shake, and he dropped the rifle as if it were afire. His eyes burned, which vaguely surprised him, because he never could remember crying in his life. Carefully and gently he moved to kneel by the little girl, taking care not to make sudden movements. "My God in heaven above, little girl!" he muttered, his voice guttural with pain. "No! I ain't a-gonna shoot you!"

Glendean frantically searched his face, looking into his eyes, desperately trying to assimilate what he said—and what he meant. Enoch stayed still and allowed her to stare at him, size him up—and felt somehow that though he burned with shame, it was important that he meet her eyes.

Glendean's mind frantically chattered, *He ain't a-gonna hurt me, he dropped the gun; he ain't a-gonna shoot me, he said so; he called God, he promised; he ain't a-gonna kill me . . .* on and on for long moments. Finally she drew a long, shuddering breath, then she sat up and looked woefully at the kneeling man.

"I'm scairt," she said in a small voice.

"I know," he nodded, "an' I'm sorry. I'm scairt too."

In spite of her fear, Glendean found it fascinating that this big man—this man her whole family had always feared, Enoch Satterfield himself—was scared. "You are?" she whispered. "Was you a-scairt I might shoot you?"

"No, darlin'," he replied gently. "I was a-scairt *I* mighta shot *you.*"

Glendean digested this for a while. "But you didn't," she finally declared. "An' I don't think you're a-goin' to no more." Scrambling to her feet, she crossed her arms across her chest, hugging herself, and backed off from Enoch a few feet.

Enoch almost smiled at the cloak she wore. Obviously of fine quality, made of some soft gray wool, it must have been a woman's cloak, cut down. It was still too large for her. The hem was wet, and dragged a full foot behind her. *Good way to conceal your tracks*, he thought ruefully.

Glendean was pale, her breathing erratic, but she looked determined. Assessing him again for long moments, she finally whispered in a wounded voice, "But you shot my pa, didn't you?"

Enoch's heart lurched, but still he didn't make any abrupt movements or attempt to rise. He only crossed his arms over his upright knee and leaned forward slightly. He might be a forbidding, stern man, but he knew instinctively how to keep from being threatening to a child. "No, I niver did," he replied somberly.

Again Glendean regarded him watchfully, with a gaze that seemed so incisive, so penetrating, it might be the gaze of a seventy-year-old woman. "You didn't?" she asked.

To his surprise, she sounded relieved, and as he answered, so did he. "No, I didn't, little girl."

"My name's Glendean," she offered. "An' I b'lieve you."

"You do? Why?"

" 'Cause I think you're tellin' the truth," she replied simply. "My ma says she kin tell if'n I'm lyin' by lookin' at me. An' I think I could look at you an' see if'n you'd lie about—about—thet. My pa." Abruptly she began to cry with sobs that sounded too deep for such a small child. She knotted up her fists and rubbed her eyes hard, but still the tears flowed.

Enoch badly wanted to take the child into his arms and soothe her, but he knew better. *She give me a chance to tell the truth,* he reflected, *an' then she believed me. Reckon thet's more'n I deserve.*

As Glendean's sobs finally subsided into sniffles, he carefully rose to his feet. Glendean's dark eyes followed him all the way up, and his shadow completely engulfed her. "Why don't we dust the snow off'n them rocks and sit down fer a spell?" Enoch asked politely. "We both had us a scare, an' I'd like to rest a minute."

After a few moments Glendean finally murmured, "Awright."

"Good," he nodded. "I'd like the company. Kinda lonely up here, ain't it? 'Specially when you're all by yourself?"

"Murdoch's down on the Ridge, waitin' fer me," Glendean replied noncommittally. Hesitantly Enoch held out his arms to lift her up to the rock, and she relented and allowed him to do it. "But this is the first time I been up here by myself. Usually my Oncle Glen brings me."

Enoch leaned up against the rock that squatted next to where Glendean sat, eyeing his rifle regretfully as it lay in the wet snow. He knew better than to touch it yet, however. "He does? Thet's good. Yore Uncle Glen's a friend o' mine, you know."

"I know." She gave him a sidelong glance, and some of the fear stole over her face again. "Are you gonna holler at me an' Oncle Glen about springin' yore traps?"

No wonder Glen's been bringin' us so much meat! Enoch thought with exasperation. "Don't reckon I'll holler," Enoch answered gravely. "But I would like fer you to tell me why yore a-doin' it."

"Aw, shoot, Mr. Enoch," she cried. "You didn't know? Since Oncle Glen's yore friend, I thought he woulda told you! Beauregard got caught in one, an' it hurt his leg somethin' awful, 'til Doctor Cheney fixed it up! An Murdoch's his brother, you know, an' I love both of 'em so much, an' so does Oncle Glen! We hate them gol-derned traps!"

Now Enoch, in his turn, took a few moments to digest this mish-mash of information. *Beauregard . . . Glen's horse! So Murdoch must be a horse!* Relief swept over Enoch with such intensity it surprised him. When Glendean had said that Murdoch waited for her down on the Ridge, he had immediately been filled with dread. *Seems like I don't hev no stomach fer shootin' Carters today*, he mused. *And mebbe not fer any days to come. . . .*

21

THE HIGH, COLD FULL MOON

"Tim Toney thinks he's so smart," Bake Conroy muttered with disdain. "Gabe Stroud's so busy boot-lickin' he's probably forgot how to get up from his hands and knees. And Mr. Day might be eddicated, and all"—he cracked the breech of the rifle with a loud snap—"but even he don't understand. Not like I do." Briskly he seesawed a rag fragrant with linseed oil back and forth in the already-gleaming breech. "I understand, because I *listen!* They just don't *listen!*"

Peering down the barrel, he clicked his tongue with satisfaction. He had found this rifle in Fort Smith, when Mr. De-Spain had sent him away in disgrace. As soon as he had seen it, he had realized that he was meant to find this particular rifle—a Sharps .52, with a telescope—so he could redeem himself.

Somberly he continued, "What Mr. DeSpain said was: we don't understand what he wants! Gotta listen! Not just to what he says, but to what he wants!" Bake shook his head regretfully as he loaded a single cartridge into the breech. Thoughtfully regarding the case head with the distinctive letter "H" stamped on it, he nodded and shoved another cartridge in behind the first.

Snapping the breech securely, he looked around his small cubicle built into the corner of the bunkhouse. It was clean and spare, with no frills or ornaments. It was solitary, but Bake didn't mind solitude. He really didn't intend for anyone to hear what he was saying, anyway.

"Feud's going good," he said, smiling coldly at the blank wall, "since I kinda got things rollin' by fixing Lige Carter. Carters and Satterfields both are starting to think Mr. DeSpain's money looks pretty good. Now . . ." He crossed his arms, leaned back contentedly on his bunk, and considered the bare white ceiling. "There's just one more little bit of business I gotta take care of . . . I think I know just what Mr. DeSpain wants."

★ ★ ★ ★

"Listen here, horse," Maeva began but stopped when she heard the sound of her own voice, tentative and weak. Clearing her throat, she began again. "Sock," she declared, "we's almost at my cabin. You done real good." She felt absolutely ridiculous, but she had the vague notion that one must reward animals when they performed tricks or did favors for humans. She noted that Sock's ears had twitched when she spoke, so she decided that she probably had done right by the horse. She had never had a pet of any sort, so she couldn't be quite certain, but Sock seemed to be satisfied.

"He might even let me git back on him," Maeva muttered dourly to herself. "Maybe even without kickin' my fool head off, or bitin' me or stompin' me or whatever it is horses do when they just plain don't like a person." Sock's ears twitched again, and Maeva grudgingly admitted to herself that she and Shiloh's horse had somehow managed to work together fairly well.

Like you and Shiloh do. The thought popped impertinently into her mind. Sternly she put thoughts of Shiloh Irons aside. *Time for that later,* she chided herself. *Right now you just make sure you know what you're comin' back here for!* Mentally she ticked off a list: woodbine—tell Josh to wind it around Sharon's head, wrists, and belly to choke off the convulsions—at least it'll keep her still. Now for Dane—what was it?

Running her hand through her straight, thick hair, she shook it free, lifted her face to the sky, and breathed deeply. *There's plenty o' time,* she repeated firmly to herself. *Get to the cabin and eat something. And feed this horse something, I reckon. Drink some cinnamon tea, hot and strong. Cool cloth over my eyes for five minutes. Then decide what you need . . . start back . . . to Shiloh . . .*

Abruptly Sock came to a halt. He was practically standing

on her doorstep. Smiling, she patted him lightly on the neck and dismounted, then stretched gracefully. She felt better already, and she had plenty of time.

★　★　★　★

"It's not that I'm nervous, or scared for her, or anything," Shiloh drawled. "I know she can take care of herself. And she knew that Sharon and the baby were all right, and that I had carbolic acid to clean out Dane's wound. And she wouldn't have gone to the Satterfields'. I think she's probably just resting before she wrestles that horse all the way back to the Carters'. Don't you think that's probably it?"

Glen did manage to keep from laughing out loud, but he had to turn around full-front to hide his grin. Behind him Shiloh glumly rode Murdoch, the look on his face contrasting sharply with his careless words. *That the third time he's said all that? Glen gleefully wondered. Or the fourth?*

"Yep. That's prob'ly it, Shiloh," he finally answered. Shiloh didn't seem to notice that Glen's voice was constricted with tightly controlled laughter.

"She knows that Cheney's taking care of the Satterfields, right?" Shiloh insisted.

"Told her so myself," Glen said faintly. "Reckon she woulda gone there?"

"Nah, I don't think so," Shiloh muttered uneasily. "Do you?"

"Nope. Do you?" Glen's voice sounded high and strained.

"Nope," Shiloh replied seriously. "And she knew Dane and Sharon were better. She's probably just resting, don't you think?"

"Yep, probably," Glen choked. "Maybe she just wanted to rest a little afore she started back on that bully horse of yourn."

"You think so?" Shiloh asked intently. "Not that I'm worried, or anything."

The two rode in silence for a while. Glen looked around at the woods, thinking how gray and dreary the landscape was. *Snow even looks dirty gray*, he thought idly. *Guess it's 'cause the*

289

light's dirty gray. Behind him, Shiloh thought sourly that Glen certainly seemed to be dawdling along.

They reached the foot of Maeva's mountain and began the slow ascent. Glen broke the long silence. "Shiloh?"

"What?" Shiloh was startled at the harshness of his own voice, but Glen seemed not to notice.

"What are you scared of?"

"Scared of?" Shiloh repeated blankly, furrowing his brow. "Well, Sharon scared me back there, when she was convulsing, just before you got there. Is that what you mean?"

"Naw." Glen shook his head impatiently. "Not like that. What I mean is—what makes you afraid?"

Shiloh was silent for so long, Glen turned in the saddle to see if he might have fallen asleep or fallen off his horse and been left behind. At his look, Shiloh grumbled, "I'm planning on answering you, as soon as I figure out what the question is."

"Lemme give you a fr'instance," Glen said helpfully.

"Oh, thanks. I'd appreciate your help."

"See, I've noticed that you won't fight—"

"You noticed that, did you?" Shiloh interrupted. "Was that at Thanksgiving, when I took off at a dead run before you could kill me to save Lorine's honor?"

Grandly, Glen ignored him and continued, "—but I know it ain't 'cause yore afraid. You got your reasons for not fightin', I reckon, but it ain't 'cause yore afraid. Jis' like back there with Miss Sharon. She mighta scared you—but I bet, deep down, you weren't afraid."

"Well . . ."

"You knew what to do, didn't you? And you done it, didn't you?" Glen demanded.

"S'pose so," Shiloh shrugged.

"So you weren't afraid," Glen declared. "What I'm tryin' to talk about is something that makes you afraid so's you don't 'zackly know what to do." Turning back in the saddle, Glen seemed lost in thought, as if he actually had asked himself the question and expected no answer from Shiloh.

Finally he heard Shiloh say in a conversational tone, "Maeva."

"Hmm?" Glen asked, startled. "What's that?"

"I said 'Maeva,'" Shiloh repeated slowly. "She's the only thing I've ever come up on that I'm afraid of, like you say. Been on my own, taking care of myself, all my life," he stated simply. "Guess I learned kinda early about making the kinds of decisions men have to face. But Maeva, now . . ." Shaking his head, he let the words trail off.

"Doctor Cheney make you afraid like that?" Glen asked abruptly.

"No," Shiloh answered without hesitation. "I know her."

★ ★ ★ ★

Sock stood in the clearing in front of Maeva's cabin, reins trailing limply to the ground. As Shiloh and Glen pulled their mounts up a few feet from him, Sock pawed the ground nervously and snorted.

Shiloh and Glen blinked in the late afternoon gloom. Something was behind Sock, something on the ground. A shapeless white hump, but what were those black patches?

At the same instant, Shiloh and Glen threw themselves off their horses and ran. Panting, Shiloh slid the last few inches on his knees, but when he came to a stop beside the crumpled figure of Maeva Wilding, he found he could not reach out to touch her. "Oh, no," he moaned thickly, "oh, no, no . . ."

Glen fell to his knees on the other side of Maeva's body. He noticed that he was holding his breath and choking. Suddenly he drew in a great gulp of air and reached out with a shaking hand. He turned Maeva over. Her dark blue eyes stared indifferently at the darkening sky. Against the white snow, her bronze complexion gave a cruel impression of the blush of life. Shiloh reached out and closed her eyes gently.

Afternoon had drifted close to evening. The two men knelt by the body, unaware of the icy snow surrounding them and the brooding darkness gathering. No words were spoken. The only sounds were those of horses milling about—their heavy steps muted, the businesslike leather saddle sounds and harness clinks deadened by the powdery snow. Once Shiloh reached out with a jerky, impatient movement to smooth Maeva's fur cloak. Glen's meaty hand hovered over the black splash of her hair for a few moments, but then he withdrew it as if he were ashamed.

Shiloh looked around, shocked at the darkness. Reaching in his pocket, he pulled out his pocket watch and opened it.

When Johnny comes marching home. . . . The tune was slow and dragging, and died out before the end.

"What—what time is it?" Glen asked in confusion.

"Dunno," Shiloh replied in a leaden voice. "Forgot to wind it."

Glen sat back on his heels and drew a long, shuddering breath. "Let's take her in. It's cold."

"Yes." It seemed to take Shiloh a long time to answer. "I'll . . . fix her. In that white dress of her mother's . . . with the red ribbons . . . and her cape." Gently he ran his hand lightly over the white fur.

"If'n you'll fix her up in thet white dress," Glen said in a faraway voice, "I'll sew up the hole in the cape, and clean it."

"Yes."

Neither man moved.

"Then . . . what do we do?" Shiloh asked.

"Tonight we sit up with her."

"What do . . . you mean?" Shiloh's words were hesitant. He seemed to be having trouble making conversation.

Glen shrugged, a slow lifting of his shoulders that seemed to cost him a great effort. "Used to do it 'cause of the wild animals, long time ago, you see," he answered woodenly. "But I reckon now we jis' do it to . . . honor her."

"Yes, I see," Shiloh nodded dreamily. "Not because of the wild animals. . . ."

But that night, for the first time that winter, the wolves called long and mournfully at the high, cold, full moon.

22

BLACKCASTLE SPRINGS

Shiloh and Glen mourned Maeva Wilding all the long night, and each honored her in his memory as best he could.

Maeva lay in her feather bed, dressed in the simple white velvet gown with the wide red sash that had belonged to her mother, and brand-new white moccasins that Glen had made for her. Shiloh spread the cleaned and mended cape over her, its voluminous folds brushing the floor on either side of the bed.

"Do you—would you mind if'n I fixed her hair?" Glen asked thickly.

Shiloh mutely shook his head.

Glen brushed her long black hair to a sheen, then pulled it over one shoulder and tied a red ribbon in it. He had to try three times before he got it right. Then they lit two white candles and placed them on the two windowsills. Shiloh brought in two straight wooden chairs from the kitchen, and they seated themselves on either side of the bed. In the gently flickering light, Maeva seemed to sleep.

Occasionally in the night Glen told Shiloh stories about Maeva. "Seems like she was allus jis' like this, even when she were a child," he mused. "She knew things about people."

"Like what they were afraid of," Shiloh sighed.

"Yes," Glen agreed. "Like that."

Once Shiloh's eyes lingered on Maeva's hands, crossed upon the thick white wolf fur of the cape. "Her hands," he whispered, almost to himself. "So cool, and soft . . . I guess she never told anyone how she kept them so soft. . . ."

Glen watched the candle's ghost-shadows in the corners of

the room. "She had healing hands," he replied, as if that explained it.

The candles flickered out long before dawn, but the cool white light of the moon seemed fitting. By unspoken consent Glen and Shiloh sat with Maeva until the sun was well up. They both seemed to know when it was time to rise and leave the tiny bedroom, pulling the curtain closed behind them.

Both men hoped to leave the shadows of their grief behind that curtain, so they walked outside, squinting in the bright morning glare and coughing as they stamped in the cold, breathing great gulps of the stinging air. Glen narrowed his eyes and scanned the clearing in front of the cabin. "I'm gonna find the bullet."

"Good," Shiloh nodded curtly. "But don't pick it up. I want to see where it is."

Glen walked over to where the bloodstain was frozen on the snow, and began to walk a circle around it, his head down. In the cold fireplace Shiloh built a fire. He thrust a coffeepot into the heart of it with savagely precise movements. A stranger, observing the two of them and listening to them, would have thought perhaps they were gunfighters or bounty hunters—cold and heartless men.

"Here!" Glen called.

Shiloh unhurriedly went outside to stand by Glen. He looked down at the inconsequential hole in the snow with anger, then turned his face upward.

"What," Glen demanded, not inquired.

"Her wound," Shiloh said succinctly, still gazing at the branches of the trees above them. "Did you see?"

Glen stared down at the ground. "I saw enough. Figure I know what we're going to find in that little hole."

"Go ahead."

Glen reached down, plucked the ball out of the snow, and held it out in an upturned palm. It was bulky, knobby, ugly, and big. "Might could be a forty-four," he said indifferently.

"It's a fifty-two and you know it."

"Yep, reckon I do. But why the devil would Enoch Satterfield shoot Maeva?" Glen's voice sounded strained.

"That's the first question," Shiloh stated flatly. "The next one is: why would Enoch Satterfield climb all the way up there"— he jabbed a forefinger toward the highest peak of Blackcastle Springs, looming close in the sky over them—"to shoot Maeva?"

"What are you talking about?"

"I'm trying to tell you, Glen," Shiloh explained so carefully that Glen bristled slightly. "Her wound. Bullet came in here"— he put his hand high on his chest, then whirled and put his hand on his lower back—"and came out here."

Glen turned his gaze up to the mountain, a jagged black imprint on the mild blue winter sky above the clearing. "Hard fer me to think of what it's like to have one of them fancy telescopes." His dark eyes seemed to mirror the smooth glint of obsidian that formed the sides of the highest peak. "Reckon I'll be a-goin' up there," he murmured.

"I'm going, too."

Glen turned on his heel and stalked back into the cabin. In a few minutes he came back out carrying two items: a copy of *McGuffey's Eclectic Reader*, worn and faded; and a small polished cedar box, obviously homemade. Wordlessly he held out the box, and Shiloh took it and opened it. Inside were a simple turquoise-and-coral necklace and a tiny gold ring. Shiloh smelled the faint fragrance of cedar.

"Did you notice these was the onliest little—personal— things in her room? They was layin' on the washstand," Glen said gruffly. "I looked at 'em all night, thinkin'. Maeva ast me oncet if'n I could read. Guess we was twelve, thirteen years old. I smart-alecked off to her, somethin' like, 'O' course! My pa woulda whacked the tar outen me if'n I didn't learn to read!' " He looked down at the book, unseeing, running his hand back and forth across the tattered cover. "I ain't sure Justine ever taught Maeva to read. Shore wisht I hadn't said that." His voice was harsh with regret.

Shiloh's mind was sharp and alert, and he was not at all tired, but he simply couldn't think of anything to say to comfort Glen. "I gave her this necklace for Christmas," he said quietly. "She never even had a chance to wear it. But this ring . . . I don't know anything about it. Do you?"

Glen didn't answer for a long time. He raised his eyes from the book, up to the peaks of Blackcastle Springs Mountain, the expression on his face unreadable. Finally he told Shiloh in a careful tone, "My pa's name was Seth."

The words made no sense to Shiloh until, frowning down at the box, he impulsively turned it over. Scratched on the bottom of the box were tiny initials: S. R.

Gingerly he picked the ring out of the box and held it up between his thumb and forefinger. It was very small and plain, but it was a perfect circle, not nicked or dented; and the gold gleamed as if it had recently been polished. He dropped the ring back into the box and replaced the smooth-fitting top. "I can't wear it," he said dully.

"Neither could she," Glen retorted. Shiloh didn't know whether he meant Maeva or her mother, or both; but he decided to keep the ring, and slid it into the pocket of his fishskin.

Glen turned to study the cabin somberly for a few moments. Then he faced Shiloh and said curtly, "I'm a-gonna chop down them three trees that's close up by the cabin."

"What?" Shiloh exclaimed sharply. Two tall, shapely pines grew on one corner, slightly behind Maeva's cabin. An old, stately oak grew almost right against the front corner. "Why? They'll fall right on top of the cabin!"

"I know." Glen nodded slowly. "Need to do it, 'cause the cabin's gonna start burnin' in a few minutes."

Shiloh was jolted into silence. Glen offered no further comment; he merely waited, watching the changing expressions on Shiloh's face.

When the shock subsided, and Shiloh was able to think clearly again, he realized, *No one would ever want to live here. And Maeva would hate— No, I would, and Glen would hate it if people came up here disturbing it, or just . . . sightseeing. . . .* With a start, Shiloh remembered that this mountain—and Blackcastle Springs, too—again belonged to Glen. He had the right.

Shiloh peeled off his fishskin and growled, "Let's get to it, then."

They felled the two pines first, then together they furiously chopped the huge oak. Even with a killing wedge chopped almost completely through the great trunk, the tree still stood, tall and unyielding. Shiloh and Glen dropped their axes and pushed mightily, sweat running down their foreheads, grunting painfully. Acrid fire-scent began to sting their nostrils, though they saw no flames as yet. Finally an explosive crack cleaved the air, and the unforgettable, seemingly unending sound of a great giant falling to the ground echoed through the quiet forest. Glen and Shiloh watched the remains of the cabin crash to the ground, and flames began to lick at the two pines. Maeva's funeral pyre would burn for two days and two nights.

They watched only for a few moments, then abruptly Glen turned and whistled sharply. Beauregard galloped into view almost immediately, followed by Murdoch and then Sock. Glen began to walk toward Blackcastle Springs. Shiloh and the horses followed.

When they got to the foot of the mountain, Glen stopped and motioned to the right, slightly downhill. "There's a little pool right on t'other side of them trees. Lead the horses over there, but don't tie 'em up. Beau'll stay, so them two will."

Shiloh led the horses to the pool and dropped the reins. They seemed to be looking after him questioningly as he disappeared, but they didn't try to follow. Soon Shiloh returned to where Glen stood moodily staring up at the sharp black crystal peaks above. Neither of them spoke as they began to ascend the cruelest face of Blackcastle Springs Mountain.

Nearly an hour passed before they came to the first sheer wall of obsidian. Glen hesitated, looking at the narrow paths to the right and left. Shiloh wiped his brow. This half climbing, half striding was hot, hard work.

He searched the valley below. An unmistakable stain of gray smoke rose from directly below them, but they couldn't see the cabin or the clearing. They hadn't risen high enough above the tree line. "Gotta get higher," Shiloh said.

Wordlessly Glen turned and began winding up the side of the mountain. After a few minutes of negotiating the steep side, he said over his shoulder, "I think this here's a path."

Shiloh seemed to use his hands much more than Glen, and he definitely was breathing harder. "A path," he repeated, panting.

"Just a feelin' more'n anything else." Glen waved his hand vaguely. "Hard to tell 'cause of the snow. But seems like you kin feel to wind your way up to the top, along where the underbrush might be beat down. You see?"

"No," Shiloh said shortly, "but I trust you. Lead on." Abruptly, a misstep caused him to come face-to-face with the steep slope, and he managed to push himself back up just before sprawling flat.

Glen didn't look around at the scuffling sounds and grunts behind him. "Yore laigs is too long," he explained. "Throws you off balance. You ain't cut out to traipse around these mountains."

"No, I'm not," Shiloh murmured quietly. "Guess I never was." Suddenly the pain of loss seemed fresh and raw again, and he and Glen climbed in silence.

Glen wound around to the left, then to the right. They didn't stop again for quite a while, and Glen seemed confident of their direction. Shiloh couldn't get much of an overview, as he had to watch his footing carefully and also keep his eyes on Glen's unerring steps in front of him. But he was aware that they climbed steadily and had managed to avoid another sheer wall of the strange black glass.

Glen stopped abruptly and Shiloh almost ran into him. "Reckon this could be it?" he asked quietly, looking down into the valley. Shiloh turned and followed his gaze. They stood on a small, flat shelf of black rock, and could see the burning cabin and the clearing plainly.

"It's high enough," Shiloh replied reluctantly, "but it's kinda hard to tell without a 'scope." Studying the view with a critical eye, he finally shook his head. "I don't think the angle's right."

"Guess I don't rightly know what you're looking for." Glen scowled.

"Think about it," Shiloh encouraged him. "Look down there and remember exactly where she was lying." Bleak realization of his loss surprised him again, making him swallow convulsively.

Glen was watching him intently, his dark eyes filled with understanding and his own grief.

Shiloh determined to go on. "Where she was lying," he repeated in a stronger voice, "and the entry and exit wound, and where you found the bullet. It has to be a straight line that ended—or rather, began," he amended harshly, "up here."

"I see," Glen nodded, "and you're right. He couldna been standin' here." Squinting up to the left, he said, "Almost has to be up there. But how the heck did he git up there, an' how'd he keep from slidin' offa that rock? Looks slippery, an' it slopes downways a little bit!"

Frustrated, the two scanned the jutting shelf above. Perhaps five more steps to their left would bring them to a sheer wall, which formed the northern crest of the mountain. It was broken only by a shiny, flat rock that appeared to be precariously stuck onto the crystal wall. The deadly straight line from this mountain to Maeva Wilding must have begun from that one inaccessible rock.

Angrily Shiloh walked the last few steps to the wall and hit it with his fist. Then he straightened with surprise, reached out his hand, and—to Glen's amazement—walked into the solid wall!

"Come here and look at this!"

Glen could hear Shiloh's voice clearly; he seemed to be only a few feet away. Hurrying to the wall, he searched the surface of it with his fingers, feeling slightly delirious. Half of Shiloh's body suddenly reappeared right by him.

"Look!" Shiloh exclaimed. "It's a hallway!" He completely disappeared again.

Even though Glen was standing only a few feet from the slender crevice, he still could hardly see it until he was directly in front of it. The smoky, shiny surface of the obsidian fooled the eye, much as a series of mirrors placed to reflect each other will. Glen stepped into the shallow depression, which appeared to be merely a high, narrow crevice; but once he stood facing the back wall, there was an opening sharp to his right, and then it cut back to the left. He found himself facing a straight pathway that seemed to have been chiseled out of the solid rock. The floor underneath was smoke-gray, and the wall on the right rose up about twelve feet. The wall on his left was the mountain itself.

Shiloh stood ahead of him, impatiently motioning him forward. They followed the strange passage upward and around, and found the outcropping of rock they had been seeking. But the shelf, for the moment, held no interest for them.

Inside Blackcastle Springs Mountain was a garden.

Shiloh thought that thousands, or maybe tens of thousands of years ago this might have been an enclosed cave. But somehow, the mountain had shifted to make a three-sided room with walls, floor, and ceiling of black glass. The open end of the room faced directly northeast, flooding the room with long hours of benevolent indirect sunlight.

At the far end of the room, a small fountain bubbled quietly from a shelf about three feet up the wall. The water cascaded down into a large, shallow basin which must have had a tiny opening back into the heart of the mountain, for it formed a small pool that evidently stayed at a constant level. *So perfect, it could be manmade,* Shiloh thought. Then he corrected himself, *No, better than manmade.*

Everywhere there were green plants and jarring splashes of colored flowers. Once again, Shiloh's and Glen's eyes were fooled, for they thought at first that the plants were growing in the mountain. But Shiloh realized that this room was made of rock, and no plants would grow naturally here. As he studied the room, he could clearly see that although the greenery at first seemed abandoned and wild, there was a barely discernible order to it. The walls were lined with plants, and in the middle of the square room were plants—but clearly a straight path led down the side, across the back, and back up the other wall.

"Maeva! This must be her garden!" Glen breathed. "Mm, mm, mm! Ain't this a sight!"

"Maeva's secret garden," Shiloh murmured. He sounded almost happy. Slowly he wandered around the room, touching the shiny leaves of the plants. As he got close, he could see that all of them were either in raised beds made of small stripped logs, or in some type of container. An old kindling box held a large, nodding fern that Shiloh had seen growing by streams. A chipped ceramic bowl such as women used for mixing bread dough held a plant with indifferent greenery but with startling orange flowers at the end of long stems. With a half-smile he saw three dented chamber pots in a corner; two of them held small, delicate pine trees and the other a plant with large blossoms that Shiloh was almost certain was an opium poppy.

Shiloh could now see that Maeva had built raised beds down the entire length of all three walls, about two feet high, and another square bed in the center of the room. The earth in the beds was almost completely covered with plants and even plain grass; but Shiloh could see glimpses of the rich, black, crumbly dirt.

How in the world did she ever get all of this done? he wondered. *How many years did it take? How many back-breaking trips?* Kneeling to examine the striplings Maeva had used to make the beds, he shook his head in amazement. *No way to get logs more than four feet long through that zigzagged entryway*, he realized with amazement, *so that means she had to cut them to four-foot lengths and haul them two, maybe three, at a time.*

As he knelt, he noticed that the floor of the cavern was very warm. *Hot springs must trickle all under this room,* he thought. *It's almost hot—and humid, too. No wonder everything grows like this.* Then he saw, right by his knee, a round, red muscadine. Looking up, his eyes suddenly picked out muscadine vines twining and curling everywhere, with fat red grapes peeping out from behind and under the flat, dull leaves. They even were beginning to run along the ceiling, he saw with amusement. Muscadine vines were hardier than the most stubborn weeds.

Glen, too, wandered the room, touching leaves and flowers with awe, trying to adjust to the shock of seeing this greenness, this life, this robust growth in the black heart of a mountain, in the middle of winter. Shaking his head, he murmured, "Nobody on this earth coulda done this but Maeva."

Shiloh stood up, and his face again grew hard. "And I'll bet nobody on this earth knew about it but her—and whoever killed her."

As if by a signal, Glen and Shiloh walked out to the rock shelf where someone, just the day before, had waited with a powerful rifle. It looked as if a column of the rock wall had broken off about chest-high, leaving a narrow break in the high wall that overlooked Maeva's cabin. The rock that Shiloh and Glen had seen jutted out in front.

"Perfect sniper's nest," Shiloh growled.

Both of them looked around the wall where the killer must have waited, perhaps for hours, to shoot Maeva. The hallway in front of the room was littered, too, with boxes and bowls holding plants. An old, dented watering can lay on its side by the opening in the wall. One large box made of old cedar shakes held dirt. Shiloh saw with some amusement that one flour sack held rabbit droppings. He had teased Maeva about collecting the small round inoffensive leavings, but she had informed him with great dignity that "rabbit tea's the best fertilizer there is."

Glen bent down, snatched up something on the floor, and held it out to Shiloh. "Copper Winchester cartridge," he muttered. "Fifty-two caliber."

Shiloh felt rather deflated. "I guess we expected that."

Glen searched his face shrewdly. "What's the matter? This tells us for sure that it was a fifty-two caliber rifle! And that tells us who killed her!"

"I don't know, Glen," Shiloh said hesitantly. "I was hoping we'd find something else, something more."

"But what? Why?"

"It just doesn't make any sense, Glen!" Shiloh insisted. "Enoch Satterfield wouldn't hide up here like a stinking rat, waiting and sneaking! You know he wouldn't!"

Blowing out an exasperated breath, Glen's eyes ran over and around the hallway, the floor, the wall, the room behind him. Finally he said mildly, "I know, Shiloh. I don't think it was Enoch, either. But there ain't nothing else here except . . . you know . . . Maeva."

Shoulders sagging with defeat, Shiloh dropped his head. On the gleaming floor by his boots were traces of a garden: little bits and dribbles of dirt, some leaves and broken stems, bark chips, a scattering of small brown seeds. Sadly he replied, "You're right. This place is just like her, and all that's here are memories of her. Let's go."

23

ELEGY AND REQUIEM

"Shiloh, I'm sorry," Cheney murmured, her face pale with shock. "I'm so sorry."

"Yes," he said simply. Rising from the kitchen table, he went to stand over the stove with his back to Cheney. The kitchen was warm and inviting, but he was still chilled. His fishskin was dirty, his boots muddy. His blue eyes were clouded with exhaustion, and a wide sooty smudge lay under his left eye, which made the "V" scar look as if it were written with heavy charcoal. "Glen went straight on down to the church. He figured the men were gathering to go up to—up on the mountain, because of the fire."

"Yes, they are," Cheney replied. "They rang the church bell, and everyone went to see, of course. I decided to come back and get ready, just in case." She paused for a moment, then in a tight voice she asked, "You aren't thinking of going back up there, are you?"

"No. No one's going back up there. Glen and I . . . Glen and I . . . made sure the fire won't spread."

This was new, this hesitation and heaviness in Shiloh's voice. To Cheney, it revealed the depth of his grief much more clearly than his words. *Why don't I know just exactly what to say to him?* she thought desperately. *He's always known how to help me— why can't I help him now?*

Rissy walked to the stove holding two coffee cups. Shiloh reached out for the coffeepot, and Rissy slapped his hand soundly. "You so tired you ain't got no sense left," she snapped, wrapping her apron around the handle of the steaming coffee-pot. "Jest go set down! I'll tend to dis heah coffeepot!"

Cheney cringed at Rissy's sharp words, but to her surprise, she saw that though Shiloh didn't quite grin, his face twisted wryly as he obediently returned to the table. "Yes, ma'am!"

Briskly Rissy poured hot coffee for them. Shiloh lifted his cup gratefully and sniffed. "Mmm . . . seems like a long time since I had a cup of hot coffee." A vision of Maeva's old, battered coffeepot rose in the back of his mind. He and Glen had never had the coffee he had so carefully made only this morning. . . .

Abruptly he turned to Cheney and demanded, "Glen told me you were at the Satterfields' yesterday." *Only yesterday?* "How bad was it for them?"

"First let me tell you about Caroline," Cheney answered with a smile. "She's doing so well, I can hardly believe it! I tried to get Leah and her to stay here another week, since all of the children are in those two small rooms at the Sikes', but they wouldn't." Shaking her head, she muttered, "It was too much like charity. The Sikes are 'family'—third or fourth cousins, I think. Anyway, Caroline wants you to come by so she can thank you in person. And she wants you to look at her leg. She said she imagined it must have been hard for you."

Shiloh closed his eyes as he remembered the chilling moment he had broken Caroline Satterfield's misshapen leg. "That's good. Think I will go see her."

"Yes, do. And take Glen," Cheney added thoughtfully.

Then she briefly reported on the injuries sustained by the Satterfields at Copperhead Gate. "T. R. has a nasty gash in the side and a badly chipped rib. He's in a lot of pain, but the wound is clean, and he's going to be all right. Levi had a concussion, but luckily they handled him very carefully and just let him rest. I don't think there'll be any permanent damage. Another brother, Caleb, got his ankle broken, a hairline fracture. His son Will's hands got burned from a rifle misfire. Latham Trask"— she hesitated and sighed softly—"seemed to have received the least serious injury, but actually I'm afraid it's going to be the worst. A bullet tore through between his fingers and exited right above the wrist."

"You can't fix it?" Shiloh asked, a glimmer of interest lighting his eyes.

Cheney shook her head. "Too many delicate bones, all smashed. I think he'll lose the use of his hand."

"So strange," Shiloh muttered, his eyes wandering out of focus. *All those men—all those bullets—all that hate—and not one of them dead* . . . "Dane Carter!" He shook himself and glanced remorsefully at Cheney. "And Sharon! I forgot! We've got to—"

"We can't, Shiloh," Cheney shook her head, and reached out to touch his hand lightly. "Bobbie Jo and Glendean came by just a little while ago to ask for some medicine for him. They said Dane's holding his own—no better, but no worse. Bobbie Jo said Katie's taken charge of Sharon, keeping her in bed, will hardly let her move. She said Katie barely lets Josh see her." She sighed deeply. "But I don't think either one of us can go up there now."

"Why not?" Shiloh demanded. "Josh let me help yesterday, so he might—"

Cheney shook her head, her face filled with pity for him. "Bobbie Jo didn't come right out and say it, but I think Josh thought that you and Maeva simply deserted them and went to the Satterfields."

"What!" Shiloh exclaimed, banging his coffee cup down on the table. "But Glen came in, and told us *you* were tending the Satterfields—and we told Josh we'd come back!" The anger in his face weakened and again his eyes dulled. "But we didn't. And I guess I should have."

Briskly Rissy mopped up spilled coffee, snatched Shiloh's cup from his lifeless fingers, wiped it, and took it to the stove to refill it. "Les' see," she scoffed, "I reckon that makes three-four places you shoulda been yestiddy, all at the same time! Whassa matter with you, Mistuh Shiloh?" Banging down the cup of fresh coffee in front of him, she snorted, "Shirkin' yo' duties somethin' awful!"

A glimmer of amusement lurked in Shiloh's shadowed eyes. "You don't have to go so easy on me, Rissy. I'm a man, I can take it."

Someone banged lustily on the front door. Cheney jumped, but Rissy gave her a warning look. Cheney sank back in her chair, smoothed her skirt, and said in a mocking tone, "Rissy'll get that door! I'm the doctor, I ain't supposed to get that there door!"

"Thass right," Rissy nodded with sly approval. "I figgered you'd learn it, did I say it often enuf, and slow enuf." Triumphantly she glided out of the room.

"Ouch." Shiloh smiled slightly. "She's got us both beat today, Doc."

Cheney's heart warmed. She could see how much effort it took for him to smile.

It was unmistakably Glen Rawlins' deep, booming voice at the door. Even from the kitchen, however, Cheney could tell by the raw timbre of it that he was weary and barely keeping his grief at bay. He appeared at the kitchen doorway, completely obscuring Rissy behind him. Like Shiloh's, his face was grimy, and he had blue-black smudges under his eyes. His great fur coat was matted with mud, and his moccasins were almost unrecognizable. In his arms he held Glendean, clad in the beloved gray cloak that had been Cheney's, the hood almost obscuring her face.

"I found a fairy out in the garden!" he announced to Cheney and Shiloh, pausing in the doorway for dramatic effect.

"Oh, bring her in!" Cheney cried. "That means we get three wishes, and she'll have to grant them!"

"Aw, it's jis' me, Doctor Cheney," Glendean said shyly, pushing the hood back from her head. "Do you mind if'n I visit you agin?"

"No, of course not!" Cheney smiled. "In fact, that was going to be one of my wishes!"

"Well, mah wish is dat I could git back into mah kitchen!" Rissy's muffled voice sounded from behind Glen's broad back. Hastily he stepped aside, and Rissy huffed into the kitchen. "I jest might be able to git some dinner cooked for ever'body, if'n peoples would set down an' git out o' mah way!"

"Sounds like an invitation to a meal to me!" Glen told Glendean, who nodded enthusiastically. Delicious smells of stew simmering and bread baking filled the kitchen.

Glen and Shiloh removed their coats and hung them up on hooks by the stove. Then they returned to the table, talking in low voices. Glendean settled herself on Glen's lap; from her pocket she produced three small, intricately carved wooden animals and began to play. Rissy's busy clatterings and mutterings in the background added to the comforting, homelike atmosphere.

"So, did you notice anything . . . anything at all?" Shiloh was asking earnestly as they settled down at the table.

"I don't rightly know," Glen answered with difficulty. "Ever'body was—shocked, and kinda—scared-lookin'." Picking up one of Glendean's animals—a clever little horse—he began to play-gallop it up and down the table. Glendean joined in with the wolf and the pig.

Glen went on wearily. "Just about ever'body was there— DeSpain, his men, the Sikeses, all the Wilkeses, Leah and Lorine, Reverend Scott, Booth Trask and Jimmy Dale Satterfield, and Bobbie Jo. All the Jessups, and the Redden boys."

"Guess I was hoping too much," Shiloh muttered darkly. "No one's going to jump up and say, 'Oh, by the way, I already know all about this because I—'" He broke off guiltily, staring at Glendean's bent head. Unheeding of the attention, her wolf jumped on the horse's back, then jumped off and began to chase the pig.

"She was there," Glen said wearily, his eyes on the little wooden horse. "She musta heard."

"I don't understand," Cheney interrupted. "I thought Shiloh told me that Maeva was—that the rifle was—I mean, that you already knew who—did it." She knew Glen told the truth about Glendean, but Cheney couldn't speak baldly of murder in front of the little girl.

"I told you," Shiloh said evenly, "that it was a fifty-two caliber rifle with a telescope."

The wolf tried to hide behind the pitcher of Rissy's Double Cream, but the pig jumped over it and trounced him soundly, with whispered sound effects from Glendean. Glen's eyes softened as he watched the animal drama. "Well, Doctor Cheney's got the same idea as ever'body else," he said quietly. "Thet fire brigade like to've turned into a lynchin' party."

"You put a stop to it, didn't you?" Shiloh asked indifferently.

"I was busy hustlin' Leah and Lorine back over to the Sikes' house. Jimmy Dale had done slipped out even afore I quit talkin'. Waylon DeSpain's the one that reminded 'em of what happened to the last bunch that rode after the Satterfields."

"Well, I'm glad he did," Cheney put in stoutly. "They're an armed camp right now! I know, I was there."

"DeSpain . . ." Shiloh said thoughtfully. "He tried real hard to talk Maeva into selling to him, didn't he? That day you took her out to the Wilkes'?"

Glen frowned down at the table. The horse was hiding behind the bowl of salt, but the wolf was craftily flanking him. "Yep. But it don't make no sense. Them mountains ain't worth squat for timber—and DeSpain's allus knowed he ain't a-gonna buy no Rawlins land. And he looked just as sickly as ever'body else, him and his lawyer—what's his name?"

"Day," Shiloh answered. "Leslie Day."

"I keep on wantin' to call him Mr. Fish, fer some reason," Glen sighed, and Glendean giggled under her breath. The wolf didn't waver, however, as he inched silently and steadily toward the horse.

"Maybe it doesn't make any sense," Shiloh countered wearily. "But I don't think somebody did this for a sensible reason."

The horse reared triumphantly; the pig had jumped on the wolf just in time, and saved him.

Dryly Cheney stated, "You're right, of course, Shiloh. Personally, I don't think any of us are lunatic enough to figure out the reason why. That's why I think you'd better stick with what you know!" A vision of Enoch Satterfield, luridly outlined by balefire and torch fire, his face twisted with hatred, darkened

Cheney's mind and hardened her heart. "You know he's a dangerous man! The only man with a fifty-two caliber Sharps rifle, and a telescope! And Enoch Satterfield wasn't home all day yesterday! Face it, Shiloh, Glen! You know he killed Lige Carter, and you know he killed Maeva!"

Glendean's head jerked up. Her eyes were dark with fright, and her face paled. The wolf and the pig suddenly lay lifeless and wooden in her small hands. "What'd you say, Doctor Cheney?" she whispered. "You mean—" she swallowed hard, and sought Glen's face. "Ya'll think Mr. Enoch kilt ol' Maeva?" she entreated him.

Glen's dark eyes met Cheney's, and her face burned with shame. Dropping the little horse, Glen stroked Glendean's dark curls. "Now, Glendean, you don't need to be a-worryin' yoreself about all this."

"But, Oncle Glen," she said unhappily, "I guess I gotta."

"Why, little girl?"

"Well, see," she began, fidgeting with one of his shirt buttons, "me an' Mr. Enoch have got a secret, see," she said reluctantly. The room fell completely silent. Even Rissy stopped her busy clattering. "But I reckon now I gotta tell it. Mebbe— mebbe—if'n I do," she went on in a small voice, "you kin tell Josh for me." Leaning back against Glen's barrel chest, she did look like a small, lost wood sprite. "An' mebbe then we kin all be friends."

★　★　★　★

Maeva's memorial service was at sunset the next day. Cheney's lifetime memory of it was one of fire and snow. Beginning shortly after noon, men and women made their way to the bonfire set on the shores of Moccasin Lake. Some people threw pieces of wood onto the fire, some logs, some evergreen branches. Some of the women threw cloth bags of herbs into the flames, and for a short time sweet smells wafted through the air. By the time the sun was low in the western sky, almost every person in Wolf County gathered on the shores of Moccasin Lake to look up to the peaks of Maeva's mountain as Reverend Scott spoke. The brilliance of the sun as it lowered toward the mountain temporarily dimmed the pale glow of fire that still smoldered where Maeva had lived.

"Maeva is gone, so we have gathered here for our own comforting," Reverend Scott said, grief and regret edging his fine tenor voice. "And it comforts us to think of her now, to remember who she was, how she befriended all of us, how she helped us—and healed us.

"So I feel that the best way we may find solace, and somehow relieve our sorrow, is to honor Maeva by taking this time to remember exactly what she meant to all of us. I've asked three men to speak to you now. I asked them to tell us all of Maeva, and how she affected their lives. I ask you to honor her by listening, and remembering."

Glen Rawlins stepped forward, dressed in solid black, nervously fingering a black hat. But when he spoke, his voice was strong and sure and commanded each person's undivided attention, even the children's.

"Maeva Wilding counted me as a friend, and I counted her friendship as a great gift."

Shiloh's attention began to wander. His mind stubbornly, obsessively, went over and over each picture, each scene, each fact, each word, that had to do with Maeva's death. As soon as Glendean had spoken the words last night that exonerated Enoch Satterfield, Shiloh's mind had clamped onto one thing and refused to let him rest: *Maeva's killer is right here. You've looked at him, you've talked to him, you know him. You just have to see him.*

With weary desperation Shiloh searched the faces around him. *It's a wonder to me that a man like that can walk among us, and we don't see him as any different from the rest of us. Seems like somehow we'd know, we'd feel it . . . seems like we'd get a chill when he passed us on the street, or we'd be able to see hellfire in his eyes, or children would be scared of him. . . .*

Unwillingly, his shoulders dropped and he shut his eyes

tightly to try and control his tiresome, helplessly repetitive thoughts. Beside him, Cheney glanced at him with concern, stepped closer to him, and started to reach for him. But at the last moment she withdrew her hand, her face torn with uncertainty, and bowed her head to say a small prayer for him instead.

Glen finished his brief words and stepped back to Lorine Satterfield's side. Even she was subdued today, dressed in a plain black dress and cape. Enoch Satterfield stood on her other side. As Glen joined Lorine and took her arm, Enoch stepped forward and faced the crowd. A shocked murmur swept over them, but quickly it was hushed to a baited silence.

"Glen Rawlins said that Maeva Wilding called him a friend," his strong, raw voice called out proudly. "That were an honor that was hard to come by. I wisht I could say that she called me 'friend'—but she didn't."

The crowd shifted restlessly, almost with fear. Enoch waited until the air was still again. "An' I ain't never said the words to her—God forgive me—but in my heart I called her a friend!" Now he let the grief temper his voice. "Me an' my family, we trusted Maeva. We welcomed her. We was allus glad to open our door and see her standing there." He shook his big, shaggy head sorrowfully. "I cain't count the times that Maeva took keer of me or my family or my kin, jis' like we was her own blood. Hit's an ungodly shame thet I waited—thet all of us waited—'til now to say how much she meant to us." He looked back up and his hazel eyes burned into the faces of the men and women before him. "She were a healer. She were our healer."

He stepped back into the crowd. Leah took his arm, tears running down her face. Awkwardly he patted her hand, his head lifted proudly.

The sun touched the highest peak of Blackcastle Springs Mountain. The light began to darken into vermilion, and the lake shimmered red. Someone coughed, another stamped his feet with cold, and a child's whisper hissed. Some sort of discussion, or confusion, disturbed the front ranks of the crowd.

Cheney strained, trying to see what was wrong, but she

couldn't see over the throng. Turning to Shiloh, she said, "Can you see what's—"

Josh Carter's voice rang harshly in the air. "I cain't! I won't! Not with the man that kilt my pa standing right there!"

The crowd parted, and Josh Carter almost ran through them, his face distorted with fury. In shock, the crowd parted, and awkward silence shamed all of them.

Suddenly Bobbie Jo Carter stepped forward, and deliberately turned her back on the crowd to face across the lake to Maeva's mountain. She began to sing, not lightly and joyfully, but slowly, thoughtfully.

> On Jordan's stormy banks I stand
> And cast a wishful eye
> To Canaan's fair and happy land
> Where my possessions lie.
> I am bound for the Promised Land . . .
> I am bound for the Promised Land.
> O who will come and go with me?
> I am bound for the Promised Land.

★ ★ ★ ★

With an icy blue gaze Shiloh watched Josh Carter stride angrily to the long row of horses, buggies, carts, and wagons lined up behind them. *Josh Carter won't listen to Glen; he didn't listen to his own sister, not to Cheney, not even to his own father's dying words. That man needs a lesson in how to pay attention and how to show respect!*

The fury he had kept tightly reined rose up in him, cold and decisive. Here was a visible, clear-cut malefactor, who openly disgraced Maeva Wilding's memory. Shiloh decided to follow the man and beat him to a bloody pulp. Disentangling himself from Cheney as she tried to hold him back, he marched after Josh Carter.

He had almost reached Josh when he noticed that Sock was stamping and biting, trying to break away from his tether, and

314

the horses around him were getting spooked. *What's the matter with that stupid horse!* he thought angrily. *If he keeps on jumping around like that, he's going to stampede the whole lot of them!* With one frustrated glance at Josh Carter's back, he veered his course toward Sock. Josh flew up into the saddle of his mount and recklessly galloped away.

As Shiloh neared the restless horse, Sock managed to break his lightly tied tether. To Shiloh's surprise, he didn't take off in a triumphant run. He merely moved close to the horse tied next to him, clamped his teeth on the saddlebag, and pulled viciously.

Shiloh stopped mid-stride, his face incredulous. *Somebody's got muscadines!* he thought disgustedly. *Stupid horse!* He moved forward to try to mollify Sock and rescue his unhappy victim.

The realization hit him so suddenly, it was almost like a steel spike jabbing into his brain. Again he stopped, his face white and intense, his eyes fierce, as Sock chewed and pulled on the gray roan's saddlebags.

Muscadines . . . in winter.

Blankly he looked down at his boots. He remembered Maeva's garden, and staring down at a small scattering of seeds by his boots, and thinking that she would have planted them, and they would have bloomed, if someone hadn't killed her. . . .

But they wouldn't, because they weren't seeds for planting. They were muscadine seeds. Someone had stood at the break in the wall in Maeva's garden and had munched on muscadines, and had spit out the seeds as he waited.

Four more steps, and Shiloh yanked the saddlebag out of Sock's strong white teeth, threw open the flap, and thrust his hand down into the dark mouth of the leather bag.

Inside was a bunch of red, perfectly round muscadines, tied up in a light blue bandanna.

Gray roan. Light blue bandanna. Who? Shiloh's mind fought to remember, his face straining with concentration.

"Whaddya think you're doin', Chickie Boy?" Bake Conroy's stance was relaxed, his expression one of ugly anticipation. Disdainfully he tossed his rifle to one side. He knew Shiloh wouldn't fight. How many times had he snarled into the smoky, whiskey-fumed air at the Nameless Saloon that "Maeva'd got her a yellow-headed chicken boy"?

He doesn't know I know, Shiloh's mind warned loudly. *Get Glen—*

But Bake Conroy was sneering at him, the juicy, fragrant fruit he held reminded him of the secret garden, and in the background he could faintly hear Reverend Scott finishing Maeva Wilding's requiem.

Shiloh hit Bake Conroy's jaw with a stunning, head-cracking force.

But in the half-moment of Shiloh's reverie, some animal instinct had made the hair on the back of Bake Conroy's neck prickle, and he managed to pull back enough to dissipate the blow. His jaw didn't break, but a hot flame of pain flared up on the side of his face. He staggered and seemed to fall as Shiloh pulled aside his coat and grabbed for his gun.

Wildly Conroy lunged and snatched up his rifle. In an instant of dismay he saw that he had grabbed it barrel-first, but again his instincts raged, and he came around and knocked Shiloh down flat with the butt.

Shiloh felt only an instant of the thundering blow, and he was unconscious before his body hit the snowy ground. He didn't see Conroy straddle him, his face distorted with fear and fury, and struggle awkwardly to turn the long rifle around to shoot.

A thundering of shouts intruded on Conroy's confusion. Reluctantly he turned his head to see Glen Rawlins rushing toward him, roaring like a grizzly as he charged. Like a flock of black crows, men ran behind him.

Conroy ran to the gray roan, fumbled with the reins, jumped into the saddle, and kicked the horse savagely as it galloped wildly up the street.

Glen reached Shiloh, and with one regretful glance at Conroy disappearing down the street, knelt and bent close to Shiloh's face. Moments later Cheney threw herself down beside him. Even as she reached for Shiloh, he opened his eyes and struggled to sit up.

"Muscadines," he said to Glen with desperate weakness. Glen's face darkened with instant comprehension. "It's Conroy! Where—"

"Lie down!" Cheney ordered. "Be still! Be quiet, and let me—"

Furiously he pushed her imploring hands away. "I'm fine! Leave me alone!" Impatiently he struggled, stood, wavered for an instant, then brushed his hand across his face. "I'm going after him."

"If'n this has to do with Maeva, Glen," Enoch Satterfield said as he stepped out of the crowd, "reckon you better tell us 'bout it."

"Conroy," Glen said tightly. "He's the one who kilt Maeva. Shiloh figgered it out. Must've got a rifle like yourn somewheres." Enoch held his rifle loosely by his side, butt down to the earth. The barrel glinted dully in the last light.

Enoch nodded thoughtfully, glancing to the north, where Conroy had ridden. "Then he kilt Lige Carter, too."

"Yep." Glen nodded shortly. "I'll be goin' after him now."

"We," Shiloh grunted. "We'll be going after him."

"Shiloh—" Cheney began, laying her hand on his arm.

Shaking his arm free, he turned away from her and mounted Sock. His glittering blue eyes were on Glen, and he said nothing.

"Doctor Cheney," Glen told her sternly, "you knew he was gonna hafta do this. Leave him alone." Turning on his heel, he stalked to Beauregard, mounted, and looked at Enoch expectantly. "We could use your help, Enoch," he nodded.

"Yes, sir." Enoch marched to his gray horse and mounted, cradling the rifle across his lap. Without looking back the three men rode up the deserted street of Black Arrow.

At the last building, Glen reined up and shouted, "Whoa! Hold up there!" They were in front of DeSpain's barracks. All the windows were black, and the door stood open blankly.

"Think he's in there?" Shiloh muttered, almost to himself. He had half dismounted.

"Nope," Enoch replied in a low growl. "Reckon he went in there to git somethin'."

"What?"

"His rifle," Enoch spat. "Kin shoot a long ways, with these here telescopes."

"Won't give him much of an advantage in this dead dark," Shiloh muttered.

"Mebbe so, mebbe not," Enoch shrugged. "Depends on his night eyes. Jimmy Dale could do it, easy."

"That's the truth," Glen muttered. "But he can't see—nor shoot—like Jimmy Dale kin. Nobody kin."

"He's a-gonna find thet out," Enoch growled with satisfaction, "if'n he tries to go through Copperhead Gate. Jimmy Dale's keepin' watch all night."

Glen turned to scan the northwest. "He'll figger that—an' he'll figger tryin' to cross the Carters' land would be 'bout the same . . ."

"An' he'd be right," a voice said in the gloom on the side of the bunkhouse. Enoch's rifle leveled toward the shadows. After long moments, Josh Carter rode forward, close enough for the three men to see him.

"Reckon you ain't a-gonna shoot me," he said in a low voice, "since it appears you didn't kill my pa."

Enoch seemed to consider it for a long while, but finally he lowered the rifle. "Reckon I ain't," he replied calmly.

Josh turned to Glen. "I was dawdlin' up the way, here, thinkin' 'bout goin' back. Heard a rider, like a one-man stampede, hurryin' this way. I stopped and waited, curious-like. It were Conroy." His face was shadowed by his floppy hat, so the men couldn't see his expression. But he seemed to nod in a gesture of placation toward Enoch, and went on in a quiet voice, "You was right, Enoch. He came flappin' outta here with a rifle. Had a long, mean barrel and a black 'scope on it. He looked right at me. Could tell he really woulda liked to have shot me, if'n he'd had the time."

"Which way?" Shiloh demanded.

Josh's arm and pointing finger were heavy black outlines against the sky. "Maeva's Trace."

"Oh, Lord," Glen sighed.

"Let's go!" Shiloh growled, and started Sock.

"Wait jis' a minute, Shiloh!" Glen barked.

Shiloh automatically jerked on the reins to pull Sock up short. *You'd think he was my lieutenant or something*, he ridiculed himself, but quieted Sock down so he could listen.

"You cain't just bolt up the Trace like a flyin' fool," Glen warned. "Now, I know what to do. Let's ride that way, but slow enough where you kin hear me."

"Yes, sir," Josh and Enoch responded instantly, then their shadowed faces turned toward each other in remembrance and recognition.

Glen's face, half-lit and half-black, turned toward Shiloh at a questioning tilt.

Quietly Shiloh nodded, "Yes, sir."

24

NIGHT FALLS ON MAEVA'S TRACE

"Walk now," Glen told Shiloh in a low but clear whisper. "But bring the horses." He hated the thought of Sock or Beauregard shielding them, but a horse's life couldn't be traded for a man's.

They took only four slow steps up the steep, pathless Trace when Shiloh hissed, "Get on my right. Left ear's buzzing loud." In truth, continual explosions still blasted in Shiloh's ear after Conroy's blow to the left side of his head. *Great help I am*, he thought with disgust. *Can't hear anything except myself, stumbling and crashing around like a buffalo herd!*

Soundlessly Glen moved to Shiloh's right side. He didn't like to, because that put Shiloh on his off side—Glen was right-handed—but he was still confident that he could take care of Shiloh. Again they began their painfully slow ascent up the Trace. Heavy clouds had gathered, so they had no light to guide them. Occasional starlight merely lightened the night from ink-black to gray-black.

Glen worried as he walked and listened. Sternly he reminded himself, *Scared worryin' turns into panic. So make it into smart worryin'.*

He stopped to listen, and within a few seconds both Shiloh and Sock had stopped also. Glen and Beauregard were so attuned to each other that they almost stepped in unison, and stopped together. Finally Shiloh and Sock were quiet. The two men and the two horses waited patiently, but the forest remained silent.

He woulda come anyways, Glen sighed to himself. *This way, mebbe I kin keep him from gittin' kilt.* Cautiously he began to lead again, reviewing his strategy as he went.

Conroy's gotta be on this mountain. No way he woulda had time to git over. Josh workin' around and up the Carter side, Enoch on the Satterfield side. Me and Shiloh workin' up the south face.

Over and over Glen repeated the steps to himself, picturing the mountain and the men on it. Finally he allowed himself a small nod of satisfaction. *We'll flush him out. Bound to. Prob'ly be Enoch—he's the best woodsman there is, even if he is the oldest.* With a small sidelong glance at the dim outline of Shiloh and Sock on his left, he reminded himself sternly that Shiloh was his friend, and he was vulnerable, unschooled in this kind of fight. Glen considered him to be as much his responsibility as if Shiloh were wounded or disabled—which, in effect, he was.

Maeva's Trace had never been cleared, and the timber grew tall and thick on the lower reaches, much too thick to be able to see up and ahead. Shiloh and Glen kept their vision short-sighted, planning ahead only enough to get man and horse around the next tree.

Occasionally Glen would glimpse the stars and the black blot of the naked crest of Maeva's Trace. The timber on the upper reaches of this mountain—the highest for miles—had been thinned by the merciless forces of wind, heat, rain, and snow. Over the ages the soil had been beaten and blown into gravelly sand. The trees had stubbornly clung to life, but they were twisted and tortured shapes. Lightning often struck the peaks of the Trace, leaving broad, erratic swaths of bare rock among the groups of stunted trees huddling together. Three deep, treacherous gorges had been formed eons ago when the mountain had shifted in its seat, deep inside the earth.

For the moment, however, Glen did not contemplate the terrain above. He concentrated on creeping stealthily from tree to tree, and listening. The night was quiet, with no wind, and the snow muted all sound—both of hunter and the hunted—as effectively as a thick quilt. Glen was confident, however, that he and Josh and Enoch had night eyes and ears much more attuned to the forest than Bake Conroy's ever would be; and that would give them a decisive advantage. And of course, he could take care of Shiloh.

A cold, sharp crack sounded above them. A whistling scream flying past Glen's left ear made his head hurt. Before he could look back, loud crashes and thrashing noises sounded behind him. Sock screamed. Glen could not seem to turn around fast enough; the jarring suddenness of all the noises had momentarily confused him. By the time he pinpointed the darkness behind him where Shiloh had been, all he could see was the outline of Sock, down on his side, thrashing and struggling to get up. Sock's hooves desperately fought air, then the horse flipped on his other side as he slid down the steep incline and out of Glen's sight. He heard more horse grunts and struggling sounds, then silence. There was no sign of Shiloh Irons.

Glen's face turned upward, and the edges of his vision seemed to waver with heat. He shouted, a barbarous roar of warning. Holding his rifle high, he ran headlong up the steep side of Maeva's Trace. Kicking aside branches carelessly, leaping across fallen trees, his breath a continuous growl in his throat, he ran blindly, guided by animal instinct.

Kill him! He killed Lige! And Maeva. Not right, not her time. Now Shiloh! I'll kill him!

The trees thinned, and he could see stars and the black cutout of the top of the Trace that blotted them. Small rocks and crumbly soil began to slide under his moccasins, and he saw the distorted clumps of trees here and there. Still he ran headlong, fighting desperately to get to the exact spot his mind had pinpointed as the place the shot came from.

A thick tree rose up in front of him. Glen barreled into it, felt it give, heard it grunt, and then began to fall.

For a moment he saw the stars, then they began to whirl in sickening circles. He fell on his gut, and the breath was forced out of his lungs. Cartwheeling, sliding, the noise of rocks falling and hitting below, he tried to separate the sounds, but his mouth and eyes and ears filled up with dirt and gravel, and he was deaf, blind, and dumb. He fell and slid, his leg turned under him with a wrenching pain, and he flipped, slid some more, and finally hit bottom with a sickening thud.

The gorge! Fell into the south gorge! Stupid—!

The pain in his head was sickening, and continual screeches sounded in both ears. His face was cold, but he felt a sticky warmth in his mouth, and he tasted the salt thickness of blood. His right leg throbbed with scalding pain, but already a part of his mind catalogued it as a wrenched knee and not a broken bone. Everything else hurt too, but as he calmed down he gingerly analyzed the pain and thought that his body was bruised, scratched, cut, and scraped, but not broken, and none of his innards were jarred out of place.

Rifle . . .

He was lying on his back. He could see nothing at all, only blackness with bright red and white spots of light that burst everywhere. Realizing that his eyes were wide, straining open, he shut them with a grimace to try and bring tears to clear his vision. The din in his ears was calming somewhat. With both hands he began feeling delicately to either side for the comforting cold steel of his rifle.

Scrape . . .

At the stealthy, gravelly sound his heart jumped erratically. Desperately he tried to calm down, to see, to listen, to feel, to be quiet, to be smart—but he couldn't seem to control his own body and mind.

He's down here . . . with me . . . he's coming!

Choking fear took over Glen Rawlins' mind. Never in his life had he been this afraid; but never in his life had he been this helpless to face danger. He couldn't see. He had no weapon. He had nowhere to run or hide. He would lie here, cowering and helpless, and Bake Conroy would crawl to him. He would feel his cold fingers touching him any minute, then he would feel a bullet's searing heat—

Scratch, scrape . . .

Glen tensed every nerve in his body and jumped, thrusting hard with his good leg. He came up off the ground in a madman's desperate lunge, and hit Conroy about two feet away as he half knelt, his arm upraised.

No rifle! Knife!

Glen saw nothing, but as he bear-hugged Conroy, he felt his stance and sensed the knife. Instinctively he grabbed Conroy's upraised arm, yanked hard, and literally flipped Conroy over his own falling body.

Momentum crashed Glen into the side of the gorge, and showers of rocks stung his head and face; a sprinkle of snow cooled and revived him for a few seconds. Then, unbelievably, he heard Shiloh's hoarse shout above. "Glen! We can't see! Call out!"

Glen opened his mouth, but Conroy flew through the air and landed square on top of him, forcing the breath out of his lungs. He rolled, Conroy rolled, Glen rolled and tried pushing, then pulling. But Conroy was fighting madly, and Glen could get no controlling grip.

A searing flame plunged deep into Glen's back. He was vaguely surprised at how quickly the pain spread across his shoulders into his arms, numbing his fingers, blazing down his legs, making his knees trembly. His hold around Conroy's shoulder and back loosened into a weak hug. *I'm afraid,* he thought childishly, *and I'm alone.*

I am here, he heard a Voice. *Remember Me? I was always here, I will always be here. I am always here. I Am.*

The stench of fear faded, the sounds of his own gasps and Conroy's guttural rasping seemed to dissolve into the background, and Glen's pain quieted into dull unimportance. He felt the cool of snow and the warmth of blood. He saw nothing with his eyes, but in his mind, he saw himself, twelve years old, sitting alone on the shore of Moccasin Lake and asking the Lord Jesus Christ to forgive him for his sins and save his soul and come into his heart.

Quietly, unhurriedly, Glen let his arms fall to the ground, and again he closed his eyes. *I'm sorry for my sins, Lord. I do remember! And now—whether it's for five seconds, or for fifty years—my life is yours. Forever . . . and ever . . . and ever . . .*

Glen thought vaguely that he was going to sleep, but an explosion of light assaulted his eyes even through his closed eyelids. Slowly he forced them open. Bake Conroy knelt by him, his right hand upraised, holding a knife dripping blackly above Glen's chest. They were outlined in lurid yellow-white brightness, and popping noises sounded strangely from inside the light. Both men turned startled faces toward the erratic, blinding flashes.

Maeva's little balefire things, those little puffball things, Glen thought muddily. *I'm sorry, Maeva . . . I wisht I woulda taught you to read . . . and about Jesus. He woulda stuck closer to you than me . . . closer than a brother. . . .*

Bake Conroy was still turning, his face distorted, inhuman, when Enoch Satterfield's and Josh Carter's bullets hit him almost simultaneously, about one-half inch apart, directly through his heart. Glen watched curiously as Conroy's face smoothed out into a blank acceptance. Then Conroy slumped face down across Glen's chest.

The light was fading, the flashes dying out, and Glen was sleepy. As he closed his eyes, he prayed. *Thank you, Lord Jesus . . . and Thy will be done . . . live or die . . . Thy will be done. . . .*

25

New Life and Old Loves

Reverend Scott's mild blue eyes searched each face as he quoted from memory: "And he shewed me a pure river of water of life, clear as crystal, proceeding out of the throne of God and of the Lamb.... And there shall be no more curse: but the throne of God and of the Lamb shall be in it; and his servants shall serve him: And they shall see his face; and his name shall be in their foreheads."

The shining water lapped gently around Reverend Scott's waist. "These scriptures are talking about beginnings, about old things passing away and all things becoming new. That's why we're here today. All of us have, in the last few months, witnessed the passing away of many things: curses ... bad blood between brothers ... old fears ... the lives of people we loved.

"But today we gather to celebrate new beginnings! We celebrate a miracle child, born two weeks ago, who lives and breathes by the grace of God. We celebrate the miraculous healing of a man who for days was more dead than alive. And we celebrate his rebirth—a miraculous renewal in the spirit!

"So now, I baptize you, my brother, Glen Rawlins, in the name of the Father, and the Son, and the Holy Ghost."

Reverend Scott was slender, youthful, but he looked wise and strong as he covered Glen Rawlins' nose and mouth with his hand and slowly lowered him into the glassy waters of Moccasin Lake. Glen's barrel chest and big head completely disappeared, the waters only slightly disturbed into shallow, wide circles. Suddenly Glen sprang straight up, jumping from Reverend Scott's cradling hands and shattering the still surface into thousands of silver glitter-drops.

"Praise God!" he boomed, shaking the water from his black hair and beard. His teeth gleamed large and white, and his eyes sparkled like jet.

Laughter rang out, full of gladness and lightness, in the cool morning air. Reverend Scott recovered from the shock and, standing waist-deep in the icy waters of the lake, crossed his arms over his chest and laughed along with the crowd gathered right up to the soft laps of water at the muddy shore.

★ ★ ★ ★

This early in spring was, perhaps, not the best for "Dinner-on-the-Ground" as the churchgoers called it. But today, for the third week in a row, Sunday had been warm, with a mild blue sky and fleecy white clouds. The sun was a benevolent, summery yellow. Only patches of snow on the highest peaks of Maeva's Trace remained. The long "white wolf winter" was finally over.

"You look very nice," Cheney said approvingly. "I've never seen that shirt before. Where did you get it?"

A shadow of old pain crossed Shiloh's face, but he answered mildly, "Maeva made it for me. For Christmas. This is the first time I've worn it." The shirt was a rich indigo blue made in the cavalry style, with a double-breasted front closure edged in brown. It fit Shiloh perfectly, the cut accentuating his broad shoulders and tapering to a fitted waist. The indigo color darkened his eyes into a more intense blue.

"Oh," Cheney murmured. "It's—wonderful, Shiloh. She did excellent work."

"Maeva could sew good when she had a mind," Glen said thoughtfully. "Glad you wore it today, Shiloh. New day—I'm a new man. Good time for starting over."

Shiloh's face closed. "I'm going to start over," he drawled, "on all the desserts."

He rose, dusted off his breeches, picked up his empty plate, and ambled over to the long tables set up behind what had been Waylon DeSpain's home. Actually the tables were pieces of lumber on sawhorses, but the women had covered them with snowy white sheets, and enormous amounts of food lined them invitingly. Everyone was beginning to slow down now, however, walking around with a last chicken leg or biscuit or a piece of cake, or carefully balancing a piece of pie on tented fingers. Shiloh seemed determined to try at least a bite of each of the dozens of desserts.

Rissy, Cheney, Glen, and Caroline were seated on the lightweight rug Caroline had woven specially for Cheney. Caroline, her splinted leg stuck out awkwardly in front, watched Cheney enviously. Her legs were gracefully tucked to one side, and she leaned on one arm, watching Shiloh, shaking her head and smiling as he licked his fingers after picking up each delicacy and carefully positioning it on his crowded plate.

"I orter go rap his knuckles," Rissy muttered. She sat stiffly erect at Cheney's side, her long legs straight out in front, her plate balanced in her lap.

"Not today, Rissy," Cheney said languidly. "Today is too— good."

"Yep!" Glen agreed, wolfing down a huge bite of pumpkin pie. "Even I ain't a-gonna preach at him today!"

"Dat's good to hear," Rissy sniffed. "De Lawd knew what he was doin' when he called you to be a shirriff, an' not a preacher!"

"You really think so, Rissy?" Glen asked anxiously.

Rissy shot him a shrewd glance, then nodded twice, firmly. "Yassuh, I do."

"Good," he nodded thoughtfully. " 'Cause I've worried a lot 'bout it, you know. I told ever'body I was God's man first, and a sheriff second. Dunno what kinda lawman that makes."

"The best kind, I think," Cheney declared.

Glen's face shone with pleasure. Droplets of water still glinted in his beard, and his thick hair was plastered flat back on his head. "Why, thank you, Doctor Cheney! I 'preciate that!"

Cheney's face grew serious, and she replied thoughtfully, "No, I think I need to thank you, Glen. In the last few months, you've been a miracle, walking and talking, right here with us. You've made me remember—remember to pray, and to lean on our Lord, and not to trust too much in our own—I mean, my own—strength."

"Well, I reckon that's the only reason I'm still here," Glen grinned. "You know that better'n anybody. You an' Shiloh kept me alive."

"No," Cheney protested, "Jesus Christ is the one who kept you alive."

"Yep," Glen agreed, "by yore doctorin' an' Shiloh's nursin'."

"That's right, Cheney," a soft voice interrupted behind her. "Just like Rose. Jesus gave her life, but He used you and Shiloh to keep us both alive."

"Sharon! And Rose! Give her to me, right now!" Cheney cried, jumping up and holding out her arms. "Oh, she looks wonderful! I can't believe it!"

"Believe it," Sharon said firmly, "and don't forget what I said. Never forget."

"No, I won't . . . Sharon Rose," Cheney whispered to the tiny pink baby. Sharon Rose yawned, her dark blue eyes puzzled at Cheney's face looming so close over hers.

"Glen, do you wanna go up to Blackcastle Springs today?" Caroline asked languidly. "Doctor Cheney said I could ride either Sock or Stocking, and use her saddle." Caroline managed very well with Cheney's sidesaddle.

"Fine with me, Caroline," Glen nodded. "I been baptized in Moccasin Lake today—think I'll baptize in Blackcastle Springs, too! Make sure it took!"

"Glen!" a loud voice called. "Git over here! I want you to come and help me beat this smart-alecky Dane Carter at horseshoes!" Lorine Satterfield stalked toward them. Dressed in a cool minty green, her dark hair shone in the sunlight and her face was flushed with a coral glow.

Behind her Dane Carter grinned, then whirled on his crutch and hopped nimbly to a tree where Wanda Jo Trask sat reading a book. She looked up, surprised, as Dane dropped his crutch and threw himself down beside her.

Glen squinted lazily up at Lorine as she stopped by the rug, her hands on her hips. "Cain't do it, Lorine," he shrugged, grinning. "Dane kin beat me at horseshoes. 'Fraid you're on yore own."

"Ain't that the truth!" Lorine retorted saucily. "Wisht my laig woulda got broke! Mebbe then you'd be carryin' me around all the time, instead o' Caroline!"

Caroline smiled her enigmatic smile up at her older sister.

"Naw," Glen shook his head. "You weigh more'n Caroline."

Lorine's hazel eyes glittered dangerously for a moment, but then she laughed merrily. "Seems like you got yore work cut out for you, little sis! A Bible-thumpin', saved-an'-sanctified, water-baptized, gun-totin' lawman!"

"That's right, Lorine," Glen replied mischievously. "So you better behave yoreself. 'Cause now I kin either arrest you or preach at you!"

The sly humor faded from Lorine's face. "Y'know, not too long ago I woulda been real mad at ya'll. But I ain't. I'm glad fer you, baby sister."

"I'm glad fer you, Lorine," Caroline said softly, and Lorine gave her a puzzled look. " 'Cause now you're a-gonna find the man the Lord wants you to have."

"We'll see, little sister!" Lorine grinned. "I got lotsa lookin' to do!" She whirled, her skirt billowing prettily out behind her.

Sharon observed, "Well, she's heading in Shiloh's direction. I hope he knows the dire danger he's in."

"What?" Cheney exclaimed, straightening and peeking around the tree. Lorine laughed up at Shiloh, pulling him by the arm toward the horseshoe field. Gently he disengaged his arm, smiled, shook his head, and walked toward the lake.

Reverend Scott appeared at Lorine's side. Frowning, he said something to her, and Lorine looked startled. Then she smiled brilliantly, locked her arm around his, and they strolled over to talk to Jimmy Dale and Bobbie Jo.

"That's interesting," Sharon observed, her gentle brown eyes sparkling.

"What?" Cheney demanded grumpily. "That's old gossip

about Jimmy Dale and Bobbie Jo. They might not have made an announcement yet, but everyone knows they're going to, any time now."

"No, Cheney, dear," Sharon laughed. "So like you not to see it. I'm talking about Reverend Scott and Lorine!"

"Hmph," Glen grunted. "Lorine might catch a bigger fish than she baited her hook for."

Cheney and Sharon giggled, but Rissy echoed Glen's "hmph" and turned back to Glen. "Speakin' of fish," she demanded, "whut 'bout thet Mistuh DeSpain an' his slippery lawyer? Neva Sikes tole me they got outta jail!"

Glen held out his hands palm-up. "Cain't help it, Rissy. They served their sentence—sixty days. And they returned everyone's land."

"It doesn't seem fair," Sharon mused. "Those two men that worked for them have to serve a year! One of them was just a boy! What was his name?"

"Tim," Glen answered. "Tim Toney. And he was man enough to be out shooting at your husband, and Lige and Dane. And he had the bright idea of setting fire to Enoch's smoke-house. He orter be hung."

"Amen, Lawd," Rissy grumbled.

"You don't mean that, Glen," Sharon chided. "I happen to know that you've been to Fort Smith twice to talk to those two men."

"That's right," Glen replied gruffly. "An' I'm a-goin' back next week. I think there's a chance for that Tim. He's young and he's smart, and I could tell he spoke truth when he come clean about ever'thing that happened." He shook his shaggy head. "All four of 'em really did feel bad about Maeva. Even thet Mr. Fish looked warm-blooded fer a minute. And Tim, well . . . I think Bake Conroy goin' lunytick like thet really made him think 'bout what kinda life he was headin' fer."

"So you've been taking food and soap and books—"

"Bibles," Caroline corrected with an affectionate glance at Glen.

"—and Bibles to them, and visiting with them," Sharon finished.

"Practicin' preachin' to 'em," Glen grinned. "They're locked up there, so they have to listen."

"Oncle Glen! Oncle Glen!" Glendean's shrill voice cut across the low murmur of people talking and laughing, and everyone turned around to see Glendean crawl out from under one of the tables of food. She scuttled along on her hands and knees until she was free of the table, then jumped up and ran headlong toward them. "Help me! Please!"

Glen jumped up in a smooth motion, startling for a man his size, and took two giant steps to meet her. Scooping her up in his arms, he demanded, "What is it, Glendean? Are you hurt?"

Glendean began to cry, rubbing her eyes with a grimy fist and sniffling. "N-no."

Glen sagged with relief. "You scared the fire outta me! What is it?"

"It's Jim-Jim," she snorted mournfully. "Mama tole me not to bring him, but he came anyway."

"Oh, he did." Glen nodded wisely. "Well, why are you crying? What'd he do?"

"He sat on Miz Sikes' fried taters," Glendean muttered, "an' washed Mama's cookies in Junie Moon's best cream."

Glen struggled to keep his face grave and concerned. "Well, I kin see how that might make Miz Sikes and yore mama cry, but why're *you* cryin'?"

"Well, when he finished with the cookies," Glendean went on mournfully, "he was headin' fer Lorine's chocolate pie. Mr. Enoch made a swipe fer him, but it scairt Jim-Jim when he hit thet big pot of possum stew instead. Then Miz Trask sorta fell down, and Jim-Jim hid! Now I cain't find him nowheres, an' Miz Sikes said she's been cravin' fer coon dumplin's!"

"Hit's all right, little girl," Glen murmured, as Glendean sobbed and hid her face in his neck. "You know he comes an' goes as he pleases. He'll be back, with all this here food left to wash."

Caroline couldn't hold herself up any longer, so she gave up and lay down flat. Startled, she saw Jim-Jim perched on a low branch of the tree right above them, but she was giggling too helplessly to say anything.

Jim-Jim stayed on the low branch of the tree until Glen stood under him, holding Glendean. Then it appeared that Jim-Jim decided to jump down on Glen—but he missed, and landed on Rissy's head.

Rissy screeched, but baby Sharon Rose lay beside her, so she dared not scramble to her feet and run. She made quite a picture, sitting with her back arrow-straight, her long legs thrust stiffly in front, her eyes wide and mouth open, and the beady-eyed raccoon perched on the crisp white ruffled cap on her head.

Cheney and Sharon turned, and they both started more violently than even Rissy had. Cheney's hand shot out, but stopped in midair, for she suddenly, helplessly collapsed in laughter. Sharon was already listing dangerously, giggling, holding her side.

Rissy's face abruptly changed to faint disgust. One strong black hand reached up and plucked Jim-Jim up by the scruff of his neck. Rising slowly, she dusted off her apron with great deliberation. Jim-Jim hung from one hand, watching her reproachfully. Finally Rissy straightened and stalked over to Glen, who looked slightly ashamed of himself, though chuckles still welled up in his throat. Still in his arms, Glendean just looked scared.

Rissy thrust Jim-Jim in front of Glendean's face. "Ah b'lieve, Miss Glendean," Rissy stated with great dignity, "that this is yore lost critter." Glendean took the raccoon, and Rissy nodded stiffly, then majestically sailed toward the church.

★ ★ ★ ★

Cheney walked toward Shiloh, desperately trying to think of what she might say to him. *Something clever? Wise? Sympathetic?* He was sitting on one of the logs by the side of the lake, placed there by Waylon DeSpain for the party on Thanksgiving. As

Cheney remembered that time, that beginning so long ago, the troubled look on her face smoothed and softened. She reached Shiloh and sat close beside him, staring out across the lake, and said nothing at all. Without thinking, she reached out and slipped her hand into his.

They sat in silence for a long time. Shiloh's eyes stole often to the peaks of Maeva's Mountain and Maeva's Trace. Cheney drank in the beauty of the spring day, the drowsy warmth of the afternoon sun, the diamond sparkles on the water.

"Today makes me think of a garden I saw once," Shiloh muttered, almost to himself. "It was beautiful. A secret garden."

"Yes," she agreed with understanding, if not with comprehension. "This place—these hills. Buried in a long, dark, bleak winter. But now . . . before long . . . it'll be like a garden."

Shiloh nodded absently, his eyes roving over the black peaks of Blackcastle Springs Mountain.

Enoch told me that this is why they stay, why they love this land so much, Cheney mused. *Because no matter how bad the winter, spring is like a new life, and they all get to start over again.* She sighed gently. *But for me, it's an ending, not a beginning. It's time for me to go. But what about Shiloh?*

"I can't stay here now," Shiloh murmured.

"I know," Cheney smiled. "Where are you going?"

Picking up her hand, he enclosed it in both of his. "I don't know," he answered absently. "Where are you going?"

"I don't know." She shrugged.

He turned to her for the first time, his eyes searching her face gravely. Then they lit up with mocking amusement. "Sounds like we're going in the same direction, Doc," he grinned. "Might as well travel together."

"All right," she nodded, then gave him a mischievous glance. "Can I carry the gun this time?"

"No!" he sputtered, and then saw Cheney's face. "But you can carry my medical bag. It's such a mess, I thought you might take better care of it."

"Well, if you'd just do as I tell you and keep it organized—"

she snapped, then stopped abruptly as Shiloh's eyes sparkled.

"You know, for once I agree with you, Doc," he nodded. "Think it's time we got organized. At least enough to decide which way to leave town."

"Let's just ask Rissy," Cheney suggested. "I'm sure she won't have any trouble expressing her opinion."

Shiloh and Cheney sat looking over the water, talking and laughing and planning as the sun reluctantly began to ease toward the western mountains. Far behind them, Glen, Caroline, and Glendean dozed under the tree, and beside them, Rissy sewed and hummed softly.

Inside the log, Jim-Jim nestled comfortably on Neva Sikes' best black hat and played with her best pearl hatpin. For a long time he listened curiously to Cheney and Shiloh, his nose twitching and his black eyes glittering. But at last he grew weary and, lulled by the gentle lapping of Moccasin Lake, he fell asleep.